"[A] terrific legal thriller . . . and even superstar John G are always surprising, the c the story a grabber from st

"He powers his latest legal thriller with a narrative engine that smashes through the barriers of coincidence and credulity, leaving readers breathless at the author's audacity . . . As expected from past Ellis performances, there is a beautifully sustained trial sequence, with several surprises. But what really makes his third book so impressive are the human challenges he sets up and conquers."
—*Chicago Tribune*

"A steady stream of twists and complications . . . a stunning Perry Mason–style courtroom shocker will knock readers right out of their seats. After they pick themselves up off the floor, the ensuing fast and furious revelations will have them flying through the final pages."
—*Publishers Weekly*

"Ellis keeps the suspense bubbling at its highest peak. This first-class legal thriller is strongly recommended for all libraries where good writing, excellent character development, and exceptional trial strategies are appreciated."
—*Library Journal*

"[A] twist sets the story's last third spinning as Ellis tightens, then ties up, a solid case. Unlike the mob of hacks who want to be the next Grisham, Ellis is never glib, hackneyed, or tiresome. In style, plot, and character, he engages and entertains."
—*Kirkus Reviews* (starred review)

"The gladiatorial trial sequences are detailed and riveting . . . [Ellis's] misdirection and plot twists will please fans of Bernhardt, O'Shaughnessy, or Margolin."　　—*Booklist*

continued . . .

Praise for the Edgar® Award–winning

LINE OF VISION

"The best suspense novel I've read in a while."
—James Patterson, author of *3rd Degree*

"A fresh take on the legal thriller. Crackles with unexpected twists." —*San Francisco Chronicle*

"Don't think you can put *Line of Vision* down—you can't. Dave Ellis won't let you go, from the first tantalizing page to the final double twist."

—Barbara Parker,
New York Times bestselling author of *Suspicion of Madness*

"The most original and exciting thriller I've read in a long time. Starts at a fever pitch and never lets up."

—J. F. Freedman,
New York Times bestselling author of *Above the Law*

"*Line of Vision* is a wicked delight . . . David Ellis's hero beguiles like Patricia Highsmith's Ripley at his most devious. The story grabs, shakes, twists up, and won't let go, all the way through to its deeply satisfying resolution."

—Perri O'Shaughnessy,
author of *Unlucky in Law*

"Almost continuous tension and a surprisingly sympathetic narrator. [Marty's] struggle is compelling and the verdict a stunning surprise. Expertly written, intricately plotted, and, of course, highly entertaining." —*St. Louis Post-Dispatch*

"A spellbinding legal drama—sexy, seductive, and full of surprises—which features a fascinating if unreliable protagonist. This is the best first novel I've read in a good long time."

—William Bernhardt,
author of *Hate Crime*

Titles by David Ellis

LIFE SENTENCE

LINE OF VISION

JURY OF ONE

JURY
of ONE

David Ellis

BERKLEY BOOKS, NEW YORK

THE BERKLEY PUBLISHING GROUP
Published by the Penguin Group
Penguin Group (USA) Inc.
375 Hudson Street, New York, New York 10014, USA
Penguin Group (Canada), 10 Alcorn Avenue, Toronto, Ontario M4V 3B2, Canada
(a division of Pearson Penguin Canada Inc.)
Penguin Books Ltd., 80 Strand, London WC2R 0RL, England
Penguin Group Ireland, 25 St. Stephen's Green, Dublin 2, Ireland (a division of Penguin Books Ltd.)
Penguin Group (Australia), 250 Camberwell Road, Camberwell, Victoria 3124 Australia
(a division of Pearson Australia Group Pty. Ltd.)
Penguin Books India Pvt. Ltd., 11 Community Centre, Panchsheel Park, New Delhi—110 017, India
Penguin Group (NZ), Cnr. Airborne and Rosedale Roads, Albany, Auckland 1310, New Zealand
(a division of Pearson New Zealand Ltd.)
Penguin Books (South Africa) (Pty.) Ltd., 24 Sturdee Avenue, Rosebank, Johannesburg 2196,
South Africa

Penguin Books Ltd., Registered Offices: 80 Strand, London WC2R 0RL, England

This is a work of fiction. Names, characters, places, and incidents either are the product of the author's imagination or are used fictitiously, and any resemblance to actual persons, living or dead, business establishments, events, or locales is entirely coincidental.

JURY OF ONE

A Berkley Book / published by arrangement with the author

PRINTING HISTORY
G. P. Putnam's Sons hardcover edition / March 2004
Berkley mass-market edition / March 2005

Copyright © 2004 by David Ellis.
The Edgar® name is a registered service mark of the Mystery Writers of America, Inc.
Cover design by Marc Cohen.

ISBN: 0-425-20145-7

BERKLEY®
Berkley Books are published by The Berkley Publishing Group,
a division of Penguin Group (USA) Inc.,
375 Hudson Street, New York, New York 10014.
BERKLEY is a registered trademark of Penguin Group (USA) Inc.
The "B" design is a trademark belonging to Penguin Group (USA) Inc.

PRINTED IN THE UNITED STATES OF AMERICA

10 9 8 7 6 5 4 3 2 1

TO MY WIFE,
SUSAN

Blood

A FEELING HE cannot escape: Someone is watching. He has no visual confirmation but it's a sense, his gut telling him that he's not alone as he stands on the street outside the athletic club on the commercial district's southwest side. The bitter air of a February evening stings his sweaty body, the light wind shooting over the top of his long black coat and filling the space inside his sweatshirt. His fellow players have left in their various directions, to high-priced condos along the city's lakefront or, in some cases, to student housing at whatever school they are attending. Not so for this young man. He will walk four blocks to the Austin bus that will transport him to the city's south side, to his middle-class home.

He looks at his watch. It's early. Seven-forty. Open gym at the City Athletic Club—every Wednesday night, the basketball courts can be used free of charge—officially ends at eight o'clock and usually goes to eight-thirty, but tonight the game broke up abruptly after a minor fracas between players turned into a heated altercation, enough so that the gym supervisor sent everyone home. He wasn't a part of the fight. He wouldn't feel so comfortable shoving or throwing punches; it's a class thing, an issue of hierarchy. He's not one of them. He's not their age and he doesn't have their pedigree. They are college kids and grad students, mostly, who live in nice housing their daddies are paying for. He's a high-school kid with a good outside shot. He understands his place.

Not one of them. He's not sure who he is anymore.

The streets on the southwest side are empty. It has been dark since five, and most of the professional buildings in the district are to the east and north, so it is quiet as he walks toward the bus stop. Quiet is not good, not anymore. These days, he prefers noise and company to drown out the howling in his head.

He hears it before he turns his head and sees it behind him, to the north. Squad cars are unmistakable even from a distance. This particular police vehicle is headed south on Gentry, toward him. The car has just crossed Bonnard Street, which puts it less than a block away from him. The boy finds it difficult to walk with his head craned back, but he will do what he can to be non-chalant. There is no reason to panic. He doesn't know the officers' intentions. More than likely, it's a routine cruising. He's a white kid in a long coat and sweats, obviously leaving the City Athletic Club after a game of hoops. They might not think anything of him. Or they might stop him. They might even ask him what's in the gym bag he's carrying. But he doesn't know this, and he can't react preemptively because that would draw suspicion, could turn a nonevent into something.

He hears the squad car stop short of him. That seems odd, because there is nothing behind him that would draw their interest, no reason to stop. He doesn't know how to respond. He listens a moment, slowing his pace. He hears another car drive by, on Bonnard Street north of the officers. That car, headed east, sounds like it's moving quickly, which might normally catch the attention of police officers on a sleepy night. But he hears no response from the cops, which means something else—some*one* else—has their attention just now.

He tries to be casual as he turns and looks back at the squad car. The illumination of the street is decent, with the towering overhead streetlights, and he sees two of them inside the car. The driver is a thick man, an Italian; his partner is smaller and Latino. The driver is speaking into a radio.

The boy turns and continues walking, stifling the instinct to run. His heart is drumming now. Perspiration on his forehead, when it's only ten degrees or so outside.

He hears car doors open, then close, one after the other.

He will not run, not yet. If nothing else, he will let them walk a sufficient distance from the vehicle, so that if he does run, it will take some time before they can return to the vehicle, if that is their choice.

He looks straight ahead now. He is walking among high-rises, so there are few options. Buildings will be closed, or open only to the extent that he could approach a security guard. Wait—an alley, before the end of the block. His mind races as he taps his recall. The alley goes through to the next street. Yes. He can cross through the alley to the next street. Yes.

"Hey," the officer calls out. It's the driver, the bigger, older guy.

It has happened in a finger-snap. He has been identified and called out. Until now, it has been something of a game, the boy ignoring the police and the police not overtly approaching him. Now a line has been drawn.

The boy runs. He's in the perfect outfit, sweats and court shoes, though a sixteen-year-old probably doesn't need such advantages against a large man pushing forty. It takes him under thirty seconds to reach the alley. He hears the officer calling to his partner, something about the car, which means that the vehicle will be coming after him soon as well.

He looks down the alley. Bags of garbage next to full dumpsters, an old fire escape running up one wall. A parked car on the next street over. Something in the shadows, maybe his eyes playing tricks. It only takes a second to make the decision. He turns and runs into the darkness.

He hears the officer again, talking into the police radio as he gives chase.

"—in pursuit—"

He looks back for signs of the officer as he's running. A mistake. He knows it before it happens. His foot catches something, a pipe probably, and he falls. His gloves rip against the uneven pavement. Worse, his knee. His kneecap, even with the protection of the wool coat, has landed awkwardly on the tattered concrete. He can't diagnose the damage. It just hurts like hell.

He gathers his gym bag and manages to get to his feet. He is shrouded in the darkness of the alley, only indirect lighting from the street allowing him to see at all. He can't run anymore, will probably need a moment before he can even put weight on his leg. He is not even midway between the two streets now. He couldn't possibly escape.

"I just want to talk to you, kid. Relax." The officer is standing at the threshold, casting an ominous figure with the light behind him. One hand on his police radio, the other extending forward. But not holding a gun. The officer shakes his head, even shows the palm of his open hand, as if to decelerate the threat. He is moving cautiously toward the boy, shuffling his feet as each one eyes the other.

"See those hands," he calls out. "Lose the bag."

The officer moves slowly, his gaze alternating between the boy and the gym bag. The boy shows the palm of his free hand as he moves backward. It actually hurts less to backpedal, but he still moves with a limp. His heartbeat drums, not from the physical exertion. He swallows hard and feels a hot, sickening taste in his mouth. He asks himself, in a flash of a moment, how it could have come to this.

The officer pulls his radio close to his mouth, speaks urgently but quietly. Then he moves closer to the boy, his index finger still extended. Do-not-move.

"I said drop the bag," he says to the boy. "Let's just talk a minute."

The boy drops the bag.

The officer's right hand falls to his side, sweeping gently at his leather jacket, exposing for the first time the holster, his weapon. The boy waits another beat, looks into the eyes of the police officer.

"I haven't said anything," the boy says. "I won't. I swear."

The officer looks at him. Then he brings his radio close to his mouth. He mumbles something into the radio that the boy can't make out.

"I repeat," the officer says in a louder voice. "Suspect is armed."

PART ONE

Offenses

I

Chances

SHE ALWAYS LOOKED into the eyes of her clients to see if the hope was still there. She wanted to believe that, for some of these children, a legal victory was the road to a better life. She needed to believe, at the very least, that she was giving them a chance.

Shelly took the boy's hand by the wrist. She would not pat it reassuringly or offer empty words of comfort. There was no need to condescend. It was a serious situation and everyone knew it. The teenager sitting next to her in the courtroom looked younger than his years, a quiet boy with coffee-colored skin, an elongated neck and small flat nose, with long eyelashes covering the wide, awed stare of his dark eyes.

It had been a three-week hearing, on and off. Over a dozen witnesses had testified, primarily for the city board of education. The school was trying to expel Rondell based on a pattern of violations of school policy. The acts alleged included acts of defiance—such as violations of the school dress code and misbehavior in class—as well as violent altercations on school grounds. Shelly, as the advocate for Rondell, had a two-tiered trial strategy. First, she tried to dismantle each of the acts in the "pattern" as not being adequately proven. Second, and in her mind more pointedly, she argued that Rondell shouldn't be expelled but transferred to one of the city's "alternative" schools, set up years ago to take in troubled students.

A chance. In the end, that's all she wanted for Rondell. A

chance. If they kicked him out of school, he would retreat to the drug- and gang-infested streets. School was the only option for this boy. The school had expelled him without much of a hearing—in these post–Columbine days, schools were increasingly embracing the "zero tolerance" policy—and by the time Shelly caught the case, the act was completed. She had run to court and now sought a preliminary injunction against the school board, forcing them to keep Rondell in school until the issue was sorted out. Some would say she was buying time. What she was really doing was seeking leverage. If the judge leaned her way, the school might decide to give Rondell the alternative school option, which Shelly would take in a heartbeat. Her client was no saint. He probably didn't belong in a traditional school. He just needed a chance.

Shelly had cross-examined school officials, students, and school security personnel. She could do it in her sleep by now. She had lost count, but in her time as an attorney representing students, she had tried over forty cases, including civil hearings such as these and about a dozen cases in juvenile court, which essentially meant criminal court for children. She felt good about her defense of Rondell, but the problem was numbers. One or two witnesses might not be credible, but over a dozen? Sheer numbers would seem to tip the balance against her client.

"All rise."

The judge, the Honorable Alfred Halston, assumed the bench. His Honor was battle-worn, a weary man with snow-white hair, a lined face and gravelly voice. Shelly considered Halston a tough draw. He was presumably next in line for presiding judge, a politician's politician who took the bench fifteen years ago after leaving the state's House of Representatives. As an elected judge, he was no longer subject to popular election—a judge only had to run for "retention" once a decade, and no judge had been ousted in recent memory—but that didn't erase political considerations. Everything was political in the city, and a judge hoping for elevation soon was always thinking two steps ahead of every ruling. Returning a violent boy to school was all he needed. If this kid turned around and shot someone, everyone would look back at the judge for blame.

Shelly had become adept at knowing the verdict before it was rendered. Look at the jurors' eyes, look at the judge's demeanor. Judge Halston looked first at Shelly's client, and she knew the answer.

"What we have here, young man," he began, "are allegations of a very serious nature. You should be ashamed of yourself."

That confirmed it. The judge wouldn't begin in such a testy manner if he were going to rule against Rondell. If he were going to uphold the expulsion, he wouldn't need to scold Rondell—the ruling would be punishment enough. Shelly nodded along, because she was never arguing that her client was a prince. Plus, when you're ahead, you let the judge feel like Solomon himself could not have divined a more exquisite outcome. The judge continued on for several minutes, castigating Rondell Moten for taking the gift of education for granted, for vanquishing this opportunity to learn, improve, find a constructive place in this world.

The judge sighed. "Nevertheless," he began.

Not a complete victory, though. The judge was only finding that Shelly had established a likelihood that she would win at a final trial—the judge was simply issuing an injunction keeping the boy in school until the matter was finally resolved.

Shelly knew what would come next. The attorney for the board of education would offer Rondell alternative school to drop the matter, to prevent the further draining of resources directed against a single student in litigation that could go to the state's highest court. The attorney knew Shelly well, knew her resolve.

Rondell's mother hugged her son. Shelly watched the mother nervously gather her child in her arms. Perhaps she was in need of a fix, or maybe she was simply fearful of what might have happened. Shelly didn't know which, and she didn't know whether keeping Rondell in some form of school would miraculously transform his life, currently straying down the wrong path. She certainly wasn't in the guarantee business. She just gave them a chance.

After parting with Rondell and his mother, she reached into her bag for her cell phone and turned it on. She almost dropped the phone, which was ringing. She answered it and heard the voice of Rena Schroeder, her boss at the Children's Advocacy Project.

"Shelly, do you know someone named Alex Baniewicz?"

She closed her eyes, standing in the hallway outside the courtroom. "Yeah."

"You remember that police officer who was shot last night?" Rena asked.

Of course, Shelly remembered. It was the headline of the *Daily Watch* today, covered as the lead story last night on television. A city police officer had been shot in the face while in pursuit of a drug dealer. The city always noticed when one of its finest went down.

Shelly dropped her head.

"He's asking for you," said Rena.

2

Dreams

JUST A DREAM. *Go back to sleep.*

A memory that is hardly a memory at all. A memory of dreams, of racing, wild, intoxicated dreams. Men running and shouting. Winter. Screaming. Crying. Stabbing. Grunting. Hands, cold hands. A voice, Shelly's voice. Don't. Stop. What are you doing? What's—what's this—? A man's voice. Relax. The cold hands, again. She is flying through the chilly air, so cold, so very cold. She is suffocating. A weight on her, pressing down on her chest, her abdomen. Tobacco and alcohol and winter—

"Relax."

Darkness. Where is she? She has forgotten. She feels the bed. She is spinning. She is nauseous. The bile rising to her throat. He is on her. Her shirt is open. Her—her bra is off. His face, whiskers scraping against her cheek. The smell. Alcohol, not like the kind Daddy drinks, cigarettes on his breath, his body odor, the flannel rubbing against her chest—

"Don't."

"Shut up and relax." *His voice. Her legs are spread and this is what it is. This is what she's heard about. He is inside her, his penis is inside her, ripping into her, back and forth, in and out, and she's not dreaming because she can feel his sweat on her face and his awful breath and he's so heavy. She raises her hands but can't make fists. She concentrates on what she can control. Her name. Her age. My name is Shelly. I am sixteen years old. I took the train from Haley. My parents are out of town and don't know. I don't know where I am.*

"Don't," she hears herself repeat.

Light, coming from her right. A voice, a man's voice, then a female, then she hears the voice of the man on top of her. "We're in the middle of something here." Laughter, muted laughter as the door closes part of the way, reducing the light, then opens again.

She remembers the name Andrea. She remembers Mary and Dina and—

She remembers now. She remembers coming in here, thinking this might be the bathroom, but it was a bedroom and she was overtaken, simply overcome with drowsiness and she thought if she just sat for a second on the bed, just for a second, she might get the energy to get up and find the bathroom because she needed to go—

She looks into the blinding light and opens her mouth but the words don't come. Laughter from the light, then darkness again. Harder now, and quicker, driving inside her. He is going to come. The phrase, she didn't know what it meant when Brandon Ainsley asked her at lunch, sixth grade, in front of a table full of boys—"Do you come when you're called?" and she said "Of course" and oh, how they laughed and now he's going to come, this person whoever he is, he's making the noise and she feels him shiver and moan, she feels it shooting inside her and she wants to return to the dream, she wants him to leave, it hurts and she wants him to leave but it's over now, he's off her, and she catches her breath and shuts her eyes and she's crying. She hears him zip up his pants and she doesn't know what it means when he chuckles and says, "Nice to meet you," and then, "Go back to sleep, it was just a dream."

3

Lost

SHELLY RACED FROM the courthouse to her car and found the jail where Alex Baniewicz was being held. She approached the police station and assumed an air of confidence. So much of being a lawyer was presentation, and she did not anticipate a warm reception.

The interior of the police station had been remodeled. The reception area was spacious, with white walls and a long bench on each side of the door. The rest of the structure was cordoned off from the reception area by a wall with a secured door. Visitors were directed to the one division along the wall, a window covered by bulletproof glass, behind which sat a uniformed officer busying herself with paperwork. Above the thick glass was a sign in black, bold letters, ALL VISITORS ARE SUBJECT TO SEARCH, with the same words written in Spanish beneath it. Shelly walked up to the window and spoke into the small microphone embedded in the thick glass. She felt like she was buying a movie ticket.

Shelly gave her name to the officer. "I'm an attorney here to see Alex Baniewicz. I understand he's being detained here."

The uniformed officer glanced over the glasses perched on her nose. The thought passed in and out of Shelly's mind, the women always got the traffic duty and reception jobs. The woman looked over a sheet before suddenly looking up at Shelly. It registered with the officer now. Baniewicz. The one who had killed the cop. Now came the runaround—*You'll have to wait, he's not available right now, maybe you should come back later*—which Shelly had been through before with a number of her clients held on juvie beefs, when the cops wanted more time to interrogate their suspect. The police were supposed to stop talking to the accused once a lawyer was requested, but the Supreme Court had goofed it up and ruled that any equivocation on the suspect's part was open game to continue the interrogation, notwithstanding the request for counsel. And if the suspect hadn't asked for a lawyer, the police weren't required to tell the suspect that a lawyer was waiting outside, trying to get in. So Shelly was accustomed to being insistent. In this context, she reminded the officer of the high-profile nature of the case and promised her that she would be taking down the names of every officer who prevented her from speaking with Alex Baniewicz. Right now.

Her presentation seemed to buy her something with the officer. Shelly sat on a bench and made a point of looking at her watch. But her mind quickly drifted from the cop to her client. What had happened to Alex in the last few months? How could it have come to this?

A small classroom on the second floor of the law school, doubling as a conference room for the Children Advocacy's Project. He was seated in a chair, looked no different from any tenth-grader learning English or math or science. Appropriately dressed in a white shirt and khaki trousers, with a long black wool coat folded in his lap—better dressed, in fact, than most of her clients. Well developed for sixteen, a strong neck and broad shoulders, a square jaw, thick curly hair. His eyes were large and expressive, something like amusement playing on his face as Shelly walked into the room.

According to his file, he had been involved in a fight in the hallway at Southside High School. No weapon, no racial epithets, and while it was not his first offense, it was far from a pattern of misbehavior. A brief suspension and nothing more, Shelly had figured.

He was white, which separated him from the majority of her clients. Most of the children she represented were younger and, from what she could see, poorer, and overwhelmingly Latino or African American.

"Alex?" she asked.

"Alex Baniewicz." He lifted himself from the chair that barely contained his frame. "Nice to meet you."

They sat in the chairs. "Your mother isn't here?"

He shook his head as he looked Shelly over. It would not have been the first time a young student leered at Shelly, but she did not recognize lust in the stare. It was more like curiosity.

"You're prettier than I thought you'd be," he said.

The security door on the wall buzzed. A man stepped out, wearing shirtsleeves. His belt held a weapon, handcuffs, a cellular phone. He was Hispanic, tall, relatively lean, with a long, worried face. He put his hands on his hips and looked at Shelly. "I'm Detective Montes," he said to her. The detective led Shelly through the squad room, refurbished like the rest of the building. It looked surprisingly efficient. High ceilings, large thick windows, steel desks, high-powered computers on some of them, typewriters on others, bulletin boards listing cases by the victim's name with assignments to various detectives, with categories for "Pending" and "C/P"—whatever that meant—and "Closed."

She saw only two women out of the nine detectives, and nothing but cool glares from all of them, regardless of gender. They took a seat at his desk, which told Shelly that she was about to receive a pep talk—the strength of the police's case, the importance of getting out in front of this steamroller, giving Alex's side of the story before things went too far and the death penalty was the only option. She wasn't in the mood, was in a hurry to see her client, but she also wanted to see the government's hand. "Your client's a drug dealer," said the detective. "If he's calling you for help, I assume you already know that."

"You sell drugs," she said to him. "You don't walk around with a roll like that working part-time at McHenry Stern." It was always best to say it as fact. If she had a dime for every denial she'd heard from a young client on issues of drugs and weapons, she could retire from the nonprofit legal profession.

"Your client was carrying drugs and a weapon in a gym bag," said the detective. "Officer Raymond Miroballi, a guy I've met, by the way"—he met her eyes when he said this; a cop shooting was personal to any detective, even more so if he was an acquaintance—"Officer Miroballi approached your client and your boy ran. Eventually he's cornered in an alley and your guy shoots the officer in the face. We have the officer's blood on your client's clothes and hair."

No. Not this fast. Blood was found, maybe, but not blood that could be identified as belonging to the slain officer or anyone else, for that matter. Not in less than a day. This guy was jobbing her.

"We have another cop who'll positively I.D. your client. And we're scooping witnesses right now from the area. Eyes and blood, Counselor. He's done. Finito. So tell your client that if he helps us, maybe he can avoid the gas chamber."

She took all of this without comment. There was no need for debate, and the police wouldn't turn over evidence to her this quickly anyway, so she saw no need for a fight. In any event, Shelly knew that there was probably a strong case against Alex Baniewicz.

"You make it sound so bad." Alex grimaced but did not contest the accuracy of her statement. He was different, Shelly thought, more comfortable with himself, more willing to open himself to Shelly than most teenage clients she had. "I mean, it's not like you think."

They were at a celebratory dinner—Alex's idea—after Shelly had represented him at his disciplinary hearing. As it turned out, Shelly felt that her presence had hardly been necessary; the school administrators were quite fond of Alex and simply wanted to give him a brief, in-school suspension for his hallway fight.

"What's it like, then?" she asked. "How is your method of drug dealing different from everyone else's?"

Shelly expected hemming and hawing, rationales and excuses, reluctantly imparted nuggets of information. But Alex, without hesitation, laid out his story for her. There were a couple of guys at work, he said—professionals, investment bankers at McHenry Stern, where Alex worked as a runner, a mailboy. "Smart, educated, rich guys," he said. "More money in a week than I've ever seen." They partied, these gentlemen, did some cocaine on the weekends as recreation. "Five, six grams a week, tops," Alex promised. "It's side money for me. That's it. It's not like I work the streets or anything. I don't sell it to junkies or children or anything. I'm, like, a middleman."

"That's an awful risk," Shelly said, "for a little side money. What do you need that money for?"

"For Angela," he answered easily.

"Angela's your girlfriend?"

"Angela's my daughter."

The door to the room was solid wood, inscribed with the block letter C. Detective Montes pushed it open and allowed Shelly in. The detective walked over to a wire cage inside the room, where Alex Baniewicz sat on a steel bench bolted to the floor. The bench was centered so that one couldn't use the wall as a backrest. There was little opportunity for comfort, which, apparently, was the point.

When Alex stood, she got her first full look at him and drew back. It was what she expected but it wasn't, in some way; maybe there was no way to prepare oneself. His face, typically cast in an amused grin, was now clouded in grief and pain. Everything, in fact, was off—the coloring of his face, the life in his eyes, the line of his mouth, his posture. He was pale. His hair was oily and disheveled. He hadn't shaved, probably hadn't bathed since his arrest. He looked entirely out of place.

Little outward signs of a physical struggle. His cheek was bruised, his hands were scraped, but that wasn't bad for someone accused of shooting a cop. Shelly thought that she'd like to see his ribs. Cops greatly preferred the midsection. Less visible and easier to explain away. That was one of the advantages of a one-piece jumpsuit like the one Alex wore—it would be difficult to take stock of bruises to the body. She could imagine their reaction when they came upon Alex, the boy they were sure had killed one of their own. She'd heard each officer was entitled to one "free one" if a suspect fled or resisted, a pop to the side of the head or the stomach; her mind raced at what might be fair game for a suspect who shot a cop.

"If we could get some privacy," said Shelly to Detective Montes.

The detective reached for Alex and put him in a chair, locked his handcuffs down onto a small metal ring bolted to the steel table. "I'm ten feet from this door," he cautioned. She wasn't sure if the point was to warn Alex or assure Shelly.

She took the other chair, across from Alex. She fought back emotion, looking at a shadow of the boy she'd grown to like so much. A boy with so much potential, a young father with plans for college, a job—so much hope, suddenly looking at no future at all.

He was stopping. He'd promised.

"Alex," she said softly. "You didn't talk to them, did you?"

He shook his head no, without looking at her. That was something at least, that Alex had kept his mouth shut. Most of the kids Shelly represented were accustomed to talking their way out of jams and took every opportunity to explain their situation to the police, almost always worsening their position in the process. She recalled Simien Carlyle, who at age fifteen was the driver for three older boys who held up a convenience store and shot one of the clerks in the process. Simien explained to the police—truthfully, in Shelly's opinion—that he didn't know his co-conspirators had a gun, much less that they planned to use it. By the time Shelly reached the boy, it was too late to explain to him that, by virtue of the law of accountability, Simien's admission to being the driver was the same thing as admitting he'd pulled the trigger.

"Not a word?" Shelly confirmed. "There was never a tape recorder or video camera? You never talked even to someone in another cell or anything?"

"I didn't say anything," said Alex, looking at her. "I've seen enough television." He smiled briefly, and Shelly's heart ached. This boy did not belong here. Not this one.

Shelly didn't know where to start. Her throat was full. She swallowed hard and thought about what she could say. Her options ranged from asking him how he was holding up to offering him a mint. Nothing seemed to make sense.

"I'll help you any way I can," she said quietly.

Alex remained still, his eyes downcast. When he spoke, his voice was drained of the typical resonance, the enthusiastic inflection. It was the shaky, weakened, deflated voice of a boy who had been beyond terror and back. "Talk to Ronnie," he said. "And Mary Ellen. Can you do that? Tell them I'm—basically okay. Ronnie must be flipping out."

She had so many questions. He was walking the streets with drugs? A weapon? He shot a police officer?

"Do you want to tell me?" she asked.

"Not now." That was not a surprising answer. *Not now* had become Alex's slogan of late, at least with Shelly. She didn't know what had happened. They had been friends. He had confided in her. He was going to quit. He was going to find a way to support his daughter and attend college at the same time. And then—nothing. He shut her out. Didn't return phone calls. Heartfelt, probing conversations replaced with distant small talk. What had happened over the last few months? Could she have helped him? Could she have prevented this?

"I want you to listen to me," she said, trying to overcome a tremble in her voice. "There is no such thing as casual conversation in here. Everything you say, they are listening, and they will use it against you. Don't talk to the guards. Don't talk to someone in the cell next to you. They'll try all those tricks, Alex, and they're allowed to do it."

"Don't talk," he repeated. "I can handle that."

"I'll go see Ronnie. And we'll figure something out."

After a few choice words for Detective Montes, reminding him that her client now had a lawyer and would not answer questions, she made it out of the police station. She exhaled as if she had been holding her breath for the last hour. She felt so helpless and confused. This simply didn't make sense. Alex Baniewicz—if she knew this boy at all, if she had even the slightest ability to read a person's character—could not have shot a police officer or anyone else.

There were a handful of reporters outside the police station. Print media, she thought; they weren't made-up and had no microphones. They knew her name, which meant that they had contacts inside who gave up the name of the lawyer who had signed in to visit the cop killer. She begged off comment, which was tougher than she'd have thought.

She eventually crossed the street to the parking garage. She had parked on the ground level and saw, even before she entered, two men sitting in a car with their eyes on her. They eased out of their sedan and moved near her car.

Shelly sized them up, their build, any infirmities, which hand was dominant, her proximity to cars, people, a weapon. One was tall with thinning blond hair, a soft stomach, wouldn't withstand a kick to the midsection. The shorter guy was muscle-bound, stronger than Shelly; she'd have to go for the face. She looked into her car quickly, then unlocked the driver-side door for easy access. Her fingers laced through her keys until her fist held several metal spikes. Then she straightened up and looked them in the eye. Always look them in the eye.

But they were no threat. They were two grim-looking men but they weren't looking for a fight. The taller one, in fact, seemed to sense Shelly's trepidation and raised a hand. He even addressed her by name, which told her all she needed to know. They knew her name and knew she was here.

"Special Agent Donovan Peters," said the tall man. He nodded toward his shorter colleague, the weight lifter. "This is Assistant United States Attorney Jerod Romero."

She held out her hand for their credentials. After she verified their authenticity—as best she could, anyway—she looked up at them. "Okay. What do you want?"

But she knew the answer, and she was beginning to understand more than a few things. They wanted to talk about Alex. She was about to learn why she hadn't heard from Alex for the last several months.

4

Never

SEE THE PERFECT *family. She sees it from the threshold of the kitchen, looking in on the family after she has excused herself from dinner. Not feeling well, she told them, which was certainly true, but instead of taking the stairs to her room, she has sneaked back to look in on them.*

How can she tell them?

The four of them are there. Edgar, the eldest, seven years her senior, who has graduated from school out east and is now completing a master's degree in public policy, looking more like Daddy every day, the same thick, cereal-colored hair, prominent nose, squared jaw. He sounds like Daddy, too, if you close your eyes and listen. Thomas, still an undergraduate out east as well, takes after Mother, a smaller nose, darker eyes, wispy light hair. Mother is there as well—Abby is her name—her sweet, round face and soothing voice, her blond cropped hair, watching Daddy with such dreams in her sparkling green eyes.

And Daddy, so proud as he watches his boys, as he dreams of greater things. He is a strong man raising strong men—and a lovely young daughter, a sweet, innocent little daughter! So aggressive and confident in all he does, the conviction with which he speaks, the old-school discipline with the boys, even the way he eats—mixing all of his food together, "like a dog's breakfast," before shoveling it all into his mouth.

It has been four weeks since it happened. Twenty-eight days. The incident in the city. The rape, yes, it was rape, no matter what anyone said! And now this. Four weeks, two positive home tests, one missed period. She is only sixteen years old and this.

How can she tell them? How, when her brothers are talking about master's degrees and girlfriends, her father has some exciting news of his own, her mother is so proud of all the men in her family?

The answer is obvious. She can't tell them. Not ever. They will never, they can never, ever know that the baby girl of the family, the darling princess, is pregnant.

5

Pinch

"WE PICKED UP Alex Baniewicz in December of last year."
Special Agent Donovan Peters pushed a file in front of Shelly.
They were sitting in the federal building downtown, in a small
conference room with a view of the state courthouse. The room,
she thought, was quintessentially government—cheap furniture,
modest artwork that seemingly was placed there only because
something was supposed to go on the wall, thin carpeting of no
discernible color.

Shelly opened the manila file before her. Her heart sank as
she viewed a mug shot of Alex, a black-and-white photo clipped
to one side of the file. A summary report written by another
federal agent was on the opposite page, explaining that, on December 5, 2003, Alex Gerhard Baniewicz was arrested in possession of seventy-four grams of powder cocaine.

She closed her eyes. Oh, how it must look to the government.
Seventy-four grams of cocaine! He looked like your run-of-the-
mill purveyor of drugs. She wanted to come forth with excuses,
that Alex only sold small quantities to some wealthy professionals, not children or junkies. She imagined that Alex had
made the same excuses to the federal authorities. The excuses,
of course, were no excuses at all. And worse yet, Shelly realized
with a shot to her gut, she couldn't even be sure they were true.

"You didn't know," Peters said to Shelly.

No, she certainly did not know. She thought back to the time
she had spent with Alex over the last year, tried to connect

conversations and dinners to specific dates. It all made sense. Beginning of December, end of November—that had been when Alex cut off contact with her. She could recall nothing since December 5, with the exception of her trip to his house in early January this year, after she hadn't heard from him for six weeks. She could see from the way he had looked at her then— or rather, hadn't looked at her, had cast his eyes downward, stuffed his hands in his pocket, as he'd stood in the doorway of his house. Something had happened. He wouldn't tell her what. *Just some things I gotta take care of,* he'd said then. *You shouldn't be here,* he'd warned. What could Shelly do? She couldn't make him tell her. All she could do was offer to help.

"I take it he cut a deal," she said, realizing that she was exposing her ignorance. But that was the least of her worries. She felt so many things at the moment, including a betrayal that these men seemed to know more about Alex than she did.

The prosecutor, Jerod Romero, looked stronger with his coat off. He was an intense man. He was standing behind Peters with his arms folded. "He cooperated, yes."

That was common enough. Catch a drug dealer and flip him, use him to catch people higher up on the chain. She looked through the file and found it, the letter of cooperation. In a circumstance like this, the U.S. Attorney's office didn't usually arrest and charge the suspect, because if they did, they would be required to put him before a judge in less than twenty-four hours for an initial appearance. That would expose the arrestee publicly, which was precisely the opposite of what the federal government wanted if they were going to use the suspect as an undercover informant. Instead, the U.S. Attorney's office had signed Alex to a letter of cooperation, in which he was informed that he was the target of a federal investigation and that he might later be arrested and charged with possession with intent to distribute a controlled substance. Alex, through the letter, agreed to cooperate and was guaranteed only that such cooperation, if it came to fruition, would be made known to the judge at his sentencing. Alex also had to agree not to violate any local, state, or federal law during this time—except, of course, under circumstances controlled by the feds—and to inform the federal government if he was going to leave the jurisdiction.

She moved the file away and looked at the men. "Okay. So?"

Romero began to pace. "So, we are in the midst of an operation that is bearing fruit. We expect to bring dozens of indictments."

"But we're not ready," said Peters.

Shelly's heart raced. Dozens of indictments? That didn't jibe. Alex only had a couple of contacts at work to whom he sold drugs. Those people, and maybe Alex's supplier, didn't add up to *dozens of indictments*. "Okay," she repeated. "So?"

Romero leaned onto the table, facing her. "So it's bad enough that he's out of operation now. We've already lost a valuable asset out there. We were hoping to contain the damage."

Shelly nodded. "Okay, I'm a slow learner. You don't want Alex testifying in open court that he is working for the G. Anyone who's been in contact with Alex will know they've been targets."

Peters, the F.B.I. agent, lifted a shoulder, as if Shelly were only half right. "It could endanger the whole operation. It could place the lives of undercover federal agents at risk."

"That's what I don't get," said Shelly. "What does the one have to do with the other? What does your federal investigation have to do with the shooting of this police off—"

She froze. The men across from her, now both seated, cast glances at each other and then at her. They were calculating what to reveal, and they seemed to understand that Shelly had figured it out herself. They also had probably calculated, correctly so, that she could get much of this information from her client, Alex Baniewicz.

"Cops," she said. "You guys were investigating cops. A drug ring of cops." She stuck an index finger into the table. "Including this one here. The one Alex is accused of shooting."

Romero opened his hands, then brought them together.

"Alex was helping you take down a dirty cop." She looked at them for confirmation. Their lack of a response was sufficient. "And—this cop found out, didn't he? He found out Alex was working for you and he tried to silence him." She looked at them again. "Am I getting warm?"

"That's all speculation," said Peters. "Every single thing that you have said, Counsel, cannot be proven. But we certainly expect that you might say it in court."

Romero concurred. "We were assuming you'd be pleading self-defense."

Shelly got out of her chair. She felt a surge of hope mixed with her confusion. She was playing catch-up but she was getting the picture now, and there might be a way out of this. Maybe. But it wasn't going to happen right now. So she would keep mum about her intentions. This was time to be gathering, not giving, information.

"Has your client spoken with the police?" asked Peters.

She shook her head no. "He won't."

"That's very important to us," he said. "I need to know if my guys on the street are safe. If your client is flapping his mouth and word spreads, my guys are sitting ducks—"

"He's not talking. He won't."

"We need your word on that," said Jerod Romero. "Everything we've told you."

Shelly looked out the window. "You need a lot from us, Mr. Romero. And it doesn't come free. Let's start talking about a deal, right now. And not just on this drug bust. I want a deal on this cop-shooting, too. I want the whole thing."

"Understand that this is sensitive ground," said the prosecutor. "The assistant county attorneys can be pretty tight with cops. We have to be very choosy about whom we share this with."

"I got that. I also have a client facing a capital murder charge. Because he was doing your dirty work."

Peters, the special agent, scoffed and made a show of it with his hands. Romero didn't accept the characterization well either. "Okay," he said. "Listen. All we're acknowledging is that you'll plead self-defense. That doesn't make your story true. If you haven't figured it out yet"—Romero made eye contact with Peters—"your client says a lot of things. Some may be true, a lot of them probably aren't."

Shelly felt a shiver run through her. She felt as if the insult somehow implicated her as well, at least her gullibility. "Well," she said, a little more testily than she would have preferred, "was Alex connected with this cop or wasn't he?"

"They had met," said Romero. "Look—do we think Officer

Ray Miroballi was using Alex Baniewicz to sell drugs? Sure. Of course. But good luck going to trial on what we *think*. Maybe if we'd had the time to fully investigate this thing, we would have gotten somewhere. Right now, you don't have much of a leg to stand on."

And they were not going to help her in that endeavor, they were saying. Okay. Regardless of the merits of a self-defense plea, the point was the federal government didn't want Shelly or Alex disclosing the federal sting. This thing would be high-profile when it was announced, and the more cops caught in the web, the merrier for the federal prosecutors. Thus, no need to debate the merits right now. Focus on the soft spot.

Shelly gathered her briefcase. "Here's what I want from you. First of all, in exchange for our silence for now, I want these federal charges to disappear."

Both of them moved on that one. They didn't appear to be falling to their knees in compliance.

"Dropped," she repeated. "Gone. Complete immunity. That's for starters. And then you do whatever you need to do with the county attorney to make this murder case a little more manageable."

Romero, still shaking his head, raised a hand. "Part of your client's plea is that he keeps quiet. So don't act like that's some gift—"

"Oh, come now," said Shelly. "My client has a constitutional right to present a defense in his murder case. If his defense relates to undercover work he was doing for you, you can't stop him from talking about it. And you'd look bad trying to."

She put down her briefcase. As she thought about it, the federal government was already looking bad. One of their undercover informants in a shoot-out with one of their suspect cops? They'd look out of control of their own investigation, to say nothing of having their entire sting halted prematurely. Yes, they had plenty of incentive to keep this quiet.

Romero stood and collected himself a moment. Shelly tried to see things from his perspective. He probably saw Shelly as somewhat reasonable—and sympathetic to his mission of ridding the streets of drugs—but also willing to stand up to the feds, and to do whatever was necessary to promote Alex's interests. She didn't intimidate easily, and if Romero had done his homework about her, he probably knew there was only so far he could push.

He framed his hands. "Those kids you try to help, Shelly? Those are the same ones *we're* trying to help. We're talking about ten-year-old kids. Strung out. Addicted. Giving blow jobs in an alley at ten bucks a pop for drug money. Child porn? Teen prostitution? That's all about drugs, Counselor. We're fighting the scum of the earth here."

"So keep fighting," she urged. "Let's call this thing what it was. Alex was fighting off a rogue cop. Get him out of jail. We'll keep this whole thing silent. And your investigation keeps going." She handed him her business card. "For now, we're on the same team. We'll keep mum. But you get us a deal. And get it fast." She moved to the doorway and stopped. "And don't you ever lump Alex in with those scumbags on the streets."

She held her breath as she walked out, ignoring the audible reaction to that last comment. She was in the dark on so many things. She needed answers.

6

Home

"YOUR FOLKS ARE *deceased*," she said to Alex. She had read it in his file. His father, Gerhard Baniewicz, died when Alex was ten years old. His mother, Patricia, had died of cancer when Alex was thirteen. Alex was taken in by Elaine Masters, the mother of Alex's best friend, Ronnie Masters, three years ago.

Alex nodded. "My dad was a good man. Came over on a boat from Warsaw. Worked his butt off. Sold machine parts." His eyes cast away as they walked along the lakefront. It was a quick walk from Shelly's law school office and it was unseasonably pleasant for March. "Problem was, he didn't have much by way of benefits. So he didn't leave us much."

"An independent contractor," she said. Not an employee, and therefore without pensions and health insurance. An inexpensive way for a company to hire workers.

"Exactly. He dropped dead. Aneurysm. Just dropped dead at a sales call."

"I'm sorry, Alex."

"Mom was okay after a while. We got along okay there for a while."

Two parents lost in three years. She couldn't fathom the sense of abandonment. Or maybe she could, but not in such a cruel manner.

"Cancer of the pancreas," he explained. "By the time they found it, it had spread to her lungs. They couldn't even operate. She lasted about four months."

"Do you get along with Elaine?"

"Yeah, Laney's all right. Good heart. Kind of a messed-up lady, but a good heart."

"How's she messed up?" They had reached a small park carved out of the shoreline, and found a bench.

"Booze," he answered. "She makes—let's say she makes bad decisions when it comes to men. There's a guy she was with. He's been gone over a year and she still thinks he's coming back." Alex cupped a hand as if to make an announcement across the lake. "He ain't." He waved off the sarcasm, leaned onto his knees as he looked out at the water. "She just needs a break, really. She needs someone to take care of her."

"So it's you and Ronnie."

"Ronnie's my guy. Only one I trust. Good role model." Alex lightened up. "This guy, he's a junior, he's already got a scholarship to Mansbury College. Smart, smart, smart. And he'd give his right arm for me." He looked at Shelly and then beyond her. "He saved my life once," he said.

Shelly drove along the south side of the city, her stomach in knots and her head full of dark images. The thing about this city, you could drive two miles in this direction or that and find completely different neighborhoods. There was a pocket, about three square miles, almost directly south of the city's downtown, that contained tree-lined streets and small bungalows. The area was known as Mapletown, consisting almost entirely of city workers—firefighters, cops, teachers, and other civil servants—who were required to live in the city boundaries but wanted to get as far out as possible. Mapletown looked more like a suburb than the city proper. But there was a decent influx of minorities in the community over the last ten years—moving into a decent neighborhood was not, after all, the exclusive province of white people. Shelly recalled the cries from minority leaders that realtors were steering blacks away from Mapletown, that homeowners had a silent pact to sell only to other whites, which had prompted a federal investigation by the Justice Department. Lawsuits had been filed, subpoenas issued, but at the end of the day, all that Shelly knew was that Mapletown was slowly integrating.

Alex lived on one of Mapletown's tree-lined streets. Shelly liked the character of the old homes, contrasted with the cookie-cutter developments sprouting up in the city neighborhoods north of the river, where every new townhouse looked the same. Here, the homes were different heights and sizes, though most were limited to small lots. Alex's home was midway down the street, a faded red-brick bungalow with a decaying yard in midwinter. She opened a screen door that looked as if it had been the object of a great deal of work to keep it fastened.

The boy answering the door, she presumed, was Ronnie. He was taller than Alex. His eyes were a bright, watery blue that stood out from an olive complexion. His hair was a thick black, combed back to expose a high hairline. He was wearing a ragged flannel shirt open to his navel, over a white undershirt and blue jeans, no socks or shoes. His face was washed out, presumably from tears and distress and sleep deprivation.

"How?" Shelly had asked him. "How did Ronnie save your life?"

Alex smiled quietly. "A couple of years ago. I was a freshman. Me and a couple of my buddies were drinking. We didn't have much experience with it, so we were pretty lit. Anyway, one of these guys gets the bright idea to hot-wire a car and go for a joyride. We drive it awhile and my buddy almost crashes it. That woke us up. So we ran like hell. Left the car where it was, on some random street corner."

Shelly opened her hands.

"Anyway, turns out, that car belonged to someone who, uh"—his face brightened—"a guy whose car you don't want to hot-wire. This guy was affiliated."

"He was in a gang."

Alex nodded. "He found out who did it and he wasn't pleased. This is the kind of guy, Shelly—we're not talking about someone who's just gonna punch you in the face." His expression straightened out. "Anyway, I didn't know it, but Ronnie went to him and said it was him, not me, in the car."

"Hm. Nice guy. What happened to him?"

"Well, he didn't get killed," said Alex. "We'll leave it at that."

"You're Shelly," Ronnie said.

"Yes."

He gawked at her. It wasn't the first time she'd been the object of stares, especially from a teenager, but like Alex, this boy seemed more fascinated than admiring. He sized her up and stuffed his hands in his jeans, narrowed his eyes. "They're saying he killed a cop?"

"Yes, they are. Can I come in?"

"Oh. Yeah."

He led Shelly into a humbly furnished living room. It was her first time actually stepping into Alex's home. The furniture was decent but old and mismatched, yellow-brown fabric couches, a black leather chair, off-white carpeting. The walls were almost empty of photos or artwork, a muted green color in need of another coat.

"Is your mother here?" she asked. She was referring to Elaine Masters, or Laney, as Alex always called her. It sounded like Laney spent many nights away from home, so she wasn't surprised when Ronnie answered in the negative. She helped herself to a seat on the couch.

Not sure of what to do, Ronnie took a seat as well, on the opposite couch. Shelly looked over Ronnie's head and saw a black-and-white photo of a man, woman, and infant. The photo would have been about sixteen years old and it looked every day of it.

"Alex's folks," Ronnie confirmed.

The man was dressed in a shirt and tie, the mother in a simple dress as she held the baby. Alex's father had died seven years ago, his mother three. Looking at this photo, it made sense. The parents looked to be midforties at his birth. Late in life to start a family. That sounded like Shelly's mother talking.

"He moved in with you after his parents died," Shelly said.

"Right."

"He was lucky to have you to turn to," she said.

"Look what good it's done him." Ronnie rubbed his hands together. He was despairing, Shelly could see, fidgeting in his chair, wanting to do something but understanding that there was little he *could* do. To listen to Alex, Ronnie was the epitome of all things virtuous. Intelligent, ambitious, compassionate, courageous. It was always interesting to meet someone after such a buildup. But the young man certainly wasn't in top form at the moment.

"Tell me what they're saying," he asked.

She answered clinically, as a lawyer, to defuse the heartache she knew both of them were experiencing. "They said he was carrying a weapon and drugs. The police tried to stop him on the street, he ran, and there was a shooting."

"Bullshit. He wouldn't walk around with drugs like that." Ronnie looked away in anger. "No way."

An interesting response. Denying the drugs but not mentioning the weapon. Shelly had had the same response about the drugs, though. It didn't fit. She wondered how much Ronnie knew. Was he aware, for instance, that Alex had been arrested by the F.B.I.? She assumed so, but she hadn't even spoken with Alex yet on the subject.

"Just"—Ronnie shook his hands—"just tell me what to say. I'll say anything."

She ignored the offer for the moment. She certainly would not take him up on it. "I thought he was going to stop, Ronnie," she said, not hiding her disapproval, as if Ronnie were to blame for Alex's transgressions. "I thought he was going to find another way to make some money."

Ronnie struggled in the chair. "That was the plan. Didn't seem to work out. Your guess is as good as mine." Ronnie was acknowledging the same feeling that Shelly had experienced of late with Alex—he was keeping his friends at a distance.

"What in the world was Alex doing with a gun?" she asked.

Ronnie opened his hands. He appeared to be giving a poker face, but he wasn't a natural. In her job, Shelly had seen plenty of them. Bottom line, he wasn't going to answer. Everyone was playing it close to the vest. "Did you ask *him* that?" he asked.

Actually, no, she hadn't. It hadn't seemed the time for twenty questions. She looked at this young man, the boy of whom Alex had spoken so affectionately, and she felt as if she really didn't know Alex Baniewicz at all.

"He was playing hoops at the open gym," said Ronnie. "City Athletic Club. He was coming home afterward."

"You were home?"

"Yeah. When he didn't come home, y'know—with all this shit he was up to, I got worried. I knew something like this would happen." He shook his head. "Can you fix this?" he asked her. "Make this go away?"

She looked at him a moment. "I can try to help him."

"But you know people, right?"

"Ronnie, this isn't something where you make a phone call and erase what happened."

He received that statement like a stubborn child. He was feeling helpless, she could see. Surely, he didn't think that she could snap her fingers and get Alex out of a murder charge.

Ronnie brought his hands together. "Tell me what to say and I'll say it."

She waved a hand and sighed. She wouldn't know where to start.

7

Life

A ROUTINE PROCEDURE, *she has been told. Not difficult, they must mean. Not risky, they must mean.*

It should just take a minute, she is told, for the anesthesia. Count backward from one hundred.

100 . . . 99 . . . 98 . . .

He can't know. No one can ever know. No one, but especially not him. Not Daddy.

Church confirmation, three years ago, when Shelly was thirteen and was upset over the dress Mother had chosen for her, a dispute that escalated into an argument about Christianity and God. How could there be a God? she asked her father, who as always had intervened. With famine and war and poverty? How can there be a—

93 . . . 92 . . . 91 . . .

When you were born, Shelly, he said. That's how I know there is a God. When you have a child of your—

We don't advocate abortion, Shelly. We simply provide this procedure as an option for young women. You were sexually assaulted. This isn't your—

Your father will never know. This is your body. Your constitutional—

87 . . . 86 . . .

He can't ever know. It would kill him.

Move on with your life.

Daddy?

Eighty-seven, eighty eighty I'm sorry eighty sorry Daddy but I can't only sixteen years old please don't stop loving me please forgive me you can't ever know if you ever knew—

Can't . . . ever . . . know . . .

8

Lessons

SHELLY WAS LATE for her class. Thoughts of Alex Baniewicz in detention, his life suddenly interrupted and steered in a different, uncertain direction, filled her as she walked into class.

No. *Interrupted, steered* were the wrong words. He was a good kid, but he'd been playing with fire. She had warned him. Damn it, she had warned him.

They were at the gym where Shelly worked out. Eleven women this week, ages ranging from nineteen to forty-seven, sat in chairs. Shelly did not know their backgrounds, did not even know their names, but she was relatively sure that many of them had been victims. That was why they were here, for a three-session seminar.

Shelly had changed into sweats in the locker room. She walked into the small room with nothing, stepped onto the gym mat in the front of the room. "My name is Shelly," she told them. "Write my numbers down and use them whenever you need them. Whenever." She listed her home, office, and cell phone numbers. Most of the women had brought pen and paper and wrote them down.

"Every minute of the day, every day of the year, a woman is sexually assaulted," she said. "And that's just rape. Add in muggings and break-ins, and the numbers go up exponentially." She looked at the women but kept her eyes moving. She wasn't going to confront anyone. Many of these women carried the secret deep within, something Shelly could certainly understand. "It's okay if you're afraid. I can't keep that from happening. But what I can do is help you be prepared. For every ten women who are attacked, at least nine of those could have been prevented. If not all ten."

A couple of the women nodded. Shelly always started with encouragement.

"Self-defense and protection starts with the three A's. Awareness, attitude, and action. In that order." She tapped her head. "It starts up here. It starts with being smart. Being *aware*. There's a difference between paranoia and awareness. If you're aware, you don't *have* to be paranoid. Okay?"

Some answered audibly, others simply nodded. She needed to empower these women. She needed to fill them with confidence.

"Over these three evenings, I'll teach you how to fight. Not like in the movies, and not for black belts, but in real life. And I'll teach you how to think, if you're attacked. But you only fight if the attacker is in a position to harm you. The key is never to allow that to happen. That's what tonight is about. Awareness. Awareness in your home, awareness on the street, awareness in the car." She paced, ticking off points in her hand.

"Someone in a uniform comes to the door and wants to use the phone, don't let him in. Tell him you'll make the call for him and he can wait outside. Don't advertise your name, or your address, on anything you wear or carry. Check every part of your car—even the backseat and underneath—before you get in. If you're at a bar, keep your drink with you, and if a stranger gives you a drink, don't drink it." She stopped. "We'll cover all sorts of things like that tonight. I'll teach you how to answer the phone. How to turn a corner. How to carry a bag. Nothing challenging. Nothing that's hard to remember. Understand that attackers are looking for an easy target. If you make it tough for them, they'll move on."

She would cover other details tonight that hit closer to home. *Don't get drunk and lose control. Don't go to a party where you don't know anyone, in a city where you don't know anyone.* She would show them how to convert their fear and shame into discipline and focus and, later, solace and confidence. They would practice her tips until they were part of their lives, part of a routine, and someday, maybe, the cries that lay dormant deep within them, that haunted them in the still of the night, someday those cries might dissipate. Shelly would try to convince herself as much as them.

9

Help

IT STARTED ABOUT four years ago and ended last year. Shelly had filed a sexual harassment claim against a school on the city's north side. A teacher had engaged in sexual relations with Shelly's client, a fifteen-year-old student. The teacher was an attractive, thirty-seven-year-old woman in the midst of a harsh divorce. She had seduced the boy, had met him on and off school grounds, had been foolish enough to write him love letters, things like, *Do you think I'm sexy? I think you're so hot.* She had regressed to a high school mindset herself.

Shelly settled with the teacher, who had little more than a small liability policy through the teachers' union, but went to trial against the school. The school was looking at damages in the hundreds of thousands, if not millions, so they hired Paul Riley to defend them. Paul Riley of Shaker, Riley & Flemming. Paul Riley, who had been the top assistant prosecutor in the city, who had sent the infamous Terry Burgos, murderer of multiple college students, to the gas chamber. Paul Riley, who defended the murderer of a prominent doctor in Highland Woods in a crazy case a few years back and got an acquittal. Paul Riley, who had represented Jon Soliday, the top aide to the Democratic nominee for governor in 2000, in the latter stages of a murder trial that had much to do with the election of the Republican candidate, Attorney General Langdon Trotter, to the governor's mansion to continue the G.O.P. domination of that office.

Paul Riley, who represented everything she disliked about

the law, had beaten her butt in the sexual harassment case, a jury verdict for the defense. An arrogant man who had the jury eating out of his hand, who developed a folksy style, a humble-country-lawyer thing that made him look reasonable when he suggested that the school could not possibly have known that one of its teachers would undergo such a transformation from respected language arts teacher to sexually ravenous predator.

Your problem was the boy, Paul had informed Shelly after the verdict, in a phone call to congratulate her on a well-fought trial. *Harder to accept that a woman can rape a boy, especially a big, strong kid like that.*

He was being kind, in her estimation. The truth was that Paul Riley had simply whipped her butt. And now she needed the best. She needed to do whatever she could for Alex. She knew Alex had money, but not the kind of money Riley would command. On the other hand, this was a hot case, a cop killing, heavily covered in the press. That might be payment enough for someone like Riley.

"Michelle!" Paul said, as his assistant led Shelly into his office. The firm was located in a lakefront building, with a lobby spacious enough to land a plane, state-of-the-art architecture, a faux waterfall, modern furniture. Walking through it, Shelly momentarily paid respect to something she would never know: the billable hour.

His office fit the bill, in the corner facing north and east, capturing the lake and the developments along it in floor-to-ceiling windows. There was little in the way of cabinets—presumably the assistants and paralegals held on to the files. One long shelf ran along the east wall to hold Paul's awards and memorabilia, some of it impressive, some of it morbid. A knife was laminated to a plaque with the inscription, *People v. Burgos.* Presumably the knife used to slit the throat of one of the many victims. Pictures on the walls featuring Riley with various officials, including one with the current governor, Langdon Trotter. Behind his desk, on the wall, was an artist's sketch of Paul Riley questioning a witness in the prosecution of Terry Burgos, with the subtitle "The Alibi." She remembered the issue in general terms. Burgos had apparently tried to create an alibi for the murders of the young women and used his boss, a university professor who owned a printing company, as corroboration. But Burgos's plan was foiled when his alibi was exposed, when it was revealed that he had doctored the time sheets. The prosecution—Paul Riley, that is—had used the aborted alibi as proof of Burgos's consciousness of guilt, which meant he did not fit the state's legal definition of insanity.

Paul came from around his desk and showed her to the beautiful wine-colored couch against the south wall. This office was big enough for casual furniture. This office was, in fact, approximately half the size of Shelly's studio apartment.

"Good to see you," he said. "How's my favorite public-interest lawyer?"

The question annoyed her about ten different ways, including the condescension she imagined, the fact that they hadn't gotten along at all during the trial, and the fact that he was greeting her so casually when she'd scheduled an urgent appointment. He was showing her his cool even in an emergency.

"You've grown your hair out," he observed. "It looks very nice."

"I think I need your help, Paul," she managed.

Paul, sitting next to her on the couch, nodded, pursed his lips, kept them from a smile. He was physically fit for an older man, looked comfortable in an expensive suit. His face was long and lined, well-proportioned, deep smile lines around his mouth and eyes. His hair was expensively coiffed and sprayed into place. "I imagine it must be important, if you're asking me."

Shelly did not conceal her reaction but kept silent.

Paul laughed, genuinely amused. "What I mean by that is, I wouldn't expect to be on your referral list under ordinary circumstances. I assume that you must feel some compulsion if you're calling me. You're probably swallowing a lot right now."

"Would you like me to tell you why I'm here, or not?" she asked.

He swept a hand. "The suspense is killing me."

Shelly sighed. Paul quickly touched her arm. "I'm sorry, Michelle. I'm operating under the impression that you don't care for me much, so I had to play with you a little. I apologize. This is important to you, obviously. Please, tell me how I can help."

Okay, he had met her halfway. "Paul, I have a client who is charged with killing a police officer."

"Recently," Paul said. "Day or two ago."

"Right."

"Sure." Paul's tongue ran against his cheek. Calculating.

"His name is Alex Baniewicz. He's a good kid—I mean, he has potential—" She swept back her hair, tucked it behind her ears. "He's basically a good kid. He also sells drugs once in a while. Apparently, the officer was chasing him and Alex killed him in a shoot-out."

Paul fingered a cuff. He wore a thick, heavily starched white shirt with gleaming silver cuff links, a gorgeous orange-and-blue tie. The guy had *lawyer* written all over him. Shelly was suddenly conscious of her blue jeans and sweater.

"You've talked to him?" Paul asked.

"Yeah."

"What's he say? Did he do it?"

"He didn't tell me. But I think so, yeah."

Paul nodded. "Has he talked to them?"

"No. And I've told him not to."

"Great. Good. What do they have? Eyes? A weapon?"

Eyes. The same thing Detective Montes said. "Both of those," she said. "They caught up with Alex about fifteen minutes later. They found the blood on his clothes. They have at least one eyewitness—another cop. I'm told they're scouring the area for more witnesses. They have a weapon and drugs at the scene."

Paul shook his head with a purpose. He seemed to do everything with a purpose, though Shelly had to concede that he made it look casual. "How old?"

"He's sixteen," she said. "So it's death-eligible. In more ways than one." Homicide of a police officer, by itself, made it a capital offense, not to mention that it was murder in the course of another felony, possession of narcotics. The United States Supreme Court had ruled that fifteen-year-olds were too young to be sentenced to death, but a child of sixteen could be executed. Which meant that Alex Baniewicz was eligible for the death penalty.

"And Elliot will seek death," Paul agreed. "For shooting a cop? No question."

Elliot Raycroft, he meant. The county attorney for the jurisdiction, which included the mammoth city and some of the surrounding suburbs.

Shelly nodded.

Paul touched her arm again. He was a very touchy sort. "Sorry, it sounds like you're invested in this boy. But we need to know that going in."

"I understand. I want you to be blunt."

"Then I'll be even more blunt, Michelle."

"Shelly," she said.

"Shelly?" He had spent the entire sexual harassment case calling her by her formal name.

"Shelly."

Paul seemed to recognize that he'd been left out of the club. He could probably figure the criteria for admission. "Okay— Shelly. If your guy hasn't told you whether he did it, do yourself a favor and don't ask him again. Not yet. Find out what the police have first. You can even ask *him* what he thinks they have. But don't ask him whether he did it."

"Sure." She inhaled. Advice she didn't need. "Paul, I was hoping you'd take this case."

He let out a small laugh, a chuckle, implying that this was a major hurdle. He grimaced, while his eyes hit the ceiling, blinking rapidly. "I'm pretty tight." He looked at Shelly. "What is the financial situation?"

"About as tight as your schedule."

Paul rubbed his hands together, studied them. "I make four hundred dollars an hour."

Shelly drew back. "I make four hundred dollars a *week*."

"Surely not."

She waved. She was exaggerating but not by that much. "Obviously, Alex can't pay that."

"Find out what he has, Shelly."

She held her look on him. She understood rationally, but could not accept emotionally, that his representation might actually depend on how much money he would make.

"This is a for-profit operation," he added, the closest he would come to apologizing.

"I'll find out," she said, quickly shaking his hand and leaving.

"Shelly," he called to her. "Take a little more advice from me?"

She dropped her arms, closed her eyes. "Sure."

"Sometimes kids—people—go bad. You don't understand why. It doesn't make sense. You do what you can to help them. And when you're done, when you've done your best, you go to bed at night, and you sleep. Because after you've done your best, there's nothing else you can do."

They have to let you help, she thought. She thanked him and headed for the elevator.

10

Schemes

Alex Baniewicz had been transferred from the police station to the adult detention center on the southwest side, which would be his permanent pretrial home, confined in a special juvenile section for those under eighteen held for adult crimes. Shelly was not informed of the transfer until she reached the police station, so she didn't reach Alex until lunchtime.

She caught Ronnie on the way out. He was more dressed up than when she met him last night, now in a button-down shirt and slacks, hair well-combed. His eyes were bloodshot and he was crying. She figured he stifled his sobbing until he was out of Alex's presence. She had caught him at the release point.

She put her hands on his shoulders. "We'll figure something out for him. You need to keep up your strength, Ronnie."

Ronnie swallowed hard and straightened himself. "I'll be fine. Just tell me what to do and I'll help. I'll do anything."

"Great. I may need that. I'll talk to you soon." She realized, after she left him, that Ronnie was supposed to be in school right now. Come to think of it, she was supposed to be at work, too.

She sat with Alex in a holding room. The table, to which Alex's hands were shackled, was a thick piece of wood on metal legs. The chairs were a hard plastic and bolted to the floor. For some reason, the walls were a pale orange. She wondered who would have made that choice, then wondered why she was even thinking about that. It was amazing how the mind worked, how random thoughts entered the radar screen even during difficult moments like this.

"You and Ronnie have a nice talk?" she asked. Alex gave her a look, as if she had said something challenging. Maybe she had. It was probably the wrong way to start, under the circumstances, but she had less information than anyone and knew that had to change.

"Well, *I* had a nice talk," she added. "With the F.B.I."

Her client looked exhausted. His skin had a yellowish tint that gave the impression of illness. His eyes were sunken, surrounded by dark rings to the point that he almost appeared to be wearing makeup. His reaction to her words was slow, two unfocused eyes eventually meeting Shelly's. She tried to shake the thought that she might lose this kid before it was over.

"I wish you'd told me when it happened," she said. "Instead of shutting me out."

Alex coughed quietly.

"This cop—Miroballi—you knew him."

Alex nodded.

"He was coming after you, Alex?"

He stretched his arms—with some effort, considering his hands were shackled to the table—and cracked his knuckles. "That's what they're saying?"

"They seem to think it's a possibility, yes. Alex, if you shot him because you thought he was going to shoot *you,* you acted in self-defense. You know that, right?"

"You said *if* I shot him."

"Right. *If* you shot him."

God, did he look awful. His hair showed no attempt at order, matted in some spots and sticking up in the back like he'd just awoken. His face was sweaty and unshaven. He ran his tongue against his cheek and stared, with some newfound intensity, at the table.

"The feds are worried about us blowing their operation," Shelly said.

Alex reacted with a humorless laugh.

"Why don't we talk about that?" Shelly suggested. "When the feds arrested you."

His shoulders hunched, his eyes closed, Alex answered quietly. "I—don't really know. I have my place where I keep—you know."

The large quantity of cocaine, he meant. Broken down into packets of one gram each.

Buy in bulk, he had told her. *Cut down on visits to my supplier.*

True, she'd responded. *But then they catch you with a bigger stash.*

They won't catch me.

On its face, his scheme made some sense. He would buy a large quantity of drugs and keep it hidden in the trunk of a beaten-down Chevy he'd bought for a couple hundred dollars. To keep the car off the street, he'd rented a parking space in an alley a couple of blocks from his home. He never drove the car. So there was no chance he would be pulled over by the police, or that the car would be ticketed or towed. Each Friday, he visited the car and removed a small quantity of cocaine to sell to the bankers at work.

"They were all over me," he explained. "I closed the trunk and didn't even make it out of the alley. A guy walked up to me and whispered to me. He tells me he's F.B.I. He points to a black car down the street and he tells me not to run. He takes me to the car and it's all over."

"How much did you have on you?"

"At the time? Four grams. I was going to take it to work. It was a Friday."

"They were waiting for you." Shelly could imagine how it happened. "They were looking at the cop as a suspect and they found you with him. They followed you, sat on you for a while, and then busted you."

"That seems to be how it happened," he agreed. "They whisked me away in that black car of theirs and took me to some building. Bunch of them stayed back and—well, they found the whole load."

Seventy-four grams, to be precise. "They didn't want to publicize their catch," she added.

"I guess not."

"So what did they say to you?"

His face played, almost into a smile. "They were very interested in what I did with that cocaine. Who I sold it to, who I got it from." He looked at her. "They were very interested in a certain cop, too."

"Raymond Miroballi," she said. The cop he shot. She stirred at the mention of the name. There was so much to learn. "Tell me about him. How you met him."

"Miro came to me." Alex shrugged. "I figure he got my name from Todo."

"Todo," she repeated. "This is the guy who supplied you."

He nodded. "Eddie Todavia. Used to go to high school with me. Anyway. So this cop—Miro—he comes to me one day and says he knows what I'm up to. Says he knows Todo is selling me drugs, and he knows what I'm doing with them. He says it's cool with him, he's not looking to bust me. He just wants a piece. A 'taste,' he says to me."

"He wanted a kickback," Shelly summarized. "He got tipped off about you, presumably from Todo, and he wanted a cut."

Alex nodded. "So what am I supposed to say? No? He'll bust me."

"You said yes."

"Of course I did. He said he wanted two hundred a month. Two hundred a month and he keeps his mouth shut. And he watches my back."

Shelly closed her eyes. It wasn't hard to believe, especially after her meeting with the F.B.I. It was right there, for any cop with a wandering eye. And scold Alex as she may wish, she could see his view of things. What leverage did he have against a cop who had caught him with his hand in the cookie jar? She brought a hand to her face. *This* was precisely what she'd warned him about. One day, he'd get caught.

"So the F.B.I. saw you with Miroballi," she said.

"Right. They followed me after that and caught me. Then they put me in a room and ran me through the wringer."

"And you told the F.B.I. what was going on," she assumed.

"Yeah, but seemed like they already knew. They told me I could help myself. Stay out of jail. They told me they wanted everyone connected to this. My seller. My buyers. And Miroballi."

"Most of all, Miroballi," she said. A dirty cop. The only thing more inviting to a federal prosecutor than a dirty cop was a crooked politician. "Give me a time frame, Alex."

He looked off again. "Last summer is when Miro came to me. I think, like, July or maybe it was August. No, it was July. He gave me some time to think about it, but not much time. By August, I was dropping off payments to him. And at some point, the feds must've been watching. They saw me make two payments, I think. End of November, beginning of December. I was dropping off money to him, as much as I could. He was—well, he was cutting into my profit margin, let's say." He sliced a hand on the table. "I mean, Shelly, I was selling at most, maybe five grams a week to these couple of guys at work. Some weeks, it was two grams. I'm not exactly rolling in cash here, is my point. Two hundred a month, this guy wants. That's fifty a week. I'm not clearing a whole lot more than that, and now I have to pay that much to this guy for starters. And then he upped it."

"Upped it? Increased his fee?"

"Yeah. That would have been about November. He said five hundred was a better deal. Five hundred! Shelly, I'm not making enough to cover that. I'm dipping into my own pocket to cover that."

"Did you tell Miroballi—'Miro'—did you tell him that?"

He shrugged. "Of course I did. He wanted to introduce me to new customers. He wanted me to sell crack. He said I was missing out on a huge market. I told him I didn't *want* a huge market. Crack, Shelly? Me? Selling crack to hookers and junkies?"

Powder cocaine was no longer the preferred drug on the street. Crack cocaine was far more addictive, and cheaper. Powder remained popular among the white-collar set, where Alex worked. Officer Miroballi was trying to push Alex onto the streets.

"I said no, thanks. No thanks."

"And I assume Officer Miroballi was none too pleased with that answer."

Alex laughed bitterly. "You assume right. He was telling me the hard time I would do if I were ever caught. He said it was him or prison. He kept saying, a nice-looking white kid wouldn't stand a chance in the penitentiary." Their eyes met with that last comment. It was the precise fate he was facing now.

"You agreed to the five hundred."

"I said I'd think about it," said Alex. "I figured I had some leverage, too. I had already paid him some cash, right? If he took me down, I could take him down, too. Plus I was a cash cow for him. I figured we could negotiate this a little. That's how we left it."

"This was in November," Shelly clarified.

"Yeah. Or early December. After that meeting—the feds got me within the week."

Right. December fifth. "But what about Miroballi?" she asked. "He didn't know you'd been picked up. Why didn't he come back to you to keep 'negotiating'?"

Alex gave her a long look.

"He *did* know," he said.

"Had to have known, Shelly. *Had* to have figured it out."

"So you never heard from Miroballi again?"

"One time after that. We met at a restaurant and talked terms." He flicked a finger in the air. "I told him I wanted to stick to the original deal. Two hundred a month."

"How did he respond to that?"

"Well, that's the thing." Alex licked his teeth. "He didn't fight at all. He just said, 'Oh, okay,' like it was no big deal." He looked at her. "You'd have to know the guy, Shel. He wasn't a guy who took something like that easily. But he did. He just went along with whatever I said. He just wanted the conversation to be done. I think he was testing me."

"Were you wearing a wire?" She couldn't believe that she was asking Alex questions like this. But she imagined that Miroballi had had the same thought of Alex.

"No," he answered. "I couldn't wear a wire. Miro would check for it."

"Was the F.B.I. listening?"

"Don't know. They didn't exactly share their every move with me, Shelly."

Fair enough. "But Miroballi seemed overly compliant with you. And that made you think he was on to your situation."

"He must have been. He *must* have, Shelly. I didn't hear from the guy again. He's getting regular payments from me, then he's upping the fee, then all of a sudden he's being all agreeable, and he disappears off the face of the earth? Of course he knew. He knew the feds had gotten to me."

She sat back in her chair. Oh, the tangled webs. Alex had

been caught and turned into a drug peddler by a dirty cop, then caught by legitimate law enforcement and flipped into a government informant. All of this, for a kid who just had an arrangement with a couple of guys at work for recreational drugs. She hadn't approved of his side business, but God—surely he hadn't deserved this.

"The feds are telling me that I won't be able to prove that Miroballi was working with you," she said.

Alex waved a hand in anger. "Bullshit. Shelly, they knew. If not, how would they ever know to find me? How would they even know who I was? They only *found* me because I was working with Miro."

"I didn't say they didn't *know,* Alex. I'm talking about proof. Did they have *proof*?"

He pursed his lips, stared at the wall. "Can I prove that Miroballi knew I had been caught by the F.B.I.? Other than the fact that he tried to blow my head off? No, I can't read the guy's mind. I can't prove it." He looked at Shelly plaintively. "He disappeared the moment I was picked up by the feds, reappears one time and barely says a thing, and he tries to kill me. That's all I can tell you."

"I believe you," she said. She couldn't possibly say that with confidence.

He shook his head. "Next time I see that cop—well, you know."

"The next time you saw him was the day of the shooting."

Alex nodded yes. Shelly had arrived at the moment, but she wouldn't ask the question yet. She wouldn't ask him whether he pulled the trigger.

Alex inhaled and looked over Shelly's head, working his jaw. "See, Shelly, Miro never just walked up to me in the open like that. He didn't just get out of his squad car and say, 'Hey, bud, where's my money?' I'd drop it somewhere and he'd pick it up after I left."

"So that day, when he got out of his squad car—"

"Oh, yeah, this guy"—Alex adjusts in his seat, animated now—"he gets out of his car and comes after me—I know what this guy's doing."

"You think he wanted to kill you."

Alex's eyes fell to the table, a haunting expression on his face. "Shelly, I swear to you—Miro knew. He was going to take me out right there. People think just because a guy's a cop, he doesn't do bad stuff."

"People don't think that," she said. At least, she certainly didn't. She reached across and put her hand on his.

II
Deliberations

SOMETIMES SHE WATCHES *him in court. He is a prosecutor, and today he is talking to the jury. He is tall and strong and speaks very confidently. If she were told that he was king of the world, she would believe it. They are drawn to him, she can see, the jurors, the spectators, even the judge. Daddy is prosecuting a man who held up a gas station in Bakerstown and killed the attendant. Felony murder, she has heard him say to Mother.*

The defendant was convicted two weeks ago. This is the sentencing phase. Her father is asking the jury to sentence the defendant to death. She can see the defendant and she's read about him in the papers. There weren't many murders in Rankin County, so everyone knew about this. He's a famous killer but she's not watching him. She's watching Daddy.

He's not moving as he stands before the jury. His hands are clasped behind his back. He can be animated, but he's not now. He is speaking quietly.

He's telling the jury about the gas station attendant. His name was Davey Humars. He was twenty-two and was engaged to be married. He liked to watch baseball. He liked to fish.

It has been two days since she left the clinic. She was discharged shortly after she came out of anesthesia. She was provided transportation from the clinic through a covert route to the train station to get her home. She never even saw any of the protesters marching outside. And they never saw her.

Davey Humars had a life, Daddy tells them. He had a life

and he was entitled to it. What do we stand for, he asks them, if we do not stand for the sanctity of life?

Her eyes well up but she will not cry. She's cried enough. She imagines the day she will tell him. She was attacked. She got pregnant. She will tell him about the abortion clinic.

He will know. A day from now or thirty years from now. And he will never look at her the same again.

12
Family

SHELLY LIVED ON the north side of the city, in a neighborhood generally described as a "developing" community, which meant, as far as Shelly could tell, heavily populated by minorities but getting whiter. She had lived here since she graduated law school. She was near the lake and the park, near a bus line that got her downtown in less than half an hour. It was a rental neighborhood primarily, mostly young gay men and Latino families with kids. It was well-lit, quiet, and affordable.

Her apartment was in a four-story brownstone in the middle of the block. It was about a thousand square feet stretching long and thin, with exposed brick walls and old hardwood floors. She got decent light from the southern exposure and a large bay window. She had no patio per se but a landing for the fire escape, overlooking the alley to the rear of the building, served the same purpose when it was warm.

She arrived home that night at nine. It had been four days since Alex was arrested. She had represented him at his bond hearing, in which the court took all of thirty seconds to order Alex held without bond. She was still waiting to hear from Jerod Romero about working out a plea for Alex. In the meantime, she was struggling to find a lawyer for Alex, someone who worked on homicide cases on a regular basis. She had visited fourteen lawyers in three days, all the while trying to keep up with her regular work at the law school.

She was beginning depositions in a case tomorrow, a lawsuit

the Children's Advocacy Project had filed against the city's board of education, seeking to increase money and resources to education for the deaf. The board said the time and manpower was needed to teach the mainstream pupils, and forcing resources elsewhere would hurt the majority to benefit the few. Shelly was stretching constitutional principles to argue that deaf kids should be "mainstreamed" with the general student population but given the necessary extra resources. The answer from the city was always the same—no money, no people, no space. Shelly was not unsympathetic. The city's position was not unreasonable, but it was unacceptable. She filed suit in federal court, where the life-tenured judiciary was far more willing to knock the city around, but even then, any remedy would take years to implement. So much work, to wait so long for what most likely would be only an incremental improvement for deaf and hearing-impaired children.

She was sitting on her bed with the television on. It was primary election day in the state, and results were beginning to pour in after ten o'clock, three hours after the polls had closed. Along the bottom of the screen, numbers were scrolling along. It was a big election primary because all of the constitutional offices—governor, secretary of state, attorney general, and the others—were in play. The gubernatorial primary on the Democratic Party side had been particularly contentious. She was watching a tape of the acceptance speech of the incumbent Republican governor, Langdon Trotter, who had not been challenged in the G.O.P. primary. Still, he had decided to hold a victory rally to get the free airtime.

"We will continue with our goals," he told a raucous crowd. "We will not back down. We will not change our positions from the primary to the general election."

The governor was referring, she gathered, to one of the Democratic Party candidates, who previously had espoused pro-life views while in the state senate but, while running for governor, changed his stance to the more conventional Democratic Party position.

"We are pro-life and we are proud of it!" he proclaimed. "We will not turn our backs on the innocent unborn!"

She shook her head and looked back down at her notes. She

had been reviewing deposition outlines prepared by the law students. CAP was part of a legal clinic, which meant that students did much of the litigation work. Shelly would often try the cases herself when they went to trial, but she usually had at least one student working with her. For the deaf-ed lawsuit, two of her third-year law students would take most of the depositions.

The portable phone rang. She considered avoiding it but picked it up off her nightstand.

"Shelly." It was her brother Edgar on the phone. Edgar, clear-eyed and serious, whose hair never moved, even as a child, whose posture never strayed from erect, who worshipped and mimicked their father. "So you're there."

"So I am," she said. "Very busy time for me," was the most she would apologize.

"Yes, I've heard. You're taking the cop killer, I see."

The news must have reached the papers. Shelly didn't read the news on a daily basis anymore. Or maybe Edgar just had the information by virtue of his job.

"He's my client, yes." Probably not for long, if it were up to Shelly, but she didn't see the need to relieve her brother's agitation. Seven years her senior and the opposite gender, Edgar had found little common ground with Shelly over the years. He doted on her as a child, truly loved her, she believed, but Shelly had found it difficult to return the affection. The love was there—it was there for all of her family—but there was no connection, no warmth. Edgar was no different from Mother, giving her little credit for original thought or substance. She would grow up like Mother, raise some kids. *Oh, a law degree? How cute! She'll meet a nice lawyer.*

"Shel, really—a drug-dealing cop killer?"

"I don't think we should be discussing this. I believe it's called a conflict of interest."

Edgar was the superintendent of the state police force. He had received the appointment three years earlier.

"I'm still your brother." He paused. "I just can't believe— Why do you spend your time— Shelly, really, is this why you got a law degree? I thought you were helping schoolkids. What happened to that?"

"I do help schoolkids. I helped Alex once. He needs my help again."

A sigh from the other end. "Okay, little sister. I don't understand it, but okay."

"I have your permission?" Shelly tightened her grip on the phone.

"Boy, you get a bug up your ass. I'm worried about you, Shel. Can't a big brother look out for his little sister?"

She closed her eyes.

"This stuff will eat you alive. This is going to be a capital murder case. And he's going to lose. You understand that, right?"

"I understand the stakes and the odds, Edgar."

"Listen, little sister. Another thing. This is a cop killing." He paused, as if Shelly were supposed to understand. "I control state police. I don't control city cops."

"What does that mean?"

"It means, drive the speed limit in the city, okay?"

She shuddered. The same thought had occurred to her—retaliation from the local force. "I always obey the laws."

"I put in a call to Fran Macey."

"Who?"

"Francis Macey. Superintendent of the city police."

"Did you now?" Her blood was boiling. "So now he knows to call off his goons?"

"Shelly, cops wake up every day not knowing if it's their last. They approach every pulled-over vehicle wondering if there's a shotgun waiting for them. We do the shit work so everyone can sleep safely at night. So when one of their own—"

"Edgar, I know what cops do. Lawyers defend people accused of crimes. That's what I'm doing." She left out her best line, the one about Edgar never spending a single day in uniform himself. "I won't give the police any excuse to harass me. I will drive the speed limit and I will only cross at crosswalks when it says 'Walk.' If the light changes and tells me to dance on one foot, I'll do it. Okay?"

"Jeez, Shel."

"And thank you, once again, for assuming I can't take care of myself."

A small chuckle from her oldest brother. He mumbled something off the record. "At least call Dad tomorrow, would you?"

"I'll try," she said. She hung up the phone.

On the taped address on television, Governor Langdon Trotter was calling for stricter terrorism laws, for an expansion of the death penalty to include those who sell drugs to our children. She placed the portable phone on the bed and watched the governor complete his short speech, then wave to the crowd. His family gathered around him. His wife, Abigail, kissed him lightly on the mouth. His two sons patted his shoulders and hugged him when it was their turn.

The screen cut back to the anchor desk at Newscenter Four, to Allison Henry. "An interesting side note," she said, "on this celebratory evening for our governor, is that Governor Trotter's only daughter, Shelly, is the lawyer for the young man charged with the murder of Police Officer Raymond Miroballi two weeks—"

Shelly turned off the television and closed her eyes a moment. Then she returned her focus to the outlines for tomorrow's depositions.

13

Company

SHE FELL ASLEEP that night sitting up with work on her lap. She popped awake when she heard the noise. The buzzer to Shelly's apartment resembled the plaintive squeal of a wounded animal. Shelly had grown used to it, though she rarely had visitors.

She turned to look at the clock on her nightstand and felt a pain in her neck from having fallen asleep sitting up. It was just past three in the morning.

The buzzer squealed again. She gathered herself a moment as her heartbeat raced. She reached under her bed for the billy club her brother Edgar had given her, a cop's club, heavy as a baseball bat but more painful on contact. She went to the intercom in her hallway and pressed the "Talk" button.

"Who is it?"

She pressed the "Listen" button.

"Are you Mrs. Trotter? Alex's lawyer?"

"Who is this? I'm calling the police right now." She was holding the portable phone in her hand.

"Manuel," he answered. "My name's Manuel. Alex told me to talk to you."

She paused. There was a sense of urgency to his voice. She held the "Listen" button down for a moment and considered her thoughts.

"Don't—don't call the police," he said.

"Why are you here?" Shelly demanded.

"Man, listen. I'm here to help you. But I can't be around here. They's looking for me."

"Who is looking for you?"

"The *policía*. You can't call 'em."

"The police are looking for you?"

"Yeah. That's what I said. 'Cause of Alex."

"Walk down the stairs," Shelly said.

"What? Lady, I'm telling you—"

"Listen to me. Walk down the stairs, out to the gate. So I can see you." The entrance to the walk-up brownstone had an awning, so Shelly's view of the visitor, if she walked to her front window, was obstructed. But she could see the gate by the sidewalk. "Walk down the stairs to the gate, count to twenty, then walk back up."

Shelly turned off the hallway light and walked in darkness to the front window. She pressed her face against the glass and looked down, watched a young man descend the eight stairs and stand at the gate. He raised his arms as if on display. After a count of twenty, he took the stairs back up to the intercom.

Shelly looked around but saw no other movement outside, a peaceful evening on her block. She walked back to her intercom and pressed the "Talk" button.

"I want you to understand a couple of things, Manuel," she said. "I have a gun up here and I'll use it. I know how to use it. You get me?"

She pressed the "Listen" button.

"—get you, lady."

With a shot of adrenaline filling her body, Shelly pushed the "Enter" button for three seconds. Then she walked to her bedroom, put on sweatpants to go with her T-shirt, removed an extra set of sweatshirt and sweatpants, went to her kitchen, and took out her camera. She opened the door with the chain still on and listened to the footsteps of the man. She watched a young man, about Alex's age, take the final staircase with a nervous glance around. He was smaller than Alex and darker, sweaty and disheveled. She saw the look in his reddened eyes. He was a junkie. He reached the top and looked at Shelly through the crack in the door.

"Stop there," she said.

The boy was wearing a black football jacket and worn jeans. He did what she asked.

"Take off your jacket."

He complied, tossing the jacket by the staircase.

"Take off your pants."

"Huh?"

"You heard me. Take off your pants or I shoot."

He shrugged but followed her instructions, first removing his high-top gym shoes, standing before Shelly in a gray T-shirt and cheap boxers and sweatsocks.

"Throw them down the stairs," she ordered.

The boy had gotten the picture now, that Shelly was afraid he was armed. He tossed his clothes and shoes down the staircase.

"We can talk here," she said. "Lean against the wall and put your palms against it."

The boy shook his head but complied. Shelly held her camera through the crack in the door and snapped his photo.

The boy flailed his arms at the flashing of the camera. "What-choo doin', woman?"

"If you move again, I'll shoot." She closed the door and looked through the peephole. The boy settled against the wall. She put the camera underneath the dishwasher, where a board was missing. Then she went back to the door and cracked it. "You'll never find that camera," she said.

"Lady, I don't want your fuckin' camera." The boy was exasperated. Nervous, strung-out, and tired.

"Talk to me."

"Man, the police's gonna kill me. They know I know about 'em."

"What do you know?"

"Man, I saw what happened."

"I don't know what you're talking about."

"Alex"—the boy adjusted the volume of his voice— "y'know, the cop gettin' shot and all."

"What do you know?" Shelly's eyes kept looking past the boy, at the stairwell.

"I saw the whole fuckin' thing."

Shelly kept her breathing even. This was exactly what she needed.

"Tell me what you saw."

"I saw it, lady. Jesus." He gathered his arms around himself.

It was always drafty in the hallway, and the temperature outside could not have been above twenty degrees.

"He didn't do it, is what I saw."

"Who shot him?" she asked. She felt a fire inside her.

"I don't know. I just know it wasn't Alex."

"How do you know Alex?"

"He's my guy, y'know."

"What does that mean?"

"He's my source, lady. Dig?" He licked his lips. He was a junkie, no doubt. "Lady—I want to help Alex, you know—but these guys are lookin' for me."

Alex was *this* guy's supplier?

"The police are looking for you?" she asked.

"Yeah, lady, what the fuck I been sayin'? Guy like me, I ain't got no protection. Ain't nobody gonna care if I go disappearin' and shit."

"What police? What are their names?"

"Lady—I need help. I need you to hide me."

"I can't hide you," she said, feeling the tone of her voice soften. What could Shelly do for this boy? He couldn't stay with her. She didn't have the cash to put him up, and even if she did, for how long? Until trial? If this boy was being straight with her, he wouldn't last that long. She would need to get him held as a material witness.

Jerod Romero, the federal prosecutor. That was the person she needed to call.

"I can get you protection," she said. "But probably not until tomorrow."

"Damn." He wasn't responding to her. The boy was shivering— could be his nerves, or it could be because he was in his underwear on a cold night.

"I have a gun," she repeated. "Remember that?"

"Yeah, I remember."

She threw out the sweatshirt and pants to Manuel. "Put those on," she said. "You can come in for a minute." She couldn't very well send this boy back on the streets.

Her alarms were going off—this was everything she told her students in self-defense *not* to do.

She opened the door and let Manuel pass her as she clutched

the door, looking down the staircase. She closed the door again and directed the boy to the couch. He looked silly in a baggy sweatshirt and pants that didn't even reach his ankles. He looked the part of a junkie, skinny frame, drawn face, eyes and mouth wet and red, his hair mussed and greasy, prominent body odor. He looked around Shelly's apartment with some fascination. This was how normal people lived.

"I don't know," he said. "Man, I don't know."

"You're safe here."

"Lady, you don't know what you're messin' with here. Cops can go anywhere, see. They can do any fuckin' thing they want."

"I'm going to talk to someone who can help you," she said. "Protect you."

"When?" he asked, still standing, moving on the balls of his feet. "Now?"

"Tomorrow," she said. "You can—I suppose you can stay here tonight."

"Nah, man." He looked around. "Not tonight, lady."

"Why not tonight?" she asked. "You think they've followed you?"

"Man, you're helpin' Alex, right? You don't think they're watchin' *you*?"

Dread filled Shelly, an enveloping poison. She went to the front window and looked out but saw nothing.

"Nah, I'm comin' back later."

"No," said Shelly. "I need your help. At least let's talk awhile."

"Man, I gotta stay mo-bile." The boy walked in circles. "I gotta get lost."

"Manuel, I guarantee I'll get you protection. I guarantee it."

"Tomorrow," he said weakly.

"Tonight, *I'll* protect you."

Manuel sighed and laughed. "No thanks. Tomorrow."

"Please." Shelly moved in front of him. She could not be sure she would ever see him again.

He brushed her aside and went to the door. "Sorry, lady."

"You'll come back tomorrow, though," she said.

He smiled at her without enthusiasm. He seemed to be telling her there would be no tomorrow.

She went to the door and took his arm. "I swear I'll protect you. Stay alive tonight and find me tomorrow. Wait." She went to the kitchen, ripped off a piece of a notepad, and scribbled her cell phone number. She stuffed it into his hand. "Take this. Call me anytime. Wherever I am, I'll come find you." Shelly unlocked the chain and started to turn the knob, but kept the door partially closed. "You trusted me enough to come here. Trust me—"

It hit Shelly the moment she felt the outside force on the door, a barreling weight pushing her backward. They had used the boy to gain access without breaking and entering. They knew enough to know that, from her view above, the awning obscured them next to the outside door. They'd been here before, probably stood by the door, measured the angles of viewpoint. They'd known exactly where to stand to avoid detection.

They didn't take the stairs with the boy initially, because Shelly would have seen them. The plan was to get the boy inside her place, at which time they would sneak up the stairs and wait for the door to open again, as the boy was leaving. She hadn't looked through the peephole, but had she done so, ten-to-one they were just outside its range as well. They were waiting to pounce the moment they heard the chain open, the moment the door opened even an inch.

They had given this boy enough information to bullshit his way in. He knew Alex, knew the cop. But he hadn't provided any detail whatsoever. They had busted the junkie and made him help them, probably in exchange for a walk.

She'd been smart but not smart enough, not sufficiently careful. She was living the one lesson she never told her students, because there was no point in doing so: No matter how careful you are, if someone wants at you bad enough, he'll probably get there.

The impact threw Shelly against the wall but she managed to keep her feet. Two men stormed in, wearing black ski masks and long coats, rubber gloves. The first man came at her, his hands raised. She gave a short kick into his crotch. He doubled over; she grabbed at the back of his coat and used his momentum to propel him forward, past her to the carpet.

The second man held a revolver with a silencer poised at her face. He shook his head slowly. He was in the doorway, with a foot jammed against the door to keep it open. She looked at his feet, then measured the distance. She was off balance against the wall, too far from the man for a kick, and she couldn't close the door on him even if she could reach it. She ignored the sounds behind her, the painful grunt of the first intruder. She measured the distance again.

"You'll be dead before you take a step," said the man. His voice carried well through the mask. "And so will Alex."

She heard the man behind her get to his feet. A moment later, a weapon was pressed against her temple.

Alex, he'd said. This guy knew the name of her client. As a juvenile, his identity had been kept confidential. Not reported in the press.

In the space of no more than ten seconds, they had entered and subdued her. And made virtually no noise doing it. They were either hard-boiled crooks or cops.

Or both.

The one in the doorway looked behind him to be sure the junkie had high-tailed it. Then, with his revolver still trained on her, he closed the door and locked the chain. He approached her with the gun aimed at her face. There were now two guns within inches of her nose.

"Open wide," he said.

She locked her jaw, grit her teeth, but he pushed the silencer hard against her mouth until she had no choice. If she resisted, it could go off.

"Here's the good news," he whispered. His eyes—the only part of his face exposed—were a dark brown, narrowed into slits. "I'm not going to kill you."

Shelly had already figured as much. If they wanted her dead, they would have killed her by now. They'd shown too much skill to be sloppy on this point.

"This gun here"—he pushed the weapon deeper into her mouth, almost gagging Shelly—"this is my insurance against you trying any more of that judo shit. Won't be my fault the gun goes off." He grunted, or laughed, it was hard to differentiate. The tough part was over, now he was confident. "Oh, yeah, lady lawyer, we know all about you."

Shelly was frozen. Her mind instinctively turned to her myriad of options, body locations for kicks and knee thrusts and punches. If it were a fair fight, she was sure she could handle them together. But there was nothing she could do with a gun in her mouth.

They had done their homework. They would deliver their message and get out.

The second man whispered into her ear. "You sure are a nice piece of ass, you know that, Shelly?"

Shelly shut her eyes, gasped for air with a mouthful of gun.

"You wearing a bra under there, Shelly?" The man touched her breast, fondled it, one then the other. "No, of course not. You were asleep. Yeah, it's too bad we don't have more time tonight. Maybe you could put on a little show for us."

Shelly squeezed her eyes shut but kept still. She thought the words with a calm that surprised her. *Not again.* They would have to kill her first.

"Aw, she'd probably put up a fight," said the one behind her. "Just for show. Before long, she'd have her legs wide apart. Isn't that right, Shelly?"

"Maybe next time," said the one in front. "Maybe, things don't work out here, we'll bring back three or four others. We'll take turns on little Shelly."

"Yeah, but you know what happens then."

They both laughed.

The second man moved his face next to Shelly's. "She'll cry rape again."

Shelly felt faint, could hardly keep her balance. They were telling her they were cops, had pulled her file, knew all about her. They wanted her to know.

The man in front moved even closer, so that his mask almost touched Shelly's nose. "If we hear a single bad word about Ray Miroballi, you both die. We'll find Baniewicz, in or out of jail. And we'll find you. We'll make it hurt, Counselor. You know how the Cans do it, right?"

She did know. The Columbus Street Cannibals killed rival gang members by cutting off a limb and letting them bleed to death.

"You keep your mouth shut about this visit, and Baniewicz pleads guilty." The gun moved against the base of her throat. "Or there's nowhere either of you can hide."

The gun at her temple moved against her ear, then around to the back of her neck, never leaving her skull. Then she felt hands on her shirt, her hair, and she was turned violently and hurled across the room. She could fight, yes, but she was small, maybe a hundred and ten pounds at best, and the force sent her face-first into the carpet.

She did a quick inventory, with her chin dug into the carpet. No broken bones, maybe a scrape or two at most. If they came at her from this position, she had several options, most of them below the belt. Some would maim. Some would hurt like hell.

But they weren't coming at her. They were done.

"Yeah, really not a bad piece of ass," one said to the other.

She heard laughter, then movement, a door closing gently behind her. She tried to scream but, once again, she couldn't.

14
Birthday

IT WOULD HAVE been a terrible day, anyway. The nineteenth of February. A day off for Shelly usually, every year. A *personal day*.

She hadn't slept after the visit from the intruders. She had called the police and spoken with officers when they arrived, saying nothing of her very real suspicion that it was police officers who had paid her a visit. Her point had simply been to show them—if they were still watching—that she wasn't afraid to call the authorities. If the burglars were cops, they would be checking the report that was filed. She wanted them to know.

She had to see Alex, as she had every day, first thing in the morning before going to work. She didn't want to shower, didn't want to move her eyes off the front door. So she had bathed in the kitchen, taking a bar of soap and running it over her underarms and chest, drying with a towel. She hadn't washed her hair but pulled it back sharply and pinned it. She could only imagine the impression she made.

She watched the clock as it hit seven-thirty. She inhaled and closed her eyes. On her kitchen table, she lit the sole candle and stared into its flame. She did the same thing she did every year on this day, asked for forgiveness and redemption.

God, of all days.

She drove to the detention center and raced to the check-in. "Michelle Trotter," she said, "here to see my client, Alex Baniewicz." She looked at the clock. It was three minutes past eight in the morning. She felt dizzy from sleep deprivation but charged with adrenaline.

"He has a visitor," said the man behind the glass window.

"Who?" Not having enjoyed her own most recent visitors, her mind raced as to who might be paying a call on Alex.

"Ronald Masters."

Oh. Okay. Ronnie.

She took a seat and felt exhaustion set in. Lack of sleep, tension, and grief had wiped her out, and her day had hardly started. But she felt some measure of relief being here, even if she hadn't seen Alex yet.

Time moved slowly as she sat in the waiting room with two other women, each of them younger than she. Each of them African American. Neither of them appeared to be filled with hope or enthusiasm. This was not a happy place. If she were her mother, she would be bouncing off the walls right now. She remembered when her mother's father—Shelly's grandfather—had passed, and her mother continued to cook the scrambled eggs after receiving the phone call, because she *needed to do something*. Shelly didn't mourn that way. She let it swallow her whole, maybe so it would go away more quickly.

Ronnie Masters emerged from a door. He was wearing a hooded sweatshirt, which struck Shelly as insufficient for the cold weather; his long, dark hair was hanging all over his face. He saw her and nodded. Shelly greeted him, gave him some empty pleasantries.

"Didn't know you were gonna be here," he said, as if there were something meaningful about that. He gave her another look. "Have a rough night?"

"Something like that."

Ronnie kissed Shelly's cheek. He probably wanted to beg Shelly to save Alex, to spare him from the consequences of his actions. Whether Ronnie was in denial, Shelly did not know. What a "brother" would feel in such a situation was unfathomable. Little escaped Ronnie, and his presence had nothing to do with Alex's guilt or innocence.

Shelly touched her eyes as Ronnie left. She felt an excruciating weight as she followed the guard into the interview room. Alex, having had a prior visitor, was already seated in the familiar position, hands cuffed before him. His eyes were swollen and red. Shelly had seen it before—little hurt a young man more than seeing the effects of his actions on his family.

Alex seemed surprised to see her. He started to speak but caught himself. He seemed overly aware of a small bag of items sitting on the floor near him. Shelly saw books, three different used paperbacks, inside the bag with a purple, frilly ribbon hanging out. Come to think of it, the bag was a small plastic one, fire-engine red. She could see a card in the bag as well, a long message in a fancy font.

She looked up at Alex. He smiled apologetically.

She pointed at the bag. "Your—is it—"

He swallowed hard. Their eyes locked on each other as she sank to her seat.

"Happy birthday to me," Alex sang, an attempt at breaking the sudden tension, with a nervous smile that evaporated as soon as it appeared.

"Seventeen," she said.

He said nothing. She searched his face, which invited her. The longer they stared at each other, the more uncomfortable she became.

"Were you—" She couldn't get the word out. "You were—"

He nodded. He smiled at her differently than ever before. The sweetness that Shelly had found so compelling for an unrefined kid, his immediate willingness to open himself to her, held a different meaning now.

"Adopted. Yes." Alex finished her sentence, pausing first, then slowly saying the words.

They stared at each other without words. She could read it on his face but she couldn't believe it.

"No," she said.

"Yes."

"I'm so sorry," she said, not even realizing she uttered the words as the realization had crashed down on her.

"I was gonna tell you, Shelly. A bunch of times."

Shelly stared at this boy as if he were a work of breathtaking art, a magnificent structure to behold. She brought a hand to her mouth, closed her eyes. Her body began to tremble, but she did not cry. A different feeling gathered over her, a feeling that certainly couldn't prevail, not under the circumstances, but one that could not be denied temporarily.

When she opened her eyes again, the trembling ceased.

Alex smiled at her, clearly more at ease with the information than Shelly. He'd had a year to digest it, after all. "I suppose it's time we talked about it," he said.

Shelly held on to the table as if a strong wind threatened to blow her away. Alex hadn't really needed a lawyer for that initial disciplinary case at school after all.

He'd just wanted to meet his mother.

PART TWO

Choices

15

Mother

SHE OPENS HER *eyes with a start, popping up on the re-clined leather chair, staring into the eyes of Dr. Sarah Karpiel. The doctor, her legs crossed, sits on a stool, reading from a clip-board. She is fair-haired, wears glasses and peers through them at her patient.*

"What—did I—?" *Shelly's throat closes.*

"No." *The doctor sets down her clipboard and leans on her knees.*

"No?" *Shelly feels a flood of relief.* "I—you didn't—"

"Shelly, we don't push abortions on people. We don't even advocate them. We simply provide a medical option at the pa-tient's request." *There is a hint of rebuke, or maybe frustration, in the doctor's voice.* "Although it would be preferable not to wait until the last moment to tell us."

"I—I told you."

"You withdrew consent, Shelly. You started screaming, as best you could, at least."

Shelly sits up, gathers her gown about her. Her heart is pounding. She places a hand on her belly and looks up at the doctor. "What did I say?"

The doctor shrugs, but surely she recalls the words. Perhaps she doesn't want to. "You said 'no.' You said 'stop.' You said, 'Don't do it.'" *She adjusts her glasses.* "At least, as best as we could understand. I wasn't going to take that chance."

"Thank you." Shelly exhales, looks up at the ceiling and maybe beyond.

"You can return, Shelly, but only if you're sure. You have some thinking to do."

Shelly manages her way out of the chair and steadies herself. She knows it now with a vision, a clarity she has never known.

16
Son

ALEX EXPLAINED THINGS, moving slowly at first before gaining some comfort. He had been adopted by the people Shelly saw in the photograph at his house—Gerhard and Patricia Baniewicz. Everything he'd told her was true—his dad was an immigrant who sold machine parts, his mother a second-generation Russian who worked at an assembly plant—except that they weren't his biological parents. They had met in their midthirties—they were only a year apart in age—and married less than a year later. They rented a floor of a small house just south of Mapletown in a heavily concentrated Polish neighborhood.

After several years attempting to conceive, the couple learned that Patty Baniewicz was infertile. They were rejected by adoption agencies because they failed the "rule of seventy" applied by many agencies, which added up the ages of the two parents and disqualified those over a cumulative age of seventy. So they turned to private adoptions—attorney adoptions—and after two years made the connection. Alex came into their lives after eighteen months of waiting, the product of an entirely confidential transaction between attorneys. They didn't know the name of the family who had brought them Alex, and that family didn't know them.

Shelly listened intently. She was not surprised at the ages of Alex's adoptive parents, because she knew well the ins and outs of adoptions. She knew the "rule of seventy" and that most parents who went the private adoption route were older, sometimes in their late forties or even fifties. She also knew that the unintended consequence was that many of these parents passed away when their adopted children were young, leaving the children in an often precarious situation—for the second time in their short lives.

Yes, she had researched it quite a bit herself. She even knew how to find her son, knew the long way and the shortcuts. Either way, it was fairly expensive and difficult. But it could be done. She knew how. She just hadn't ever done it.

Gerry Baniewicz died, as Alex had originally told her, of an aneurysm when Alex was ten. Three years ago, Patricia died after a very short and unsuccessful bout with pancreatic cancer. By the time it was discovered, the cancer had spread to her lungs and was inoperable. She died 137 days after getting the news. She had made what preparations she could for Alex. Financially, she would leave little behind. Elaine Masters had agreed to take Alex in. She was an alcoholic and everyone knew it, but she was also a kind woman who simply could not keep up with her troubles. It was because of Ronnie, Alex said, that Patricia could die knowing that someone would be looking out for Alex. Alex recalled his mother, at home and near death, grasping Ronnie's hand and making him promise that he would stay by Alex's side.

Shelly sat next to Alex. She searched his face as discreetly as possible, for evidence of her parents' traits, her own characteristics. His strong chin—maybe that was a Trotter trait, like Shelly's father. The eyes, she could see some of her mother, the shape not the color. His features were primarily dark, however. She didn't want to say it, even think it: Alex probably looked more like his father, whoever that was.

It had been ninety minutes now, since Shelly had learned. The first hour was a fog; neither of them spoke more than a handful of words. Shelly was absolutely transfixed by him, this boy who had sought her out a year ago under the ruse of needing help with a disciplinary proceeding, when all he really wanted was to meet his mother. This boy who sought Shelly's approval, who seemed to be making an effort to comply with her wishes for him—at least until—well, that could wait. Her mind, her heart was enough of a tidal wave already.

Oh, look at him! He was a sensitive, compassionate kid.

He was a drug dealer who shot a police officer.

"Tell me how you found me," she said, though she could probably guess herself.

"Hired a guy," he told her. "Some of the I-bankers use private investigators when they're doing due diligence. I used one of them. Put me back about twenty-five hundred. He went to some agency—"

The Department of Public Health, Bureau of Vital Statistics.

"—and got someone to give him a peek at the birth certificates."

There was a birth certificate for every child born in this state. The certificate contained the birth mother's name and age, as well as the place of birth. For adopted children, an amended birth certificate was then placed on top of the original, with the adoptive family's name. The procedure Alex's investigator undertook was a routine, though technically illegal one, looking at the original birth certificate to find the name of his biological mother.

"So then we knew your name, and it didn't take us long to find *you*."

She nodded. For such a loud-mouthed, opinionated attorney, she was suddenly without words. She knew more about the process of locating a parent or child than he did. She could have found Alex. All these years, she could have and didn't.

"I just wanted to meet you," he continued. "That school thing—that fight. That was kind of my excuse. I just wanted to see you in person. I didn't know if we'd ever get to know each other. I didn't know if I'd ever tell you."

She had never felt so disarmed. She wanted to duck under the table in shame. All of the rationalizations she'd lived with seemed empty. She was without excuses or words.

"It's okay," Alex said.

Was her remorse that obvious? She couldn't know. She couldn't think rationally now. What could she say to this boy? What *should* she say?

A knock on the door. The five-minute warning. Their time was up.

Shelly could recall the conversation almost verbatim. Last May, before the warm weather had broken. She and Alex were walking along the lake on a Sunday, only a short walk from Alex's offices at McHenry Stern. She was cold and Alex had given her his long black coat.

She didn't know, in hindsight, why she had told him. Maybe because she had known, of all people, he would never repeat it. They didn't share friends or run in the same circles. So he was safe. Yes, that would have been the easy way to rationalize it. But that wasn't the truth. The truth was, she had always opened herself more to children than adults. She had few close friends, perhaps by choice. The truth was, in the four months she had known Alex up to that point, she had come to rely on the friendship as much as Alex. She'd never told anyone, other than the police, of course. She'd never told anyone and she suddenly felt the urge.

The truth was, she wasn't just helping Alex get his act together. She'd needed his friendship as much as he needed hers.

I was raped when I was sixteen, she'd told him.

She'd told him everything. The reaction of the police. Her thoughts of abortion. The reaction of her parents. Her life afterward.

I had the baby, she'd said. *I gave it up for adoption and never saw it. Not then or ever again. An attorney came in, had me sign the papers, and it was over.*

And now, as she sat across from a boy who was her son, she recalled Alex's reaction. The loss of color to his cheek, the catch in his throat when he tried to vocalize a response. She didn't discern the subtleties then, the difference between shock and disappointment, or perhaps the mingling of the two.

How, she wondered with the knowledge of hindsight, had that information affected Alex? When she told him of her rape last May, she was telling him he would never know his biological father. And worse. She was telling him that his birth, his very existence, was the product of a criminal act.

It came to her now, the reason for her need to purge to him that day. That hadn't been just any old Sunday in May. And—yes, now that she thought about it—it had been Alex's idea to meet on Sunday. He had bought her lunch and given her a small gift, a pair of earrings. She had accepted it for what she thought it was, a gesture of appreciation for everything she had done for him. It had never occurred to her then that it was a Mother's Day present.

The guard entered the room and unlocked Alex's handcuffs from the table. Alex stood up in his handcuffs and looked briefly at Shelly before being led out of the room.

17
Plea

JEROD ROMERO HAD a series of routine matters in court this morning. For some of the cases, prisoners in orange jumpsuits were shuffled in, joined by their defense counsel. Romero was all business, no humor, even when the judge was not on the bench.

He finished about noon and saw Shelly as he was gathering his papers. "Ms. Trotter," he said in his formal courtroom voice.

"I need to know you're protecting Alex."

"We are." Romero looked at her with curiosity. "Why do you mention it?"

Shelly had thought about it over the nine hours that had passed since the two men ambushed her in her apartment. She'd run to Alex to ensure his safety—only to be broad-sided by his revelation—then to work, to do a final run-through for the depositions that would begin today in the deaf-ed case—and then to the federal courthouse, where she had found Jerod Romero.

With the constant shift in focus, she felt punch-drunk, delirious, driven only by adrenaline. She could only imagine the impression she was making on the prosecutor.

She had decided she would not reveal what had happened. Not yet. She couldn't prove anything and she could only make matters worse. There was always time to do it. Ways to do it.

"Something happened," said Romero.

"Just make sure Alex is okay. I'm putting you on notice."

"You have to tell me if someone threatened him," he said. "Or you."

"No, I don't. But if you don't give me assurances, right now, that Alex is safe, I'm going to the press. I'm going to the judge. I'm going to tell everyone in town about your operation."

The prosecutor raised his hand, looked around the emptying courtroom as if he were afraid Shelly might divulge the confidential information right now. From Romero's perspective, Shelly held a real card here. She had every right to change Alex's plea to self-defense and to explain in detail the facts of that defense. The federal prosecutor, with all his powers, could not stop her. The U.S. Attorney's office could not prevent Shelly from revealing the sting operation.

And that was not only important to the U.S. Attorney's office as a whole, but in particular to this Assistant U.S. Attorney standing before her. This would be a major case, perhaps a career-maker, for Jerod Romero, depending on how many cops were snared in the operation.

"He's safe," he told Shelly. "You have my word."

She was too exhausted to sufficiently read the prosecutor. She took him at his word, mostly because she had no choice. She didn't want to expose the drug sting, either, and more to the point, she didn't want to hurt Alex's chances for a negotiated deal with the county attorney on the murder charge.

Romero motioned for them to sit at one of the rows of spectator seats, which resembled pews in a church. He seemed to appraise her outward appearance more than consider strategy. "You're right," he admitted. "I can't make you tell me. But if someone's getting nervous about Alex—I need to know that, Shelly. I can help you. And I need to know."

She refused to elaborate. Romero could fill in the blanks, anyway. A covert visit from one of the city's finest, threatening her and/or Alex. Perhaps Romero would consider tailing Shelly now—not so much to protect her but to catch a nervous cop looking to harass her. But more important, he would be watching Alex, hopefully more closely than ever. Surely the federal government had ways, even in a county-run facility. She certainly hoped so, because she had few options. She needed to keep it a secret as much as he did.

Romero ran a tongue against his cheek, folded his hands. He lingered in that position as if he had something to say but wasn't sure. Finally, he looked at her and said, "Sixty years."

Shelly stared at the floor, her breath whisked from her lungs. "Sixty," she repeated. "The county attorney agreed to sixty years?"

"State time is one-for-one," he said. "With good behavior he's out in thirty."

She ran her fingers through her hair. Her vision was spotty. She felt herself swooning.

"Sixty years is a godsend, Ms. Trotter." The prosecutor's tone held a rebuke. She was supposed to be grateful.

She *should* be grateful. Sixty years—really only thirty—for shooting a cop in the face? So why wasn't she thrilled? What had changed? Nothing should. Whether she was Alex's mother or defense attorney, her interests were the same. Weren't they? Alex's best interests.

Was it easier when they were looking at the death penalty, or life in prison? Did it make the solution easier? Fight it out. All or nothing. Now, with a compromise, she was looking at giving him willingly to the state.

Giving him up. Again.

"Where?" she heard the lawyer in her ask.

"Where—does he serve his time, you mean? Downstate, I assume."

"Federal prison," she said. "Has to be."

"I can't do that. For shooting a—"

"Do it," she said. "And I'll discuss it with my client."

"Ms. Trotter—Shelly." The prosecutor opened his hands. "I hope you'll tell him he'd be crazy not to take this deal."

"We'll have to discuss it," she managed, getting to her feet. She walked down the aisle and gently pushed against the swinging door.

"Maybe I can get a federal correctional center," Romero called out. "Would that do it?"

"I don't know."

"Come on, Shelly. Thirty years, easy time."

"Mr. Romero," she said as she hiked her bag over her shoulder, "there's nothing easy about thirty years."

18

You

SHE WAS BACK to Paul Riley. Shelly had started with him and, after meeting with over twenty defense lawyers across the city, had returned to him. Because he was the best. Because his practice was thriving, unlike many of the state-court criminal defense attorneys, so he might be more willing to take on a case that didn't pay. Because he had been the top lieutenant at the county attorney's office back when he put away the infamous killer, Terry Burgos. Because he'd been an Assistant U.S. Attorney before that, and probably knew better than anyone how to navigate the murky waters between the two prosecutorial offices.

Because she detected something in the way he looked at her? She thought of herself as rather plain-looking, tall and athletic, her mother's curved face and pointed chin, thick hair that fell to her shoulders with little ado. But she wasn't blind to the looks on the faces of many gentlemen who made her acquaintance, and Paul, who otherwise managed a passable poker face, hadn't done a good job of concealing his opinion. Maybe he wasn't trying to.

"So the shooting of this cop falls right in the center of an undercover federal sting," said Paul. Shelly had broken the oath of secrecy but felt perfectly secure in doing so, in this context, one lawyer to another, explaining the merits of the case to the lawyer who might be handling it. Did Paul know that this was the scenario?

"Timing is a question," he said. "We don't know how much time they want to wrap up their investigation of the dirty cops. Could be months. Could be years. The more time they need, the better your leverage." He snapped his fingers absently. He and Shelly were across the street from Paul's office. It was a primarily carry-out diner with a small counter. Paul lifted a slice of chicken off his plate. He clutched a napkin in his other hand.

Shelly had a fruit plate before her but couldn't touch it. The men behind the counter were shouting to each other in Greek. Piles of sliced chicken and burgers sizzled on the grill. The place reeked of fried foods.

"I don't want to plead him out," she said.

Paul wiped his mouth. "Premature. Investigate first. Find out about the dead cop. See what the feds have on him."

Shelly looked at him. "I didn't come here so you could tell me to investigate the case before I plead out my client."

He smiled briefly, then turned to her. "Shelly, I start trial in less than thirty days. It will last eight weeks at least. It's a multiple-defendant Medicare fraud case. And I have a civil RICO trial scheduled for four weeks after that. Even bigger."

"And those clients pay," said Shelly. She immediately regretted the comment. She couldn't impose her priorities on Paul Riley.

Paul let it slide. "What I would be happy to do is help. Anything you don't understand, or if you want some advice or my opinion, I'll be available. Evenings."

"Won't you be preparing for trial in the evenings?"

"Yes, but there are plenty of lawyers I'm working with. It's a pretty big defense team."

Paul Riley, in other words, was the showboat who took the labor of the toiling attorneys and wove magic in the courtroom. Shelly gave up all pretense of attending to her food and swiveled on her chair. "Tell me what I need to do to change your mind."

Paul found this amusing. "There is nothing you can do, Shelly."

"We'll move the trial date," she offered. "To fit it into your schedule."

"Shelly—"

"I'll find a way to get you paid."

Paul held up a hand. "I'll help, Shelly. No charge. But that's it."

"That's not good enough."

"There are dozens of first-rate trial lawyers in this city. I would be happy to recommend one."

Shelly deflated. A road already traveled. Her mind angled for the right words, but Paul was not even close to equivocating. "Fine," she said. "Recommend someone."

He wiped his mouth and threw the napkin on his plate. "You," he said.

"Me." She spat the word from her mouth. "I've never handled a capital murder case."

"You're one of the best lawyers I ever opposed, Shelly. You don't even realize it."

"I'm not better than you."

"That's a matter of opinion," he said. "And perspective." He touched her leg, just a tap, in a way that Shelly found inoffensive. With his movement, Shelly detected a hint of his cologne and felt a stirring. "That case we had, you and me? I walked in thinking there was no way I could lose. But I'll tell you, Shelly, I had a little sweat on the back of my neck when that jury came back. I actually thought you had talked a jury into giving millions to a fifteen-year-old who played out a schoolboy's fantasy, screwing a beautiful teacher."

"That was a civil case," she answered.

"But I was under the impression you had handled a number of criminal cases."

"Juvies, Paul. Not an adult case."

He waved his hand, as if that ended the conversation.

"Not a capital case, Paul."

"Oh, look." He swiveled on his chair to face her. "Shelly, there are a few details that are specific to a criminal trial, compared to juvenile court. With those, I can help you. Otherwise, it's just putting twelve in a box and trying to convince them your side is right." He looked over her head. "There are a handful of good lawyers who could do this, I suppose." He shook his head. "But they'll want to be paid, and even if you find a good one willing to work pro bono, you offer some things that they don't."

She grimaced but did not take the bait.

"For one," said Paul, happy to answer his own point, "you hate to lose. That case we had? I've never seen anyone so upset at losing."

"Every trial lawyer hates to lose."

"True, but it usually comes down to money. Plaintiffs' lawyers hate to lose because they want in on the award. Guys on the side of the deep pockets, they want more business, and that comes from winning. You? You weren't going to take any of that kid's money, if he had won. There was nothing in it for you at all."

"Fairness," said Shelly. "Justice."

"Oh." Paul waved at her. "Sure, fine. But there was more there, Shelly. You have a chip on your shoulder, and I mean that in a good way. You take losing personally. You absolutely hated losing to me—in part because you thought I was a pompous ass, sure, but more than anything because you just hate losing, period." He smiled at her. "Tell me I'm wrong."

She shut her eyes. This guy was right on in his analysis. She seemed to spend her life fighting one battle or another.

"The other thing you offer," he continued, now enjoying himself, "is passion. You care about this kid more than anyone else will. You'll work harder than any of them. And I'll be there to lend a hand."

Shelly felt a tremendous tightening of her shoulders, a shot of anxiety to her heart.

"If I didn't think you were capable, Shelly, I wouldn't have recommended you. I don't give false praise."

It was the last thing she wanted to hear. What bothered her most was, she knew Paul was right. Despite herself, and somewhat surprisingly to Shelly, she had few doubts about her abilities as an advocate. She had already come around to Paul's way of thinking. A jury was a jury. A case was a case. She had tried countless cases, some to a jury and some to the bench, and she had won most of them. She might need assistance with forensics, or particular rules governing criminal cases, but at the end of the day she was merely shaping the evidence to support her client's position, something she had done a dozen times before a judge or jury. The only difference was the stakes. That had been her reason for seeking out Paul. She was trying to pass the responsibility. But Paul had been right when he said that Shelly would bring a determination to this case that no one else would—and he didn't know the half of it. Maybe that's what Alex saw, too, why he wanted Shelly to defend him. Given the options, Shelly was hard-pressed to quarrel.

"Can I trust this federal prosecutor, Romero?" she asked Paul, and she realized in doing so that she had made the decision. She would defend her son in a capital murder case.

"Don't know the guy personally." Paul waved to someone who walked into the joint. They exchanged jocular pleasantries before Paul leaned into Shelly. "This much I can tell you. A.U.S.A.s don't think much of county prosecutors, and vice versa. It's a turf thing. This guy Romero's not going to be thrilled at the prospect of sharing confidential information with Elliot Raycroft or any of his underlings."

"Meaning—"

"And that's doubly true," said Paul, lifting a finger, "if they suspect that county prosecutors are involved in this drug operation."

She looked at Paul.

"Cops are pretty insular, yes. But protecting your drug dealers on the streets is a lot easier if you have some help from the guys who charge crimes. Is it the most likely scenario? No. But if it's even a possibility, Romero is not going to want to tip anyone off." Paul threw some money on the counter and called out thanks to the owner. "All I'm saying, Shelly, is this. Make sure you're seeing things with your own eyes."

19
Farewell

THE FUNERAL FOR Officer Raymond Mitchell Miroballi, which had taken place two weeks ago, had been covered extensively in the television and print media. At the time, Shelly couldn't stomach reading or hearing about it. Instead, she had held on to the papers and now, for the first time, pored over news accounts.

The photograph of Raymond Miroballi in the paper was from the neck up. Miroballi was in uniform and cap, probably from several years ago when he became a cop. He had full, high cheeks, small eyes, a powerful neck.

The Miroballi boys were all cops. Ray was the baby at age thirty-eight, the youngest of three brothers, the other two also members of the city police force—Detective Second Grade Reginald Miroballi, forty-two, and Lieutenant Anthony Miroballi, forty-four. Ray Miroballi was the father of three children, ages ten, eight, and seven. He was married to Sophia Miroballi for twelve years and lived on the city's south side, only a block away from where he grew up.

There were no pictures of Ray Miroballi's brothers in the articles. She wouldn't be able to provide identification anyway, given the ski masks they wore. Was that it? Had it been Ray's brothers who had paid her a visit last night? She knew they were cops—they made a point of letting her know that—but they could have been other cops working with Ray Miroballi in their drug scheme. The only thing she knew with certainty was that anyone smart enough to concoct that scheme to break into her apartment had brains enough to craft an alibi as well.

She read again about the life of Ray Miroballi and his children. The paper listed facts. The details, Shelly Trotter would never know. His sense of humor. The things he did with his kids. Was he tyrannical? Did he spoil the children? A devoted husband? Happily married? How would his kids grow up now, having lost their father?

This was why she didn't relish being a criminal defense attorney. She believed in the system with all her heart but didn't want to be part of it, couldn't be a part of it. What was the saying? A liberal was a conservative who had never been a victim of a crime. Well, she was probably considered a flaming liberal by most conventional standards, but not when it came to the rights of the accused. Who had protected her when she needed it?

Maybe her views had softened over time, but she made a distinction in any event with children. For them, the presumption of innocence was a multilayered concept. Kids who had turned down a wrong path at a young age could not be fully blamed for their actions. At such a young age, could the connection between their upbringing, their influences, be so casually severed from their actions? They shared fault, of course, but so often only their share was addressed by the justice system. Defending them was not so much seeking absolution for their acts but giving them another chance at an age when they still had so many options. Locking kids away in a delinquency home was rarely the answer. Kicking them out of school was never the answer, yet it had become, increasingly, the chosen course for school systems. Burdened with shrinking budgets and depleted resources, a school board simply found it easier to say to hell with some problem kid. That was just not acceptable to Shelly. Every kid deserved a shot at a good life.

She found herself reading and rereading paragraphs, her eyes passing over words as her thoughts were consumed by Alex. Alex, her client. Alex, her son. How was she supposed to react to that news? Neither she nor Alex seemed to know. Maybe in a normal setting, they could slowly move toward a relationship that was appropriate to the situation. But they were already friends, and now she was defending him from a capital murder charge and wondering what he wasn't telling her. She had always loved her child, from the moment she gave him up, not even knowing it *was* a "him" as opposed to a "her." But now, seeing this boy in the flesh, was she supposed to flip a switch and feel maternal love?

She shook her head harshly. If she couldn't get Alex off these charges, there wouldn't be much of a point to any of this talk of mother and son. She had to be his lawyer first. She looked up and saw Rena Schroeder standing in the threshold of her door. She had been there, Shelly sensed, for a lengthy moment. Shelly blinked out of her trance.

Rena was wearing an oversized sweater and a skirt. Her earrings hung down to her shoulders, below her cropped dark hair. Her arms were crossed; she leaned against the doorframe. Her eyebrows arched in concern. This was something to see with Rena. Fifteen years representing children in an enormous city, she had seen it all, wore a weathered, seasoned expression that, to an outside observer, resembled indifference. Shelly sensed it was a defense mechanism.

So why the frown?

"The dean got a call from the I.R.S.," she told Shelly.

Shelly cocked her head.

"They want to investigate our 501(c) status," she continued. The Children's Advocacy Project, though affiliated with the school, was technically its own nonprofit entity. A nonprofit entity was allowed tax benefits so long as it maintained its mission, which in this case meant work for children in education, housing, and juvenile court proceedings.

"Shit," Shelly said. She scolded herself for not thinking of it. Defending Alex Baniewicz for an adult crime fell outside CAP's charter. A nonprofit had to be damn careful about exceeding the scope of its mission. The I.R.S. could pull the tax-exempt status in a heartbeat, with financially crippling results. The project would be shut down.

"Have you done anything from this office?" Rena asked. "Filed any motions?"

"Yeah. Nothing major." She chewed on her lip. "But yes." She softly pounded her desk and looked up at her boss. "Did they mention the case by name?"

"No."

"No," Shelly repeated to herself. "Of course not. God, it didn't take them long."

"What does that mean?"

It meant Jerod Romero, the federal prosecutor, looking for some leverage against Shelly and Alex in his bid to keep his snitch in line. A quick phone call to a sister federal agency.

"Shelly—"

"I know, Rena. God, I understand." Defending Alex from the offices of CAP could wipe out the entire project.

"A lot of people could handle this case," Rena offered. "You always said you didn't like handling criminal stuff, anyway."

Shelly nodded agreeably, but she had only one option here, and there was no point in delaying the inevitable. "I have to represent him, Rena."

"Shelly, we don't have a choice. It's not like we can ask the I.R.S., 'pretty please.'"

She looked at her desk. "I would never ask CAP to be a part of this. Not now."

She looked up at her colleague, who was getting the picture. "No," Rena said.

Shelly shrugged.

"Shelly, this is crazy. You're going to—to quit? So you can be this kid's lawyer?"

What could Shelly say? Certainly not the truth.

"Oh, God, you're really considering this." Rena came over to Shelly, sat on her desk. "We need you here. This is—this is what you were meant to do."

"I feel like this is something I have to do." Shelly reached for Rena's arm. "I know it sounds crazy. But he trusts me. He needs me."

Nine years working for the rights of children. Nine years working with law students helping disabled and emotionally disturbed kids, finding ways to keep troubled children in schools when no one else cared. Nine years and it was over.

Rena continued her protests, refusing to accept Shelly's position. But the more Shelly thought about it, the more her conviction grew. Who else but Alex's mother would be willing to go to the wall for him? *Passion,* Paul Riley had said, and he was never more right than now.

"I'll be gone by the end of the day," Shelly said.

20
News

SHE APPROACHES THE *door of the study in much the same way she once did as a young girl, after her bedtime, eavesdropping on conversations not suitable for the ears of little Shelly. Politics mostly, gun control, the death penalty, taxes. She recalls several of them, one in particular where her father explained the evils of abortion to his two sons, Edgar and Thomas. That was back during Daddy's second term as the chief prosecutor for the county. Shelly herself, at age nine then, had read the newspaper accounts. Rankin County Attorney Langdon Trotter had led the charge of protestors outside the Anthony Center for Women's Health Care, which had brought the option of abortion to the downstate county for the first time since the Supreme Court had cleared the way. Her father hadn't succeeded in stopping the clinic, not through protests and not through lawsuits.*

Only three days ago, Lang Trotter's only daughter, Shelly, had walked into that very health center, secure in the notion that her father would never know what had happened to her. But now he will have to know. There is no hiding it. She is pregnant and she is going to stay pregnant. She is going to have the child. She has few answers. She doesn't know how she will manage her next year of school, much less the rest of her education. She doesn't know if she will keep the baby. She doesn't know the gender. She doesn't even know if the baby is healthy. These things she will figure out with time. The first step comes now, telling her parents.

As she approaches the study, she hears bustling, drawers

*opening and closing, her mother and father talking with anima-
tion. She walks in and sees files pulled off the bookshelves, piles
of paper on the normally orderly desk. Her father is leafing
through papers.*

*They turn and see Shelly. There is a glow to both of them.
Her mother, Abigail, looking so youthful in a sweatshirt and her
cropped blond hair, her light green eyes beaming with pride and
excitement. Her father, in a T-shirt that exposes his large shoulders and arms, his hair slightly disordered.*

*It is a Saturday morning, just past nine. The phone rang
thirty minutes ago. Now she knows who it was and what they
said. The top brass in the state Republican Party has had several conversations with County Attorney Trotter over the last
several months. The current officeholder, a Republican, has privately given notice that he would not seek re-election. Now is
the time, in June 1986, to begin the process of building support.
By early 1987, candidates will be creating something called
"exploratory committees" to begin their runs for the February
primaries in 1988. The statewide party is disciplined, Daddy
has told her, and they want to get behind a candidate to avoid a
messy primary.*

*Thus, the phone call. Shelly looks at the documents her par-
ents were gathering. Tax returns, financial documents. Vetting,
something Shelly has known well as the daughter of a politician
since she was a small child. Checking out a candidate's background before endorsing him.*

*"We might as well tell her, Lang," said her mother. Then
to Shelly: "Honey, you're looking at this state's next attorney
general."*

*Her mother squeals and hugs Daddy, rubs his arm. Her fa-
ther smiles and blushes but quickly fixes on Shelly. The steel-
blue eyes narrow and focus on her.*

"What's wrong, pistol?" he asks.

21

Different

RONNIE MASTERS ANSWERED the door on the first knock. He wore jeans with no socks or shoes, a purple sweatshirt with a towel over one shoulder. Didn't appear to have visited a barbershop since Shelly last saw him, with thick strands of dark hair kicking out on all sides of a reversed baseball cap.

He was holding Alex's eighteen-month-old daughter, Angela. He was the babysitter while Mary Ellen, Angela's mother, was at work. "Hope you don't mind," he said, nodding to the toddler on his arm. "I thought you might wanna meet her."

She did. She had thought about Angela—her granddaughter; she was thirty-four and she had a granddaughter—constantly since Alex had broken the news. This little creature, who stared at Shelly with gigantic amber eyes, a pacifier stuck in her mouth, was her blood.

Ronnie moved back to let her in. Shelly extended her arms and Ronnie handed her Angela. She took after her mother, Mary Ellen, whom Shelly hadn't met but had seen in photos. A tiny, soft face with enlarged brown eyes, flyaway dark hair standing on end in some spots. She was wearing a tiny pair of beige overalls.

Shelly lowered her head and nudged her nose against Angela's. The toddler was at the grabbing stage, and she took temporary hold of Shelly's nose. "Hello, little Angela." She looked at Ronnie.

Ronnie gave her some space. He had called her to discuss the case, but he could see she wanted a good long look at the newest member of her family.

She held the baby close. Angela, with those faraway eyes, seemed content to be held by her. Shelly spent all of her time with children and teens, but little with infants. Still, it felt right. Better, certainly, than she had felt with Alex after he dropped the bomb on her. She'd been speechless. With an infant, there was little need for the intelligible word.

She sat on the couch with Angela and rocked her, made noises with her lips, tickled her. When she wanted down, Shelly watched her stumble around the living room like a drunken sailor, grabbing things at random, throwing them or handing them to Shelly. What an amazing thing a child was. It unleashed such an outpouring in Shelly that all of the emotions canceled each other out, and she was left with utter astonishment. This girl was her blood. This one, no matter what else happened, would have a future.

Ronnie wandered back into the living room after a while. He walked over to the table by the couch. For the first time, Shelly noticed the open scrapbook. Photographs of Ronnie and Alex at various times throughout their lives. Ronnie had been going through it. That was the sort of thing you did when you lost a loved one, cling to the memories. She felt a pang of remorse for both of the boys.

Ronnie slid the scrapbook under the couch and looked at Shelly. "I'm going nuts here," he said. "I gotta do something. I gotta help. You need any help? Organizing or making phone calls or—something?"

Shelly bounced the baby on her lap. For starters, she could use a salary and an office. She'd said her abrupt goodbyes to the people at CAP only two hours ago. Two boxes of items from the office sat in her car.

"I'm sure I will need that kind of help," she said. "Thank you."

"Do you think you'll be able to work this all out? With the feds and all?"

"That's kind of complicated, Ron."

"Too complicated for a kid." He clenched his jaw. He seemed to share some of Alex's attitude. She had certainly heard that

Ronnie was a smart one, academically accomplished. A scholarship, Alex had said, and Ronnie was only a junior.

"Well, all right," she conceded. "I think the federal government is reluctant to discuss the matter with the county prosecutors. Why, I'm not entirely sure."

"Probably think they're in on it with the cops."

She cocked her head. That was a rather astute observation, she had to concede. "In any event, they are very worried about this. I imagine I can secure something favorable with the federal government, on their end. But frankly, a few years in a federal penitentiary is small potatoes compared to murder."

Ronnie nodded. He watched Angela, who was getting antsy. Ronnie lifted her off the floor and walked her around the room. "Take care of the federal problem," he said quietly as he kissed Angela's cheek and hummed to her. He seemed to be accustomed to caring for her. "I'll take care of the rest."

"Tell me what you mean by that," she said.

"I'm going to put her down." Ronnie walked out of the room with Angela in tow.

I'll take care of the rest. What did Ronnie mean by that?

He returned to the room, wiping his hands with the towel. "Never washed my hands so many times in my life as I have since she was born."

"Where's your mother?" Shelly asked.

He pursed his lips, indicating he didn't know. "She's usually out at night. Some bar or another. She's more a social drunk. Likes to go out and get bombed, sometimes meets a guy. She doesn't drink during the day. She has a job and the two—it hasn't interfered."

"Is she around Angela much?"

"Nah. If she's had even one drink, I keep her away. So what do you think of my idea?"

"I want to know what you mean."

"The drug thing," he said. "The stuff with the feds. I can't help him there. Get him off that, and I'll get him off the murder charge."

Shelly felt a charge, as much physically as emotionally; she was on the verge of collapse. "Explain yourself," she demanded.

He sat down next to her. "I'll say whatever I have to say."

Shelly looked at this boy, the earnest expression, and believed him. "Alex says you have a scholarship."

Ronnie seemed thrown by the change of topics. "Yeah. Legislative scholarship."

"I didn't know that," she said. "From who?" Each member of the state legislature was given a few scholarships a year that they could award to constituents. As she understood it, there were no fixed criteria, and she knew that several of the representatives and senators in the city gave them out based on need.

"Sandoval," he answered. Shelly had met State Representative Santiago Sandoval. A good man. She had discussed legislation with him to reform the state's school code, the disciplinary section. The bill had passed the Democratic-controlled senate, which was run by a city boy, Senate President Grant Tully—the guy Daddy beat in the governor's race. But the House was still Republican—most of its members were not elected from the city and had little use for it—and the legislation never even got out of committee.

"Going to Mansbury," Ronnie said. Mansbury College was a liberal arts school at the western boundary of the county. "Keeps me close to home. I can commute."

She liked this kid. She liked all children, she supposed, always tried to find the brightness in their soul. It was always there, somewhere, but with Ronnie, you didn't have to look too hard. He was doing it the way everyone told him. He wasn't bemoaning his fate, growing up in a single-parent house where the single parent was a drunk, attending a school where he was a minority. He was studying hard, working a job at the grocery store, planning a life. And planning, no doubt, to take the ones he loved with him.

"Well, Ronnie, I imagine you had to work pretty hard to get where you are. You are a year away from college with a bright future. About the only way you can blow it now is to start playing games with the legal system. And with me. Perjury is a crime, pal—"

"Oh, don't give me that shit." Ronnie left the couch. He pointed to the adjoining room. "That little girl's daddy is sitting in jail right now because he was trying to support her. You got that? You think I'm gonna let that little girl lose her dad?"

"He broke the law," she said, immediately regretting the comment.

"At least he tried," he answered, his voice rising. "At least he was there for her."

She sat back in the couch as if a spear had pierced her heart. Apparently Ronnie had been in on the secret as well all along. Or maybe Alex had talked to him today.

Ronnie, for all his frustration, seemed to immediately sense the impact of his words. He raised his hands. "I didn't mean it like that."

"No, I—it's all right." She shifted in her seat, composed herself. "You're right, actually."

Ronnie returned to his seat. "Really, I didn't—"

"The point I wanted to make, Ronnie, is that if you think you can lie to protect Alex, you're wrong. All that will happen is that both of you will go to jail. Then where's Angela? Without a father *or* an uncle." She exhaled slowly. Better to focus on the case.

"Got it." His missteps had quieted him.

"Just—please. Just tell me the truth."

He considered her for a moment, then threw up his hands. "Alex was selling coke to some asshole at work. Some young rich guy with so much money to spend, he can pick up a couple grams of blow on the weekends and get wired. I think there were two guys. He sold, like, five grams a week, I think. I didn't like it but he didn't exactly ask my permission. I said, just keep it away from the house. Which he did. You can ask the feds that, because they came through here like a tornado. Turned the place upside down."

"The F.B.I. searched your house."

"Yep. Alex kept the stuff in his car, see."

Right. She knew that. "Go on."

"I knew he had this thing with a cop." Ronnie adjusted in his seat. "The guy had figured out Alex's deal, I guess. He wanted some off the top."

"Alex told you about this," she confirmed.

Ronnie nodded. "Made his situation tougher. He had to sell a little more to clear the same profit." He shrugged. "That's what happens when you do that shit. I told him."

Shelly had, too. "Did you know the F.B.I. was interested in the cop? Miroballi?"

"Yeah. That was Alex's ticket. Only way he could stay out of prison."

"And did you—did Alex ever indicate to you that the cop, Miroballi, had gotten wise to the F.B.I. operation? Or that Miroballi seemed suspicious? Started to act differently? Threatened Alex? Anything like that?"

Ronnie followed her questions closely, leaning in. He paused. "Did Alex say he told me about that?"

"I'm asking you, Ronnie."

He scratched his chin. "Okay, I get it."

"Get what?"

"You're saying self-defense, so you need proof that Miroballi had figured out that Alex was working for the feds."

She had never said the words *self-defense* to Ronnie. She felt a burn in her chest. "Ronnie, you and Alex can't talk about this case when you visit him."

"He's my bro—"

"They can listen to you." She touched his knee to deflate her words. "You aren't his lawyer, Ronnie. There is no confidentiality. They can listen in on your conversations. Legally. You aren't his lawyer and, technically, you aren't family, either. You have to watch your every word in there."

Shelly wasn't entirely sure that Ronnie was disqualified from familial confidentiality. He was the son of Alex's legal guardian. Maybe that *would* qualify. That was a legal question that required research into the Department of Corrections regulations. Easier to play it safe and tell the boys to keep their mouths shut. "If you want to discuss something, do it through me," she advised. "Okay?"

"Okay." Ronnie, she could see, was not accustomed to feeling dumb.

The front door swung open. Shelly recognized Elaine Masters from the one time they had met. Shelly put her at midfifties but had to discount her estimate for the effects of alcohol. Laney appeared to be losing the battle with age, and perhaps with life. Her eyes were bloodshot and sad. Her cheeks had dropped considerably. Her hair was a bad color-job of red. The smell of alcohol spread immediately through the room. She cast a look at Shelly.

"Who're you?" she managed.

Shelly got to her feet and offered a hand. "We've met, Mrs. Masters. I'm Shel—"

"Oh, yeah." She waved at Shelly and staggered past her. Ronnie was on his feet and standing in front of the room that served as Angela's nursery. He shifted his feet, as if he were guarding her in a game of one-on-one. "What's *your* problem?" she asked him.

Ronnie took her arm and directed her away from the makeshift nursery, toward the hallway. "Sleep it off, Laney," he said gently.

Laney wrested her arm free. "Tell *me* what to do," she mumbled, but she kept moving.

Shelly glanced at her watch. It was close to eight o'clock in the evening.

When Laney had made it down the hallway, Ronnie looked at Shelly. His face was flushed. "She just needs to blow off some steam after work. She's got a job as a dock clerk at a parcel service. She got promoted last year. It's just, after work, sometimes she—"

"Ronnie, it's none of my business." She raised her hands. "Really. I should get going."

Ronnie looked down the hallway. Shelly, from the doorway, could only hear the sounds of his mother banging a door. "Okay, well, I'll see you later," he said.

22

Sunlight

ALEX BANIEWICZ HAD been indicted by a grand jury two days earlier on two counts of felony murder, which covered murder in the course of another felony—possession of cocaine—as well as murder of a peace officer. The prosecution was required to show probable cause to hold Alex over for trial and had two choices in doing so—they could go to a grand jury for an indictment, or have a preliminary hearing, at which the prosecution would present evidence to a judge and give the defense the opportunity for cross-examination. Shelly had hoped for the latter, not because she expected to beat the case but so that she could watch the witnesses testify against Alex, observe their demeanor, and begin to formulate strategy. The county attorney had opted, as he often did in high-profile cases, for a grand jury, where the likelihood of obtaining a true bill was about as strong as the sun rising in the morning.

Shelly got to court early for the arraignment. Alex was brought in and escorted to the seat next to her. He had been deteriorating on a daily basis, she thought, showing immediate and perhaps permanent wear from the incarceration and pending proceedings. She spoke words of encouragement to him, lawyer-client stuff, which remained the only basis on which she was able to conduct a conversation with the young man. It was ironic that, since Alex had shared the information with her, she'd grown more distant from him. It had been easier, apparently, to be his friend than his mother. She couldn't make sense of such things, but she settled herself with the knowledge that beating this case was paramount, and her focus on that was excusable. Win the case, then figure the rest of this out.

Dan Morphew, the assistant county attorney handling the case, took his seat and nodded to Shelly. She left Alex and walked over to Morphew. He was a hearty man, large and round, middle-aged. No ring on his finger, so either single or divorced. He had the look of a big Irish drinker, she couldn't help but think, washed-out pale as they came, with splotches of red dotting his long cheeks and his nose, flakes of dry skin on a formidable forehead. His hair was cut in military fashion, probably the best choice with a receding hairline and a bald crown, but she assumed he chose the style so he wouldn't have to bother. His clothes were no different, inexpensive and not well pressed.

He got to his feet with some effort and offered a hand. "Dan Morphew."

"Shelly Trotter."

"Keeping busy?"

"Hasn't been hard." She handed him her new business card. She would be using office space at Shaker, Riley & Flemming. Paul Riley had offered her an open office. His idea. Another way he could help, without committing his own time. Shelly had found it difficult, somehow, to accept this arrangement gratis. So they worked out a deal. The young lawyers at Shaker, Riley were required to do pro bono work each year, yet there was little structure in place, no single lawyer supervising their work. So Paul, who had realized that Shelly was without a paycheck now, hired her as a pro bono consultant. She would be the lawyer to whom the associates would turn for advice on their public-interest work. "My temporary home," she said.

Morphew's reaction showed he recognized the firm. "Riley's place. Impressive."

"Oh, yeah, I'm really moving up."

"Have a seat a second?" Morphew returned to his chair and grimaced. "Back problems," he explained. "Two surgeries." He shook the card in his hand. "You know Paul?"

She nodded, sitting next to him. "Tried a case against him."

"Won or lost?"

"Lost."

He chuckled. "Most people do. He's as good as they come. I helped out a little on the Burgos case. Saw the guy in action."

The Terry Burgos case was probably the most infamous case in the county in Shelly's generation. She was in college at the time, but the case was covered throughout the nation. Burgos lived on the southwest side near a small liberal arts college where he worked odd jobs. He managed to lure six young women to his house—some of them students at the college, if memory served—murdered them, and performed various sex acts on them as they died or after they were dead. Shelly recalled the television coverage, the small home where Terry Burgos lived, the campus auditorium whose basement he had used as a personal graveyard, police cars and construction crews as they combed and excavated the house.

"I remember," she said.

"Yeah, who doesn't? All those girls. Women, I guess, some of them. I've seen plenty of crime scenes, but that one—" He shook his head. "Anyway, the whole thing was a circus. Burgos had this public defender, Jeremy Larrabie—remember that guy? Wanted to make a name for himself with the case. Had that big head of hair, and those crazy suits? Always ready to talk to the media, and they were everywhere. We always said he was crazier than Burgos."

"Paul was kind enough to lend me some space for this case."

"Yeah? Hell of a guy. God, was he cool in the face of all that. I mean, he had some serious pressure on him, but you wouldn't know it." He evened a hand in the air. "Cool as they come. Really made a name for himself after that case. Every damn law firm in the city was bidding for that guy. Instead, he goes in with Judge Shaker and starts his own firm. Good for him. So anyway." He looked at her. "What do you think of Petey?"

"Who? Oh." The trial had been assigned to Judge Pietro Dominici, a former assistant county attorney. Most of the criminal court judges were former prosecutors, because the presiding county judge would only assign judges with experience in criminal law to the criminal courts. It made sense, and yes, occasionally a criminal defense attorney would win a judicial election, but it seemed rather daunting that most of the jurists presiding over criminal cases used to be prosecutors themselves.

"Good draw for you," she said.

"Yep. He's tough." He laughed. "Guy's family comes over on the boat sixty years ago, from Sicily. They've got this real Italian name, right? So they change it. His dad's got the same name—Pietro Dominici. He moves here, he changes his name to 'Peter Dominic.' You know, just drops a coupla vowels." He jabbed a finger at the bench. "Petey here, he's in our office, Peter Dominic, Jr., right? Real gunner. He runs for judge and loses. Peter Dominic loses. So he moves over to Brighton Village—you know, where all the Italians live?—and he goes back to his father's original name. Yeah, now he's 'Pietro Dominici' and he's running in a subcircuit that's at least forty percent Italian. He took it easily."

Shelly looked at her watch as if she were unimpressed with Morphew's familiarity with this judge. It was one minute to ten. "I better get over there, Dan. I don't want the judge seeing me consorting with the enemy."

"Aw, Petey's never on time. We got at least five minutes." He said it with the confidence of a man with power. This guy was her father without the polish or ego.

She wanted to ask him whether he ever worked with Dominici at the county attorney's office, but the answer was probably yes. No matter how large the office was, Morphew was a lifer, a career prosecutor, and he supervised hundreds of prosecutors over the years. He slipped Shelly one of his business cards. "I'll get discovery over to you today," he said. "If you have any problems, you call me. Okay? Any problems at all." He waved at the bench. "Make a motion to preserve your record but I'll have it to you today."

She thanked him and considered the unusually generous nature of the prosecutor. Could be he recognized the profile of the case and didn't want any missteps. Prosecutors, to preserve their convictions, often had to do the defense attorneys' preliminary work for them. But she assumed otherwise. The county attorney, Elliot Raycroft, was the political protégé of Governor Langdon Trotter, and Morphew was probably under orders to treat the governor's daughter right.

"Who'd you use in the grand jury?" she asked Morphew.

"The partner. Sanchez. Did everything through him." In

probable-cause hearings, hearsay was permitted, so often the prosecutor would simply put on the investigating police officer— or in this case, the dead cop's, Miroballi's, partner, Officer Julio Sanchez—and ask him what his investigation turned up. It obviated the need to bring laypeople before the grand jury, who were less practiced witnesses and who could be more easily tripped up at trial if they contradicted their previous testimony.

Shelly leaned back, looked behind herself at a sea of blue. There were approximately twenty uniformed police officers in the spectators' seats. They had come out in force to show the judge that they were behind their fallen comrade. "Alex doesn't deserve this," she said.

"He shot a cop, Counselor. You had to expect this. But I'll tell you what." He leaned into her. "We might consider life. Just to get it done."

"Won't happen," she answered as the door in the back of the courtroom opened. The bailiff, sitting in the corner, got to his feet.

"Don't say I never offered," Morphew whispered as Shelly walked away.

"The court will come to order," said the bailiff. "The Honorable Pietro Dominici presiding."

Judge Dominici walked with a purpose to the bench. He was a short man who filled out his robe. He had the face of a boxer, squarish, a pug nose, small but fiery eyes behind wire-rimmed bifocals, thick graying hair.

The court clerk, sitting to the right of and below the judge, a young heavyset man, called out the case—*People v. Baniewicz.*

"Good morning," said the judge. His voice was softer than Shelly expected, free of emotion and almost difficult to hear.

"Good morning, Judge *Dominici.* Daniel Morphew for the People."

The judge cast a furtive glance at the prosecutor, suppressed a smile. "Good morning, Mr. Morphew."

"Good morning, your Honor. Michelle Trotter, for the defendant."

"Good morning, Ms. Trotter." The judge opened a file before him, adjusted his glasses.

"We'll waive reading, your Honor," she said, allowing the clerk to forgo an official reading of the indictment handed down against her client.

She'd been waiting for this moment ever since those two intruders left her house, left her wondering about the safety of her client as well as herself. Four nights now, sitting upright on her bed, watching the clock, listening for sounds. She had moved her couch in front of the front door. She had broken glass and sprinkled it on the patio next to the sliding glass door in back. She had placed a small glass full of marbles on the handle of the sliding glass door, where it loomed precariously and would fall with a rambunctious sound at the first hint of jarring. And as the hours of fitful sleep and meditation had passed, she found that she was angry with herself. She hadn't given in right away. She had taken the first intruder and sent him headlong to the floor. She didn't back away from the second one, she just couldn't reach him, and he had a weapon trained on her. Yes yes yes, she could tell herself all of that. But she had been overtaken. Shelly Trotter, who had coached hundreds of pupils on the art of self-defense, had thought she was invincible herself. The moment had come and she had failed.

"Are you prepared to enter a plea at this time, Counsel?" the judge asked.

"Your Honor," she said, "the defense pleads not guilty by reason of self-defense."

A stirring behind her, mostly from the city's finest sitting behind Dan Morphew. Morphew himself did not react, simply wrote something on a pad of paper.

This might, or might not, be Alex's defense at trial. She could withdraw it, or ignore it—the state would have to prove guilt beyond a reasonable doubt, anyway. Based on what she knew so far, this was the best bet. But she could have waited to make this announcement. She wanted to do it in open court, which was not technically required, and she wanted to do it now. The intruders had wanted to push her in a closet, to keep her quiet about Officer Ray Miroballi's off-duty work as a drug dealer, and now she was telling them, as much as she could, anyway, that she would not be quiet. Here it is, everyone. A cop wanted my client dead. It would make the papers. It would ruffle feathers. Should anything happen to Shelly or Alex now, the scrutiny would be unbearable. A little sunlight was just what Shelly and Alex needed right now.

The judge adjusted his glasses again, not, it seemed, out of surprise but by habit. Shelly's words had an impact, no doubt, but he went a long way to show disinterest. "Very well. Mr. Morphew, you acknowledge notice."

Morphew had been watching Shelly. Did he know any of this already? She assumed he might have. "We do, Judge," he said. "And if we could handle the 311 notice now."

Shelly nodded solemnly, sneaked a look in Alex's direction. She wished that this could be handled in writing, but so many things these days had to be acknowledged on the record in open court. Several years ago, there had been a bit of a scandal when a defense attorney showed up for trial claiming to be entirely unaware that the state was seeking the death penalty against his client. If it had been something else, maybe it would have been chalked up to a snafu, but the anti–capital-punishment establishment had a field day with it. *Will they at least tell them first before they try to execute them?* So now such things had to be done in front of the judge. This had worked to her advantage today, allowing her to announce her self-defense plea to the entire city media.

"That's fine," said Shelly.

"Your Honor, pursuant to Section 311 of the criminal code, the People hereby give notice to the defendant of our intent to seek the punishment of death."

"We acknowledge notice," said Shelly, with another glance to Alex. He had fallen into a now-familiar look, his eyes set in a hard, unemotional stare. The thought hit her again—she might lose him before they got to trial.

"Very good," said the judge. "Have you two discussed a trial date?"

"We haven't had that chance, your Honor."

The judge worked his lips while he read his calendar. "Ms. Trotter?"

"Yes, your Honor."

"Is the defense waiving a speedy trial?"

"Yes, your Honor. We would seek leave to take the depositions of a number of individuals." In criminal cases in the state, depositions—the questioning of witnesses under oath prior to trial—were rare. In civil cases, lawyers took depositions for months, if not years, to prepare for trial, and this typically came after written discovery, where each side answered questions in writing from the other side. The civil litigator's creed was to know everything before a trial started, to know the answer to every question asked of a witness at trial, because the witness was already asked the question under oath at the deposition. The civil litigator's other creed was to bill as much time as possible on a case, which made depositions still more desirable. In criminal cases, on the other hand, depositions were almost never used, despite the fact that the stakes were higher—a person's liberty as opposed to money. It had always been a bitter pill for Shelly to swallow. How could it be that lawyers fighting over a contract dispute could employ endless resources to uncover information before trial, but a lawyer defending a boy accused of capital murder was not allowed to question witnesses under oath?

"You're seeking leave to take depositions?"

"We are, your Honor."

"Have you filed a motion?"

"No, your Honor." Shelly had been kicked out of the law school before she could put it together. She had just moved into her temporary office. "We will be happy to do so."

"Your Honor," said Morphew. "If counsel will let us know whom she wants to depose, perhaps we could dispose of this now."

"That would be fine." Judge Dominici focused his small eyes on Shelly.

"Your Honor, we would like to depose Officer Julio Sanchez, the partner of the decedent. Officer Sanchez was present the night of the shooting. We would like to depose other police officers as well. We would like to depose the decedent's wife. We would—"

"His wife?" said the judge. "Why do you want to depose his wife?"

Shelly had anticipated the question but had never come up with a good answer. "Judge, it is our theory that my client was defending himself from an attack on his life."

"I understand that, Counsel," which was the judge's way of saying she hadn't answered his question.

"We're trying to build a case for why the deceased officer wanted to kill my client."

The judge was not pleased. Shelly imagined that a former career prosecutor, now on the bench, did not enjoy hearing such allegations, to say nothing of the fact that Shelly's comments would shine the spotlight still brighter on this case.

"Judge," said Dan Morphew. "If I could respond."

The judge ignored the prosecutor. "Serious allegations," he said to Shelly.

"Yes, your Honor. But they are true. We are entitled to explore them."

Judge Dominici settled his hands before him. "The requests for deposition are denied."

"Your Honor—"

"You have full subpoena power for documents," said the judge. "And you can bring anyone into trial. The rules for criminal procedure do not contemplate free-wheeling discovery like the civil code. Mr. Morphew, other than telling me that these allegations are outrageous, do you have anything to add?"

Morphew paused a beat. He knew to shut up when he was ahead. "No, Judge."

"Your Honor—"

"Ms. Trotter, I've made my ruling. Do you have anything new to say?"

"Yes, Your Honor."

"Very well."

"We withdraw our waiver of a speedy trial."

The judge stared at her. He showed no indication of surprise, but he seemed to take the response as a rebuke. Shelly had settled on the decision last night. Clearly, option one was to depose witnesses before trial to build her case. But if she was not entitled to do so, she felt the advantage of surprise favored her. She had no control over when the federal undercover operation might come to an end—she assumed later than sooner, but she simply didn't know. The best plan, then, was to go to trial, having pleaded self-defense without any elaboration, without any specificity to Dan Morphew. The F.B.I., of course, would have its hand forced by then, and would be announcing a major arrest of city police officers at precisely the time that jurors were being empaneled in the case of *People v. Baniewicz.*

"The defense demands a speedy trial," she said.

The judge held his look on her a moment longer than necessary, before looking at his calendar. "Very well," he said evenly. He chose a date in mid-May and did not ask either side if it was workable. "Anything else?" he asked.

"One more thing, Judge," said Shelly. "I request protective custody for my client." She couldn't come out and discuss the real reason that police officers might want to harm her client, due to her promise to the federal government, so she focused simply on the fact that Alex was accused of killing a cop. The judge was not receptive. If anything, Dan Morphew noted in response, being a cop killer would elevate Alex to some level of acclaim. In the end, the judge denied the request but left the matter open for reconsideration if circumstances warranted it.

Shelly heard the voices of the lawyers for the next case, issuing their "good mornings," as she moved to the table where they kept the orders, to be filled out by the lawyers and handed to the judge for his signature. Dan Morphew shot her a glance, something subtle yet hostile, and over his shoulder Shelly could see a number of reporters gathering and heading outside, where they would await her for more tidbits into this case. She inhaled deeply and looked at the press gathering at the door. For the first time, she would have some choice words for them today.

23

Offer

"JEROD ROMERO, PLEASE," Shelly said into the phone. She was in the law offices of Shaker, Riley & Flemming, in the office Paul Riley had generously donated to her. She had spread out her files, arranged her folders, set up a computer password, played with the Dictaphone on her desk, swiveled in her chair and looked out the window at the view of the elevated train and small glimpse of the river. It was an office for an associate, not a partner, but it was nicer than anything at the law school.

He came on the line a few moments later. "Jerod Romero."

"Mr. Romero. Shelly Trotter."

"I'm hearing interesting things, Shelly. A self-defense plea?"

"Just exercising our constitutional rights. Don't worry, nary a word about drugs or dirty cops. So far."

"Did you—"

"And by the way, Mr. Romero, I'm calling you from the law offices of Shaker, Riley and Flemming, where I'll be working. You can call off your I.R.S. goons."

Silence. She didn't expect a response. "I'm not sure what you're suggest—"

"I'm suggesting that if you think you can get me off this case, or coerce us into a plea, by going after CAP's tax-exempt status, you are wrong. I'm not going anywhere and it's time for put-up or shut-up."

She detected an amused chuckle. "Sixty years is a great deal, Shelly."

"Well, then, why don't we get together and discuss it? You, me, and the county attorney's office. Let's all get in a room together and hammer this thing out."

"We don't work that way."

"Let's cut the crap," she said. "The A.C.A., Dan Morphew? He offered life today."

Romero cleared his throat.

"You haven't said a single word to the county attorney," she continued. "They don't know anything about this sting. They don't know about any deal for sixty years. So let's do it this way. You have your reasons for not wanting to talk to them. I don't care. Let's just focus on the federal charges."

Romero didn't answer, which meant he was listening.

"Complete immunity," she proposed. "Rip up the letter of co-operation. It's meaningless now, anyway. You haven't charged him yet. I want an agreement that you will not prosecute him at all, in exchange for his silence about the drug sting until this thing goes to trial. That gives you almost three months to wrap things up."

"You've thought this through," he said.

Paul Riley walked into the doorway and tapped lightly on the door. She nodded at him.

"That's it, Mr. Romero. Take it or leave it. And nothing about cooperating or anything else. No conditions except that he doesn't talk about the sting until trial."

"Well, I can run this up—"

"Run it up your ass, for all I care," she said. "You have until the end of the day tomorrow. I want a written agreement and all the discovery you have on Ray Miroballi by tomorrow. Or I hold a press conference."

She hung up the phone and smiled at Paul.

He raised a finger to her, as if he had something important to say. "Middle-aged guy walks into a confessional," he said. "He says, 'Father, I have sinned.' The priest says, 'Tell me, my son.' The guy says, 'Father, I just spent the entire night with two gorgeous runway models I picked up at a bar. We did drugs all night and had the raunchiest sex I've ever had. We were doing things I've never even heard of.' The priest tells him to do some Hail Marys and seek forgiveness from the Lord. The guy says, 'Oh,

Father, I'm not Catholic.' The priest says, 'Well, then why are you telling me all this?' The guy says, 'Are you kidding, Father? I'm telling everybody!'"

She smirked at him. "Very nice, Riley."

"You looked like you could stand to smile." He leaned against the door. "Putting the screws to the G, are you?"

"Something like that. Listen—thanks so much for this space."

"You already thanked me." He was wearing a charcoal suit with an expensive shirt, a light shade of red with a white collar and cuffs. *If I were a client,* she thought to herself, *I'd feel at ease with this guy.*

"You talk to Joel?" he asked.

"Put him to work right away." Joel Lightner was an investigator whom Paul used, and whose services he'd offered gratis to Shelly. Paul had gone a long way to assuage his own guilt for not taking the case—or for trying to please Shelly. She didn't know which one, but she could hardly say no under the circumstances. She had a client who needed a good investigator.

"Hm. Good." He opened his arm. "We eat."

Lunch was at a popular steakhouse, but Paul ordered fish and Shelly went with vegetables. It was more than she usually ate for lunch. She felt comfortable in the nice setting, the good company—yes, she was beginning to warm to this big-shot corporate lawyer—but somehow uneasy at the relaxed setting while something so urgent was at stake, while her son sat in a holding cell and watched his back in the jail yard. He was looking over his shoulder every moment of the day in a dreary, sunless hole, while she was ordering marinated vegetables at an upscale eatery.

"You're going to miss the law school," he said. "The children's project."

"I am."

"It moves you. Your work."

She nodded. "School is everything to a kid. Especially the ones I'm helping."

"Knowledge is power, right?"

She rearranged the lettuce in her salad. "It's more than knowing who the tenth president was," she said. "It's about socialization. It's about skill-building. It's about nutrition."

"Nutrition. Really."

"Oh, sure. Most of the city schools serve breakfast as well as lunch now. Sometimes it's all these kids eat during a day."

Paul took a second look at the breadstick he was about to break in half.

"You know what day of the school week has the highest student attendance?" she asked him. "Every week, every year?"

Paul shook his head.

"Monday," she said. "Because a lot of the kids are hungry."

Paul's eyebrows raised. "I guess I didn't know that."

"I don't expect everyone I keep in school to become doctors or lawyers, or go to college, or even graduate high school," she said. "But they learn things in school—or at least, it's the only chance they'll have to learn things. History and science, fine. But I'm talking about things like—I know an English teacher who spends a few days each year on telephone skills. A lot of these kids don't have phones at home at all. They don't know basic conversational skills on the telephone. How are they going to hold any kind of a decent job?"

He raised his hands. "You've taught me something."

She sighed. She could really get going when prompted. And it was preferable to revisiting the events of the last week. "I'm preaching," she apologized.

"Not at all, no." Paul wiped his mouth with a napkin. "Give me an update on the case."

Well, my house was burglarized, my client and I were physically threatened, I got kicked out of my law school, they're seeking the death penalty against my client, I have the distinct feeling that Alex and Ronnie are playing games with me.

"Just getting started," she said.

Oh, and it turns out my client is the son I gave up for adoption.

"I think I've cleaned up the federal mess. I think they'll let him walk if we keep quiet about the undercover operation until trial."

"Good. Great. What else?"

She felt a bit like one of Paul's associates reporting to the senior partner. "They gave their 311 notice today."

"Not surprising."

"We have a trial date in May."

"That should work out well." Paul picked at a roll on his plate. "Just as you're about to pick a jury, the feds will have to round up the bad guys. There will be headlines about drug-dealing cops just before the trial starts, and you tell them about one particular drug-dealing cop."

She nodded.

"I gather you already thought of that," he added.

She smiled. "Hopefully, Morphew won't know what hit him."

"Danny's a good guy." Paul waved to someone across the room.

"He sure speaks highly of you."

"He's top brass now," Paul said. "Third, fourth in command. They brought in a heavy hitter."

"Wonderful." She sighed. "My problem is, I'm having a reliability problem with my own client. And his brother."

"How so?"

"They're holding back, I think. They both seem to be protecting each other. I think the feds are, too."

"Hate it when people hold back." Paul held his stare on Shelly. "Hate that."

She put a hand on her chest. "Am I being accused?"

He sat back against the cushion and gave her a playfully scolding look. "I remember a case I had a few years back. Had a real fireball on the other side. A tough, solid lawyer. Tells me her name is Michelle Trotter. I say, 'Oh, any relation to our new governor?' She says, 'No.' "

Paul winked at her. No doubt he had read the papers, the stories of the governor's daughter defending the accused cop killer.

"Did I do that?" She didn't remember. But she didn't doubt the veracity of the story; it was her standard routine. That case with Paul, she recalled, headed to trial just as Attorney General Langdon Trotter was being sworn in as governor.

"First time I met you. First court appearance on the school case."

Her face colored. "Old habit."

"Silly," Paul said. "If you don't mind my saying so."

"Why should I tell you that my dad is the governor?"

"Why *shouldn't* you?" he answered. "I mean, you don't have to wear a sign around your neck, but you lied when I asked."

"Well, why did you ask?"

Paul shrugged. "Just making small talk."

She shook her head. "It would have made a difference."

"Oh, come on."

"No, Paul—really. If I had told you I was Lang Trotter's daughter, it would have bought me something with you. Right?"

"Of course not. I still would have thought you were a whiny public-interest lawyer."

"Funny," she said. "That's very amusing. Really, though—it makes me a commodity. I can help you. I can hurt you. At a minimum, I have a bit of celebrity. It would change how you interact with me. Maybe something subtle, maybe something overt. But it's there."

"Hm." Paul pursed his lips. "Maybe."

"I don't need that. I don't want that. I didn't ask for that."

"Okay, okay." He raised his hands. "Tough, independent, get-there-without-using-the-name. I get it." He grabbed his glass of water. "Want me to throw this in your face to show you it doesn't matter to me who your dad is?"

"Enough abuse."

He laughed. "You certainly are refreshing, Ms. Trotter."

"I'm here for your amusement." She was enjoying herself. The vegetables arrived at the table and were delicious, mixed with olive oil and garlic.

"So tell me why you think the U.S. Attorney's holding out on you," Paul said.

"Oh, in part I think it's just their nature. They're protecting their investigation. They don't want me to know any more than I have to."

"Sounds about right."

"But with Miroballi—they don't want to concede anything. To listen to them, you'd think Miroballi was clean."

"Maybe he is." Paul could be so matter-of-fact about topics of importance.

"That can't be," she said.

"Sure it could."

"No, I mean, it *can't* be." Because that would mean she had no case.

"Right." Paul put down his fork. His halibut was half-eaten. "Listen, if one of their snitches gets mixed up in a shoot-out with one of the bad guys, they have egg on their face. Right?"

"Right."

"And they can't deny that Alex was one of their snitches."

"Right."

"So they deny that *Miroballi* was one of the bad guys."

"And given his untimely death, they don't really care about him anymore. Which is why it's so hard to cut the deal with them."

"Oh, you'll get your deal. He'll give you a walk for your silence." Paul brought a napkin to his mouth. "Alex doesn't mean anything to them anymore, Shelly, except that he can expose them. They were looking at a cop who's dead now, and even if Alex could connect them to other bad cops—"

"That's a big if."

"—but even if he could, he can't now, not in jail. So what do they care about him? He had, what, seventy-four grams of coke, you said? We're talking about maybe a year in prison if it's a first offense."

"Eight to fourteen months," she said, having reviewed the federal sentencing guidelines. "Probably a Level Sixteen."

Paul waved a hand. "Judge would probably give him three hundred sixty-six days so he could get good time off." For any sentence that exceeded one year, federal prisoners could receive a percentage reduction for good behavior. Shelly had figured that Alex would probably get either eight months or a year-and-a-day for his crime, which ended up almost equivalent with good time.

"The point being, they'll take it," said Shelly.

Paul stared at her, in that thoughtful, discerning way he had. She wondered if he had even heard what she said. He took a moment to poke his food, as if he were debating, then looked back up at her.

"Do you like men?" he asked.

"Do I—like men?"

"Yeah. I mean, a lot of you public-interest lawyers are lesbians, right?"

Shelly laughed, threw her head back, clapped her hands together. It felt good, such a welcome release. "Oh, God." She caught her breath, her body still trembling, tears forming in her eyes. "I should be really pissed off at you for saying that."

"I have a problem with being direct." Paul was enjoying her enjoyment. "Have you answered my question?"

Shelly took a deep breath and expelled one last burst of laughter. "I really couldn't tell you if the majority of my colleagues are gay or straight."

"No, not that question." Paul held his smile but with some effort.

"Yes, Paul, I like men. How about you?"

He cleared his throat. "I've been divorced for years. Haven't gotten around too much since then."

"Sorry," she said. "I didn't know that."

"How about you? Ever married? Kids?"

"No," she said quickly. "And no." It felt like a needle was piercing her heart.

"Are you serious with anyone?"

"Are you asking me out, Paul?"

"Well—" His face colored. Paul Riley was blushing. "Why don't you answer my question first?"

"Okay." Shelly placed her hands together. "The best answer I can give you is that I'm not ready for a relationship right now."

"I understand perfectly—"

"No, wait, Paul. Let me explain." *Wasn't* she ready for a relationship? Did she really intend to spend her life alone? And she couldn't deny her attraction to this man. Paul Riley, tall and distinguished—handsome, yes, broad-shouldered, the first signs of thickening of the torso but still well-built, his thick, sandy hair flecked with gray, rough, lined skin and a strong jaw. A man who represented wealthy clients who lied and cheated and stole to make and keep their money, who provided every legal maneuver to protect the most powerful, provided that they could pay. A man she would stereotype as shallow, arrogant, materialistic.

But a man who provided her counsel, an office, hope during a time of need. Oh, it didn't make sense, but these kinds of things didn't make sense, did they?

Stop. No. She couldn't be foolish. It was no time for frivolous behavior. She was playing too many cards too close to her vest. Story of her life.

"Believe me, Paul—believe me when I tell you that there's a long list of reasons why you wouldn't want to get involved with me at this moment. Can I just say—no for now?"

"Absolutely. Of course." Paul was being overly accommodating in his assurances. "It—probably wasn't a good idea, anyway. You know, we're working together, in a way. You probably shouldn't mix work and—y'know, not love but, well, romance or—" He sighed, fell back against the cushion of the booth. "For God's sake, I'm not very good at this, am I? I'm fifty-one years old and I feel like I'm fifteen."

"Actually, you're better than most," she said. "You're straightforward. That's rare."

"Rare," he repeated. "Okay, I'll take rare."

"I would've guessed ten years younger, by the way."

"Oh—" Paul brought a hand to his face. "Now she's letting me down gently. Where's a good bolt of lightning when you need it?"

"How about this, Paul." She waited until his eyes peeked through his fingers. "You made my day by asking."

"That, I like. You could smile a little more." He seemed to calm down a bit. He had a self-assurance that was rare in men, in her opinion—the fact that he was able to move on from rejection without brooding or self-pity.

"By the way," he added, "this whole thing was a ruse, just to cheer you up."

She raised her glass. "It worked."

24

Skeleton

BLANK FACES, INITIALLY, *the look of shock and disbelief. Waiting for the punchline. Waiting for their darling sixteen-year-old daughter to explain that she isn't serious. They watch her, search her face, wait for a smile or laugh.*

She tells them again. Yes, she is serious.

"How—who—who did this to you?"

There. The question she has anticipated, from her father. The first question, notably. "It's not important, Daddy."

She has no good reason for her refusal. It's bad enough she has to tell them she's pregnant—that much cannot be helped. She can't tell them how. She can't.

Todd Brisker? Rick Logenthal? Wally Josephs? Jed Arnold's boy—what's his name—Billy? Benji Carol?

Her father is suddenly pacing, small circles, jaw and fists clenched, throwing out the name of every teenage boy that comes to mind.

Her mother, Abigail Trotter, the lively facial features that still danced, her bright green eyes and tiny nose, animated eyebrows, now rendered into a blank expression, staring at her only daughter, her special beautiful precious daughter, as if she is a museum exhibit, something fascinating and unknown. Teenage Barbie got knocked up.

"It's not important," she tells them again.

"Shelly." Her father, the powerful, promising politician, hands open, almost pleading. "How could you let this happen?

How could you do this—" He flails for a moment, looks around the study helplessly, at the tax returns he has compiled, the financial statements ready to be sent to the state G.O.P. powers, then finds his wife quietly sobbing.

"*How could you do this to your mother?"*

25

Reports

DAN MORPHEW CARRIED through on his promise and turned over the prosecution's evidence by messenger to her office. She spread out the file on her office table with a rush to her heart. She would now begin to learn what kind of a case they had on Alex.

The police had two witnesses to the shooting aside from Officer Miroballi's partner. One was a forty-two-year-old homeless man who had been south of the alley, on the opposite side of the street where the shooting occurred. According to the police report, the man saw Alex Baniewicz walking southbound on the 200 block of South Gentry Street on the commercial district's west side, which put him south of the City Athletic Club and south of Bonnard Street, the nearest perpendicular street to the north.

According to the report, the homeless man—one Joseph Slattery—saw a police squad car slowly follow Alex, then turn on its overhead lights. Officer Raymond Miroballi left the vehicle and followed Alex on foot. Alex began to run, and the officer pursued him into the alley. Mr. Slattery moved further north to watch and saw Alex open fire on the officer and flee through the alley on the opposite street.

The other witness was a thirty-three-year-old architect named Monica Stoddard, who had an office on the nineteenth floor of the building across the street from the alley. She had a view of the alley from her window, the report said, and she looked out when she saw the sirens flashing. She saw a man—whom she obviously could not identify as Alex—running from a police officer. She saw him turn into an alley and watched the officer pursue Alex.

She saw Alex shoot the officer.

The report of Miroballi's partner, Officer Sanchez, indicated that he and Miroballi saw a young man carrying drugs on the 200 block of South Gentry Street. The squad car pulled over, but when the suspect began to flee, Miroballi gave chase while Sanchez returned to the vehicle to pursue by automobile. Miroballi radioed in a call for assistance as he turned down an alley after the suspect. Before Sanchez could reach the alley, he heard a gunshot. He found Miroballi dead in the alley and no sign of the suspect. Sanchez then called for assistance—reporting an officer down—and stayed with the fallen officer.

All available units had converged on the area. They cornered Alex about a half-mile away, unarmed and compliant. It was a miracle that Alex had survived that confrontation, she thought.

Back at the scene, they found two one-gram packets of co-caine and an unregistered firearm with the serial number scratched out. A fingerprint analysis did not turn up any identi-fiable prints, certainly not those of Alex Baniewicz, and a bal-listics test showed that the gun was not the one used to kill Ray Miroballi.

So they had a weapon, but not the murder weapon.

Weird.

Blood spatterings were found on Alex Baniewicz's sweat-shirt and in his hair that were matched to Officer Miroballi. Miroballi's blood was A-positive and Alex's was O-negative. So that negated any argument that the blood was Alex's. For good measure, the lab had run a DNA test to confirm that the blood was Miroballi's.

Shelly rubbed her eyes and stretched. She got up from her chair and looked out the window, just to change the scenery for a moment. This case, she thought, was defensible. She had pleaded self-defense to squeeze the U.S. Attorney and to scare off any cops who might want to hurt Alex or her. But she could always change the plea to a straight not-guilty. The woman was a problem. She had seen Alex pull the trigger, according to the report. If she could crack that nut, the state, thus far, would not even be able to put a gun in Alex's hand.

Which reminded her. She found the results of the residue test. The police performed a gunpowder residue test on Alex Baniewicz the evening of his arrest. Residue often, though not always, found its way onto the person or clothing of someone who fired a firearm. The results in the county attorney's report were characterized as "inconclusive," which to Shelly meant that they didn't find any residue but didn't want to admit that fact. She sighed. This was one of the fun details with which she was unfamiliar. She would need help on this.

She turned next to the transcript of the officers' radio calls to police dispatch. She had been supplied audiotapes as well, but didn't think it necessary—or savory—to listen to them just yet. The first exchange came at 7:44 P.M. on the night of the shooting.

SQUAD 13: Dispatch, this is Thirteen. We got a white male, late teens, appears to be holding narcotics.
DISPATCH: What's your location, Thirteen?
SQUAD 13: 200 block of South Gentry. Southbound.
DISPATCH: Do you need assistance?
SQUAD 13: Don't think so. I'm going to check him out.
DISPATCH: Watch your back, Thirteen.

That was the first call. The next call came two minutes later, from Officer Miroballi's handheld walkie-talkie, which appeared to be coded "Radio 27."

RADIO 27: Dispatch, we have a white male on the run. I'm in pursuit.
DISPATCH: Do you need assistance, Twenty-seven? Do you copy? Twenty-seven? Officer, we are sending available squads.

The next call, one minute later, at 7:47 P.M.

RADIO 27: Dispatch, advise all units that suspect is armed. I repeat, suspect is armed.
DISPATCH: Copy that, Twenty-seven. Vehicles are

responding. Where is he running? Twenty-seven? Twenty-seven, do you copy?

The next transcript must have been from Miroballi's partner, Julio Sanchez, from the squad car the next minute of the hour, 7:48 p.m.

SQUAD 13: Dispatch, this is Radio Twenty-six. I'm in the squad car.
DISPATCH: Give us your location, Thirteen. Thirteen, advise of your location. 200 block of South Gentry? Thirteen?

The final transcript, from "Radio 26," was obviously Officer Sanchez's handheld. The call came two minutes later—7:50 P.M.:

RADIO 26: Dispatch, we have an officer down. Officer down. Officer—we have an—oh, God, Ray.
DISPATCH: Twenty-six, paramedics and ambulance are responding. Keep your man alive, Twenty-six.
RADIO 26: 200 block, South Gentry. We're in an alley. We have an—Ray Miroballi's been shot. One suspect, I think. I think there's only one. Oh, God help him.
DISPATCH: Stay with me, Officer. A white male?
RADIO 26: Late teens, early twenties. Oh, God, come on, Ray. Ray. Ray.
DISPATCH: Twenty-six?
RADIO 26: White male, black coat, green cap, headed west—he went through the alley. He's going to be headed—oh, there's so much—probably south on—on I guess Donnelly. Maybe north. I don't know where he went.
DISPATCH: Stay with your officer, Twenty-six. Stay with him.
DISPATCH: All units, we have an officer down at the 200 block of South Gentry. That's a Code Blue. I repeat, this is a Code Blue. Suspect is a white male, late teens or early twenties, black jacket, green cap. Suspect believed to be headed north or south on Don-

nelly. Suspect is armed. Suspect is armed. We have a Code Blue, officers. Suspect is armed.

Shelly had been holding her breath, she discovered, and let out a long exhale. She made note of her personal reaction, because it would be the same one the jurors would feel. Revulsion. Horror. A desire for justice for the fallen officer. Dan Morphew, if he had any sense, would put this transcript front and center in the trial.

She had a defense, she thought, and maybe more than one. But she knew how the men and the women of the jury would feel after hearing these tapes and hearing the eyewitness accounts of the shooting. They would want to punish someone. And they would only be given one choice, only one young man sitting in the courtroom.

26

Reason

"Shhh. she'll hear *you*."

"Well, I don't really give a damn, Abby. I really don't."

She is in many ways an adult now, but she feels like a child again, sneaking down the stairs and listening. It is close to midnight now, and she went to bed over an hour ago. They have been talking since that time. They talked all day yesterday—Saturday, when she told them—and they have talked all day today. Their big discussion this morning, after a tense breakfast, a talk that didn't go so well.

"It's over. That's it, Abby. It's over."

"It's not—"

"It's down to me and Justin, Ab. They can go either way. Why on earth would they go with me now? They just need a reason. We just gave them one."

"That's shortsighted."

Shelly hugs her knees but doesn't move for fear of a squeaking stair. Her heart pounds, echoes so furiously that she wonders if they will hear it. The staircase is cold, drafty, owing to the air escaping from under the door to the garage. She is staring at the door and the floor mat at its base, which she cannot see in the dark but which reads HOME. She smells the change of seasons creeping through the door, the smell of freshly cut grass still clinging to the lawnmower in the garage, which Daddy used today for the first time this year. She closes her eyes now in the belief that she will hear them better.

"Listen. I'm a downstate prosecutor. Anyone south of the interstate has to overcome the impression that he doesn't have a piece of hay in his mouth and a first cousin for a wife. My sixteen-year-old daughter is sleeping around and got knocked up? Come on, Abigail."

"That's just a stupid stereotypic—"

"It's an impression. Maybe the voters wouldn't care, but we're not talking about voters right now. We're talking about the slatemakers. They want to get behind one candidate this fall and run with him. Whoever that is has the nomination. And it won't be me. Not now."

Glass tapping glass, liquid gurgling. Daddy is pouring himself a drink. Shelly feels a tear squirt out of her shut eye unexpectedly. They are coming so easily. Emotions so raw and at the surface. For her parents, too, she realizes, not just her.

"Then we wait four years," Mom says. "You're still young in '92."

"Oh, don't talk to me about '92. What if Justin wins? Then he's the incumbent in '92. I run against him then, I'm a pariah. I lose and never get another chance." Footsteps. Daddy is pacing.

"Lang, honey—"

"This was it. You see that, don't you, Abby? I was their first choice. This was our chance. We might not get another one now."

She stands up slowly. She is practiced by now, moving gingerly to avoid a crack of the knee or ankle. She takes two stairs at a time, placing the foot down first, then applying the weight. She returns to bed and prays that sleep will come quickly.

27

Inquiry

SHELLY LAID OUT copies of the prosecution's evidence on her bed. Her apartment was arranged like it had been since the intrusion—couch in front of the front door, the glass of marbles balanced on the handle of the sliding glass door, the alarm fully armed—but it was her hope now that there would be no more visits. She had made a point, in court, of announcing that Officer Raymond Miroballi had tried to kill Alex, of requesting protective custody for her client on the theory that his life might be in danger in detention. She had repeated these claims to the press outside and read about them in today's paper. She had stayed within the confines of her agreement with the federal government but had made her point, nonetheless, to rogue police officers who might want to do harm to either Alex or her. The spotlight was shining now, and she felt safe.

The intruders *were* cops, weren't they?

Shelly jumped at the sound of the phone ringing, the portable phone lying next to her on the bed bellowing out its shrill cue.

"You're a hard one to get hold of," said Governor Trotter.

She held her breath. If ever there were a time, even on her meager budget, to spring for caller identification, this was it.

"I meant to call," she said. "Congratulations on the nomination."

"Since when did you leave the law school, Shelly?"

Without telling you, you mean? Well, he was certainly cutting to the chase. "Long story," she said. "Recently."

"You're working for Paul Riley now?"

"No, not really. I've taken a leave from the school. I'm representing someone outside the parameters of the law school."

"So I've heard." A somewhat icier tone.

"Is that why you're calling?"

"Shelly, I'm calling you because I haven't spoken with you since Christmas. I want to see how you're doing."

"I'm doing fine. How are things at the capital?"

"Shelly." Her father seemed to be struggling. "Edgar's concerned about you. I'm concerned. You're defending a capital murder case and representing a cop killer."

Oh, and he's also your grandson.

"What exactly is it that worries you?" she asked. "That I'm out of my league? That I'm turning the spotlight on the city police?"

"Why are you handling this case, Shelly?"

"He needs my help."

"Lots of boys need criminal defense. You don't help them."

Shelly recoiled. "I have to justify why I'm representing this boy?"

"No, of course not. Hold on a second, if you would." A woman was speaking in the background to the governor. He responded as he typically did, with a decisive, crisp answer. "Sorry about that. Listen, Shelly—you leave your job to take on some drug peddler's case? Why do that? What's so special about this kid?"

"So you *do* want me to justify it."

"I admit I'm curious." She could picture him in his high-backed leather chair, his jacket off and sleeves rolled up a tuck. He cut the perfect model of the state's chief executive.

"He deserves a chance," she said, and winced as she played that over in her mind.

"Just tell me you're being careful."

"I'm being careful," she promised. "I always am."

28

Testing

SHELLY STOOD AT the intersection of Bonnard and Gentry downtown. It was only three short blocks from the offices of Shaker, Riley & Flemming. "There's the City Athletic Club," she said, pointing to the northeast corner of the intersection. "He was at the open gym that night." The club had its own building, a fourteen-story edifice wedged between two newer buildings double its size. Flags of the city, county, state, and U.S. waved above the entryway, along with a flag bearing the club's crest. "He walked down Gentry, crossed Bonnard, and was heading south. He was going to the bus."

Joel Lightner, a private investigator whose services Paul Riley had lent for this case, nodded. He was not the prototypical investigator, in Shelly's eyes. He was tall and gangly, with an oval face and tight curly, gray hair. His long olive coat was open, and he seemed not to notice the whipping winds that came out of nowhere in this city.

They crossed Bonnard Street and headed southbound on Gentry, on the east side of the street, tracking the path Alex took. "About here," said Joel. He had reviewed Shelly's notes, taken from her several conversations with Alex. He was carrying a gym bag, presumably because Alex was carrying one on the night in question. "Give or take, this is where the squad car kicked on its lights." They both stopped and looked around. Gentry Street, between Bonnard and Newberry, extended the length of a traditional city block, one-eighth of a mile. Shelly and Joel were standing almost equidistant from Bonnard Street to the north and the alley where the shooting occurred, to the south.

"About midway down," Shelly concurred.

"Miroballi calls it in," Joel continued. "White male, holding drugs."

"Alex keeps walking." So they began to walk as well. "He hears a car door open and close. One of the cops has gotten out. Miroballi."

"Sanchez's report says they both got out."

"Whatever. Alex keeps walking a few steps, then runs." She broke into a decent jog. She couldn't replicate the speed of Alex's stride, she was sure, and would not attempt to do so anyway in the middle of the day downtown.

"By now," said Joel, keeping up with her and breathing with some effort, "Miroballi's giving chase—and telling dispatch that—and the other cop has returned to his squad car."

They jogged into the alley. They both saw the blood stain, cleaned up to some extent but still very present. Shelly stopped before it. "Alex falls," she said, going to her knee. "He gets up"—she turned to face Gentry Street—"and turns and sees Miroballi standing there."

"Miroballi's just called in that the suspect is armed," said Joel. "Right about when he reaches the alley."

"Alex puts his hands up." Shelly followed suit. "He starts to backpedal."

"Miroballi's walking toward him."

Shelly and Joel, walking backward, passed the blood stain and kept moving. Joel stopped a few feet from that spot. "No closer than here," he estimated. "We know Miroballi was there," he said, pointing to the blood stain. The principal amount of blood hitting the pavement came after Officer Miroballi had hit the ground, falling backward. Much of it had spilled on his person and soaked into his uniform. Some of it had sprayed forward and to the side when the bullet hit his nose. Not all of this could be seen now, weeks after the shooting. But knowing where he fell, from the principal blood stain, meant knowing where he had been standing. The question was, where was Alex standing?

"I'd say about eight feet from the cop," said Joel. "Shoot a guy in the nose, blood's gonna spray everywhere. But they didn't find much on Alex. A little blood in his hair, right? And a couple specks on his sweatshirt. But his jacket was clean. So for the most part, he wasn't hit with the blood. About eight feet."

"Medical examiner will tell us." Shelly looked around. "So he pulls the gun and shoots him?" She mimicked the act herself, using her hand for a gun. "Shoot-out at the O.K. Corral?"

"Miroballi saw a gun," said Joel. "So I assume Alex had it in his hand, or stuffed in his belt or jacket." He shook the gym bag he was holding. "Not in here."

"Neither of the witnesses saw Miroballi pulling a gun." Shelly looked up at the Forrester Insurance Building on the west side of Gentry, where the witness Monica Stoddard had been working that night. "So that means, I assume, that Alex had his gun, Miroballi reached for his, and Alex shot first."

Joel looked up, as if he were trying to retrieve data. "Yeah, Miroballi's weapon was holstered when he was found."

"That's no good," she said. "That doesn't sound so much like self-defense."

"What has Alex told you?"

"He hasn't." She paced in a circle, looking around. "I haven't asked him."

"You pleaded self-defense, I thought."

"You can comb these walls, Joel? For bullets? Take some pictures?"

"Sure. Shelly, you pleaded self-defense without knowing whether Alex even shot him?"

"Yes." She walked along the wall and looked. The bricks were in terrible condition, but to the naked eye, there were no signs of lodged bullets that would have come from Miroballi's angle, past Alex. That was consistent with all the police reports and forensics, which showed that Miroballi had not fired a weapon, and that only one gunshot had been heard. But she was certainly not going to limit her knowledge to what the police had told her.

"The second gun," she said. "The .38 on the ground." The other gun, besides Miroballi's, that was found at the murder scene but which had not been fired.

"Serial number scratched off, of course." Joel rubbed his

cheek, then moved his hand around to the back of his neck. "And they never found the murder weapon."

"The question is, who's the second gun belong to? And why leave it?"

"The why-leave-it part is easy." Joel shrugged. "Shit happens. This is no career criminal. He shoots, he wigs out and runs. That happens every day of the week."

"But that's the thing, Joel. He *took* the gun he shot with."

Joel conceded the point. He walked over to the spot where the gun had been found at the crime scene, approximately ten feet from the dead body in the direction of Alex's flight. "Looks like it fell off Alex, or he dropped it, as he was running away. Same with the coke, right? Right about the same spot?"

Shelly nodded. The two packets of cocaine had been found near the gun, all of them in the direction that Alex fled after the shooting, ten feet to the east of Miroballi's body.

"Could be intentional or accidental," said Lightner. "That stuff could've fallen out of his pocket when he ran. Maybe he just wanted to dump the illegal contraband."

"Except the murder weapon," Shelly repeated.

Joel wiped his mouth. "Murder weapon could've had his prints on it. Could be, in a moment of panic, he thinks it's just better to keep it with him." Joel removed a handkerchief from his pocket and blew his nose. He looked at Shelly. "You don't like it."

"I don't like it." She put her hands on her hips. "Not sure I believe it."

"We should go." Lightner tapped his watch.

They walked to Joel's car, parked in a lot near Shelly's office. "When did you leave the force?" she asked.

"Ninety-five," he said. "Eleven years in E.P. Four here in the city."

Joel Lightner had been the chief of detectives for a suburban police department when the Terry Burgos murders took place in the late '80s. Mansbury College, the site of the killing spree, was within the county but outside the city, in the rather diminutive town of Englewood Park. Lightner had been the lead detective on the Burgos case. He was the only law enforcement officer, as far as she knew, who ever interrogated Burgos. That case, presumably, was how he and Paul Riley had met.

"Do you know the Miroballis?" she asked him as he started the car. It was a towncar with creamy leather seats and plenty of accoutrements. The private sector seemed to be treating Joel Lightner well.

"Not really. Ray, no. Reggie—he was the second-grade, right?"

"Right," she said. Reginald Miroballi was a detective, second-grade. The middle child at forty-two, four years older than Ray. Anthony Miroballi, at forty-four, was a lieutenant.

"Heard of Reggie but didn't know him. Tony, I met once. Political guy, from what I heard. Ass-kisser."

Shelly looked out the window as they drove along the west side. Once you left the commercial district and headed west, things changed in a hurry. The west side was the poorest of the city's poor. The streets looked like the objects of target bombing. Scattered throughout every block were humble but well-kept homes, but every third lot was empty or had a house on the verge of collapse. It was the result of home-mortgage fraud, in which unscrupulous lenders gave out high-interest loans for home "purchases" that vastly exceeded the true value of the home—thanks to fraudulent appraisals. The "buyers," in on the scheme with the lenders, bought the house but pocketed the remainder of the proceeds—say $200,000 for a home worth maybe forty—while the lender sold the mortgage on the secondary market to an unsuspecting lender who jumped at the prospect of a high-interest loan. By the time the new holder of the loan was the wiser, the buyer had skipped town, and the loanholder's only recourse was to foreclose on collateral that did not even come close to covering the loan amount. Yes, sometimes the new loanholder went back to the originator, but with the vast numbers of loans bundled on the secondary market, it was becoming just another cost of doing business. One out of every hundred will be bogus. Factor it into the cost, like a department store factored in the cost of shoplifting.

The real victims were the neighborhoods. Abandoned houses on the verge of demolition became crack houses, or dangerous playgrounds for children, and in any event an utter blight. Property values remained depressed, and any attempt at revitalization was thwarted. The deregulation of the '80s was paying dividends, in spades, in the new millennium.

"Shelly, just so you know," said Joel. "This is business to me. Yeah, a cop was killed and I used to be one, but don't count me out of the inner circle here. I got one and only one loyalty, and that's to you. You need *someone* you can trust."

She wondered if he was referring to Alex in that last comment. A former cop would naturally have plenty of skepticism built up. She looked at him. "I pleaded self-defense for many reasons," she said. "One is that I think Alex may be in danger."

"Retaliation."

Close enough. She wasn't sure whether she should share the undercover drug operation with him yet. "So now, anyone thinking of going after him will have to think twice. There will be a lot of questions now, if something happens to him."

"Good enough."

"Plus, I'm throwing the state off the scent. They think I'm conceding the facts, or at least most of them. They think I'm conceding Alex shot him, and just arguing the details. That may be true. But it may not be."

Yes, he was right. She had to trust someone. She removed the photograph she took of the boy—Manuel, he called himself— who had helped the armed intruders get into her apartment.

"What the heck's this?" Joel asked, holding up the photo as he drove. "Junkie porn?"

She would laugh, under different circumstances. "This kid came to my house and told me he had information about Alex. I made him strip down to his undies to make sure he wasn't armed. What he didn't tell me was that he had brought some friends."

Joel glanced over at her.

"They gave me a little pep talk about not smearing Ray Miroballi."

"No shit."

"I don't know if they were cops, Joel. But it's the best guess." She pointed at the photo. "They rousted some junkie and used him to get in."

"You want me to find this kid."

"If it's possible. It's probably a needle in a haystack."

"I'll start with the morgue."

The thought had occurred to Shelly as well. Whoever used

this boy, if they were ruthless enough, might dispose of "Manuel" once his role was over.

Joel pulled his car into the lot across the street from the criminal courthouse. They went through a detailed security process and made their way to the fourth floor, home of the County Attorney Technical Unit. The CAT Unit had been set up about ten years ago, after one too many questions about one too many cases, amid accusations of evidence tampering by the city police. The county's criminal investigation procedures were revamped, and the county attorney took over crime-scene work.

"Nothing great on the background," said Joel as they left the elevator. "I don't see anything dirty about Miroballi at all. Or his partner, Sanchez. But I'm working on it."

"I need to talk to Sanchez next," she said, as much to herself as him.

"Ask him how his girlfriend is doing."

"What does that mean?"

"He's got a thing on the side. He's married. Got a hot little mama on the sly." He cast a glance at Shelly. "It's my guys' bread and butter. That stuff pays the bills while I handle these highfalutin cases that Riley shoots me. They got some photos, even, if you want them."

They reached the door. Joel Lightner knew several of the people inside. Their familiarity with a former colleague seemed to be sufficient for the officials to leave Joel and Shelly alone with the physical evidence, in a small room that had been prepped for them. Nice, she thought, to be with someone on the inside. And funny, she noted, that the daughter of the most powerful man in the state considered herself an outsider.

"The .38," said Joel, pointing at the weapon wrapped in plastic. Next to it in similar wrapping was Officer Miroballi's firearm. Hanging from a metal, stand-alone hanger set was the black leather jacket Alex had been wearing. The thought passed in and out of her mind, that she had never seen this jacket, which only reminded her of how little she knew of this boy.

"No blood spatterings on the jacket," said Joel, putting his nose almost against the plastic. He touched the next item, Ray Miroballi's uniform top. "Plenty of it here."

"The gunpowder residue test was negative," said Shelly, referring to the test performed on Alex the night of the shooting.

Joel uttered a dismissive grunt. "That's not uncommon," he said, "if you were getting your hopes up. Doesn't mean Alex didn't shoot the firearm."

Doesn't mean he did, either.

"When the fuck's the coroner gonna do the autopsy?" he asked.

"No idea." In a case like this, where cause of death was so obvious, autopsies were not necessarily of primary import. The only critical issue, as far as Shelly could tell, was the distance between Alex and Miroballi when the shooting occurred.

"Pardon my French, by the way." Joel moved away from the hanging rack. "Back in my old haunts, I get my old mouth back." He wiped his hands, for some reason. "Actually, in this case, I don't know how much the distance matters. Closer the better, I suppose, if you're thinking self-defense. Especially if he never drew his weapon."

He walked back over to the table. Shelly was looking around, too, but not with expert eyes. She felt more like an escort than a technician. Joel pointed to the plastic baggie containing the two grams of cocaine. "No prints," he said. "But on a night like that, Alex was probably wearing gloves. Or he was smart when he packaged it."

"Or," Shelly offered, "they weren't his drugs."

"The ol' drop-and-plant." Joel smiled. "Drop the perp, put a gun and some drugs in his hand. We used to do it all the time."

She assumed he was kidding but didn't respond. "That would make the .38 his, too. Miroballi's, I mean."

Joel cocked his head to allow for the possibility. He didn't seem to think too much of it.

"And Alex wasn't wearing gloves," she added.

"You mean they didn't *find* him wearing gloves."

"You think he dumped them?"

"Certainly a possibility, Counselor. Same place he dumped the gun." Joel reached into his gym bag, his briefcase for the day, and removed a camera to photograph all the evidence. "They'll find that gun, by the way," he added. "They found

him—what—a half mile away? That's a very workable radius."
He closed an eye and started photographing items one by one.

"You're assuming he shot him," she rejoined.

"So are you." He moved the camera from his face. "Until you
ask him."

29
Schemes

It was after another week, courtesy of an extension she had provided him, that Jerod Romero had delivered a copy of a plea bargain to Shelly's attention at the law firm. It had arrived in an 8½-by-11 envelope, emblazoned with the seal of the Department of Justice, United States Attorney's Office. A letter agreement, already signed by Jerod Romero at his line. A yellow Post-It note had been stuck to the agreement with the words, *You get the discovery when you sign this.*

She'd looked it over. The U.S. Attorney had agreed not to prosecute Alex Baniewicz for any offenses, including but not limited to possession of not less than fifty grams and not more than one hundred grams of cocaine with intent to distribute, on December 5, 2003, as previously referred to in a letter agreement dated December 6, 2003. In consideration of said promise, neither Alex Baniewicz nor his counsel, Michelle Trotter, Esquire, and/or any counsel that may join or succeed her would disclose any facts relating to an undercover federal operation probing the activities of city law enforcement in the distribution of controlled substances until such time as the matter of *People v. Alex Gerhard Baniewicz,* Case Number 03 CR 4102, commenced trial.

More details. She'd taken her time with it, spent a day looking it over for loopholes. In the end, she had been satisfied. She had secured full immunity for Alex. She'd taken the agreement to Alex for his signature, a meeting she'd cut short under the pretense of needing to get it immediately to the federal prosecutors, and then did just that, delivering a fully executed copy of the agreement two nights ago.

She looked over the agreement again now with butterflies in her stomach, now that it was fully executed, waiting for the word or phrase that she had missed the first six times around and that would suddenly doom her client. But she was satisfied and felt content. On its face, there was little reason to break out party hats. Alex was looking, at most, at maybe a year and a half in a federal camp, a rap on the knuckles compared to the death penalty that state prosecutors were seeking. It was the terms of the agreement she appreciated. No conditions on his further cooperation with the feds, who no longer needed him anyway. No condition of truthfulness. It gave Alex wiggle room. It gave Shelly, as his lawyer, wiggle room.

And it gave her indigestion, at how little she trusted Alex's word, that she found it necessary to cover him through this agreement from any lies he may have told. This was, after all, her son she was talking about.

Son. Just a word. It lacked feeling. Why? She had cared so much for this young man before she knew the truth. Why did she have to look at him differently now? Alex hadn't lied to her. A crime of omission, perhaps, but how could she judge him for that? She'd left him at birth, given him up, and now she was irked at him for the manner in which he found her?

She brought her hands to her face. She didn't cry. She was less a crier than a weller, emotions rising to the surface with some ease, eyes filling, but tears rarely falling. A powder keg inside but a cool exterior. Could be a defense mechanism. She was looking at the boy as nothing more than a client because she needed to, right? She needed to keep the objectivity that would make her an effective advocate. Would she ever be able to embrace him for who he was? Or was it easier to feel connected when he was an abstraction, a genderless, nameless somebody with no faults or virtues?

"For God's sake," she mumbled.

She heard footsteps a moment later, and she got to her feet in the small room. Alex was escorted into the room, wearing the ever-present shackles and moving slowly.

"We got the stuff from the F.B.I.," she said quickly. "Lots to do."

Alex looked at her a second. "Okay." He'd barely sat down, the prison guard hadn't left the room yet, and they hadn't even said hello. Shelly busied herself removing the folders from her bag. She knew what she was doing, as she had every time since she learned the news, using an excuse to avoid any personal interaction with him.

She pushed a file in front of him as she continued to remove items. Alex opened the folder and held each photo in his shackled hands, as if seeing the concept of photography for the first time. He was the object of attention, probably something he was not accustomed to. Shelly had seen it before, in the children she had represented, a perverse enjoyment from all the fuss about them.

"You hadn't seen these?" she asked him.

He shook his head no. "They told me they had me meeting with Miro but they didn't say much more." He continued through the pictures, an eager child.

Shelly moved her chair so she could view the photos along with Alex. A number of grainy black-and-white, 5-by-7 photos, pictures taken in a park. Close-ups, though Shelly guessed the photographer was far away, probably across the street. One man sitting on a bench in a light jacket and slacks, leg crossed, heavyset, wearing a baseball cap and smoking a cigarette. Looking at these snapshots yesterday, she had matched up the face, out of context, with the newspaper photo and shuddered. It was Raymond Miroballi. The next one, Miroballi was standing by the bench, hands stuffed in a thick jacket as another person had approached, seen from the back. Shelly had recognized the long black coat and stocking cap. It was Alex.

She watched Alex go through them and nod with recognition. Miroballi patting Alex down, making him remove his coat, hands tapping his ribs, his stomach, the insides of his thighs. Alex talking, one hand waving as he spoke. Miroballi, leaning into Alex, a finger jabbing the air, a close-up of his stern expression. Near the end of the set of snapshots, Alex was handing Miroballi a letter-sized envelope with a bulge. The first of this sequence showed Alex holding out the envelope; the second and third, Miroballi was looking around in different directions; the fourth one, Miroballi took the envelope; finally, Miroballi stuffed the envelope inside his jacket.

On the back of each photograph in this series were the words RAYMOND MIROBALLI / ALEX BANIEWICZ, ABBOTT PARK, 11-24-03, 6:26 P.M.

"So let's talk about that meeting with Miroballi."

Alex looked at the photo and held his breath.

"You're giving him the money there," said Shelly. "The envelope has cash?"

Alex continued to stare at the snapshot. He slowly nodded yes.

"He seemed upset with you," Shelly observed.

"Yeah, what was that—November? Yeah, that's when he upped it to five hundred."

"Tell me about the conversation," she said, scrolling through the photos again. Miroballi punching the air with a finger, a grimace on his face.

Alex nodded at the photo. "He's telling me he can mess me up good. A kickback of five hundred is nothing compared to going away for twenty to life."

"What did you say?"

"I said I wouldn't go alone."

She studied him. It was hard to imagine the Alex she had come to know, a gentle soul, talking tough. But it was his life he was talking about. His daughter's future.

Alex made a face. "He said I couldn't prove a thing. Said the money couldn't be traced."

"But you agreed to bumping up his fee?"

"Said I'd think about it." Alex shrugged.

She looked at him a moment, then continued on. After the photographs was a typewritten report by F.B.I. Special Agent Constantine Padopoulos. It noted that Officer Raymond Miroballi ended his shift at 5:00 P.M. on the day of Monday, November 24, 2003, and left the police station in plainclothes at 5:22 P.M. He drove in his personal vehicle to Abbott Park, which he circled in his car three times before parking and getting out.

At 5:52 P.M.—and this matched up with the photographs; Shelly went through them as she read the narrative, a process she had repeated over and over again into the wee hours last night— Miroballi sat at a park bench and waited. He was approached by an unidentified male, Caucasian, midtwenties, at 6:02 P.M.

Unidentified. That confirmed Shelly's assumption that the F.B.I. found Alex when they were looking at Miroballi. They knew about Miroballi before Alex. They caught her client because of the cop, in other words, not the other way around.

The report continued. The federal agents followed Miroballi afterward as he drove in his vehicle to his residence on the city's south side. The last of the photographs in this sequence showed Miroballi's car parked on the driveway, up against a garage that was occupied in part by a second car and in part by assorted construction materials, a vanity sink lying on its side, a garden hose wound up and hanging on the wall.

She braced herself as she considered Raymond Miroballi, family man. To his children he was probably a hero, a man who helped others, fought the bad guys. She imagined his wife, a woman she didn't know, presumably satisfied with her husband's stable income and their young children, who dreamed of more for them than she ever had, now wondering about the irreparable damage to their lives, lives without a father.

Alex was next followed by the federal agents after a rather suspicious meeting with a police officer under surveillance. Alex was shown walking, getting on a bus, leaving the bus and walking again, pulling up the collar on his black coat, finally going into his home.

A kid, really, with no idea that he was being watched by agents of the federal government. A kid who couldn't see beyond the next week, the extra cash for his daughter. She looked at Alex in the pictures helplessly, begging him to turn back, quit the drug business, don't let the government catch you and get yourself in a position that you have to defend yourself on the streets, in an alley—

"They skunked me pretty good," Alex conceded with a humorless laugh. He had been incarcerated for six weeks and the effects were clear. His neck and face were thinner, the veins in his arms more prominent. His eyes were perpetually rimmed in redness, a dark shade circled them. His hair was flat, looked greasier than before. His posture was less confident, an ever-present slope to his shoulders. They were slowly breaking him.

She imagined Alex—her son, yes, her son—she imagined her son in the penitentiary, maximum security, an unfortunately handsome youth. He'd join a gang inside probably, for protection, assuming a white kid had a gang to join; she wasn't familiar with the intricacies of prison affiliations. He'd probably enter into the drug trade in prison, maybe even start taking them himself. He would get hurt and hurt others. He would boast about how he killed a cop, a badge of pride inside.

She looked away for a moment, as if Alex could read her thoughts. He wouldn't stand a chance inside, not for the long haul.

"So you two met again a week later," she said, going to the next set of photographs. Precisely a week after the first meeting, on Monday, December 1, 2003, federal agents captured Alex and Miroballi meeting again, at the same time and place—Abbott Park. Again, Miroballi arrived first and sat at the bench. Again, he patted Alex down when he walked up. Again, the exchange between the two seemed heated. The conversation took less than twenty minutes, ending with the passing of another envelope.

"November twenty-fourth and December first," said Shelly. "Why two meetings within a week?"

"I told him I'd think about the five hundred. So we hooked up again. He wanted to know what I decided."

"And?"

"I told him okay. Five hundred."

"Pretty steep," Shelly estimated.

"You are correct about that."

"What else did Miroballi do or say?"

"He was all nervous. He was like, 'You keeping your mouth shut about this? You're not playing games with me, are you, boy?' Stuff like that."

"What did you say?"

"I said I wasn't saying a word to anyone. I mean, I didn't even know about the F.B.I. at that point."

The perfect segue. The next set of photographs showed Mr.

Alex Baniewicz walking through an alley behind his home, to his car parked at a spot next to a stand-alone garage. The date, inscribed on the back, was Friday, November 28, 2003. Alex opening the door of his car, apparently reaching under the cushion in the backseat, surreptitiously stuffing something into his jacket, and then leaving the alley for the bus.

"That was after your first meeting with Miroballi," she said. "Imagine their excitement."

"I'm surprised they didn't bust me then."

"They wanted to see where you'd go. They weren't done yet."

The next set of photos showed the same thing, more or less. Alex removing packets of cocaine from the car, but this time not making it out of the alley. A special agent of the F.B.I. stopping Alex covertly. Escorting Alex to a car. This was the following Friday, December 5, 2003.

"That was after your second meet with Miroballi," Shelly said.

"*That's* when they were done," he said without enthusiasm. He put a hand to his face. He'd probably replayed these events hundreds of times in his head, but it was another thing to see them. "They got me in a room. They did a real number on me, three or four of them. They said I was looking at ten years, minimum. They said since I took the drugs to school"—he worked part-time after school three days a week, including Friday— "that it would triple my sentence."

Shelly winced. She wasn't intimately familiar with federal drug laws. The state's drug law had an enhancement for selling drugs within a certain promixity to a school. No doubt, the federal one did too, but ten years' minimum? They were blowing smoke. And that was permissible. Cops and federal agents could deceive a witness repeatedly as long as they respected *Miranda*. And in this context, the feds hadn't even attempted to use his statements at trial, so they had virtually no restriction on what they could do.

"I was pissing in my pants, Shelly. I mean, they know how to scare. They had me eating out of their hand."

"It wasn't an ideal situation," she acknowledged. The first words of consolation she'd ever given him when it came to drugs.

"I told them I'd help them catch Miro."

"So that was the first week of December." She flipped the final file of photographs toward Alex and got out of her seat. She was never good at sitting for too long. Her mind worked better when she was moving.

The final sequence showed Alex Baniewicz and Raymond Miroballi arriving separately—Miroballi first—at a diner on the corner of Forty-third and Green. The date was January 21, 2004. The photographer captured each of them entering the establishment and then sitting in a corner booth. The cameraman had zoomed in through the window and captured some good detail. Miroballi, at one point, jabbing his finger at Alex. At another point, slamming his hand on the table. "The last time I met with him," said Alex, "they put us at the corner table."

"They," Shelly repeated. "The F.B.I.? What do you mean, they 'put' you there?"

"They told me that's probably where Miroballi would be sitting."

Shelly looked again at the photographs. The diner was crowded. The F.B.I. probably had people populating some of the tables, and probably spoke covertly with the restaurant owner to keep the corner booth open. Easier to photograph, and more likely to give Miroballi the feeling that he was in a secure spot.

"How'd that meeting go?" she asked.

"I told him that five hundred a month was no good. I said two hundred—the original deal—had to be the plan."

"Why, Alex?" This took place after the F.B.I. had flipped Alex. Why would he play tough guy?

"I figured he was suspicious," he answered. "If I walked in there with a big smile on my face and five hundred in my hand, he'd know. So I acted like we were still negotiating. Reverse psychology." He waved a hand, as if the notion had been silly. Or at least unsuccessful.

"And Miroballi went along with that?"

"He was a little too eager to please. He couldn't have cared less about money. He just wanted to know if I was keeping my mouth shut. I'm telling you, Shelly. This guy was on to me. Either he knew or he suspected."

"Okay." She looked at the photographs. "So between December first and January twenty-first, no contact?" she asked. "Nothing for seven weeks?"

"Right." Alex closed the file. "About seven weeks there, nothing. I see this guy probably twice a month every month, and then he disappears. You tell me, Shelly. Don't you think this guy had figured out something was wrong?"

Alex was making sense. She had been relieved to learn that the evidence obtained from the U.S. Attorney's office corroborated his story. It didn't prove much of anything for the purposes of the trial, but it was a start.

"I imagine those must have been seven long weeks for you," she said. "You've got federal agents waiting for you to lead them to Miroballi, and suddenly he takes a powder."

Alex shook his head. "You'd think they would know this stuff better than anyone. It's not like I just see Miro on the street and toss the money in the air to him. It was secretive. And he was the one setting things up, not me."

"Miroballi dictated the time and place of meetings."

"Yeah. Sure. But they were getting pretty agitated. They were asking, 'Why hasn't he called?' 'Where's Miro?' 'How come he's all of sudden disappearing?' " Alex's face colored. "They thought I told him."

Shelly stopped her pacing. "They thought you tipped off Miroballi about the feds?"

Alex's head inclined.

It made sense now. The comments from the prosecutor Jerod Romero, from Special Agent Peters, about Alex's reliability. *Your client says a lot of things. Some may be true, a lot of them probably aren't.* And Shelly had always been a little surprised at their unwillingness to stand behind one of their witnesses.

"The feds thought you double-crossed them," she said.

"I guess."

"Did you, Alex?"

"Of course not. Shelly, the guy's no dummy. You don't think he's on the look-out? I can't tell you how, but he had figured it out."

Shelly sat down again, choosing the chair at the opposite end of the table. "It's not that I don't believe you, Alex."

"But you need proof."

"Did you have any sense of whom Miroballi was working with? Other cops on the take?"

He shook his head slowly. "If he had partners in this, I don't know."

"What about his official partner?" she asked. "Sanchez?"

"Don't know anything about him. My guess was always that Miro was a lone ranger."

"That just doesn't work, though. The feds are looking at a ring, right? Not a solo practitioner."

Alex framed his hands. "It's not like the feds told me what was going on. But I always had the sense that they couldn't figure out how Miro fit in with everyone else. Like he didn't make sense or something."

"Who were you talking to? Peters?" Special Agent Donovan Peters was the only agent she had spoken with.

"Peters and this other guy. A younger guy. Rafey."

"Rafey." She went to her notepad.

"Rafael. I'm pretty sure that wasn't his real name. Young guy. Midtwenties, probably. He was undercover. He was on the street as a junkie. Sounds like he was buying crack."

Crack. A crack cocaine ring was more likely than a powder cocaine ring, in this day, especially if the feds were involved. Another reason why Miroballi didn't make sense.

"Alex, I have to cut to the chase with you. We haven't really covered it." She settled her hands and took a moment. "It's my policy to gather the evidence as best I can before asking you outright. I think we're at that stage now. We've pleaded self-defense but I can withdraw that. It's still an open field. But I have to tell you, there's not a whole lot of suspects here. It was close to eight in the evening when this went down, and the streets were empty."

"Nobody was around."

"They haven't found the gun and they don't have hard evidence that you even fired a gun that night. All of that is good. I'd be happy to point the finger at someone else but—"

"There's no one else to point at." He shrugged. "It was just him and me in that alley."

She ran her hands over the table and did not look at him. "Then we need to talk about it."

"It's like I've told you. It's him and me. He reaches for his weapon and I beat him to it."

"Did you have drugs on you?"

"No, ma'am." He opened his hands. "The feds had my drugs."

"You could have gotten more."

"Well, I didn't."

"Where was your gun?"

"In my jacket pocket." He made the motion of reaching into a jacket and removing a gun. "I pulled it out and shot him. If I didn't, he would've shot me."

"Tell me why you thought that."

Alex's eyes drifted off. "Why? Because there was no other reason for him to be all over me like that. Why was he coming after me? To talk? Why reach for his gun? To show it to me? Why did his partner stay behind? The guy was back in his car. Why?" Alex adjusted himself in the chair. "He was going to kill me and claim that I was going to kill him. He had the whole thing set up. He just didn't expect me to *really* have a gun."

"So he brought the coke," she said. "And he brought that other gun that was found."

"Part of the plan."

"He needs the other gun to fire it, after the fact." She nodded. "He'll kill you, then go over to you, put the gun in your hand and fire it, put a bullet into the wall, and then claim that you fired first."

"And put the cocaine in my pocket to give him the excuse for coming after me."

Shelly held her breath a moment, then gave a decisive nod. "That's our case," she said. "We just need to find some corroboration."

"Right."

"And what about the gun?" she asked. "Where is it?"

"I dumped it." Alex chewed on a lip. "They haven't found it, huh?"

"No," she said. "Will they?"

He shrugged. "I threw it in a garbage bin a ways away."

"Which one?"

He shrugged. "I was running and I saw it. Somewhere in the

direction I was running. If they can't find it, that's their problem."

Not for long, she thought. They would have it any day now.

"So you think we can win?" He said it with a hope that wrapped around Shelly's heart. He looked at her now, much in the way he had when times were simpler between them, when they were two friends getting to know each other, when they talked of college for him and a solid future for his daughter, Angela. How Shelly longed to return to that time. How urgently she wanted to rip the shackles off his wrists and run away with him. How desperately she wanted to undo the many things that had led to this moment.

30
Distance

OFFICER JULIO SANCHEZ left the police station at twenty minutes after five in the evening in civilian clothes, blue jeans and a leather jacket, a baseball cap atop his head. Shelly got out of her car and approached him. He seemed interested, looking her over.

"Officer Sanchez."

"That's me."

"My name is Shelly Trotter. I represent—"

His expression went cold.

"—Alex Baniewicz—"

"I know who you are. Didn't recognize you at first." He stuffed his hands in his jacket. "You wanna know something? You got a lot of fucking nerve coming to a cop house."

Shelly stopped a little short of the officer. "I need to speak with you."

"I'm not saying shit to you, lady." Sanchez waved at her like she was a gnat and started down the sidewalk. He was being impolite but not angry, not violent. She found that interesting.

A little early to play the card. "Please, Officer." She tried to keep up with him, not approaching him but staying within earshot. "I'm just doing my job. I just need five minutes."

"Beat it, lady lawyer."

She stopped. "Okay," she called out. She didn't have weeks and months to play around, and she was quickly tiring of everyone shutting her out. "Maybe I'll just go talk to Marta."

He stopped, too, but didn't turn.

She walked up and stood next to him, facing forward like he was. He wouldn't respond, wouldn't look at her, but he wasn't walking away, either. "I know about your girlfriend. I've got photos. And you know what? All I ask is that you talk to me." Her heart pounded. She was extorting a cop. Maybe that was debatable, as long as the only thing she was seeking was truthful answers from him. She hadn't researched the legal issue. She didn't care, in any event.

Sanchez mumbled something in Spanish.

"Threaten me if you'd like," she said evenly. "You wouldn't be the first cop to do it."

"You got a lotta *cajones,* lady."

She looked at him. His face was a bright crimson. What options he was considering, she didn't know.

"I don't care about your love life, Officer Sanchez. I care about defending my client. Besides, wouldn't you rather hear my questions now, instead of for the first time on the witness stand?"

That seemed to make some sense to the officer. "Not here," he said. "Not now."

"Not here," she agreed. "But now. There's a restaurant on Broadway by Rosemont. Be there in fifteen minutes." She walked away from him, to her car.

Sanchez showed up a few minutes late. Shelly had found a booth near the corner and made eye contact with him.

"I meant what I said," she told him after he took a seat across from her. "I have no use for those photos if you help me." It was important that Sanchez knew he had an out. The problem with blackmail was you could never trust the blackmailer. She had to let him know, if he played ball, he could sleep well at night. "If anything happens to me between now and the trial, however, those pictures go to your wife."

"The hell you talking about? Happen to *you*?"

"Yeah. Any of your buddies in blue come looking for me, these pictures go to your wife." She certainly couldn't rule out Officer Julio Sanchez from the list of men responsible for breaking into her home. All she had seen of the men were their eyes and maybe a small hint of skin on the periphery. She'd certainly assumed they were white, whereas Sanchez's skin was closer to coffee with cream. And he had a bit of an accent—second-generation Mexican, she guessed, comparing him to many of her clients from CAP—which seemed to further disqualify the officer from suspicion. But if he hadn't been there, maybe he knew who was. She was covering as many bases as she could.

"Talk to me," she said, "and live your life however you want."

"You don't know shit about my life."

That was true. But Sanchez had agreed to meet with her, which meant that his wife didn't know about Marta.

"We're getting a divorce," he said. "You happy?"

Interesting, that he would explain himself. Interesting, really, that he would have agreed to talk with Shelly at all. Just because she had some incriminating photos? She sensed that it must be more than that. Or maybe there was some rancor in the legal proceedings and she was hitting a sore spot.

"You got a wire under there?" he asked. "You recording this?"

"No," she answered. "That would be illegal." Law enforcement could wiretap, but private citizens could not record a conversation without the consent of the other party. "Even if I wanted to break the law, I'd never be able to use it in court."

Sanchez seemed to already know the law in this area. "If he says I knew him, he's full of shit." He tapped the counter with two fingers. "Didn't have a single conversation with the guy."

He was talking about Alex. This was how he was introducing the topic, by denying that he knew Alex. His statement was loaded with inferences that Shelly couldn't grasp.

More significantly, Sanchez was showing his hand here. This was a sensitive point for him; he seemed to be making a point of distancing himself from Alex and Miroballi. There was a reason for that.

Sanchez was growing impatient with Shelly's silence. "Is that what he's saying? That punk is saying *I* was working with him?"

Actually, Alex had said exactly what Sanchez was saying—they didn't know each other. But she didn't need to tell Sanchez that.

"Because he's a fucking liar," said the officer. "If he said that, he's a liar."

"Maybe he is a liar." She smiled helplessly, opened her hands. "You know how it is with these clients, Officer. They lie all the time. That's why I'm here. I don't want to hear it from Alex. I want to hear it from you. In your own words, not his, tell me what role you played."

" 'Role,' " he snorted. "I didn't *have* a role. I didn't even know what they were doing, those two."

That point, Shelly figured, was debatable. The problem was that Sanchez had to *say* he had no idea, because knowledge of illegal activity by one's partner obviously had to be reported. This was the jam Sanchez was in, guilt by partnership.

"Ray was an okay guy," he said as he looked out the window of the diner. He was a bit odd-looking, a thin man with a head that was disproportionately large, a skinny neck cropping up from an oversized leather jacket, a baseball cap that seemed too big. "I think he just got too full of ideas."

Coffee arrived, and he smiled at the waitress. Shelly had the thought that perhaps Julio Sanchez was a decent sort, an honest cop partnered with a different sort of officer. Just because he smiled at the waitress? No, you couldn't judge someone so simply, but still, it was the small gestures that said so much.

"The Cannibals," he continued. "They run A-Jar. You know A-Jar?"

Shelly nodded. The Eduardo Andujar housing project on the west side, he meant. He was referring to the Latino gang that controlled A-Jar. The Columbus Street Cannibals took their name from a speech delivered by the former mayor about ten years ago, who referred to gangs on the west side as "cannibals" who preyed on their own.

What was Sanchez talking about?

He put his hands around the coffee mug. "He was having a tough go of it," he said. He was jumping out of order, from Shelly's perspective. She was more curious about what he'd just said about the Cannibals and A-Jar. "The last few months. He'd been moody. Edgy."

It was as if he were talking to himself. She wanted to go back to the Cannibals and A-Jar. But she would let him dictate the topics for now. "When did that start?" she asked. "The moodiness and agitation?"

His eyes glazed over. He was playing images over in his head. "Christmas. Before that. The holiday season, I guess."

Shelly felt a surge in her chest. Alex was nabbed by the feds on the fifth of December.

"I asked him what was wrong. Ray, he just says he's got family problems. I figure, he's arguing with the wife or something. One of his kids is acting up. Or maybe he's sick. Or maybe the department's coming down on him. How do I know?"

"Tell me what you *did* know."

Sanchez coughed, brought a fist to his mouth. He didn't look well. Shelly had no idea if Sanchez was a good cop or not, but if he was, he might become an innocent victim, forever tainted by association with a cop who would be accused, postmortem, of corruption.

"He was stressed out, I guess." Sanchez sighed. It occurred to Shelly that Sanchez had probably already talked to Internal Affairs, which meant he was free to tell her whatever he told them. The question was whether he'd go further. "He kept saying, 'I'm a good cop, right? I don't live in a mansion. I don't drive a Ferrari.'"

"Did you know why he was saying those things?"

He shook his head no. "I figured someone was looking at him. But he wouldn't say."

"What makes the Christmas season stand out in your mind?"

Sanchez nodded to himself. "Ray always liked Christmas. He dressed up as Santa and all that for his kids. Said it was getting harder to fool the little one."

Shelly nodded, prodding him along, trying to ignore the sudden discomfort. It was easier to think of Miroballi as pure evil, not a doting father.

"But last year," Sanchez continued, "he kept saying, 'Merry fucking Christmas.'"

Good. This was good.

"At first, I thought he was sick," he said.

He had mentioned that earlier. "Sick? Why?"

The officer cocked his head. "Dropped off a urine sample once. Wasn't his normal doctor. We have the same one. Lot of us go to the same guy. Y'know, same medical plan." He motioned off in the distance. "One day, he has me pull over by this medical center. Says he needs to drop off a urine sample. Had it in a pa-per bag."

A urine sample made her think of drugs. She got the name of the center from Sanchez and would follow up. "He didn't say anything else?"

"Nope. I was a little worried about that."

"You guys are drug-tested, right?"

"In the station, though. Not some center. It's not on our med-ical, that's the thing that got me. He'd have to pay out of his own pocket."

Now she would definitely follow up, though she realized it would be exceedingly difficult to get information from any medical center on a patient.

Was Miroballi taking drugs himself?

"What I really think it was—I think he had a thing with his brothers. He was the baby. I think he thought he was going to be stuck in patrol his whole life. His oldest brother's a lew, Reggie's second grade, and Ray's thinking he's always gonna be in uni-form. It bothered him."

"But Ray was the youngest," she said. "Of course he was lower rank."

"Yeah, but they moved up faster. He seemed to think he wasn't on the way up. I think that's what it was with the Cans."

The mention of the gang again. He was saying it as if Shelly knew what he was talking about. He was assuming that Alex had told her. She had to let him keep believing that, while she extracted the information from him. Was he saying that Ray was bitter and turned corrupt as a way of rebelling? He was getting into drug dealing with the C-Street Cannibals?

With Alex's help?

"I think he just wanted to talk to him," Sanchez said, looking at Shelly. "I think he thought Alex was fucking with him or something."

Now he was talking about the shooting. God, he was all over the place. She could see that Sanchez was pained, maybe with guilt, over what had happened. He probably had been asking himself the same questions about his partner, with a slight vari-ation, that Shelly had asked herself about Alex. *Maybe if he had talked to Ray more. Maybe if he'd gotten Ray to open up.* Shelly had to use blackmail to get Sanchez to talk, but once he started, he was spouting information.

"Ray radioed in that Alex had drugs on him," she said. "Did you see that?"

"I didn't, no. But that doesn't mean he wasn't carrying. I think he just wanted to talk to him. He was scared, I think."

"Ray was scared."

Sanchez nodded. "I think he thought Alex had given him up."

Shelly nodded. It was as if a bomb had detonated in her stomach. These were the words she had wanted so desperately to hear. *Miroballi thought Alex had flipped on him.* Would Sanchez say this in court?

"Ray said that?" she asked cautiously. "That Alex had given him up?"

Sanchez shook his head no. "He never said the words. But that's always the fear in something like this. We're talking about the Cans here. You know them?"

She did. A few of her clients, over the years, had been Cannibal recruits. Young kids, who often were used for the roughest stuff for the very reason that they were juveniles and couldn't be prosecuted to the same extent as older kids. And all she had ever done for these kids was keep them in school. It was putting a bandage on a gaping wound.

"I think Ray just wanted to talk to Alex," he said again.

"He was afraid of the Cannibals," said Shelly. Not the federal government?

Sanchez blurted out a laugh. "He thinks with one big bust, he's going to make detective. He wants to be this cowboy." Sanchez looked at her. "I didn't know the details. Ray said he was working on it. But then, he starts thinking maybe this kid—Alex—he's getting smart. Too smart. That's always the fear with C.I.'s. They're playing both sides, right?"

Shelly replayed the words she had just heard. She felt as if she were sliding down a hill she had just climbed.

C.I., he had said. Did he mean—

"I told him to register him," said the officer. "But Ray, he wanted the whole thing to be a big surprise."

"Alex was Ray Miroballi's snitch," she said. She tried to say it as fact, not a question. "An unregistered confidential informant."

"And not a very good one, to hear Ray." Sanchez looked out the window again. "Yeah, they met a couple times at a park. It was all secretive. Alex was real careful about being seen. Ray would be off-duty so you couldn't tell he was a cop. I just watched from a car. Y'know, watching his back."

"Alex was helping Ray take down the Cannibals," Shelly said, unable to get past that point.

Sanchez looked at her; it seemed to dawn on him that Shelly might be learning this for the first time. "This is news to you?"

She raised her hands. "No, I just want to hear it in your words."

Sanchez raised a finger. "One word from Alex to the Cannibals, and Ray's toast," he said. "One word. Those guys have killed a cop over less."

She was suddenly claustrophobic in her seat. She wanted to leave and run. Run to another state, another country. Run to her client, her son, and grab him by the hair.

"Just to be clear," she said, trying as best as possible to pretend that she hadn't been blindsided here. "Officer Miroballi was planning a drug bust on the Cannibals' turf. Something big. Alex was giving him information. They would meet at a park"—this was the one thing Shelly already knew—"and you were there, too, watching from your car." She paused. "Miroballi thought Alex had switched sides and given him up to the Cans. And you think that's what Ray was doing that night. Checking on his snitch."

Sanchez nodded. "Ray said he was a smart kid," he said. "I mean, he could be telling Ray one thing and telling the Cans another. Y'know, playing both sides off the other. How hard would that be?"

Shelly felt the air deflate from her lungs. Not hard at all, she thought to herself. Not hard at all.

31

Fun

SHE IS NOT *supposed to be here. But isn't that what makes it fun?*

Her parents are not home anyway this weekend, off to some fund-raisers a few hours away. Daddy is "collecting support," as he likes to say. He is going to try to run for attorney general and it sounds like the people who make such decisions—you would think it was the people of the state but apparently not— seem to want Daddy to be the one.

She is happy for him, but envious as well. She wants adventure, too, and wouldn't Daddy understand? A train ride into the city, unsupervised, unapproved. She met people on the train from Haley to the city—eighteen stops in between, she counted—and she introduced herself as "Andrea," she had just moved from out east and had been visiting a sick uncle in Haley and was now heading back to her home in the city, "near the park," she had said. There was a park but she didn't know where it was, precisely; she had been fearful that someone would pin her down on specifics but that was the beautiful thing about people in the city, they didn't ask such questions, they didn't have to pry into the minute details of one's life. Andrea— she had not given a last name—will exist in the city in perfect anonymity.

Her watch says that it is half past eight in the evening. She has been to the museums and to the shops on Atlantic Boulevard—she only has a little over a hundred dollars in her pocket so she was only looking, not buying—and now she has taken a taxi to the baseball park. It doesn't look like they're playing baseball today but the activity level is still high. People of all ages, all races, all speeds of stride—some busy, some relaxed. A hot dog vendor shouts out. Kids on skateboards, young teenagers like Shelly, jumping the air with their boards, trying to perfect this move or that one. More black people than she has ever seen in one place up close. Different languages spoken. Cars driving recklessly, pedestrians veering with abandon across the street.

The sky is bruising as the sun falls and storm clouds gather. She will probably run out of things to do and will make her way back to the train station. She is a block north of the baseball stadium now, on a residential street. She sees a gathering of people heading up a block of concrete steps. They don't have housing like this in Haley. They are all freestanding homes with lawns and driveways. The houses here are jammed together with no outdoor space that she can see.

She reaches a cluster of three people who are reaching the stairs. She looks at the first woman—she is probably no older than twenty-one but to Shelly, at age fifteen, she seems so old. She is taller than Shelly and beautiful; her face reveals a certain breeding, her high cheekbones, skin so smooth it seems to glisten, long flowing hair much darker than Shelly's cinnamon.

She looks at Shelly as she adjusts the purse hanging on her shoulder. She speaks to Shelly, and Shelly wonders if there was something in the way she was looking at this woman that made her feel compelled to do so.

"Going to the party?" she asks.

Shelly nods. Then smiles. She has been so immediately accepted. "I'm Andrea," says Shelly. She moves into the group as they take the concrete stairs.

"Dina," says the woman. Such a wonderfully elegant name. "Are you in art school with Steve?"

"Yes," she says quickly. "I just graduated high school out east and I'm trying to decide what to do." This much she has already said several times to various uninterested travelers on the train.

"Cool."

The door at the top of the stairs has been propped open; a sign on the door signals visitors that Steve's place is on the top floor. Shelly's heart drums as she hears the angry music blaring down the staircase and the smell of alcohol—beer, she assumes. She has never had a drink but there is a first time for everything. She looks at Dina and she thinks that this is who Shelly Trotter will be some day, a beautiful, graceful, confident woman. Oh, if her father could see her now.

32

Victim

SHELLY LEFT HER apartment and went down to the building's front door to allow Ronnie Masters in. She was no longer comfortable using her buzzer to blindly open the front door. She was relatively sure she was safe now, but she would take no chances.

Ronnie was hopping in place. The temperatures were below freezing and he was only wearing that hooded sweatshirt.

"Is that warm enough, Ron?" she said as she ushered him in. He shook himself out. "I'm fine."

She immediately regretted the comment. Asking him about the sufficiency of his clothing was tantamount to highlighting his lack of financial resources. Of course he would prefer something warmer, but he could not afford it.

She showed him inside and quickly made some hot chocolate. She brought two steaming mugs into the living room—this was what she called the room that was not the kitchen or the bedroom, a small space with a couch and chair, a fireplace and mantel.

"Thanks." Ronnie sipped the cocoa and nodded at the photographs on the mantel. There were two plaques Shelly had received for outstanding public advocacy, a photo of her with the rest of the CAP staff, some law school graduation photos of Shelly with her grandmother.

"Your grandma's who you stayed with," he said.

"Yes." Alex had apparently informed Ronnie of the details. When she had become pregnant at age sixteen, Shelly had moved from her house in Haley to Otter Lake, where her Grandma Jeannie (her mother's mother) lived as a widow. The stated purpose for leaving Haley was that people could be cruel, and Shelly would have a lot to deal with as it was, without the comments from her fellow students. Sure. Shelly would attend high school in Otter Lake, get a tutor when she became "too pregnant," and have the baby down there. There would be an excuse given—her grandmother was ailing, and Shelly, who was closest to Jeannie, wanted to stay with her to assist. No mention of Shelly's pregnancy.

It was, of course, pure nonsense to believe that the ruse would hold. It would only take a single leak and the news would spread throughout the small town of Haley. No one would believe that Shelly went down to Otter Lake in the middle of her high school career—where she was on pace to be valedictorian and one of the state's top tennis players—just to look out for her grandmother.

No. Shelly was not sent to Otter Lake to make life easier for *her*.

She never knew if the secret got out, because she never went back. She remained at Otter Lake after she had the baby and graduated with the rather small class down there. She obtained a scholarship to the state university and went to college, returning only sparingly, and then almost always to Otter Lake.

She had some fear of this whole ordeal coming to light when her father ran for attorney general four years later. She assumed that his opposition discovered the secret, but what could be done with such information? His daughter had become pregnant and given up the baby for adoption? Was that not precisely what a pro-life candidate like Langdon Trotter would support? What, exactly, could they accuse of him of—being consistent? And how ugly would the Democrats look, picking on the daughter?

"That must have been hard," said Ronnie.

Shelly felt a wound open inside her. When that happened, periodically over the years, she would do as she did now: take a deep breath and plow through it. "You deal with it," she said.

"This whole thing." Ronnie waved his arm. "Kinda brings it all back."

"Don't worry about that."

"Are you, like—" Ronnie's eyes dropped.

"Am I what?"

"Ashamed or something, like, I don't know." He rubbed at a stain on his blue jeans. "Forget it."

She watched this boy struggle, and it came to her what he meant, exactly.

"I'm not ashamed of Alex, Ronnie. I may be ashamed of certain aspects of my own behavior, but I am absolutely *not* ashamed of Alex."

Ronnie managed a peek at Shelly but did not confront her. "I mean, 'cause of how it happened."

"Because of how it happened?" She recognized the heightened volume of her voice but made no adjustment. "You mean that I was raped? You think I blame Alex for *that*? He was just an innocent little b—" Her throat closed on the words. She felt the heat in her face. She got up from the chair to give herself some space.

Did she, on an unconscious level, blame this child? Was she punishing the rapist by punishing the offspring? No. It was inconceivable. No. But then—why *hadn't* she ever looked for this boy? She was consumed suddenly, overcome, with shame and guilt.

"Hey, I'm sorry," Ronnie said.

She held out a hand but she was not prepared to speak. She could see what was happening. Alex and Ronnie had been talking. Alex had reported that Shelly was keeping a distance—more of a distance than when they had simply been friends. The revelation of her motherhood had opened a chasm between them. Shelly knew this to be true. She couldn't explain why and, really, had made little attempt to. She was doing the same thing now as she had her whole life, wasn't she? She was hiding.

"I can't blame Alex for this," she said simply. "Alex is the victim. The greatest victim of all. His only crime is that he wanted to find his real—"

The worst part was that she could not see the finish line. She didn't know if or when she would feel maternal love for Alex. And Alex could sense her struggle, she knew.

"Maybe," said Ronnie, "it would have been better if he hadn't looked for you."

"Is that what he thinks?" It was her first acknowledgment of her suspicion that Ronnie was speaking for Alex now, that he was interceding to discuss a topic on which Alex and Shelly could not personally converse. She found her way back to her seat, across from Ronnie on the couch. "I need time, that's all," she decided. "I don't mean to make Alex feel worse about this. This is—this is just not an easy situation for anybody."

"No."

"I know I let Alex down—"

"Join the club."

That stopped her. "How did *you* let him down?"

He shrugged. "I didn't keep a close enough eye on him."

She smiled. This kid thought he had to be Alex's brother and father, at the same time. "That's not your job, Ron. And I can tell you that Alex doesn't see it that way."

He waved that off.

"You saved his life, he told me."

Ronnie rolled his eyes.

"Alex told me," she said. "He got himself into a jam a couple years back. He was a stupid freshman who hot-wired the wrong kid's car. He said you saved him."

"Yeah, I'm a real hero. How am I helping him now?"

"Well, that's why I asked you over, actually." She was moving now to an issue that was at least as serious and important as the prior one. She had left Officer Julio Sanchez feeling that her client had been deceiving her. "I have some reason to believe that Alex may have been working with Officer Miroballi, but not in the way that had been explained to me."

Ronnie opened his hands. She detected little from his expression. She had spent years giving hard truths to young people, mostly male, and she had challenged them many times. If her experience were any guide, Ronnie was not hiding anything from her.

"I'm wondering if Alex was working for Miroballi as his informant."

Ronnie paused a beat, as if he were waiting for more, then grunted a chuckle. "C'mon."

"It's not exactly a flying leap, Ronnie. He was the feds' informant. They caught him and flipped him. There's no reason why Miroballi couldn't have done the same thing."

"No." He shook his head. "I don't know where you're getting that kind of bull—"

"I got it from Miroballi's partner."

"No." Ronnie would not be moved. "That's nuts. What the hell's Alex gonna tell this cop, anyway? It's not like he's some big-time dealer or something. He doesn't have the kind of information a cop would be looking for."

"No?"

"No." Ronnie reached for his sweatshirt and got to his feet. "You're taking a cop's word over Alex's? You think this guy wouldn't bullshit you, Shelly? Are you that big a fan of cops all of a sudden?"

It was like he had punched her in the throat. She looked at him, the breath temporarily whisked from her lungs. He left on that note, triumphant in his closing remark. She listened to the door close behind him, and it was a long time before she could leave the chair.

33
Liar

I WAS RAPED.

She had said it the first time a week after it happened, while her parents were away and she could steal off to the city again, this time under far more humbling circumstances. She didn't know if she would say it. She hadn't even said the word to herself. But she had done it, filed a report with the city police, to a very understanding detective named Jill.

It has been two weeks. Give us two weeks and come back, said Jill, who had agreed to respect Shelly's privacy in the matter. She would not call Shelly at her home or contact her in any way.

So Shelly has taken her third trip to the city in a month. She thinks of the comforting words of Jill the Detective. And the other words, too. Shelly should be tested for "STDs," she had advised. Syphillis. Gonnorhea. Herpes. AIDS. Take a pregnancy test, too.

Precautions, all of them. Probably nothing to worry about. Shelly hasn't been able to schedule a visit to her doctor yet. She can't imagine doing it.

She closes her eyes as she approaches the police station. She turns and walks away, then stops and looks back. Twenty minutes doing this, which is okay because she is early anyway, she doesn't want to seem too eager, but that doesn't make sense, either.

Will there be a line-up of suspects? She can't identify her attacker. Tests performed? Maybe the man confessed!

Two women race by Shelly on roller blades. A vendor on the corner is arguing with a woman over the price of a hot dog. The sun has come over the buildings to rain rays down on the police station. Summer is in full bloom in the city, even if hasn't officially started yet. She should appreciate the energy of the city's north side, but what had passed for cosmopolitan and vigorous now seems cold and heartless.

She walks again past the rows of blue-and-white squad cars parked along the street. Two uniformed officers are standing by a car smoking cigarettes and looking with disinterest at Shelly. She draws a breath and returns to the police station. There is a different person at the front desk, an older woman with a saggy chin and bifocals resting in the middle of her nose.

The man who emerges from behind a door is large, old-looking for an officer, closer to her father's age, dressed in a shirt with brown stripes and a plain tie. He has large, scaly hands with dirty fingernails and a stomach that hangs over his belt. His neck is thick and stubbly with whiskers. "Hello, Shelly," he says. "I'm Officer Stockard." He motions to the back room. "Let's have a talk, okay?"

Where's Jill? Shelly returns to the same conference room where she spoke with the female detective. Something doesn't feel right. Something in the officer's expression, his tone of voice, his curtness. There is a file folder resting before him and a fresh notepad. He looks down at the file and starts to speak, then catches himself and looks up. "How you holding up?"

"I'm okay."

"Sorry to hear about what happened."

"Thank you."

"Shelly, we've looked into this thing. I've talked to a lot of people. We have some problems. Some—" He strokes his chin, then levels his eyes on her. "Some real inconsistencies." He opens his file, which contains about a dozen sheets of paper. He seems annoyed. "We get a lot of these," he explains. "A lot of people who say they were assaulted."

Say they were assaulted? Her stomach seizes.

He raises his hands, then places them together on the table. "Who's Andrea, first of all?"

Shelly clears her throat.

"You told your friends your name was Andrea. Why did you do that?"

She shrugs. "I was just—I don't know. I wanted to—" She draws her arms around herself.

"You wanted to be eighteen, too, I guess. Didn't you tell your friends you were eighteen?"

She nods. Yes, she did that.

"You said you were a high school graduate, just moved here from out east?"

"I said that." She wasn't looking at him any longer, just staring into the desk.

"So you see what I'm starting with here? You lied about everything."

"I—I guess I wanted to be different."

"You wanted to pretend."

Her eyes fill.

"They said you looked eighteen, too." She doesn't respond to that. "Have you talked with your friends? Ms."—papers shuffle; he bends back a page and struggles with the name—"Patriannis, for example?"

Dina, he means.

"Or Ms. Winters?"

Dina's friend. Mary.

"No," she answers quietly.

"Your friends aren't too happy with you, Shelly. They said they never would have taken a fifteen-year-old to that party. They're mad. I don't blame them."

Shelly loses control of her emotions. She weeps quietly, covers her face with her hands.

"Is there anything else you lied about, Shelly?"

She shakes her head no.

"I'm not saying I don't believe you, Shelly. But if we take a case like this to trial—assuming we could ever find out who is responsible—that person would have a very smart lawyer who would ask you some very hard questions. You know what I'm talking about?"

She manages to say yes.

"He'll say you lied, over and over again, to your friends, to your parents. He'll say you looked like an adult. He'll say you can't identify who did this to you. He'll say you're lying under oath. He'll say you're committing perjury. You know what perjury is?"

She nods.

"You can get in trouble if you lie about it. I want to make sure you don't get in trouble."

A moment passes. Shelly grinds her teeth and fights hard not to sob. She will cry but will do so alone.

"Listen to me, Shelly. Sometimes—girls your age." He leans forward and struggles a moment. "You make decisions and then you regret them. You want to take things back. So you think about them differently. A week later, things you did—they look different. You want them to be different. So you decide they were different. You make up a story—"

"I didn't make it up." The firmness of her tone surprises even Shelly.

"No one's going to believe a liar, Shelly."

She looks at the officer again, her emotions raw. "You think I made this up?"

"Oh, listen." He breaks eye contact. "It doesn't matter what I think. It matters what we can prove. Rape—rape is a difficult thing to prove." He opens his hands. "Look. Did you ever say no? Did you ever say stop?"

Her breathing uneven, tears pouring down her cheeks and into her mouth, she says, "I'm not sure if I said it or thought it."

"Was he supposed to read your mind?" He slashes his hand like a knife onto the table. "Listen. You lied to your friends. You lied to your parents. You claimed to be eighteen. You looked like you were eighteen. You had sex with some guy, you don't know who, and you never told him you didn't want to." He shrugs. "Even if I ever find the guy, what am I supposed to do with that?"

I had passed out, she wants to say. He got on top of me. I couldn't stop him. She wants to defend herself but this officer already knows these facts. He already knows these things and it doesn't matter.

She is cold in the warm room. Shivering, uncomfortable. She looks at the single bulb over the table where they sit. She looks at the officer's scaly hands.

The officer speaks gently. "I never said I didn't believe you, Shelly. But we have a large case load, and prosecutors do too. No one is going to prosecute this case. And if they did, you could be damaged a lot worse than you already have been. And your parents will know."

She wants to leave. She wants to run from this station, from this city.

A sheet of paper appears before her. "If you want me to keep investigating, you have to put that in writing and sign it. If you want me to stop investigating, you have to put that in writing, too. It's up to you."

"I wanna go home," she mumbles.

He slides a pen next to the sheet of paper. "I'm sorry about this, Shelly. I wish we could erase what happened. But you put yourself into an adult situation, and you have to think like an adult. You have to decide."

34

Details

SHELLY STOOD AT the window and pressed her face against the glass. The sun shone brightly on the street below, on the pedestrians moving along the sidewalks. It was a little early for most people to be heading home for the day. Gentry Street was a main thoroughfare for the commuters, as the train station was just to the west and south, at the edge of the commercial district.

The alley where the shooting took place was in Shelly's view to the north, across the street. As it was perpendicular to the street, she could not see all the way through the alley to the street over to the east—Donnelly Street. She estimated that she could see about fifteen feet down the alley before the view was obscured.

"There," she said into the cell phone as she saw her private investigator, Joel Lightner, come into view in the alley. Joel stopped in his tracks and looked up in the general direction of where Shelly was standing, in the nineteenth-floor office.

Shelly turned to the woman next to her, Monica Stoddard. "Do you see him?"

"Yes," she said.

"Okay, Joel. Thanks. Come on up." Shelly closed the cell phone. "He'll just be a minute," she said to the woman.

"What are you guys doing?"

"We need to know how far you could see into the alley. Joel is going to measure the distance from where you could see him to the sidewalk. That gives us an idea of how far into the alley everyone was."

Monica Stoddard nodded absently, looked off toward the window. From the look on her face, Shelly guessed what she was thinking—that they were planning a cross-examination of this woman who had witnessed the shooting of Officer Ray Miroballi.

"It's just standard," Shelly said. "We weren't there, so we need to know everything we can."

"Well, I saw what I saw." The woman shook her head as if to empty it of those thoughts. "I didn't exactly enjoy seeing it, but I saw it."

Shelly nodded and gestured toward the drawings in the corner of the room. Monica Stoddard, age thirty-three, was an architect with a small development company. The sketches Shelly saw were plans for construction of what appeared to be residential housing.

"You know the cemetery up north?" asked Ms. Stoddard. "We're buying half the block north of it, on Kesseller. You know the area?"

"I live in that area. About five blocks north, by the lake."

"Oh, sure." The woman smiled. She was taller than the average woman, gangly, in fact, with the look of a former athlete. Or maybe Shelly was taking that from the plaque on her wall, which showed that she was a Division III pole vaulter in college. Shelly couldn't even imagine leaping so high in the air with an elastic pole. "We're looking at a lot of projects up there."

"I'm sure." Shelly had watched with a sense of dread as the neighborhoods around her had slowly gentrified, as old rental units had been bought up, knocked down, and replaced with expensive condominiums or single-family homes with price tags that were in the high six figures. She certainly had nothing against white people, who predominantly purchased these homes, but she mourned the loss of character to the neighborhoods as the yuppies invaded northward. Small Korean grocers were replaced with state-of-the-art, Internet-ready coffeehouses. Small Mexican diners moved out in favor of fast-food establishments.

And this was to say nothing of the fact that her rent continued to rise every year.

Joel Lightner appeared in the doorway and knocked. He introduced himself to Monica Stoddard and set down his briefcase. "Nineteen feet," he told Shelly.

They all sat and discussed architecture for a moment. Shelly sensed that this woman was intelligent enough not to be snowed by flattery, and principled enough not to be persuaded about her account of the scene. Yet there was nothing wrong with putting the woman at ease, and there was no easier way to do so than by talking about her. Joel, more than Shelly, seemed to have a knack for the game. He spent much of his life retrieving information from people under circumstances that ranged from adversarial to shady to something other than friendly, at best. Joel skillfully segued into the facts at hand, and Shelly noticed that the woman was speaking to Joel, not her.

"I was walking by the window," said Ms. Stoddard. "The lights were flashing. It catches the eye."

"Sure." Joel flipped open a notepad. "You mind? I'm no good relying on my memory."

"That's fine. So I looked down and I saw a boy running."

"How would you describe him?"

She shrugged. "I saw a boy in a coat and a cap. And holding a gym bag. He was running down the street. There was a cop chasing after him. The kid had a pretty good lead. He was fast." She looked at the window. "He went into the alley and ran out of my sight. The cop turned into the alley and stopped, where I could see him. Just a few steps, I guess. He was talking to him, it seemed like." She tucked her hair behind her ear as she concentrated. "I mean, I couldn't hear them, but it seemed like he was talking to him. Then it seemed like he moved closer." She looked at Joel, then at Shelly. "It wasn't well lit. I could only see so much."

"No, that's fine," said Joel. "Can you tell us what happened next?"

"What happened next was—the reason you're here." She held on to that memory for a moment. Most people in their lives never saw such a thing up close. At least this woman had been spared the noise, Shelly thought, the sickening sound of a flying object penetrating the skull. Well, who was *she* to talk? She had never seen such a thing, either. What she did know, from years of karate, was the sound of fighting—the sound of fist to skin, foot to skull—and it was nothing like the *pow*s and *ka-blam*s on television.

Having gone through the entire scene once, Joel went back and covered details. Did she see the officer draw his weapon? The woman thought not but couldn't be sure one way or the other. "The best I remember, he had a walkie-talkie in his hand, but I don't know about the other hand." Did she see Alex with a weapon? "I didn't see one," she said, "but then again, he had a bag and pockets in his coat, so it's possible."

Lightner asked about Miroballi's partner, Sanchez. "He went back to the car, at first," said Stoddard. "I wasn't really watching him, to be honest. What was happening with the other cop and the kid sort of held my attention." She drew a line in the air from one point to the other. "He came jogging down afterward and found his partner. He was holding him and talking into his radio. I assumed he was calling for backup, or whatever they say. An ambulance."

Shelly regarded this witness as relatively neutral, and she wasn't sure how to react to that. Positively, she supposed. This woman used the term "cop," which may have been a reflection of the fact that the people interviewing her were on the other side, but it could be that she was no friend of the city's finest, which was fine with Shelly. In any event, she did not appear to have been cowed into a story.

"Just to confirm," Shelly said, taking a role in the conversation for the first time, "you didn't see who shot the officer."

Monica Stoddard looked at Shelly. "No, I guess not."

The police report had indicated that Monica Stoddard had seen Alex shoot the cop. So this was different. She was saying she saw Miroballi shot, but she couldn't say who did it, because the shooter was out of her line of sight. Shelly had seen that before, a cop opting for a favorable spin on the events.

This woman seemed to appreciate the purpose of the question for the first time. She had apparently assumed—everyone would assume, probably—that Alex had fired the shot. Shelly was not prepared to make that assumption, and she wasn't sure why not.

What kind of a scheme could she concoct in which Alex was not the shooter? And if Alex hadn't pulled the trigger, why did he admit to doing so? It was one thing to deny guilt in the face of overwhelming evidence—something Shelly had seen often with her young clients—but how many innocent people claimed to be guilty?

"No eyewitnesses," said Joel as he and Shelly left the building and walked across the street to the alley. "Unless that homeless guy saw something. And that will be marginal at best."

Joel opened his briefcase and removed a tape measure. He marked off nineteen feet, three inches and stood facing west, as Officer Miroballi would have that night. They were going to reenact the scene again, as best they could.

Shelly sighed. "Distances and measurements are nice, but I wish we could fill in the details."

"I'll say again, no eyewitnesses." There was a twinkle in Joel's eye. "So you *can* fill in the details, Counselor."

35
Jump

DINNER WAS LATE tonight, close to nine P.M., at a Chinese restaurant that Shelly had never patronized, but where they knew Paul Riley by name. Shelly had to concede, she enjoyed walking into a swanky restaurant where the owner ran out to say hello, gave them a nice window table. And she had to admit that she was enjoying Paul's attention.

"Try to look at the internal investigation," Paul said to her. He gestured with his fork, which held a piece of kung pao chicken. "If Internal Affairs has worked Sanchez over, there should be some documentation."

Shelly had a vegetable stir-fry, and scooped healthy portions of the hot sauce into the bowl.

"Wish I could do that." Paul pointed to his stomach.

"Ulcer?" she asked.

"Something like that. Certain things I have to avoid. I'm pushing it with the kung pao." He smiled. "I guess I'm not helping my cause too much, am I? I sound older than fifty-one."

She gave him a generous smile. Something about this guy. She turns him down romantically, he doesn't run or even brood. He maintains an appropriate demeanor, professional and friendly, and makes no secret of the fact that he's still making his play. This promise of his, to give Shelly tips throughout the process, had worked nicely for him, giving him the excuse to wine-and-dine her.

"You have to try this, Shelly."

"No, thanks."

"Oh." He wiped his mouth. "Let me guess. Vegetarian."

"We public-interest lawyers have to be either lesbians or vegetarians. There's a test."

He opened his hands. "Forgive me. I'm a Neanderthal. It's a stereotype, I bought into it."

"I'm a single thirty-three-year-old," she said. "I don't think you're the first one to think I'm gay."

"Actually." He waved a finger, his mouth full of chicken. He thought better of it, shook his head.

"C'mon, Riley. I'm asking."

"Well"—he wiped his mouth—"I thought you were pretty hard on the teacher. At our trial."

"The teacher who was screwing her fifteen-year-old student?"

Paul dropped his napkin. "Yeah. You beat her up."

"And that made me a lesbian?"

Paul laughed. "You seemed hostile to her. That's all I'm saying."

Sure, she thought. A man who is hostile is doing his job. A woman who does it is "icy," or has some other character trait that must explain this very unfeminine trait—*maybe she's a lesbian*!

"I *was* hostile to her," Shelly said. "She had taken advantage of the boy. She wasn't exactly sympathetic, Paul."

"Sure she was. *Sure* she was." Paul's hands gripped the air. "She was thirty-seven, going through a divorce. She was troubled. And she was cute. She was petite."

"She gets a pass because she was cute?"

"That's not the point. Listen. Forget about the lesbian thing. But let's talk about this. I think this might be helpful. If you don't mind."

"Trial advice? No, go ahead."

"Okay, good. A good trial lawyer always listens to other people's impressions. That's what the whole thing is about, right? Impressions."

Shelly nodded.

Paul was animated. "This woman *was* sympathetic, potentially. Everyone is potentially sympathetic, and everyone is potentially *un*sympathetic. It's how you handle them."

"Fair enough."

"You had this woman passing these bizarre love letters. Unzipping the kid's pants on school grounds. Ridiculous stuff. She was leading this boy by the hand. Calling all the shots. I think she would have hanged herself in front of the jury. But you tried to do it to her. You were hostile, Shelly. You came on very strong."

"I suppose that's true."

"You had already settled with her. You were after the school. So why brutalize *her*?"

"Because I wanted the jury mad about what happened. I wanted them to see what had been done to this boy."

Paul nodded. "Do you think it worked?"

Shelly deflated. "Apparently not."

"I think the jury felt sorry for her, after you crossed her. And maybe not so pleased with you." He pointed his finger. "Third guy from the left, back row. Remember him?"

"No."

"The banker. Most educated guy on the jury. Personable guy."

"Okay, yeah. I remember him."

"He raised his eyebrows three or four times during your cross of the teacher. He thought you were going overboard. You lost him. And I think he was the leader of that jury."

"Hmm. Okay. So he bought into your laid-back, folksy charm."

"He agreed with my attitude. Do you know what my attitude was, Shelly?"

"Just what I said."

"No. No." He shook his head. He stirred the air with his fork. "Put it into a sentence. Put my demeanor into a sentence that summarizes my theme. The entire theme of my case."

"I—your theme." She opened her hands. "Your theory was that the school couldn't have known what this teacher was doing."

"That was my legal argument, sure. But what was my theme? What was I saying with my attitude?"

"I feel like I'm back in law school," she said.

"*It was no big deal.*" He sat back in his chair. "We had eight men and four women. We were upstate, where people are more conservative."

"More conservative," Shelly agreed. "As in, *less* likely to stand for what happened."

Paul grimaced. "Maybe if the roles were reversed. A male teacher seducing a fifteen-year-old girl? Sure. You would have won that case. But a petite, troubled woman seducing a strapping, athletic, confident fifteen-year-old middle linebacker on the football team? He had a girlfriend he was having sex with, right?"

"Right."

"So add sexually experienced. If he were a girl, you'd be picturing a lovestruck adolescent, under the spell of a predatory man. With your client, you're picturing him telling his football teammates and high-fiving." He shrugged. "It was no big deal."

"That's disgusting."

"Maybe so. I wasn't trying to win an award. I was trying to appeal to the jury in the primitive sense. I never actually *said* those things, did I?" He took another bite of his food. "People aren't as progressive as you think. And juries do what they want to do. Have you ever seen a jury deliberate?"

"No. How could you?"

"In a mock setting," he answered, wiping his mouth again. He wiped his mouth after every bite. A gentleman and a scholar. "Before trial, you do a mock run-through. You try your case to a cross section of ordinary citizens, and then watch them deliberate. And interview them afterward. It's incredibly enlightening."

"Tell me."

"Half the time, they've had so many facts thrown at them, they don't remember them all. Or worse, they remember them *wrong*. We, the lawyers, know the case inside out, but we have to remember that these people are hearing it for the first time. So what are you left with?"

"Their guts."

"Exactly. With our case upstate, their gut was that there was no harm, no foul. And that, Ms. Trotter"—he poked his fork at her again—"is why I won."

Shelly shook her head.

"There are cases with a lot of factual disputes," Paul continued, "and cases where the hard facts are basically agreed upon,
and you argue inferences. With our case, you didn't have any direct evidence that the school knew about the affair. You had to
argue that they *should* have known. With cases like that, juries
go with their guts."

Shelly considered her case, Alex's murder trial. She felt like
she could not pin down even the most basic of factual points at
this moment. But his point was valid nonetheless.

"My case sucks, Riley." She pushed away her food. "I have a
client whom I don't trust. He might have been the dead cop's
confidential informant, like Sanchez says, or he might have
been forced to deal drugs for the dead cop, like my client says."

"Or both."

"Yes, or both. And I'm pleading self-defense, and I don't
even know if my client is the one who shot the cop. He says he
is but I don't know."

"Personally, I thought that was a good move," he said. "The
self-defense plea. You're not wedded to it."

"I wish I could take credit. The F.B.I. gave me the idea."

"But it was your idea to use it as misdirection."

She groaned and ran her hand over her face. That was one of
the reasons. The other was to keep Alex, and herself, safe from
unscrupulous members of the city's law enforcement. God, how
tangled this case had become.

She peeked through her fingers and saw that Paul was watching her. His look was free of any social restraint or subtlety,
something faintly primitive and longing. He was checking her
out. Men stared so much and always seemed to think that they
were doing so covertly. Most of them had the subtlety of a
chainsaw. Paul, in fairness, at least had thought he had a free
shot.

"Get men on the jury," he said. "They'll fall all over themselves trying to please you."

She looked at him differently than before, a slight narrowing
of her eyes, an adjusted set to her mouth. If she could hold up a
mirror, she might use the word *flirtatious*.

Paul, unable to hold the stare, chopped his hand on the table.
"Alex is caught in the middle. He's got the federal government

pulling him one way, a dirty cop pulling him the other. He's an—" he looked up at Shelly and froze. This respected trial lawyer, who had stared down ruthless killers and cross-examined mobsters who could have someone killed with a wink and a nod, could not continue with Shelly looking at him so intently.

"—an innocent victim," he continued. "I think that would— You could—you could sell that, I think."

She nodded slowly. She appreciated his assistance and the stroking of her ego. Paul returned to eating his entrée and Shelly watched him. He was a tad abrasive, but he had real substance, and he took pride in his work. He wasn't looking for gratitude or praise. He genuinely enjoyed talking trial strategy, imparting some wisdom. Maybe she had completely underestimated him. Yes, that's what she had done. Paul had stereotyped her, but she had done the same thing to him. Maybe, in varying degrees, she had stereotyped every man, found or assumed the existence of a flaw and highlighted it to the exclusion of all else.

Her heartbeat was racing. But for once, it was not born of confusion or anxiety. The word was *clarity*.

"This kung pao is good," he said, without looking at her.

"I think we're ready for the check," she said.

Paul looked up, with a quarter of his plate still covered, a mouthful of rice. "You want to go home?"

"I want to go to *your* home," she said.

Shelly had seen many feats of athleticism in her time. Karate teachers with lightning-quick reflexes. Athletes who could jump higher or run faster than anyone on the planet. Men who could throw a football sixty yards in the air and hit a receiver in stride. But in her three-plus decades on this earth, she was relatively sure that she had never seen a human being move so quickly as Paul Riley raised his hand and called for the check.

36

Hide and Seek

HE WAS NERVOUS. The great trial lawyer, Paul Riley, who had stood with confidence before scores of tribunals, dozens of juries, under the gravest of circumstances, could hardly get his keys into his door. He lived in a high-rise overlooking the lake, an expansive split-level condo with floor-to-ceiling windows, beautiful white furniture, expensive artwork, Persian rugs.

"This is beautiful," she whispered.

"Had a decorator," said Paul. "If it were up to me, I'd have college banners all over the walls and one of those old recliners."

"A sports fan?" Shelly spun around, looking at the furnishings.

"College basketball," said Paul. "Only pure sport left." He smiled, shrugged, then looked around, nervously clapped his hands together. "Pro ball's too controlled."

Shelly turned to him. Paul blushed and looked away.

"Shot clock's the problem," Paul continued.

Shelly walked toward him slowly, watching his eyes as they diverted to the window.

"They don't call traveling, either."

"No?" Shelly walked up to Paul, looking up at him.

"Never liked the three-point shot."

She touched his suit jacket, ran her hand down to the button.

"Course, college ball has the three-pointer, too. But in the pros, they just feed it into the center. There's no, um—no strategy left."

She unbuttoned his coat, opened it until it fell off his shoulders.

"Do you, uh, want a drink?"

Shelly looked back up at him. His face had turned a light shade of red. A trickle of sweat ran from his hairline.

"No," she said. She reached for his tie.

"I"—Paul hiccupped a laugh—"Shelly, I have to confess that I'm a little, uh, out of practice."

She reached up and kissed him, gently, ran her tongue along his lip, then his teeth, then their mouths locked. She tasted the spice of his food, the oaky cabernet. His cologne, strongest on his neck by his ears. She pulled off his tie without missing a beat, hurling it wherever. He brought his hands to the small of her back, then one cupped her head, massaged her hair. A small humming noise, a quiet groan, left his throat, echoed in her mouth. They moved awkwardly, their faces smashed together, as she removed his clothes, knocked away his hands as he tried to remove hers. There was the magnificent Paul Riley, pants at his ankles, his erection slicing through the opening in his boxers, struggling to keep his balance as he kicked off his shoes, lifted one foot after the other out of his pants.

"I have to warn you," he said, as their mouths attacked one another. "I'm half Italian, but I'm a hundred percent Irish between my legs."

She laughed. The things that concerned men. Everything was about measurements, the size of her tits or ass, or his penis. For good measure, not literally speaking, she put her hand on him. She made eye contact with him, though his eyes were hardly open, smiling at him while she gripped his penis like the handle of a slot machine.

"Jesus," he mumbled. "You do that much longer and we'll be done."

She pulled him to the floor and climbed on top, first removing her panties. She ran her fingers over his chest, flattened by gravity, but she could see he took care of himself, a couple of fairly defined pecs between a patch of curly gray hair. His stomach was somewhat rounded but hard, a middle-aged man's successful fight against time.

She reached for her purse, near the couch, and removed a condom.

"Good idea," he mumbled, reaching for her.

"I'll do it." She removed the condom and unrolled it onto his erection, which stood at an angle in salute. "Irish, my ass," she said. He smiled, though he was facing the ceiling for the moment. She hiked up her skirt and positioned herself, then fell down on top of him.

He let out a measurable noise, his head lifting off the carpet. "You're not"—he spoke through a halting breath—"not gonna take off your clothes." He reached for her sweater, ran his hands over her breasts.

"You have a problem with this, Riley? You have some kind of objection?"

"Hey, whatever"—he thrust upward, held himself in that position—"whatever you kids are doing these days."

She closed her eyes, arched her back. His hands cupped the small of her back again, pawed at her sweater, as she bobbed on top of him.

"Shelly—I'm warning—you—it's been awhile."

Something she could do better than Paul? That would be something. Oh, was she being ridiculous? She hadn't been with a man for over a year. No, it was more than two years. Why now? With everything swirling around her—why now? She moved slowly on Paul, and the answer came to her in the form of a question.

Why *not* now?

"You're gonna give me a heart attack," he said.

She smiled to herself as she quickened the pace again. Sex was just not the same for men and women—or at least, this particular woman. She'd never had an orgasm and was resigned to the fact that she didn't know what she was missing. It was something else, not intimacy but some connection between two people, however brief, however casual, a reminder that she was a woman. And there was something with Paul. Something plaintive in his affection, something entirely unaffected about his corny chivalry.

His body shuddered into a spasm. His eyes shut, his mouth opened. He omitted a slow, tortured noise. He held his breath as his body moved uncontrollably. She rested on him and waited for him to open his eyes.

He went still, then smiled, peeked at her. "Sex in the twenty-first century," he managed.

"Welcome," she said, climbing off him. He sat up, removed the condom and didn't seem to know what to do. They sat there a moment, admiring each other, then he motioned to the contents of his hand and went to the garbage. She watched his pale, freckly frame, his bare ass, move out of the room.

She found her panties and put them back on. When Paul returned to the room, he was still naked as a jaybird, but carrying a bottle of wine and two glasses. "We drink," he said.

She waved a hand. "None for me."

"You mind if I have one?" he said. He placed the bottle and glasses on a side table and threw on his boxers. "I think I need to lower my blood pressure."

"Really, Riley. You make it sound like you're a virgin."

He took a quick sip of wine. "No, far from it. But never—can I be blunt?"

"Have you ever been anything but?"

He smiled. He was at ease now. The pressure, she imagined, had probably been substantial. In her experience, men took their sexual performance very seriously. At least the good ones did.

"Never with anyone like you, Shelly."

"Oh, God." She rolled her eyes. "You were supposed to use that line before you had me, Riley, not after."

He looked at her as if he had missed the joke. Because, she came to see, he had been entirely serious. He laughed it off, anyway, playing the good sport. After all, this had not turned out so badly from his perspective.

"I should go." She was already dressed, and needed only to throw her purse over her shoulder.

She had caught Paul in midsip of the Merlot. "You're going?"

"No rest for the criminal defense lawyer."

"Shelly—" He moved in front of her. "Was it that terrible?"

She patted his chest. "No, Counselor. It was really wonderful. I just have to go. I'd really like to do this again. I really would."

"Well—" Paul appraised the situation. He was standing in only boxers, holding a glass of wine, his clothes dangled over the couch or strewn across the carpet, while his date for the evening was on her way out. He seemed momentarily at a loss for words, and somewhat confounded by that fact alone. "I would, too?"

"Good answer." She put her hand on his cheek. "I really, truly enjoyed it. I'll see you tomorrow."

She went to the door and looked back. Paul was searching for his shirt. "And then she left," he said, loud enough for her to hear but, in Shelly's mind, more to himself.

37

Hindsight

"MATERIAL WITNESSES," SAID Shelly to the guard. She signed in at the desk and moved over so that Joel Lightner could do the same.

"Joseph Slattery," said the man behind the desk. He scanned a sheet of paper that was kept in a plastic sleeve, looking for the location of the prisoner.

Twenty-five minutes later, Shelly and Joel Lightner sat in a room with Joseph Slattery. The report Shelly held told her that Mr. Slattery was age thirty-six and homeless. He had a sheet but little of significance. Criminal trespass was the primary violation in the last ten years. Before that, there had been an aggravated battery pleaded down to simple assault.

The man didn't look like a homeless man, because, of course, he was not homeless for the time being. Joseph Slattery was being held as a material witness by the county attorney. This was an option that the prosecutors reserved for people whom they suspected would be unwilling to appear at trial. Often, the unreliability of the witness was due to the fact that they were criminals. Here, the prosecutors were probably afraid that Joseph Slattery might simply disappear off the face of the earth.

He was clean-shaven and fair-complected. His hair was clean and combed. His clothes—standard prison garb—were undoubtedly an upgrade on his normal attire. Shelly detected an occasional alertness in his eyes. He was clearly a troubled man, like most homeless. Very few people rationally chose to live on the streets, which was the true tragedy. Walk along the city's streets and check out the vagrants and beggars, and nine out of the ten—if not all ten—are either mentally disturbed or addicted to something, be it alcohol or drugs. People crying out for help who don't know how to cry out. Or who cried out but no one listened.

Joel took the lead, as he did with the other witness to the shooting. He had probably spoken to people like this hundreds of times, and he had fixed on the proper angle and tone. Besides, he was the "prover"—that, after all, was the reason he was here, to corroborate what was said, in case any of the interviewees decided to change their testimony when it came to trial. Shelly would call Joel, if need be, and show that the witness had spoken inconsistently on an earlier occasion.

Joseph Slattery spoke with a soft, hoarse voice. He did not immediately appear to lack credibility, which could cut either way for Shelly, depending on what he said. She could not suppress pity for this man, who had had some major complications in his life to turn out this way. Worse still, she realized that she might be required at trial to destroy his credibility, depending on how things turned out. She would have to put aside her emotions and, as the ruthless defense attorney, equate this man with a sideshow freak in a traveling carnival.

"Highland Woods," he said when Joel asked him where he grew up. Shelly, who was practiced enough not to jump from her seat, noted that this particular suburb was among the most affluent in the city, and possibly the country.

"I'm a two-time loser," he told the room. "I'm bipolar and an alcoholic."

This much Shelly already knew. The prosecution was required to disclose such things when they proffered their witnesses to Shelly. Technically, the witness lists had not been exchanged yet in this case, but there was no reason for Dan Morphew to hide these facts from Shelly, and he had not done so. Alcoholism had overtaken this man five years ago, sending him from a decent job as an office manager to the city's streets.

"Are you medicating in here?" Joel asked, though he already knew the answer.

"Lithium. And I'm drying out."

The problem with bipolar disorder, from Shelly's perspective, was that it did not necessarily attack the witness's perception. It caused enveloping mood swings—from a heightened state of euphoria to, more often, acute depression. But it didn't mean that Slattery didn't see what he claimed to see.

Alcoholism was another story, obviously. If this guy was loaded when the events went down, Shelly could rip his testimony to shreds.

"What about when you're on the street?" Joel asked.

"Pretty much nothing." He looked at each of them. "I don't get violent. I don't do that. It's more, just—I'm uneven."

Shelly smiled warmly at the man.

"I hang out on Gentry Street a lot," he said without solicitation. "Near the train station. I was over there when this stuff happened."

"Why don't you tell us what happened, Joe," Lightner suggested.

"See, I see this cop car. That didn't mean much, 'cause I see them a lot. Usually they leave me alone. I'm not one of these guys they gotta worry about. Me, I don't get violent."

"Right," said Joel, "you don't get violent. We get that." Shelly could see that Joel had dealt with these kinds of witnesses before, and she realized that this could be a liability. He sounded like a cop playing the heavy. She had to assume Joel knew what he was doing, but she felt that this man was intelligent enough not to be subjected to condescension, something about which a woman working in the legal system knew plenty.

"This kid's running from the cops and they were chasing him. The kid went into the alley. The cop ran after him and the kid shot him." The man lit a cigarette and chewed on his lip. He seemed uncomfortable, but not because of the presence of Shelly and Joel.

"Where were you?" asked Joel.

"I was on Gentry. I was on the other side of the street."

"To the north or south?"

Mr. Slattery thought a moment. "South. Yeah, south."

"How far, would you say?"

"I don't know."

"Fifty feet away? Hundred feet?"

"Close enough to see."

"Give me a distance."

"I don't know."

Shelly touched Joel's arm, and he deferred to her. "Mr. Slattery, the boy who was running? Can you tell me what you remember about him?"

Slattery rubbed his cheek. His skin was rough and blotchy. You could clean off the dirt but you couldn't erase years of malnutrition and poor hygiene. "He had a bag. He had a gun."

"He had a gun," Shelly repeated in a soothing voice. "Where did he have it?"

"I don't know. He shot the cop with it."

"You saw him shoot the cop?"

"Yeah. The cop didn't have a gun."

Well, that last point was unsolicited. But the time for that issue would come later. "The cop hadn't removed his gun from the holster."

"Right. The kid shot him. The cop was just standing there."

"This was in the alley."

"Yeah, in the alley. Yeah." The man nodded enthusiastically.

"The cop had nothing in his hands?"

"No, sir," he answered, even though he was addressing Shelly.

"Okay, so—the cop had nothing in his hands and the boy had a gun."

"Right," he said. Shelly saw Joel scribbling in his notepad. This was good, because the witness was wrong on this point.

Shelly took a chance. "And who else was there?"

Slattery blinked. His eyes narrowed.

"You said the cop who was shot," she said. "You said the boy who shot him. Wasn't someone else there?"

"There was another cop."

"Yeah, but I don't mean him. I mean the other person in the alley."

Slattery looked off to the side and inhaled. Shelly, of course, was bluffing. She had no concrete knowledge that any other person was in the alley. This was tantamount to a cross-examination, suggesting an answer and trying to force it on the witness. She wanted him to know that she "knew" of another person, so he would feel free to tell her. The witness's face contorted, and

Shelly couldn't tell if she was tripping the man up or confusing him.

"Can you describe the other person in the alley for us, Mr. Slattery?" she asked.

"Don't know. Don't know about another person."

She wanted to come across the table and grab him. "There was another person."

"I said I don't know. I don't know about that." He began to tap his foot.

They went back and forth like that a while longer. She wanted to sound as if she knew it to be true that another person, besides Miroballi and Alex, had been present in that alley. She wanted Slattery to think there was no reason for him to deny it. But he didn't take the bait, either because it was not true or he was afraid to say so.

Finally, she sat back in her chair and let Joel continue. Joel went through a number of subjects over the next half-hour. Slattery adamantly denied that he was either intoxicated or suffering from his bipolar disorder at the time of the shooting. Shelly couldn't know, on any topic of importance, whether he was telling the truth. He certainly seemed to be sympathetic toward the government, who was temporarily housing, feeding, and medicating him. But she knew what she needed to know. His testimony would be damaging, which meant that she would have to go after him at trial.

As to whether another person was present at the shooting, she considered it an open question.

38

Cannibals

SHELLY HAD LEFT Joel Lightner with several assignments. First and foremost, she wanted him to find Eddie Todavia—Todo—the young man who supplied the narcotics to Alex. He was probably a peripheral player in this affair, but she had come to the conclusion that Alex's word could not be trusted on any particular subject. To hear Alex tell it, he sold to only a handful of professionals at the investment banking firm, and he bought in bulk, only periodically, from Todavia. To hear Officer Julio Sanchez tell it, Alex was a confidential informant who possessed critical information about the drug operations of the Columbus Street Cannibals, information that Officer Miroballi dearly wanted in order to make a career-enhancing arrest. This kid Todavia might not be the answer, but he was a start.

She heard a knock at the door of her office and blinked out of her funk.

"Don't you ever leave your desk?" Paul Riley asked.

Her thoughts ran to their moment two nights ago. She had enjoyed it on many levels, but she was not unaware that their feelings for one another were not mutual. There were men who were looking for the door the moment the sexual encounter had ceased, but Paul did not fall into that category. Shelly, in fact, had been the one to leave.

Why couldn't sex just be sex?

She opened her hands. "Just a hard-working stiff."

Paul cleared his throat. "This guy, this doctor's at a medical convention. Meets this woman doc, and they decide to go up to his hotel room."

She sat back in her chair with an anticipatory smile.

"So they do what they're gonna do, y'know, go at it for a while. Then he says to her, 'I'll bet I can guess what kind of medicine you practice.' He says, 'You're a pediatrician. Because you're very gentle.' She says, 'Wrong, I'm a proctologist. But I'll bet I can guess what kind of doctor you are.' He says, 'Okay.' She says, 'You're an anesthesiologist.' He stands back and says, 'That's amazing! How'd you know I was an anesthesiologist?'

"She says, 'Because I felt a little prick, and I was asleep five minutes later.'"

She covered her face. "Riley, don't you have any clean jokes?"

"Sure." He folded his arms. "But you need something edgy."

"Do I?"

"You're too uptight. Relax a little."

She laughed to herself and stared at him. He seemed to have a renewed confidence after their time together, a break in the tension. Then again, it was hard to read him. The reason he thrived, she realized, was that he wore so many faces. When he was arguing before a judge or negotiating with her during the sexual harassment case, he was all business, bold and somewhat intimidating. When he was in front of a jury, he wore the aw-shucks humility like it was second nature. She could imagine him at a table of his colleagues, former prosecutors, telling jokes far more profane than the ones he told her, lifting a beer and violating twenty rules of political correctness. She wondered where, exactly, she fit in, what face he wore with her. And what his real face looked like.

"Let's grab some dinner," he suggested.

"I don't know, Riley."

He raised a hand. "Just dinner." He nodded at her paperwork. "Your trial's, what, seven weeks away?"

"Forty-seven days," she corrected.

"Plenty of time."

"Doesn't feel that way. I have lots of catch-up to play." Shelly was preparing a subpoena to the city police department to obtain records of their internal investigation of the shooting. For backup, she was also filing a FOIA request—a request under the city's Freedom of Information Act—seeking the same information. She was relatively sure she would be denied this information but it was worth a shot, and maybe she could add some public relations pressure down the road.

Paul nodded. She could see his disappointment, that he sensed she was giving excuses. Maybe she was. She was trying to be reasonable, trying not to give false hope. Because it was like she had said to him initially—this was not the time. Maybe she had been caught up in the moment the other night, but when it was all said and done, she wasn't ready for a relationship with him, not on a level other than sex. How would he react if he knew that Alex was her child? What would he think of what she was doing on an emotional and professional level?

No. Not the time.

"Any way I can lend a hand?" he asked.

"I do have a question, if you don't mind."

Paul took a seat across from her desk. He seemed to enjoy the opportunity, on any level, to spend time with her. His coat was off, as it usually was within the office. She noted the breadth of his shoulders, highlighted by the dark blue braces strapped over them. The guy knew how to dress, give him that. It was more than just matching colors; he looked comfortable.

"Tell me about the Cannibals," she said.

"The Cannibals." Paul's chest heaved. "This has something to do with your case?"

"I'm just trying to educate myself on the drug trade and things like that."

"Well—these guys are about the scariest thing around right now. They've got about a thousand recruits, I'd say. They use the kids to do the hard stuff, the enforcement—"

"Right."

"—because we can't give them much time inside."

"Why are they so scary?" she asked.

"Because they are very organized. Very disciplined. The higher-ups don't even acknowledge who they are. They don't drop signs or wear colors. The higher-ups, you could pass them on the street and you wouldn't know it." He crossed a leg. "The point is, they are very smart and very hard to bring down. The

U.S. Attorney has tried. The county attorney has tried. Everyone's tried. They get the occasional lieutenant, but no one's been able to crack the principal structure. They are considered to be the most effective Latino street gang in the nation."

"Do you—"

"And they're ruthless, Shelly. You know how they kill—at least when they want you to know?"

She nodded. "They sever limbs."

"Exactly. They cut a guy's arms off and leave him to bleed to death. Does your case involve them?"

"I don't know. Do you think the Cans would kill a police officer?"

Paul's face went white. "You think the Cans killed this cop."

"I don't know. I really don't."

"Well, for Christ's sake, let me in here."

She could have taken that comment in more ways than one. "The dead cop's partner—Sanchez is his name—Sanchez says that Miroballi was looking to make a big bust on the Cans' turf. He says he was using Alex as a C.I. to get in there, and Miroballi was becoming concerned that Alex was flipping on him. So I'm thinking, what if that's true? If it's true, and Miroballi's hunch was correct—well, that means Alex told the Cans what Miroballi was up to. And if *that's* true, maybe the Cans ambushed Miroballi."

Paul stared at Shelly, his mental machinations working over this information. "Killing a cop," he started. "That's a big attention-getter. The premeditated slaying of a police officer. I mean, it's not as if Miroballi would be doing this solo. It would be a decent-sized operation, I'd expect. So you kill one cop, you just whet the appetite of the cops to come after you."

"Assume it wasn't a big operation," she posited. "Assume that it was one cop, frustrated that he isn't moving up the chain, looking to make a name for himself. A big bust."

"Not realistic. If it's big, there's protection. Miroballi couldn't waltz in like Rambo and take down the entire place."

"Okay, so I don't know the details. Maybe he gets it set up and calls in the cavalry. He still gets kudos for the bust. Just play along with me."

Paul sighed again. "Well, listen, if that's what he was thinking—if the Cans thought this was a single, renegade cop, then sure, it might make some sense to take him down."

"And not in their signature way," she added. "No arms severed. In fact, they can put the whole thing on Alex. They don't leave any fingerprints at all on this thing."

"Then I'd take out Alex, too, if I were them." Paul played with his cufflink, rotating it around the cuff of his shirt. "He's the one guy remaining who could tell a story."

Shelly felt the juices flowing. It always helped to bounce things off a colleague, especially someone as well versed in gang crimes as a former state and federal prosecutor. "Maybe they know he won't talk," she offered. "Maybe they've made it clear that it would be a bad idea."

"They're holding something on him."

"He has a daughter," she said, and she felt nausea grip her stomach. Her granddaughter, Angela, whose guarantee of safety could be the reason Alex would remain silent.

"Let me step out of the theoretical to state the obvious, Shelly. Alex is white. The Cannibals are a Latino gang."

"A Latino gang that's smart, you said. The best. They don't work with anyone who isn't Latino? They wouldn't pay off a white cop, for example, just because of the color of his skin? Or a black politician—"

"No, I see your point." Paul scratched absently as his jaw. "I can't say that doesn't make sense. You said your guy—Alex—he was working at some I-banking outfit."

"McHenry Stern."

"Sure. I know it well. Yeah, I suppose the Cans could find out about a guy like that and want to diversify. They make a deal with him. They let him know what happens if he turns on them. Then he gets approached by a city cop, Miroballi. So what does Alex do? He tells the Cannibals all about this cop, and they take him out. Alex gets caught and he remembers what the Cans have said. He talks, Alex's little girl—hell, maybe his whole family—gets the full-throttle Cannibal treatment."

"He talked to the feds, though," said Shelly. But she answered her own comment, as the idea took shape. "But all he told the feds about was Miroballi. He never mentioned the Columbus Street Cannibals."

"A kid like that is playing a dangerous game."

"Dangerous, sure, but what choice does he have?" Shelly came out of her chair. "He's out of good options. If he drops on the Cans, his family is in danger. So he drops on Miroballi. He tells them what they want to hear. Miroballi is a dirty cop. And then he knows what's going to happen. He knows Miroballi is going to get killed. Maybe he's part of the whole ambush."

"He could have gotten federal protection for his family," said Paul.

"Sure, if he's thinking straight. He's just a kid. And the F.B.I. wasn't even thinking about the Cannibals. They wouldn't even know to bring the idea up to him."

When she had finished, she was still. So was Paul. This was an entirely plausible scenario. It depended on a number of variables, none of which Shelly could prove or even knew to be true.

Paul got up so that they were both standing now. "Shelly, I want you to promise me you'll tread lightly here. The Columbus Street Cannibals do not take prisoners."

She raised her eyebrows.

He pointed at her. "Promise me that."

"I promise, I promise."

Paul tapped the door and left the room. Shelly wanted to collapse, but she realized that her night was just getting started.

39

Silence

ALEX BANIEWICZ LOOKED relieved upon seeing Shelly. Relieved but haggard, his many weeks in pretrial detention obviously showing their wear. In the seven days since she had seen him, Alex had lost weight that he could not afford to lose, which added a pronouncement to his eyes and nose. His hair was flat, probably owing to the hardness of the water—and to the fact that Alex probably took few, and very short, showers for obvious reasons. Shelly's first impression, whenever she arrived to visit, was always the same—an utter helplessness, the knowledge that even if she could get him off these charges somehow, she could not spring him right now. Over forty days still remained until trial, and a smart attorney might ask for more time, waive the right to a speedy trial and take more time to investigate. For strategic reasons, she was unwilling to do so. She felt that a quick trial worked to her advantage. Yet she had to concede that another reason to speed things along was the fact that she had serious doubts that Alex could survive an extended term incarcerated.

Her second impression, always, was that she was going to lose this case, and he was going to end up incarcerated anyway. She had theories. She would tell a story that would be supportable, but at the end of the day, a police officer was shot and there was no particularly strong evidence—that she had seen so far, at least—to justify that act. She thought she had a decent chance of beating the death penalty and maybe even getting a reduction down from murder in the first degree, but outright victory seemed so far from her reach at the moment that it was hard to even consider. And yet that was all that she was doing, looking for the smoking gun or the magical piece of evidence that would irretrievably alter the course of this case.

"What's wrong?" Alex asked, which was an interesting reversal of roles.

Shelly sat in the chair next to Alex's chained position at the edge of the table. She did not hug him or even touch him. The rules of contact, since the change in their relationship from friends to mother-son, had not been defined. "How are you doing?" she asked. She knew how she would answer that question.

"Hanging in there," he said. His voice was weak. His expression indicated exactly what she had feared—hardened features, lifeless eyes. Alex was apparently no more optimistic than Shelly about his future.

"Alex, I think it's time for us to stop dancing. I've been afraid to ask you some questions, and you have been unwilling, for some reason, to be straight with me."

"I haven't been straight with you?" he asked.

She tapped the table lightly. "Alex, you have to understand that I am your lawyer first. And as your lawyer, I don't judge. I simply look out for your best interests. If you've done something you're ashamed of, or you wouldn't want anyone to know, you still can tell me. I don't care. But I—"

"Shelly, come on. Cut to it." Alex seemed to lack the energy for speeches.

Fair enough. "I think there is more to the story than you've been telling me. I think someone else was there with you that night. I think maybe someone else pulled the trigger, even. And I want to know why you won't tell me about it."

"Oh, Christ." He looked away with a pained expression.

"Are you a Cannibal, Alex?"

He dropped his head and made a noise that could indicate laughter or a punch to the gut. "A Cannibal, Shelly? Do I look Mexican—"

"Cut the shit, Alex. You know what I mean. Were you working with them? Do they have something to—"

"No!" His voice cracked. "Jesus Christ, Shelly, a Can? Are you out of your freaking mind?"

"You sell drugs," she said calmly. "You travel to the west side to get your stuff. That's the Cans' turf. I wouldn't be at all surprised to learn that your supplier, Todavia, is a Cannibal. And I can find that much out without your help. So it makes me think, hey, maybe the Cans sunk their claws into you."

Alex shook his head.

"You said Miroballi found out about you from Todo. You said that, Alex."

"Yeah? So?"

"So if Todavia is a Cannibal—and I'll bet my life he is—that means there's a connection. And Miroballi knew about it."

"So? So the fuck what, Shelly!" She recognized the look on Alex's face. She had seen it a hundred times. It was the expression of a boy in a corner, out of smart ideas.

"Miroballi's partner said that Miroballi was looking to make a name for himself. He said Miroballi wanted to make a bust on the Cannibals' turf. And he was using you to do it. He was using *you* to get at them."

"Me." Alex grunted a pained laugh. He was going with the obvious response—he was a white kid from the white part of town, a small-time dealer not working the streets. What in the hell use could *he* be to a cop taking down a drug empire on the west side?

And no, she didn't have a response for that, exactly. Miroballi could use Todavia to get at the Cannibals, but he already had Todo—he didn't need Alex for that. She was missing a piece of the puzzle. But that didn't make her wrong.

"Miroballi's partner—Sanchez—he says Miroballi was worried that you had tipped off the Cannibals. And I'm thinking, maybe the Cannibals *did* know about Miroballi's plan to go after them on his own. So *they* took him down, Alex. Not you. But you're afraid to give them up. You think they'll hurt your family. They'll hurt Angela. And I'm here to tell you, I won't ever let that happen."

"Oh, good." Alex clapped his hands together. "I tell you, Shelly, I had my doubts, but now that you make that promise, I tell you, I don't have a care in the world." He fixed on her. "I really hope you can come up with something better than that. Really, I'm willing to go with something that works. But that is the biggest pile of shit I've ever heard."

"You make me guess, Alex, I'm going to guess. You want me to keep shooting in the dark? Keep me there, and I'll keep shooting. I'll probably miss. Hey, it's only your life."

Alex grabbed at his hair with both hands, squeezed his eyes shut. She was being hard on him but she felt she had no choice.

"Alex, understand that you have control here, not me. If you don't like what I'm going to say in court, you can fire me. I can't force a defense on you. Tell me the truth and I'll tell you what I intend to do. If you don't like it, fire me. And I'll keep what you say confidential, either way. Get what I'm saying? There's no down side to telling me the truth."

Alex appeared to be on the verge of losing his composure, but he slowly deflated and lowered his hands. "Don't ever talk about the Cannibals again," he said. "They don't have anything to do with this. You start nosing around there and you *will* get my family in danger."

"Tell me who shot Miroballi, Alex."

"Why, Shelly—why in the hell don't you think it was me?"

"The gunpowder residue test was negative."

"You said that doesn't prove I didn't shoot the gun."

"It doesn't prove you did, either."

"I shot him," he said. "I shot him I shot him I *shot* him." He patted his chest. "Want me to announce it to the whole city?" He dropped a finger on the table. "Stick with that, okay, Shelly? Okay, lawyer? Stick with that and figure out this fucking self-defense plan. I wasn't this guy's snitch. This guy wasn't some crusader. This guy was a scumbag and I will swear on my mother's grave"—he stopped on that comment, glanced away from Shelly—"I will swear that this guy was going to take my head off if I didn't do it first. Or just—" He turned away from her. "Or just walk away and forget the whole thing."

Walk away *again,* he meant. And she certainly had no response to that.

40

Digging

JOEL LIGHTNER AND Shelly drove along the city's west side, past the graffiti-laden buildings and the residential areas that tugged at her heart.

"I'm just not getting much," said Joel, referring to his attempts to dig up information on Officer Ray Miroballi and his partner, Julio Sanchez. "If Miroballi was working the drug trade, he wouldn't be stupid enough to deposit huge sums in his bank account."

She looked at him. "What would you do?"

"I'd either spend it, bury it in my backyard, or hide it in a safe-deposit box."

Shelly considered that. "Maybe I should subpoena the bank to see if he has a safe-deposit box. Most families do."

"He does."

"He does? Then I'll issue—"

"Not worth your time," he said.

"Why not?"

"Not worth your time, Counselor." He looked at her.

Oh. Okay. How Joel Lightner had managed to get a look inside Miroballi's safe deposit box was not something she cared to know. She might not approve of his tactics generally speaking, but she was heartened to know that she was working with a pro.

"That other thing we discussed," he said. "Should have an answer soon."

"Thanks, Joel."

"I showed Alex's photo around the open gym at City Athletic," he said. "Some of the guys knew him. You can imagine, it's a different group every week. You never know who's playing when. Used to play there myself, about a thousand years ago."

"What did they say about Alex?"

"Nice kid. Quiet. Doesn't call pussy fouls."

"Good. I'll try to work that into my opening statement."

She felt her heartbeat increase as the car pulled over to a curb. Joel nodded down the street to a house with tarnished aluminum siding and a front porch that looked like it had lost a fight with a bulldozer. Joel raised a cell phone to his mouth. "We're here, Teddy." Joel waved his hand in exaggerated fashion, and Shelly saw two men in a sedan down the street wave back. Joel listened to the response, which Shelly could only faintly hear through the phone. "Good. Alone? Good. Yeah, sit tight."

"Our backup," she assumed.

"It's probably nothing, Shelly. But why be stupid?" He put away his phone. "Especially if Riley's footing the bill."

"Don't remind me. I feel bad enough."

"Oh, c'mon now. Riley's loaded. Besides"—he nudged her—"not for nothing, but I think Paul would hire a small army to protect you."

"Oh, yeah?" She looked at him. "What's it to you?"

He held up his hands innocently. "Hey, nothing, ma'am. I just work here."

She reached for the door and Joel caught her. "Hey, Counselor, for real now. You never know what's behind a door, know what I mean?"

Shelly had probably visited as many of these homes as Joel. Maybe not under precisely the same circumstances, but she knew what it meant to be unwelcome in these parts.

Joel, who was licensed to carry a firearm, kept one hand near his jacket and looked over the home as he approached. The sun had fallen behind the housing projects to the west, leaving this dilapidated neighborhood in darkness. The temperatures had warmed over the last few days but it was still dropping to near freezing outside.

Joel removed his credentials from his pocket and held them out as he gingerly took the three steps onto the porch. Shelly followed and mimicked his movements. Joel banged on the door with no hesitation or caution, as if he were selling encyclopedias door to door.

Shelly had expected a peek through the window, or a question through the door, but the door opened a moment later. The words that came to mind when she looked at the young man were *tough* and *hard*. He had a wide, lanky frame with tight but small biceps that emerged from a sleeveless shirt. His head was shaved bald, the only hair an erratic goatee and bushy eyebrows. He had a fierce stare, narrow eyes, an intense frown.

Joel held up his credentials, which Shelly hadn't seen. He was a licensed private investigator, of course, but that hardly held sway. She assumed he had something that gave the impression he was still a cop. "Need to talk to you, Eddie," he said.

"No hablo inglés," he answered with no expression.

"No?" Joel put down his badge, such as it was. "You 'hablared' okay when you went to Southside."

Eddie Todavia had gone to Southside High School briefly with Alex. It was, as far as Shelly understood it, how they had met. *As far as she understood it,* these days, had become quite the qualifier.

"Let us in, Eddie. I need a couple of minutes."

*"What-*choo need?" he asked, and for the first time he looked at Shelly, spreading his gaze up and down with no embarrassment.

"Eddie, let us in or we come back, and we don't ask so nice." He looked at his watch as if he were annoyed and didn't have time to quibble. "I don't give a shit what's inside. *No me importa lo que está adentro.* Okay? *Solamente para hablar.*"

Todavia did not look particularly concerned, save for his instinctive reaction to anything remotely related to law enforcement. He was, after all, a drug dealer. But Shelly had had dozens of clients from these neighborhoods, and out here, in the minds of these boys, there was a presumption of guilt, not innocence. She assumed Todavia was assessing his options, which ranged from zero to none. Presumably, he wasn't so stupid as to have a mountain of cocaine sitting on his kitchen table.

Joel walked past the boy without invitation, and Shelly followed.

"Sit," he said to Todavia, pointing to a couch with dirty laundry spilled onto it. The young man—Shelly knew from a police report Joel had obtained that he was nineteen—complied. Shelly and Joel sat on the opposite couch.

"Alex Baniewicz," Joel said. "Tell me what you know."

"No lo conozco."

"Eddie, you speak one more word of Spanish to me and you'll be wearing a cop's baton up your ass."

"You ain't no cop."

"Used to be," said Joel. Shelly hadn't been sure if Joel would lie about that fact. "I have friends on the force, pal. *Amigos.* One phone call." He held up his cell phone.

"Don't know him, man."

"You sell him blow. I don't care about that. I want to know his story."

"Man, his story." Todavia leaned forward and laughed. "He was born in a castle and he kissed a frog or something. You mean like that?"

Joel stood up slowly. He eyed the table that was between them, a small wooden thing holding sports magazines and two plastic cups from fast-food restaurants, each of them partially full of soda. "No, that's not what I mean," he said. He put the toe of his shoe on the table and tilted it up, so that the contents began to shift toward Todavia.

"Man, why you gotta be like that?"

With those words—or more to the point, with Todavia's lack of a physical reaction—Shelly could see that Joel had established the upper hand. The boy believed, and probably correctly so, that Joel could make life difficult for him, cop or not.

Joel tilted the table so that everything slid off, including the two cups of cola. Then, for good measure, he pushed the entire table over, so that it toppled at the feet of Eddie Todavia.

Shelly felt her body tense. She assumed that a physical confrontation would not come about, but things had escalated. Truth be told, she wouldn't mind a shot at this kid. He was the first falling domino that cascaded down to Alex being held for Miroballi's murder.

"Who does Alex work with?" Joel asked.

"Man, nobody. Alex don't come with other people."

"Who do you work with?"

"Me?" Todavia shook his head firmly. "No way, man. No fuckin' way."

Nobody in the room could have expected Todavia to part with that information.

"Does Alex know your friends, Eddie? Did you arrange a meet with them?"

"No." He folded his arms. "*Huh*-uh."

"I'll let you go on the other stuff," said Joel, removing his firearm from his shoulder holster. "But on this one, I have to be a little more insistent."

Todavia showed his hands. "Man, I fuckin' tell you. The man comes to me once a year, maybe, maybe twice a year. We do our business and that's all. You think I'm gonna let him meet my boys? I'm a businessman, see. We make our deal and that's all. I don't know his shit, he don't know mine."

"Your friends are C-Street, right?"

"See, man." He held out the palms of his hands. "So why I'm gonna let this white boy hook up with 'em?"

"You're not the only one I'm asking," Joel said, still fondling the weapon. "If I find out Alex was talking to your *hermanos*, I'm coming back with my friends. Dig?"

"You talkin' crazy now. Ask, man." He waved Joel off.

"Tell me about Ray Miroballi, Eddie."

"Don't know—"

"He's a cop, Eddie. You know him."

"Don't know no cop Mira-whatever-the-fuck."

Joel cocked his gun. This did not escape the notice of the young man he was interrogating. Shelly felt herself steel. Surely Joel wouldn't bluff this far? Surely Eddie Todavia would see this as an over-the-top gesture. But he didn't. She saw the fear in his eyes. The thought occurred to her, maybe she *didn't* know this neighborhood like Joel did.

"Did I load this thing today?" he asked himself. He pointed the gun at the wall off to the side, waved it a bit. "Hard to tell by the weight. Might have a couple of bullets in here."

"Man, I don't know no cop with that name."

"He's an old partner of mine," Joel lied, bringing the gun back to his open hand. "He says you know each other."

"Okay, then whatever he says, man."

"That's right," Joel said. "I *did* load this thing this morning." He held the gun upright, then slowly moved the barrel downward in the direction of Todavia.

Todavia's hands were out in surrender. "Man, I tell you I don't know this fuckin' guy. I swear to Christ I don't know this guy."

"He says you do, Eddie."

"Man, I don't know the name. Maybe I see him, I know him."

Shelly held her breath. She kept her eyes on Todavia, who kept his eyes on Joel.

Joel dropped the gun to his side. "Okay, Eddie." He pointed to the window. "You see that car down there? Those are my guys. You move off this couch before I drive away and—"

"Man, go already. I don't need your fuckin' shit."

He was upset. She figured he couldn't have really thought that Joel would put a bullet in him. But she didn't know these people nearly as well as she had thought. Maybe they had seen such things happen. In any event, this man's pride was wounded. She saw the fire return to his eyes the moment that Joel retreated.

Shelly got up to leave. Todavia stood as well and gestured toward her. For a guy who had just had a gun pointed in his face, he rebounded remarkably. Apparently it wasn't his first time. Or maybe he was just trying to buy back some of his pride. "Hey, li'l lady," he said to her, "how 'bout you hang back so's we—"

The distance was about right, about the length of an extended leg thrust. Her precision was not at top form. The heel of her shoe—yes, she had worn gym shoes for just this opportunity—flew into the abdomen of the drug dealer and sent him flying against the couch.

"Not just now, Eddie," she said. She followed Joel out of the house. They moved briskly to the car and didn't linger at the curb.

"Remind me not to piss you off." Joel threw the car into drive and sped off. He nodded to his associates in the sedan as he passed them.

"Don't supply drugs to my client."

He looked at her. "You know, Shelly, no one put a gun to Alex's head."

Interesting choice of phrase, she thought. And it reminded her of something her father might say. Free will, the favored expression of conservative politicians. Your circumstances are tough? Pull yourself up by the bootstraps and make it happen. Yes, sure that was true to some extent. But when you grew up knowing nothing but absentee parents and gangbangers all around you, you hardly even knew what it was you were supposed to be aiming for. It was a lot easier to pull yourself up when you were attending respectable, and safe, schools, when your friends and parents shared the same aspirations as you.

But Alex didn't exactly grow up in gangland, so Joel's point carried a little more weight. In fact, all Alex had to do was look across the dinner table at Ronnie to see the right example.

"Alex went to someone he knew," she said. "I doubt he has a boatful of friends who sell drugs. He wouldn't have gone to a stranger. If it weren't for this piece of garbage, Alex might not be in the mess he's in."

"Maybe yes, maybe no. Not always so simple." Joel—both of them—seemed to relax as they put distance from the neighborhood. They were quiet for a while as they traveled toward more familiar haunts.

"Well, that guy doesn't help me."

"No, he doesn't really back up your idea," Joel agreed. "He says Alex didn't know any of his associates, so we can't put Alex with the Cans. And he didn't seem to know Miroballi."

"Miroballi could know *him*," she said.

"Sure, that's true. What's"—he looked at Shelly—"what's Alex say about all this?"

"Alex says it was self-defense. He denies all of it."

"So you don't trust him."

"It's more like I think he has some reason for not telling me everything. I feel like I have to figure it out myself."

"Don't fuck around with the C-Street Cans, Shelly."

"So I've heard."

"Well, hear it again. Don't go busting balls in their camp. Let it go."

"Let it go, even if I'm right?"

Joel wet his lips. "Your own client won't even back it up, Counselor. So what do you think is going to happen? You're going to get YoYo to waltz into court and confess that he decided to have Ray Miroballi whacked?"

Jorge Joaquinto—referred to on the streets as "JoJo" but derisively by law enforcement as "YoYo"—was believed by the government to be the top leader of the Columbus Street Cannibals. Joel had a point here. She had no way of making a Cannibal admit to hitting a police officer, at least not one still wearing his arms.

"So let me get this straight," she said. "Even if it's true that this gang killed a cop, made Alex take the fall, and is threatening Alex's family to keep him quiet—even if all of that's true, I should let it go."

"You should be realistic. What, you're going to put Alex on the stand and treat him as an adverse witness? Cross-examine him? Come on." He glanced at her. "What's your great plan?"

"Don't have one," she conceded. "But I'll tell you what I'm *not* going to do."

"You're not going to give up on this."

"Damn straight."

Joel pulled the car over at the curb by Shelly's office. She had another late night ahead of her. She had been working with a forensic pathologist on the distance of the gunshot. She was drafting an appeal of Judge Dominici's ruling two days ago that she could not make the city police department open its internal investigation to her. And she felt, in many ways, like she was just getting started on this case, constantly starting back up a new hill.

"That kid really thought you might shoot him," she said. "Just like that, for no reason other than the fact that you weren't getting the answers you wanted. And I thought I knew their world."

"Say, Shelly," Joel called to her as she left the car. She poked her head back in through the passenger's window. "That was a cheap shot back there. Nice kick, but cheap shot."

She couldn't disagree with that. But she had felt less than charitable toward the young man. And the element of surprise was always the most effective weapon of all.

41

Shadows

SHELLY SIGHED WHEN she returned to her office. She not only had the appeal of Judge Dominici's ruling on the police investigative file to finish, she had promised to look over a complaint that one of the law firm's associates was planning to file with the state Human Rights Commission, alleging racial discrimination against a company in town. This extra work was the price of these nice offices and resources—a price that she had insisted on paying, but still, it was keeping her away from full-time concentration on Alex's case.

Her cell phone buzzed. She recognized Joel's number.

"We were followed tonight," he told her. He sounded breathless. He was in the car, she could tell, from hearing the radio in the background.

"Who?"

"Well, I don't know. My guys picked it up. A pretty good tail, I have to say. I had no idea."

"You weren't looking for it," she said. "But who?"

"Well, I'd assume law enforcement. Probably the feds."

She didn't know how to react. There was something creepy about it, no doubt, but she felt a measure of validation. It told her that she was onto something here. Maybe.

"We lost them," said Joel. "In fairness, we weren't ready for it."

"Sure. No problem. What do you suggest?"

"I'll put a tail on myself," he said. "If I'm followed again, we'll get 'em. But I don't think they'll make that mistake again, Shelly. They probably know we outed them."

"Don't be sure." If it was the F.B.I., enforcing Shelly's promise that she would not expose the operation prematurely, they might *want* to be noticed.

She hung up and noticed the newspaper sitting on the corner of her desk. Paul Riley had written a note from his personal stationery—"FYI"—and she saw the article. The *Daily Watch* was following the closing days of the state legislative session, in which the Democratic-controlled House and Senate had passed legislation to repeal the ban on abortions funded by public aid. The law banning publicly funded abortions had been passed in the late '90s, when the G.O.P. controlled the Senate and there were enough conservative Democrats in the House to pass the bill. That law had effectively ended any state funding of abortions—with the necessary exceptions to satisfy the Supreme Court—which meant that it had affected only the indigent, those who needed public aid to pay for the procedure.

The Democrats, now in control of both chambers, had passed a bill two days ago to end the ban, to open up the taxpayers' wallets once more for this particular procedure. Governor Langdon Trotter had vowed a swift veto. His challenger in the November election, Anne Claire Drummond, bitterly criticized the governor's response. This was not about abortion, she said, so much as it was about treating the poor differently.

The story accompanied an article that showed a surprisingly strong showing for the Democratic nominee. Anne Claire Drummond was a former state legislator and congresswoman from upstate. She had made a name for herself as a proponent of universal health care, which was probably not the way to endear herself to the state's voters. Drummond was the liberal among the Democrats vying for the nomination and was not, as far as Shelly could tell, the preferred choice of a party trying desperately to break the G.O.P. stronghold on the governor's mansion. But she had run a series of snappy television ads that got her out to an early lead, and women crossing over from the G.O.P. had provided the necessary votes for Anne Claire Drummond to hold on against two male opponents.

If the election were held today, the *Daily Watch* said, Governor Trotter would receive 51 percent of the vote, and Congress-women Drummond would receive 47. That wasn't bad. Shelly assumed a lot of that was attributable to Drummond being the new kid on the block. When they went to the polls, most voters in the mainstream voted for comfort, and that usually went in favor of the incumbent. And her father was no lightweight. He seemed to know exactly where to draw the lines in an election year. Short of a major scandal, Governor Trotter could expect to be re-elected by a comfortable margin.

Short of a major scandal, she repeated to herself.

The *Daily Watch,* in an editorial, agreed with the Democratic nominee Drummond on the governor's promised veto of the abortion bill. Abortions should be safe and rare, it said, but not based on disparities in income. And didn't an abortion spare the taxpayers from supporting this child born to a dependent family? Whether from a cost-benefit analysis or an issue of fairness, the governor was wrong.

We will say this much for Governor Trotter: He is at least consistent. He has opposed abortion from the first day he took public office as the Rankin County Attorney. He tried to close women's health clinics back then; supported protestors as Attorney General; and as Governor, he has quickly signed anything that remotely limits abortion rights and vetoed anything that even hints at supporting the cause. He is wrong, but at least we know where he stands.

Shelly took the newspaper and ripped it in half. She threw it across the room, then went over and retrieved it. She continued to tear at it until it was reduced to tiny rubble. When she was finished, she gathered some material, turned off the light, and went home.

42

Wounds

USUALLY SATURDAYS FLY *by. This one, yesterday, slowed to a crawl, beginning with their discussion in the morning, when Shelly dropped the bomb on them. It was an hour or so before her parents could even gather themselves to provide a meaningful response—a response, that is, other than questions about the father of her child, or the rhetorical how-could-you-do-this question. Private discussions took place, phone calls (Shelly was relatively sure, presumably to her grandparents), a long walk in the evening.*

The matter was postponed, finally, for the following day. Today.

She awoke this morning with the same grief and remorse, but with an indignation as well. Why hadn't she been included in these conversations, this intricate mapping of the next step?

Her parents are already seated in the living room, with the obvious position on the sofa open to Shelly. She apologizes again, immediately, before she has even taken her seat. She realizes that she has acted irresponsibly. She realizes that her actions affect everyone, not just her. She has some ideas of her own about how this can be worked out. Above all, she is very, very sorry.

Her father, in particular, looks at Shelly as if he's never seen her before. Or, worse, like he has known her his entire life and can't believe the depths to which she has sunk. "Well," he says, opening his hands. "Now we have to clean up the mess, don't we?" He is calm. There is no trace of the anger and disappointment, of the passion from yesterday.

She looks at her hands. "If you want, I could stay with Grandma Jeannie until—"

"I'm not sure that's the best option." Her father crosses a leg. He avoids eye contact, swings his foot nervously. "There are some choices that we don't like, Shelly, but that make sense. Under the circumstances."

Shelly looks at her mother, who avoids everyone's stare. She blinks away tears, staring off in the distance. Shelly feels her mouth open.

"I don't think I'm ready to be a mother, Dad—"

"That's not what I'm talking about, Shelly, and I think you know that."

She recoils. She is hearing this wrong. She is looking at a man who marched with the protestors outside the Anthony Clinic. A man who has brutally criticized an activist Supreme Court for creating a "right" that doesn't exist. A man—

"You're a young woman, Shelly. You have your whole life ahead of you. This would change everything."

"It already has," she whispers.

"But it's not too late, Shelly, to keep this from—"

"I tried, Daddy. I couldn't."

He freezes. He looks at Mother, who has snapped to attention as well.

"What does that mean?" he asks.

She tells them. She tried. She went to the Anthony Center and something made her stop. Yes, of course she gave her real name.

"Well." Her father flaps his arms. "My daughter went to an abortion clinic without telling me." He is talking to Mother. "I bet that gave them a real chuckle."

"It's confidential, Daddy. They won't tell."

"They won't tell, she says." Again, to Mother. "Shelly, you don't know these people."

"I didn't know what to do."

It is a moment before he speaks again. He leaves his chair and paces, into the kitchen and back, his hand over his mouth, then the back of his neck. Mother is silent but seems to be keeping watch on each of them. She is nothing more than a spectator.

What does she think, Shelly wonders. Why won't she give an opinion? Shelly feels anger herself now. A wave comes over her, something she can't put into words. Change, is the only word she can use.

"All right. Fine." Father washes the air with his hands. "I had a place in mind out of state, but as long as they already have your name, it's as good a place as any."

"As good a place as any for what?" Shelly is startled by the control in her voice.

"Shelly, it's okay now. I'm telling you, it's okay with me."

She gets to her feet without realizing it, reactively. It is different. She will remember it always as the single defining moment of her life. Yet she is not overwhelmed, because the change is coming from within. "You think I stopped it for you?" She spits the words in a fury she has never known, that grows with each syllable.

She leaves the room and goes upstairs. She will apologize to them again, and again, before she leaves their home. She is so very sorry this has embarrassed the family, that she has injured Daddy's political aspirations. But that cannot be reversed now. Nothing can be. The looks on their faces. The words. She will leave. She will leave and never return to this place, to these people she has never truly known until now.

43
Notice

SHELLY'S PHONE WAS ringing when she walked into her office after eight o'clock. She picked it up before it went to voice mail.

"Jerod Romero, Shelly. From the U.S. Attorney's office."

"Jerod. Your ears must have been burning."

"Is that right?"

"Yeah, I have to disclose my witnesses for trial. Should I just use your work address?"

The prosecutor's laugh was less than sincere. "It goes without saying, I assume, that you will not be listing me as a witness just yet. Which brings me to the reason I'm calling. Are we abiding by our agreement, Ms. Trotter?"

"You mean, am I running around telling people about your undercover operation?"

"Yes."

"No, Jerod, I'm not. Why do you ask?"

"Because it occurred to me that, in proving self-defense, you have to show that Miroballi was part of a drug scheme. And if you start asking around about cops selling drugs, you are touching on our operation. See what I mean?"

"Yeah, I see that."

"So?"

"So. I have managed to provide Alex his constitutional right to adequate representation while at the same time preserving our plea agreement, such as it is."

"People's lives could be at stake, Counselor."

"That's been true for the last two months. What prompts the call now, Jerod?"

"Just making sure."

"You can tell your goons I didn't mention your operation to Eddie Todavia. He's the guy who supplied Alex the cocaine, if you didn't recall."

"I do."

"You're not denying that you're having me followed."

"As long as you understand how seriously we're taking this," he said, which was not quite the same thing as an admission. "We'll violate your client, and if I have the slightest indication that *you're* jeopardizing undercover agents out there, I'll have a half-dozen agents at your door, too."

"That must be fun," Shelly opined. "Saying things like that."

"You're on notice, Counselor. The F.B.I. doesn't have a sense of humor about this."

"Duly noted."

"One more thing, Shelly. About your case. Obviously, there is going to be a point in time when you are going to discuss our operation in open court."

"Yes." Which meant that the federal government would have to make their arrests within the next month or so, before Alex's trial began. Shelly sensed that it irked Jerod Romero that Shelly knew this, that the prosecutor enjoyed having the element of surprise.

"My question to you is, do you plan on doing it right away? With the voir dire? An opening statement?"

She had had the same question. As she had begun to develop her trial strategy, she was leaning toward postponing her opening statement until the beginning of the defense's case, which the state's criminal procedure rules allowed. Her thought was to ambush Dan Morphew with the information. But she might need to ask certain questions of the state's witnesses that touched on the subject.

"I probably wouldn't mention it to the jurors," she said. "But beyond that, Jerod, I can't guarantee anything. The state will have to try to disprove self-defense because I've pleaded it. So I expect it to come up."

"And you won't consider moving the trial date."

"I won't. You really need more time, huh?"

"Well, obviously. We weren't planning on ending this operation so soon. We will probably miss the chance to put away a number of people."

"I'm sorry about that," she said. "Really. I hate to think that we're messing with an operation that takes down dirty cops. But I have to do right by Alex. I think a quick trial date is what we need here."

Romero sighed. He understood, of course, but that didn't mean he liked it.

She hung up the phone. She was not entirely sure why she had been so glib initially with the prosecutor. She was going with her gut. She had the feeling that she had to keep everyone on edge and wait for something to happen. She had the feeling that a lot would happen between now and the trial date.

44

Continuance

THE VIEW TO the east. The city was really a breathtaking sight so late at night, when most of the downtown buildings were dark, the shoreline alive with the goings-on at the pier, the restaurants and lighted carnival rides. She leaned forward and pressed her nose against the window. There was so much promise, so much energy, so much emotion in this enormous metropolis.

Paul thrust himself inside her further. "I'm telling you, Ms. Trotter, you're going to give me a heart attack."

With the lights out in Paul's corner office, she could see the reflection of him standing behind her, pants to his ankles, tie pulled down, applying the same dedication that he brought to any task. "Are you always going to whine like this?" she asked.

He cried out like a wounded animal, gripped her waist for another few seconds. "Damnation, Shelly Trotter." He left her and attended to his business. Moving quickly, he was dressed and presentable within two minutes. "Sure, a little danger. Why not?"

"Danger, sure." She had pulled up her panties. "You checked every office on the floor to make sure everyone was gone. On a *Sunday.*"

"Baby steps." He opened his hands. "Now can we eat?"

"Back to work," she said.

"Shelly, really." He was blocking the doorway. "The sum total of postcoital time you've spent with me"—three times, so far, they'd been together—"I wouldn't have time to fry an egg."

She gave him a look. "I thought we discussed this."

"Look, I'm not talking about a lifetime commitment. Or even a one-*week* commitment. But"—he looked down at himself—"am I nothing but a piece of meat to you?"

She stared at him. They laughed at the same time.

"You know, Riley, a lot of guys would think they hit the gold mine here. No-strings sex?"

Paul threw his hands up. "Yeah, I'm starting to feel like the girl in this relationship."

"That's 'woman,' not girl."

"Whatever. I can't keep up anymore." He shook his head. "So can we eat?"

"I really have to get back to work," she said. She ran her hand along his shirt. With a presumptive pat, she left the office.

45

Questions

To ARGUE SELF-DEFENSE or not to argue self-defense. That was the question.

Technically, she could argue both at trial. Alex didn't shoot the officer, but if he did, it was in self-defense. That was a ridiculous position, practically speaking, but it did allow her to wait out the prosecution's case before making her decision. That would be a walk through a mine field at trial, but she might be able to pull it off. She had already begun to draft examinations of witnesses. She had written two closing arguments, one arguing that Alex was the wrong guy, the other that he acted with legal justification.

The "innocence" argument was straightforward. There was no credible witness that put the gun in Alex's hand. The other cop, Sanchez, didn't see the shooting. The architect, Monica Stoddard, didn't see who shot Miroballi. The homeless man says he did, but he was not credible. The gunpowder residue test was negative. Alex was there, but he didn't pull the trigger.

If Alex didn't shoot Miroballi, then she had to have some explanation that someone else did. The Cannibals? She had to admit that she would never be able to prove that. She was trying to shake the trees but nothing was falling out, and she couldn't very well march onto their turf and demand that they confess. She needed to point the finger at someone, but she wasn't exactly full of ideas.

The self-defense argument looked something like this: (1)

Alex was being forced by Officer Raymond Miroballi to sell drugs and kick back some money. We know that from Alex's testimony and from the photographs of them together, taken by the F.B.I. (2) Alex was picked up by the federal government, which was investigating a drug ring run by police officers, and Alex agreed to work for them and against Officer Miroballi. That can be shown from Alex's testimony and from the F.B.I. agents she would call. (3) Miroballi found out that Alex had flipped. And what did she have to prove *that* fact? That Miroballi seemed nervous, according to Alex. That he was willing to go along with Alex's "demand" of a smaller kickback—that he "must" have known because he was never so agreeable in the past. Yeah, that was a real winner.

Supposition laid upon supposition. She couldn't decide which case was weaker. There were so many holes. Defense attorneys, in theory, didn't need to fill in all the blanks, because they didn't have the burden of proof. But the more implausible your story, the more you had to provide corroboration.

Her cell phone rang. "Shelly Trotter."

There was no response on the other end. In the background of the caller, there were noises. It was busy. She heard a car horn. People yelling in Spanish.

"Hello?" she said.

Then she heard a *click*. With a cell phone, it was sometimes hard to tell if she had hung up on the caller or vice versa. She looked at the antenna icon on her phone and the signal appeared to be strong. "Hello?" she tried again, but the call had been terminated.

She picked up her land line and dialed the numbers. She looked at her watch. It was past eight o'clock on Sunday.

"You've reached Joel Lightner's cell phone. Please leave a message."

"Joel, it's Shelly," she said. "I need a trace on a call. As fast as you can."

46

Searches

SHELLY SPENT THE day preparing for her afternoon argument to the state court of appeals that she should be allowed access to the city police department's internal investigation. She had sought an expedited appeal, which was allowed for in cases such as this. She had made sure that various members of the city's media were aware of the hearing—political pressure, in the end, might be the best way to get to these records—and some of them had shown.

The hearing had gone about as she expected. The judges—three of them, all political types from the city—had focused on the fact that the internal report had not been completed. The city's Freedom of Information Act exempted preliminary internal investigations from disclosure. "Do you contest that this report is still preliminary?" one of the judges asked before Shelly had barely said her name. And of course, she could not dispute it. Her principal argument was that Alex Baniewicz's right to a fair trial trumped a nondisclosure law on general policy grounds. "But if the report is preliminary, how do we know it contains accurate, complete information?" asked another judge. "Isn't that the reason FOIA exempts it? Because the information is not yet reliable."

"I don't care so much about their conclusions as their underlying facts," Shelly had said. "And even if they're not reliable, proven facts, that's up to me to investigate. Let me take the ball and run with it. But if they can throw a blanket over this and drag it out until after my client has gone to trial—"

"Do you have any evidence that the police department is stalling?" asked the same judge.

Of course she did not.

The third judge piped in. She had been in front of this one before; he had a reputation for dozing off on the bench. "Why can't you discover the same information that the police department can discover?"

"They have power I don't have," Shelly had argued. "They tell a police officer to talk, and the officer has to talk. I can't depose these officers, and they don't want to talk to me."

"But you can subpoena them for trial."

"For trial?" Shelly had thrown up her arms. "Then I have to interview these officers for the first time in front of the jury."

After the half-hour argument, Shelly knew she had lost. When the police department's attorney went through his presentation, the judges hardly touched him. She would make a request to the state supreme court, but they wouldn't agree to hear this case.

Shelly, dressing for an ordinary day in mid-May, was cold standing with two reporters, arguing her cause outside the courthouse. The sun was out but it was just over forty degrees. When she left them, she turned on her cell phone and called Joel Lightner.

"I think it was 'Manuel,' Joel. The kid who helped the cops break into my house."

"What did he say?"

"Nothing. He didn't say a word."

"So how can you possibly make that assumption?"

Shelly almost walked into an oncoming car. She stepped back to the curb but got a splash from the tire. "I think he was checking up on me," she said. "He was worried about what had happened to me. He felt bad."

"And he waited two months to call."

"Just check it out, Joel. Okay?"

"I will. I'll get a consent form to you. This is your phone, so we don't need a subpoena."

"Great."

"And, Shelly? If this kid is calling you now, maybe that means there's a *reason* to worry."

"Wonderful." She hung up the phone and braced herself against the wind. Ronnie was coming to her office today to help manage the growing pile of material for her. He would make photocopies, organize and catalogue files, run any errands she needed. Shelly probably could have used the firm's paralegals, but she felt like a bit of a freeloader as it was—the deal she had worked out was rather lopsided in her favor—and Ronnie seemed so eager to lend a hand in whatever way he could.

She saw him. He was walking north on Donnelly toward her. He stopped as he got to the alley and looked in. She turned and walked toward him, but he didn't see her. He was looking into the alley. And then he disappeared into it.

She quickened her pace, once again narrowly avoiding an oncoming vehicle. It was after four o'clock now, so the streets were just beginning to fill with people. She walked up to the alley and peeked in. Ronnie Masters was squatting down near the west end. Slowly, he got up and looked around. Then he turned in her direction and began to pace.

She had pulled back in time, she thought, so Ronnie didn't see her. Now she turned and walked into the alley.

Ronnie stopped. "Oh, hey."

"Hey yourself." She gestured behind her. "Saw you back there."

Ronnie had already turned back around. He pointed back at the area where he had been on his haunches. Shelly saw a piece of the pavement that had splintered badly, a fragment that had popped up.

"That must be where Alex tripped," he said.

"Tripped." She didn't know anything about Alex tripping.

"Yeah, when he messed up his knee."

"I didn't know Alex messed up his knee," she said. "I didn't know he tripped."

Ronnie looked at her. This meant that Ronnie had been talking to Alex about the case. She had already warned him that their conversations could be recorded, legally, by the authorities. She assumed that this particular talk had taken place before her warning to him. And she wasn't up for scolding at the moment; she was more concerned with why everyone seemed to know more about this case than she.

"He fell while he was running?" Shelly asked.

"You don't know this?"

"No, as a matter of fact, I don't. I didn't notice a limp or anything."

"Well, you know how it is when you bang up your knee. For five minutes, you think you'll never walk again, then it's fine."

They walked to her office. Ronnie was still wearing that ratty hooded sweatshirt for warmth. She dearly wanted to buy him something warmer, but she knew he would not react well to the offer. He was a proud young man, she could see. And besides, it would warm up soon enough.

She could see the weight of the last two months in Ronnie's eyes, which were puffy and dark. He seemed like a boy who kept a lot to himself—like his "brother," Alex, but in a different way. Alex, at least before the shooting, radiated an optimistic glow. Ronnie seemed darker. Two boys who essentially grew up together but were different.

They reached the office, and Shelly put him to work. He sat on the floor of her office and began to place things in their proper places, which was no small chore. Shelly was no neat freak. Quite the opposite. Her office typically was chaotic. She had made a point to do better this time, with this case, but there were only so many new tricks she could teach herself.

"Christ, you're messy," he said, as if she needed the tip.

She smirked at him and poured over her notes again. She thought of the alley, of the fact that Alex had apparently fallen and hurt himself. Why hadn't he mentioned that? What else didn't she know? No, it was not exactly a crucial detail, but it made Shelly wonder about the completeness of her own understanding of events that night.

"You two got a communication problem," Ronnie said, as if he were reading her mind.

"Tell me about it. I have to learn information from you."

He stopped what he was doing and looked at her. "You don't plan on—after this is over. You don't really plan on being a part of things, do you?"

"That's not true." She felt her hair rise. "That's not true at all."

"Well, you're treating him like a criminal, Shelly. It's like you find out you're related to him and you like him *less*."

She sighed. "Ronnie, I've told—"

"You know he used to talk about you? When he was younger? He used to wonder what was wrong with him. He wondered what was so bad about him that made you give him away."

She set down the report.

"I know it must've been tough, Shelly. But it hasn't been easy for *him*, either."

She brought her hands to her face. "What do you want me to say, Ronnie?"

He looked up at her. "I want you to act like he wasn't an accident. Or a mistake." He got up from his work, wiped at his hands. He left under the guise of needing some things from the supply room.

Shelly had a headache. She was, she realized, getting tired of apologizing. If Alex didn't beat these charges, it wouldn't matter whether she accepted him into her life, or she into his. She had every right to be focusing on his defense.

Her phone rang. It was Dan Morphew, the prosecutor.

"Seventy years, Counselor. Let's make this go away. I need to get back to all that paperwork they give me these days."

"I can't buy that, Dan. Not even close."

"Think on it," he said. "Let's keep talking."

Shelly stared at the receiver a moment before hanging up.

47

Break

WHILE SHE WAITED to see Alex, Shelly opened the small package delivered from the prosecution. The prosecution had to go first and disclose its witnesses. Shelly had two days thereafter to disclose hers. Neither party was required to accurately predict whom they would call as the trial evolved, but each party had to identify potential witnesses or risk having the judge exclude their testimony. So the rule was, throw in everyone who could even conceivably touch upon the case; leave out witnesses at your peril.

The prosecution would call Officer Julio Sanchez, Miro's partner, as a witness to the crime. The two eyewitnesses, Monica Stoddard and Joseph Slattery, were listed. The prosecution listed Dr. Mitra Agarwal, the county's chief deputy medical examiner, to testify as to cause of death and the distance between Miroballi and Alex at the time of the shooting. Detective Alberto Montes, with whom Shelly had spoken at the police station that night, would testify about the investigation and about some of the testing performed on the suspect. Other than that, Morphew would only call people to testify as to chain of custody to show that various pieces of evidence were properly handled and preserved.

It would be a straightforward prosecution, which was exactly how Assistant County Attorney Dan Morphew wanted it. Nothing fancy or complicated. No doubt that Alex was there, no doubt that Alex was the shooter. Morphew would have the opportunity to supplement this list once she disclosed her witnesses, because Shelly was pleading an affirmative defense, but he probably could do all he needed to do with Officer Sanchez.

What would happen, she wondered, when the F.B.I. closed in on the dirty cops, when the sting became public? Morphew would be caught flat-footed. Or did he have some inkling now? Had he discussed things with the federal prosecutors? Is *that* what prompted his offer of seventy years?

That was a possibility. And not one that the F.B.I. would confirm, even if she bothered to ask.

Shelly also would identify Officer Sanchez. She would disclose Officer Brian O'Sullivan, the officer who first arrived on the scene after Miroballi was shot and who had canvassed the crime scene. She disclosed Ronnie Masters but kept the description of his testimony deliberately vague, which she found interesting about herself, because she realized that Ronnie would probably say just about anything to help Alex. She might consider naming the man who supplied drugs to Alex, Edward Todavia, but the jury was still out on that one; by doing that, Morphew would go to Todavia immediately, read his sheet, and figure out that he was probably connected to the cocaine that Alex had that night. She did the boilerplate as well, identifying any and all witnesses mentioned in any of the materials produced by the prosecution or before the grand jury.

And for the heck of it, she would throw in the names of Ray Miroballi's brothers, Tony and Reggie.

She wished she could trade sides with Dan Morphew. He had cops, good eyewitnesses, an accomplished forensic pathologist. She had a hostile cop, a kid who was obviously biased (and probably wouldn't testify, anyway), and down the road, perhaps, federal prosecutors and special agents who were not exactly friendly to her cause, who in fact had told her informally that she would never be able to prove that Miroballi was forcing Alex to work for him.

Alex was brought in. He needed a haircut, she realized, which made her think of his appearance at trial. He would need a couple of suits, or at least sport coats, and clean shirts and at least two ties.

The guard locked Alex's wrists down to the table and patted

his shoulder. "Thanks, Joe," said Alex. It was the same old story now with Alex. She was beginning to forget the Alex she had first known, the sunny disposition and wry sense of humor. This was Alex now. One part scared, two parts hardened, bracing himself for every day that he spent inside and preparing for a long stay. She couldn't even fathom the erosion to one's psyche from being confined, from wearing shackles whenever one consorted with outsiders. He would never be the same, she realized with a pang of regret. No matter what happened next. He would never get this time back, and he would never get this time completely out of his system.

"How's your knee?" she asked.

"My knee?"

"I didn't know you had tripped, Alex. When you were running from Miroballi that night."

"Oh. Well, yeah. I guess it didn't seem too important."

"Oh, it probably isn't," she said. "But you shouldn't be making those judgments. You have to tell me everything. This might not be such a big deal, but it makes me wonder what else you have left out."

"I haven't left anything out." He played with his fingers. "So tell me how things are going."

Shelly had always been honest to a fault with her clients. She remembered feeling, as a child, that she wasn't given enough credit by adults. So she gave Alex her best assessment of the self-defense case and the "innocence" case. Alex seemed distressed as he listened, and Shelly thought that maybe he could use a dose of that emotion. He needed to hear her say, in a coherent presentation, how weak his case looked.

"The problem with arguing you didn't shoot Miroballi," she told him, "is that we have to show that someone else did. And I need your help with that."

She was giving him yet another chance to add information. She made a point of emphasizing that the case for Alex being the shooter was largely circumstantial. Other than the word of a homeless man, it simply came to down to the fact that Alex ran into the alley, Miroballi chased him, and Miroballi ended up with a bullet in his head. Yes, sure, Alex was the obvious suspect, but if they could put someone else in that alley, too, the prosecution could do little to show it wasn't true. She was practically begging him to put a third person in that alley.

But he wouldn't. Maybe it was because this third person was a gang member, and Alex was afraid of naming names lest his family be harmed. Or maybe there was no third person, and Alex refused to make up a story. Maybe he was still that nice young boy she saw the first day, dressed in his Sunday best, his long black coat folded in his lap, an honest boy who had made some mistakes but refused to compromise his principles by making up a story just to beat the rap.

Or maybe—

She bounced out of her chair, almost tripping over herself in the process.

"What's wrong with you?" Alex asked.

"I—I just thought of something I'm supposed to be doing." She gathered herself. "I'm sorry, Alex, I just realized I'm supposed to be somewhere." She looked at her watch for good measure. "I have to go but I'll be back."

She was not entirely sure of her destination, but she felt, for the first time in a long time, that she knew the direction.

48

Breaking

"THIS ISN'T THE kind of thing we should talk about," said Joel Lightner. They were standing on the porch of Ronnie Masters's home just after noon. Joel removed a ring of keys from his pocket and tried a couple of them. "They don't have an alarm, now you're sure?"

"I'm sure," Shelly said. She looked up and down the street.

The door opened. Shelly walked into the Masters house and moved to the couch. She reached under it and opened the book of photos she had seen Ronnie place there on one of her visits. She went through them quickly and removed two photos of them last winter, when Alex was holding up his daughter, Angela, showing her a snowman that Ronnie had made.

She went to the closet in the hallway and fished through the hangers. She went to Ronnie's room and went through everything. She rifled through Ronnie's drawers, went through his closet, looked under his bed, and almost killed herself tripping over a basketball before she made her way out of his room. "Stupid ball," she muttered, thinking of the open gym from which Alex had left on the night of the shooting. She was ready to blame the City Athletic Club for holding an open gym that set this whole series of events in motion. She wanted to blame the inventor of the automobile, because it allowed Alex to travel to the west side and get dope from a gangbanger. She was ready to blame everything back to the day he was born—

Ouch.

She moved quickly to Alex's room and gave it the same workover, going through everything, even the laundry that still remained in a ball on the floor of his closet. She stopped for a moment, but only a moment, to see the photograph taped on a mirror on the wall, a small Polaroid of Shelly that Alex had taken one day along the lake when they were walking. She remembered that day. It was winter. He had stopped behind her pretending to tie his shoe, and when she finally turned around impatiently, he hit her in the chest with a snowball.

"Okay, let's go," said Joel, who was eager to leave. They had been inside less than thirty minutes. He wasted no time getting back to the car they had parked down the street and speeding away.

"You want my opinion?" Joel asked. "Go with self-defense. Your client's not going to back up anything else."

"Probably not. But I'm not letting him rope me in anymore."

"I wish I could be more helpful. I can't find squat on Miroballi. Nothing funny on his finances. Nothing about drugs. Nothing about being sick. I couldn't get the results of his urine drop at that clinic, but even if I could—what would it prove? We find cocaine in his system, it doesn't mean anything."

"Nothing on Miroballi, nothing on Sanchez," Shelly summarized. "I have no way of proving that Miroballi had figured out about Alex talking to the feds. I have zilch. Except the word of my client, on trial for murder."

She realized that she was giving herself a pep talk, trying to convince herself of the reasonableness of the theory she was formulating.

"But like I said, Shelly, your client's not going to go for this."

"So I'll prove it. With or without him." She looked at the photos of Ronnie and Alex, mugging for the camera, and slipped them back into her bag.

49

Switch

SHELLY PLACED THE photocopy of the police dispatch transcript on her desk, focusing on a portion of the final communication between Officer Julio Sanchez and headquarters:

RADIO 26: White male, black coat, green cap, headed west—he went through the alley. He's going to be headed—oh, there's so much—probably south on—on I guess Donnelly. Maybe north. I don't know where he went.

DISPATCH: Stay with your officer, Twenty-six. Stay with him.

DISPATCH: All units, we have an officer down at the 200 block of South Gentry. That's a Code Blue. I repeat, this is a Code Blue. Suspect is a white male, late teens or early twenties, black jacket, green cap. Suspect believed to be headed north or south on Donnelly. Suspect is armed. Suspect is armed. We have a Code Blue, officers. Suspect is armed.

She turned to the copies she had of Joel Lightner's notes when they spoke with the architect, Monica Stoddard. She had said, speaking of Alex, that she had seen a boy "in a coat and a cap," according to Joel Lightner, and Shelly remembered this the same way. When talking of where Alex may have hidden a gun, Stoddard noted that he "had pockets in his coat."

She looked at the photographs Joel had taken in the evidence room at the County Attorney Technical Unit. There, wrapped in protective plastic, was the black leather jacket that Alex was wearing when he was caught. She held up the photos she had taken from Ronnie's house, photos of Alex and Ronnie together. And there she saw the same black leather jacket.

On Ronnie Masters.

"Every time I've ever seen Alex in cold weather," Shelly said to Joel Lightner, "he's worn the same long black wool coat he's wearing in this photograph."

"So he wore something different that night."

"I don't think so. Look at what the architect said. Look at what Sanchez said."

"A coat," Joel read along. "A coat." He looked up at her. "So what's the difference between a coat and a jacket? It's inter-changeable. Even the dispatch operator called it a 'jacket.' "

"Not really, Joel. Not really. You see someone in a long wool garment, you call it a coat. You see someone in a leather gar-ment that stops near the waist, you call it a jacket. It's a visual thing. The dispatch operator didn't see anything. He was just re-laying information and he confused the terms."

Joel sat down in the chair opposite her desk. "You're going to base your defense on *that*?"

"I looked in the closet, Joel. At Ronnie's place. I looked everywhere, in fact. That wool coat is gone. Nowhere to be found. And Ronnie has been wearing some dinky sweatshirt with a hood every time I've seen him. He'd wear that coat if it were around."

Joel bit at his fingernails. He was quiet for a moment, allow-ing for the possibilities.

"They switched them," Shelly said. "Ronnie was there that night. Ronnie was there, and after the shooting, he and Alex traded what they were wearing. Not all of it, but the stuff that counted."

"The cap," Joel said.

"Right. The cap that everyone saw Alex wearing but that was never found. His long coat. His gloves."

"The gun," he added.

She nodded. "Ronnie took the gun and Alex's cap and gloves and coat, and left with them."

"Left Alex, too."

"He had to leave Alex behind," said Shelly. "They knew Alex. Sanchez knew who he was. Alex was never going to escape. But Ronnie could."

"And take all the incriminating evidence with him." Joel straightened in his chair, his investigatory juices flowing. "He takes the coat and gloves and cap—anything that has blood spatterings on them—"

"—and gunshot residue—"

"—right, and he leaves. No one knows that he was there."

Shelly was pacing now. "And the case against Alex is all the weaker for it. There's no murder weapon. There's no gunshot residue on Alex." She flapped her arms. "It's the best they can do. The cops are going to get Alex one way or the other, but at least this way they get him without all of the incriminating evidence, like you said."

"Christ." Joel slowly nodded. "That works."

"I think it does."

"The problem, Shelly, if you're right—that means Alex pulled the trigger. Alex shot Miroballi, and Ronnie tried to cover it up by removing the gun and the clothes."

"Alex shot him," she agreed. "Right." She looked out the window of her office.

"So you've got a third person, but he doesn't help you."

"Maybe not. Maybe so." Like anything else, there were always more ways than one to use certain information. He must have driven his car, she thought. He drove his car to pick up Alex and drove him away—but not too far away—from the crime scene, in the meantime exchanging clothes with Alex.

Joel looked at his watch. "I hate to run."

"No. Go. No problem."

"Tomorrow, Shelly? Seven-thirty?"

"Right. Thanks, Joel."

"Sorry about the delay. You said it was high priority."

"No, that's fine, Joel. Really."

"You know where you're going?"

"Yep."

"And you're anonymous, obviously."

"Right. I'll be invisible."

"Definitely." He gathered his bag and headed for the door.

"Joel," she called out. "Put someone on Ronnie?"

He knocked on the door and nodded. "You read my mind."

50

Conflict

"NICE TO MEET you." Shelly offered her hand to the man who stood with the warehouse door propped open. She didn't offer her name and he didn't offer his. He led her into the spacious facility, with rows of tall metal cabinets and a twenty-foot ceiling. He moved briskly and she followed him without saying a word.

"Here you go." He opened a drawer and pulled it out. His hand moved directly to the tab she was looking for. He had obviously already looked for it and found it. He held his finger on the file until Shelly replaced it with her hand.

The man whistled as Shelly ran through the file once, then twice. She almost jumped out of her skin as her cell phone rang.

She looked at the man, who seemed alarmed at any prospect of delay. She held up her finger and answered the phone.

"Shelly, it's Joel. Hey, where are you?"

"You know where I am."

"Oh. Oh, right. You find everything you need?"

"What do you want, Joel?"

"We got something on Ronnie."

"Hang on," she said. She put down the cell phone, removed a business card and scribbled on the back of it, using her thigh as a backstop. She handed it to the man.

"Joel didn't say anything about this," said the man.

She pointed to the phone. "You want to talk to him?"

He sighed and shook the card in his hand. "Is this it?"

"I promise." She picked the phone back up. "What is it, Joel?" She began to follow the man as Joel spoke.

"My guy followed Ronnie. Today was the first day. Pretty good first day."

The man stopped and started, then turned down one of the high rows of documents.

"Ronnie headed out to the west side today."

The man tried several drawers, pulling them out and comparing them to the card Shelly had written on.

"He went to the projects. You know the A-Jar projects?"

She did. The Eduardo Andujar projects were on the city's west side, a predominantly Hispanic neighborhood. Shelly had represented some kids from A-Jar.

The man opened a drawer and held his finger at a space midway through the drawer, wearing a bored expression.

Shelly balanced the cell phone between her shoulder and cheek and went through them. There was more than one. She rifled through them, forcing herself to move more slowly.

"We saw him go into this consignment store," said Joel. "He came out of the alley a few minutes later. Know who he was walking with?"

She found it. She opened the file slowly.

"Eddie Todavia," Joel said over the phone.

She read the original birth certificate slowly.

```
Birth mother: Michelle Ingrid Trotter
Date of birth: January 10, 1970
Age: 17
```

"Ronnie knew Eddie Todavia from school, too," Joel continued. "Alex and Ronnie and Todavia all went to school together. We forgot about that. You know what this means?"

```
Adopted child: Baby Boy Trotter
Date of birth: February 19, 1987
```

She flipped the page. "I think I do," she said.

"It was Ronnie, Shelly. Ronnie was working with Todavia. He was working with the Cannibals."

```
Adoptive parents: Franklin Masters.
Date of birth: March 5, 1947. Elaine
Masters. Date of birth: March 29, 1950.
```

"Ronnie was working with the Cannibals, Shelly. Alex must have told Ronnie he was helping Miroballi take down the Cannibals. And Ronnie killed Miroballi. Alex is afraid to give him up."

```
Adopted child's given name: Ronald
Franklin Masters
```

"Are you there, Shelly? You getting this? This is unbeliev—"

She moved the phone from her ear and turned in the direction of the man, without looking at him. "Thank you," she said. "I'm done." She left the man standing there and then brought the phone back up to her ear.

"—thought he was pulling your leg, Shelly, I really did. I thought your guy was guilty six ways to Sunday. But we've got this kid Ronnie now. I have him on tape. We can put him with Todavia and if we keep watching, he'll probably fuck up some more. Jesus, this is really something."

"Sit tight for now," she found herself instructing Joel as she pushed open the door to the document storage warehouse for the Department of Public Health, Bureau of Vital Statistics.

"Shelly, what's up? This is what we've been looking for. We finally got him. Ronnie's your boy, I swear he is."

She laughed bitterly and punched out the phone. "He certainly is," she mumbled into the evening air. She got into her car and drove without thinking. It was several miles before she realized that she had been traveling in the wrong direction.

51

Future

THE NIGHTS A *young woman lies awake, stroking her swollen belly, dreaming of the child she will never know. She knows nothing about this child. She can't even give it a name, for she doesn't know if it's a boy or girl. She thinks of gender-neutral names like Pat or Sam, and she plays the games with other shortened names as well. Andy or Andi. Joe or Jo.*

She will not name this child. It will be another family, a family with a lawyer who will meet with the lawyer Daddy has provided. A family who desperately wants a child of their own. She will not know their names. They will know hers. Will they tell the child someday? Will the child know how special it is?

Will the child be compassionate? Giving? Will she—or he— love life? Live for the moment and prepare for the future? Take chances? Be ambitious?

She goes to the window and looks out over Otter Lake. The lake is frozen now, two days after Christmas, a blanket of snow providing a tranquil cover. She longs for the summer days when she would take Grandma Jeannie's boat and rock with the gentle ebbing of the water, staring up at the stars and thinking of this child.

Her child will have children—Shelly's grandchildren—that she will never know. And they will have children. An entire family will come from this child whom she will never know.

She knows it in a way that a mother who will not raise the child knows it. Yes, the child will be special. It will be intelligent and self-assured and will do great things. She knows these things because she has to know them. They have to be true.

It will be about two months now, give or take a week. They tell her that the first one usually does not come early. Mid-February, they are saying. She will only have about forty-five more days with her child and then she will say goodbye forever.

She will not return to Haley. She knows that now. For the same reason she did not return there for Christmas. It is not what everyone thinks. She is not ashamed. She does not care if her friends would snicker or gossip. She does not want to see them anymore. She will move on now and do it her own way. She will stay with her grandmother for her senior year of high school and, if her grades remain on pace, she will get a scholarship to college. She will not live under their roof nor accept their money. Her father will overcome this temporary setback and get what he wants, someday. Attorney general, governor, president—he will find a way. She will not be proud but she will be relieved, because when this happens, she will be free of all debts. And then she will live without them.

And without her child.

52

Privileges

PAUL RILEY WAS leaning back in his chair reading a transcript when Shelly walked into his office.

"Been out today?" he asked.

"Yeah. This and that."

She had spent the day walking along the lake, pondering the events of the prior evening. She thought of Alex Baniewicz showing up at her office a little over a year ago, ostensibly for legal representation on a school disciplinary matter, when in fact he'd only wanted to meet her. But why Alex? Why hadn't Ronnie come? Why send Alex?

She had been unable, at times today, to overcome her anger as well. Did they think she was an idiot? Did they think she wouldn't check on this eventually? Didn't they realize that one day, she would do the same thing they had done, take a peek at the adoption records to confirm the name of her son? They thought she would spend her entire life taking Alex's word for it that he was her child?

It had taken her the better part of an hour to answer that question. Yes, they had to know that eventually she would go to the trouble of checking the records and confirming the facts. They were just hoping that she wouldn't have time to check until the case was over, that the magnitude of this case would distract her. They wanted her to go through this trial thinking that she had to save her son. What she did afterward was of little consequence. They wanted a desperate lawyer who would lie, cheat, and steal to save her flesh and blood from a death sentence.

When she had walked into the office late this afternoon, she had found a series of photographs that Joel Lightner had left for her, taken of Ronnie Masters walking alongside Eddie Todavia somewhere on the city's west side. She had seen a street sign and recognized it, anyway, as Venice Avenue, a major east-west thoroughfare that ran along the A-Jar projects, among other things. Ronnie didn't live near that neighborhood and Todavia didn't, either.

"I need a lawyer," she said to Paul.

He looked over the glasses perched on his nose. "You might need a priest, Shelly Trotter. Why do you need a lawyer?"

"I'm not kidding. I need a good old-fashioned attorney-client conversation."

Paul looked her over a moment, then set down the transcript and sat up in his chair. "Okay, you're not kidding. What's going on?" He motioned for her to sit.

She first closed the door behind her. The last time she had done that in this office, it had been pleasure, not business, and she guessed that the same thing had just run through Paul's mind.

"I need advice. More like confirmation."

He opened his hands.

"Let's say a hypothetical lawyer is defending a client on a criminal charge. That lawyer has some reason to believe that she can point the finger at someone else."

"Okay."

"Okay." She sighed. "Now let's say that she has a conflict of interest. Let's say that she might have some inherent bias in favor of that person—the one she wants to point the finger at."

Paul's eyes narrowed. "What kind of bias?"

"She has a reason to—to not want to point that finger."

"What kind of reason?"

"A reason, Paul. A reason."

Paul shifted in his seat, pushed himself back from his desk and crossed a leg. "Then she has to recuse herself. Withdraw from the case."

"Recuse herself, and what? Not tell her client, before she leaves, about this other person?"

"No, she has a duty to tell her client what she knows. Then she gets out."

"What if the client already knows most of it?"

"Most of it? The client has to know all of it."

Shelly deflated. She already knew all of this, and she wasn't entirely sure why she was burdening Paul with a rather elementary lesson in legal ethics.

Paul got up from his seat. "The lawyer has come upon some evidence that implicates a third party. She has a conflict with regard to that third party. She has to tell her client what evidence she has uncovered and then get out."

"Unless the client waives the conflict."

Paul cocked his head. "As long as the client is fully informed of the conflict." He lingered on that point, because, she knew, he was going beyond the hypothetical. He wanted to be "fully informed" himself.

"I would also tell that hypothetical lawyer," he continued, "that if she came into another lawyer's office and asked for legal advice that is protected by the attorney-client privilege, then she should not feel constrained to keep things hypothetical. She should tell her lawyer what the heck is going on. Because he would be forbidden from repeating it."

She dropped her head. "Not necessarily."

Paul moved to the window and looked out over the lake. She assumed he caught her meaning. The one hole in the attorney-client privilege was that a lawyer could not keep quiet about future criminal conduct that a client might commit. Past crimes, fine. But a lawyer could not stand idly by and listen to a client explain a crime she was about to commit and do nothing. He was obligated to report it.

"Shelly, be careful," he said.

The thought ran through her mind again—why had she come here? She didn't need him to explain the rules of conflicts of interest. She watched this man, in a bit of conflict himself, and she scolded herself for placing him there. And then she felt her mouth open and heard words come out.

"Ronnie Masters," she said. "Alex's brother? Or kind-of brother?"

Paul turned to her.

"He's my son. He's a boy I gave up for adoption seventeen years ago. I found this out last night. I saw the birth certificate myself."

Paul stood frozen against the window. She sensed a look of surprise, of course, but also relief. She imagined what he had been thinking—that this hypothetical "third person" was someone with whom she'd had a romantic relationship.

"And I think Ronnie killed that cop. Or at least had a big part in it."

Paul closed his mouth and made a noise. "Ronnie's your—"

"It was hushed up at the time. I got pregnant, moved downstate to live with my grandmother, and my father and his team of lawyers worked out some confidential attorney adoption. I never even knew the gender of the child. I never laid eyes on him. I don't even know how they found the Masterses. Older people can't do traditional adoptions so they go through lawyers. They skip the agencies. Or maybe my dad just wanted it hush-hush."

She stopped herself. She was gushing. Too much. Overload. She felt Paul's hand on her shoulder and she recoiled. He held up his hand tentatively, wounded, probably, and moved back to the chair behind the desk.

She took a moment to compose herself. Paul was giving her the floor here. Finally, she continued, staring at the floor at first. "I told you about Officer Sanchez? The partner? He says Miroballi was trying to make a big bust or something—"

"He was trying to make a high-profile drug bust on the Cannibals' turf," Paul said. "He was using Alex to do it. And Miroballi thought that Alex had tipped off the Cannibals. Which was why Miroballi wanted to talk with Alex that night."

Shelly nodded. "Now I'm thinking that Alex didn't knowingly tip off anybody. I think he confided in Ronnie, and *Ronnie* told the Cannibals."

"Why would Ronnie do that?"

"I don't know. But Joel Lightner has been following Ronnie, and we've seen him with the guy who supplied Alex the drugs. A guy we're pretty sure is a Cannibal himself. Maybe Ronnie works with them. I don't know. But you see what I'm saying?"

Paul shrugged, as if his answer was no.

"I can put Ronnie at the scene," she continued. "I think Ronnie was there. I think he and Alex switched the clothes they were wearing afterward. Ronnie gave Alex his clothes, so the blood and gunshot residue wouldn't show up. Ronnie drove away and left Alex there. Because Alex was going to get busted anyway. Sanchez would identify him in a heartbeat. But this way, Alex doesn't look as guilty. No gun, no blood spatterings, a negative residue test—"

"But I thought they found some blood."

"Yeah, in his hair. A little on his shirt. That just means that they didn't do a good job of cleaning up. It doesn't make me wrong."

Paul stared at the ceiling a moment. She had to admire his focus after the bombs she had just hurled. But it mattered to her, obviously, he could see that, and he was doing his best to come through for her. "I'm not sure you can put all those things together and say for sure—"

"For sure?" she interrupted. "No. But that's not the standard. That's the thing. I have more than credible evidence putting Ronnie in the soup on this. I can make a pretty damn good argument that he was there, that he played at least some role, and I can put him next to the Cannibals. Add that up with what Sanchez will say and I have an empty chair. I have a great person to point the finger at." She opened her hands. "This is far and away the best thing I can come up with for reasonable doubt. I can't walk away from this."

"No, you can't. What does Alex say?"

"Alex." She laughed, of all things. "If I'm right, then obviously Alex knows all of this. The fact that he hasn't breathed a word of this should tell you what he thinks. He won't go along with it."

"He'll testify to the contrary," Paul surmised.

"Sure. He'll fall on the sword. That's what he's done so far."

"Then you don't call him," he said. "Take five."

"But he'll insist on it," she said. "If he sees me at trial pointing the finger at Ronnie, he'll either fire me on the spot or he'll demand to take the stand. He'll say it isn't true. It will just get worse for him then. I don't know what it is with him, but he wants to be a hero."

"You have to tell Alex that Ronnie—" Paul caught himself. "Oh. Alex knows that you're Ronnie's mother."

"Of course. Yeah. He doesn't know *I* know."

"Well, you have to *tell* Alex that you know. And you have to tell him the evidence that you have against Ronnie. And you have to tell him that you plan on relying on that evidence to clear him of these charges."

He was right, of course. She left the chair and moved into the center of the room. She turned back to Paul. "Hey, you know— I realize I'm coming in here like a hurricane. Lots of fun new information about Shelly Trotter today."

He held up his hands. "Go do your job. Don't worry about me."

She smiled at him.

"But hear me on this, Shelly. Sounds like you don't know these boys as well as you thought. Don't think, if things go south, they won't turn on you. Cover yourself here. Full frontal disclosure. Don't lose your law license over this."

She raised her hand in acknowledgment. She was beginning to wish she had never obtained a law license.

53

Round-up

SHELLY GRABBED THE newspaper on her way to work the next morning. It was a stand-alone newspaper stand by the bus stop—insert the change and open the door. She liked seeing these things around the city. These little contraptions were the last bastion of the honor system. The *Daily Watch* was trusting purchasers to take one and only one paper. Good for them. A little trust never hurt anybody.

This was her favorite time of day, unlike most people. She grabbed a paper and, getting on the bus as early as she typically did—around seven—and being as far north as she was, she always had a seat. Among the bumps and car horns and crowds of people as the bus headed south, Shelly found a tranquility diving into the news of the day. The Internet was fine, but put a paper in her hands any day of the week.

She saw the headlines through the glass before she had dumped the coins in:

FEDS NAB COPS IN DRUG CONSPIRACY
PARTNERSHIP WITH STREET GANG ALLEGED

She threw in the coins and pulled on the handle to no avail, finally having to remove the change and try again after almost yanking the stand off the ground.

She removed the paper and started reading. She was vaguely aware of a bus stopping but she was too absorbed to think of it.

The United States Attorney, Mason Tremont, was pictured standing with authority before a bank of microphones. In the background, according to the caption on the front page, was the F.B.I.'s special agent-in-charge in the city, as well as the profile, out of focus, of Assistant United States Attorney Jerod Romero. The headline was supported by three separate stories covering the police officers, the federal investigation, and others caught up in the federal probe.

According to the story, late yesterday, federal agents arrested six officers on the city police force, along with a number of others allegedly involved in a wide-ranging conspiracy to promote and protect the drug trade on the city's west side. The charges against the officers would range from providing a safe harbor for the narcotics traffic, to receiving kickbacks, to outright selling the drugs themselves.

She swept the coverage looking for the critical names— Raymond Miroballi; Alex Baniewicz; Miroballi's partner, Julio Sanchez; Eddie Todavia; even Ronnie Masters. She finally found a bullet-point list of individuals picked up in the sting. There were six police officers but she did not recognize any of their names. There was one sergeant and five patrol officers. The paper listed sixteen other people, whose roles in the scheme were not detailed. In some cases, because they were juveniles, their names were not even listed. Some of them—many of them, probably—had been smaller players who were busted and flipped. Many of them were undoubtedly members of the Columbus Street Cannibals.

It was a wide-scale scheme to distribute crack cocaine on the west side. That made sense, if you wanted to sell drugs on the street on a volume basis. Cops were skimming off the top in drug busts—if not stealing the entire stash—employing runners to do the selling, helping out the bad guys when they got picked up, tipping off their cronies, even recruiting buyers. The implicated police officers came from more than one precinct on the west side. Shelly didn't know one precinct from another. She'd have to consult with Joel Lightner or Paul on that point.

By the time she walked into her office, she had read every article twice and used a pen to mark relevant portions. Another copy of the front page was sitting on her chair, courtesy of Paul, no doubt. She put in a call to Joel Lightner and left a message on his cell phone.

She looked again at the photograph of United States Attorney Mason Tremont. He was the first African American named to this jurisdiction as the top federal prosecutor. He was appointed by, and served at the pleasure of, the president, like all U.S. Attorneys. But in reality, the rule was that the president turned to the highest-ranking member of his political party in the state to give the nod. It was a courtesy extended in nearly every jurisdiction in the country by both political parties. And because the two state senators were Democrats, the Republican president turned to Governor Trotter to suggest all federal judges and United States Attorneys.

Tremont was the governor's guy, or one of many. He was a former federal prosecutor who had made a nice career for himself in white-collar criminal defense and commercial litigation. But his greatest attribute was fund-raising. It was estimated—because such things could not be directly attributed—that Mason Tremont had been responsible for raising as much as three million dollars for Lang Trotter's gubernatorial campaign in the 2000 race.

She looked at her watch. She was supposed to see Alex this morning, but that might have to wait. She went to the copier and made duplicates of the articles.

She was twelve days from trial and she had a lot of people to interview, or at least try to interview. She would have to revise her witness list based on this "newly discovered" development. It was not new to Shelly, of course, at least not entirely. The judge would not be happy with her. But she would explain the necessity of her silence, and the judge at least would have to let her add the arrested police officers to her list, because she never knew their names until now. That was really all she needed. If the judge did not allow her to call the federal investigators and prosecutors as witnesses, that would be acceptable to her. They didn't seem too thrilled in helping out Alex, anyway.

The key was she could not let the judge move the trial date.

This was, more or less, what she had wanted. A big splash of publicity, talking about city cops on the take, illegal and rough stuff, only days before her trial started. It made her chances of showing self-defense all the easier. The jurors from around the county would not exactly be bowled over with shock when she told them Ray Miroballi was a drug-dealing cop.

Assuming she was going to say that. Assuming she was pleading self-defense.

That particular theory was looking better and better the more she read the stories. There would be follow-ups. Hopefully— though not likely—even a guilty plea or two before Alex's trial started. Cops *admitting* they were on the take.

The only person more excited than she, Shelly assumed, was Jerod Romero. This was his baby, and what a baby it was. Public corruption cases were the top-selling ticket in this town. Yes, this would make for excellent drama. The public—the jury in Alex's case—would be in the mood. Suburbanites in the county would only feel validated in their already tainted view of the city's finest. The city dwellers on the west and south sides would be outraged. There was no one, in fact, who wouldn't feel either disgusted or more disgusted.

She had a winner. Right?

Right. It sounded better today, with this news, than ever before. Ray Miroballi was a dirty cop who forced a kid to sell drugs. Miroballi was getting nervous about Alex, because Miroballi had discovered Alex was working with the feds against him and he needed to silence him. Alex shot him in self-defense. Miroballi's partner, Sanchez, says differently? That's because he was a part of it. He was a dirty cop, too—*like those other cops you read about in the papers,* she would not be able to directly say.

She felt a surge of adrenaline—positive juice—for the first time in a long time. Maybe Ronnie had nothing to do with this. Sure, it seemed like he was there. But he didn't do anything but try to help Alex out of the jam afterward. No reason to implicate him. Irrelevant, is what it was. A textbook case of self-defense. She'd been foolish to think otherwise.

Her phone rang after ten o'clock. It was county prosecutor Daniel Morphew.

"Haven't heard back from you," he said. "I thought we were talking here."

"What was that, Dan? Seventy years? I don't think so."

"Well, that much I figured. I'm saying, come to the table."

"I need something more enticing than seventy years to get me to the table. Okay, you want a counteroffer? How about time served?"

Morphew made a noise that resembled a mischievous laugh. "Okay, Counselor. I'll give you a discount for the headline today. Everyone hates cops, right? So take fifty. And I'm bidding against myself here."

"I'll take it to my client, Dan, but no way."

"He killed a cop, Shelly."

"A scumbag."

"Listen—I'm not arguing merits with you here. I'm saying, he killed a cop. There's only so much we can do here, even if we wanted to make this go away. We have to work with these guys every day of the week. Cops have to trust us. See what I'm saying?"

Of course she did. "After today's headline?" she said. "They'll be on their heels for quite a while. You guys are big boys."

"Then tell me no, Counselor. Tell me that there's no way we can deal."

She didn't catch the meaning.

"Tell me there's no deal you will take. No middle ground."

He needed to hear the words. Okay. He was saying this wasn't his idea. He had orders from on high to make this case disappear. He needed to be able to report a resounding "no" from Shelly Trotter. This could be a bluff. Most lawyers wanted to appear reluctant to make a deal. The best settlements were the ones where both sides walked away unhappy, or at least pretended to be unhappy. But she hadn't seen much of that bullshit in Dan Morphew. She was betting that he was being straight with her.

"Elliot wants to make this go away?" she tried, invoking the name of Morphew's boss, County Attorney Elliot Raycroft.

The grunt again, Morphew's version of a laugh, only this time it seemed less sincere, less pleasant. "Okay, Counselor. If that works for you."

She felt her blood boil. She had expected something like that answer but it didn't reduce the sting. Morphew wasn't directly saying the words because he couldn't afford to be quoted. He assumed they were speaking the same language. The county attorney wasn't calling the shots either, he was saying. Elliot Raycroft was heeding a call from higher up.

"Every one of those guys in the federal sting is going on my witness list," she said. "I'll have it to you by the end of the day."

"The cops rounded up? C'mon, Counselor. One has nothing to do with the other."

Shelly smiled to herself. Dan Morphew, to date, had absolutely no idea what Shelly was going to do with her self-defense argument. He didn't know about the plea arrangement Alex made with the F.B.I. He didn't know that Alex had ever been picked up by the feds at all. Shelly had played a game with the prosecutor. She had counted on the fact that she could prove everything she needed through Alex, her client, whose testimony she was not required to disclose to the prosecutor. But since the feds had made their bust a little sooner than she had expected, she would now disclose Jerod Romero, the federal prosecutor, as well as everyone else involved in the sting. She had already begun to put together the supplemental disclosure. But she was feeling a little mean right now, bitter, after Morphew had all but told her outright that Governor Langdon Trotter was interceding to help plead out this case. So she wanted to deliver her news to Morphew personally.

"Alex was part of that sting," she told Morphew. "He was working for the feds trying to nail a certain drug-dealing cop. A cop by the name of Raymond Miroballi. Miroballi was one of those guys, Dan. And Alex was trying to help put him away."

Silence at the other end of the phone. She wondered if Morphew had swallowed his tongue.

"This was coming out through Alex," she continued. "But since the feds decided to move on the other cops, I might as well—"

"You haven't disclosed shit about this," he said.

"Well, as I was saying, Counselor, I didn't have to. Moreover, as you will soon learn, we had a confidentiality agreement with the federal government."

"That doesn't mean squat to me—"

"No, I suppose not. Like I said, I was going to put this on through my client. But now that the U.S. Attorney has gone ahead and made his bust, I might as well go full throttle. The judge isn't going to stop me."

"This is an ambush, Shelly. This is—this is bullshit."

"Name a rule I violated," she said. "You can't. I'll have a disclosure to you by day's end."

She heard papers ruffling on the other end. She had just made Dan Morphew's next two weeks much more difficult. She had considered not naming these new people, sticking with her plan of putting on this evidence through Alex. But she decided against it. She wanted the jury to see as much of the grime as possible. She wanted to parade corrupt cops to the witness stand and ask them technically relevant questions—*Did you work with Ray Miroballi to sell drugs and protect drug dealers? Did Ray Miroballi tell you that my client, Alex Baniewicz, had flipped to the feds? Did Miroballi tell you that he had to kill my client to keep the operation going?*—knowing full well that the witnesses would refuse to answer any of the questions. They would take the fifth, while Shelly threw all of these vicious accusations at these cops for the jury's benefit. She would have at least six opportunities to do this, and by the end of the trial, the jury would have heard these suggestions so many times, they would certainly have to wonder.

"We're adding a witness of our own," Morphew said.

"Yeah?" Shelly felt the familiar heart palpitation of a lawyer near trial.

"Eddie Todavia. Ring a bell?"

She didn't respond. She felt a slow burn in her chest.

"Getting back to an earlier point," he continued. "You're telling me there's no chance of a deal."

"Tell him whatever you want to tell him," she answered. "Tell him to kiss my white Irish butt." She hung up the phone and went for her coat.

54

Cross-Examination

Two PHONE CALLS was all it took. Two calls to Mari Rodriguez, the governor's chief of staff. Sixty minutes later, she was walking into the Maritime Club, one of the exclusive, predominantly male clubs in the city. Shelly did not walk among these people generally speaking, but Governor Langdon Trotter certainly did.

She knew he was in town today. It was a rather inconsequential fact to her, not because she was too busy to see him but because, busy or otherwise, neither was likely to make much of an effort to see the other. Fine. That was fine. Stay out of her way, she would stay out of his. It had been an unofficial truce for years. Anger had turned to indifference, and usually stayed there, or at least she wanted to think so.

She took the elevator to the eleventh floor, where she had scheduled her meeting. You had to schedule with the governor. But if you were an irate daughter almost screaming into a cell phone, adjustments were made. Shelly was relatively sure that the offices nearby had been cleaned out. You're governor and you want privacy, snap a finger and it happens.

Mari wasn't around. All she saw when the elevator popped open were two members of his security detail, wearing suits and grave expressions, phone cords winding from their waist into earpieces.

"Hello, Ms. Trotter," one of them said. "Right this way." They led her to an ornate set of double doors that opened into a posh library.

"Thank you, boys."

Shelly followed the direction of the voice and saw her father sitting in the corner, reading a report of some kind. The doors closed behind her and they were alone. The whole floor was probably cleared.

"Well, hello there," he said. The governor's jacket was off and his sleeves were rolled up to his forearms. He removed the reading glasses perched on his nose.

She felt her hands curl into fists, but she had vented much of her anger in the hour that she had waited. She had done plenty of thinking and her calculations had produced a measure of calm.

"You know," she said simply.

He didn't leave his chair, which told her something. He placed a bookmark in his report and took his time setting it down on a nearby shelf. "What do I know, Shelly?"

"You know about Ronnie."

He produced an exaggerated sigh and got to his feet. She had almost forgotten how large he was. Wide shoulders, broad neck, still the full head of white hair offset by the steel blue eyes. His lack of an immediate answer was an answer itself.

"You put the I.R.S. on my legal clinic," she said. "I blamed the federal prosecutors for that. But it was you. A quick call to your buddies in the administration. You jeopardized a nonprofit clinic that helps kids who have no one else to help them. Classy. That's really something."

Her father's tight lips parted, but he didn't speak.

"Then you tell your little puppet Raycroft to cut a sweet deal for me. Anything to keep this quiet. Right? Anything to keep *me* off it, at least."

Her father looked her over. In part, it had to be a father's curiosity, the soulful way a man looks at his grown daughter. Was he proud of her? Impressed with her accomplishments? She couldn't pretend that she didn't care about his opinion. Why, she could not say. She did not understand the quirky human trait that made a grown, independent woman crave her father's approval, even now.

"You couldn't have me ruin *another* election," she concluded.

"Oh." Her father looked at his hand a moment, rubbing his thumb and index finger together, an old habit. "That makes it easier for you, I suppose."

"That is exac—"

"And it never occurred to you"—he raised a trembling, angry hand while keeping his voice even—"it never occurred to you that I was trying to protect *you*?"

"That makes it easier for *you*." She shook her head. "You could have told me—"

"Yes."

"—and let *me* make that judgment."

"Yes. And if you had ever come to me over the last seventeen years and asked me if I knew where your son was, I would have told you. But you didn't, Shelly."

"I didn't know you knew. I thought it was confidential."

"I've held state office for fourteen years. You're a lot of things, Shelly, but you're not dumb. You knew I could find out."

She deflated.

"But you never asked."

"And when it was clear that I wasn't getting off this case, no matter what you did?"

He nodded. "I could have told you. I didn't." He sighed and stuffed his hands in his pants pockets. "The boy knows?"

"Yes."

His jaw clenched. The information was coming loose now. The dam had sprung a leak.

"Do you see this information becoming public?"

Her shoulders rose and fell. "I can't control Ronnie."

"Try," he said.

"I'll ask him but it's his choice."

He didn't seem to take that well but, as always, he hardly gave a visible reaction. The Trotter family was adept at outward appearances.

"All it would mean is your daughter chose adoption over abortion," she said. "That works for you politically. As long as no one knows which option *you* wanted."

She saw the fire, momentarily, in his eyes. She had stung him with that one. She felt the rage building, not from her father's reckless interference in this case but from many years ago. That was the real reason she was here, she now realized, to say these words to him.

"You feel better now?" he asked.

"Not really. You?"

"Me?" He laughed. "No, Shelly, as always when it comes to you, I'm just waiting for the other shoe to drop."

A nice counterpunch. She felt like she was back in that room, watching the expressions on her parents' faces as she broke the news. The shock. Disappointment. Anger. Amazing, how quickly these feelings could return to the surface.

"It wasn't my choice for you to get pregnant when you were just a girl," he said. "That was your choice. And it was your choice not to tell me who the father was. And your choice to move away from home."

She felt the heat rise to her face.

"But I dealt with it," he continued. "I found your son a home. Maybe things didn't turn out perfectly, but who can ever guarantee such a thing? And yes, when this young man was arrested for shooting a police officer—"

"Alex."

"Yes, when Alex was arrested, I was aware that he lived with—" His eyebrows lifted, as if the entire matter disgusted him.

"With Ronnie," she said.

Her father wet his lips. "Yes. Of course, I was concerned. I didn't understand why, of all people, *you* would be involved. I thought maybe you knew about—the situation with the boy."

"Ronnie," she said again. "His name is Ronnie."

"Okay, fine." He spit the two words violently, as if they were one. He lifted his hand. "In any event—it turned out that you didn't know anything about it. You happened to know this boy Alex, and so there you were, defending the quasi-brother of your son. Of course, I was concerned. So yes, I tried to use some persuasion to move you away from it. And yes, maybe I put in a word to Elliot Raycroft. You were sitting next to a loaded grenade, young lady, and apparently you didn't even know it."

She looked away from him. He had not lost his ability to persuade. But he was rationalizing. She felt her teeth grinding, which also brought her back to her teenaged years. It had all come back like an avalanche. She could see the shame even now, as he struggled even to utter the name of her son—his grandson. His complete, unadulterated disappointment. And beside her anger sat a feeling she struggled to identify. She felt, on some level, completely ridiculous. Ashamed of herself? Not quite. She realized that she had viewed herself, her life, through the lenses of her father. Was that the reason she had refused, these years, to acknowledge the existence of her son? Because it reminded her of the person who had let her father down so severely?

The issue, to use a legal term, was moot. Done. Inescapably over. And that, more than anything—that overwhelming sense of regret, of the inability to change past events—whisked the breath from her lungs.

Her father mumbled something, took a step to the side, slowly paced. He made his way over to the window. "First time I ran for this office," he began. "There was that mistake in my nominating papers. A mistake big enough to topple my entire candidacy. I assume you heard about that."

She had. Everyone had. When her father's nominating petitions were filed for the governor's race, one of his staff had failed to file the original of a particular document. The issue had been raised in the context of a murder trial involving the chief aide of her father's Democratic opponent. By the time the information was public, the deadline for challenging nominating petitions had expired, so there was nothing anyone could do about it. The fact that her father had to ask her if she'd heard about it highlighted the gulf between them.

"The truth is, I knew about it before it was public," he continued. "About a week after our papers were filed. I'll never forget the look on the staffer's face when he told me. My jugular was fully exposed. If I had been knocked off the ballot for a rinky-dink mistake like that, I would have been finished."

She looked at him.

"And you know what was the first thing that went through my mind? The very first thought, after the staffer told me? As I was looking at the end of my political career?"

She blinked. Her eyes cast down on the carpeting.

"I thought how pleased that would make *you,* Michelle Ingrid."

She watched him a moment, staring out the window, rubbing a hand over his neck. She grabbed her bag and headed for the door. "Goodbye, Dad," she said.

55

Ready

THE GUARD BOLTED Alex's cuffs onto the table. Shelly realized that she could no longer remember what Alex used to look like before everything went south for him, the radiance in his expression, the gentleness in his manner, the humor. She moved to him and kissed him on the cheek. It brought a measure of life to his face.

"How you holding up, kiddo?" she asked.

He nodded. He was a bit disarmed, she could see.

"You know about the F.B.I. bust?"

He nodded. Shelly showed him the list of names of the people arrested. "Do you know any of these people?"

Alex directed his focus on the sheet with an intensity she had not seen in him before. He sat back. "No."

"You seem relieved."

"I thought the guys at McHenry Stern would go down."

"Oh." She hadn't thought about that. "The guys you supplied at work."

"Yeah."

That made sense, perhaps, that the F.B.I. left them alone. First, because they hadn't arrested—and wouldn't be arresting—Alex, which could lead to some sticky cross-examinations at trial. Second, because these guys were buying three to five ounces a week, which was far beneath what normally interested federal agents. They might, on the other hand, refer the case to the state prosecutors.

"I don't know any of those folks on this list," Alex said.

"Okay." That might or might not be okay. Shelly might well prefer that Alex was on a first-name basis with all of the crooked cops and gangbangers. "So listen, Alex. We have ten days until trial. We've got two different theories we've talked about. We have to make a call. At least between us, we do. I might be able to play some games up there, but we have to be straight what we're doing."

His chest heaved. "Okay, so what do you think?"

She had taken the seat nearest him. How was this for an icebreaker? "I know that Ronnie is my son and not you."

His mouth opened.

"Don't—please, Alex. Just don't deny it, okay? I saw it for myself." She focused on the table and kept talking, to take the spotlight off Alex while she exposed his undeniable dishonesty. "You had your reasons, I assume. You wanted me fully invested in this case. But I still am. I'll do anything I can for you. I would have all along, by the way. But anyway. That's done. So let's put that behind us. Okay?"

She saw the pain in Alex's face, saw him begin to burst forth with a string of apologies that were probably near the surface for a long while. He spent the next ten minutes apologizing and explaining. Shelly had already forgiven him and repeatedly assured him of that fact.

Finally, if for no other reason than time being short, she slapped her hand on the table. "Apology accepted. Let's move on." She looked at him. "Ready to move on?"

He laughed.

"This next part isn't quite as funny. If we claim that you're innocent—that you didn't do it—then we have to play this game. I was in here before, saying it was the Cannibals. You say no, and that handcuffs me. I have to give them someone, right? The jury has to have some reason to think that someone else was in that alley."

His face hardened. He was following the map now.

"No," he said.

"Ronnie was there, Alex. I know it and I can't shake out my mind and suddenly *not* know it. I know he was there, as sure as I'm sitting here."

"No. Shelly, no."

"Alex, you have to hear me out. You have to hear me out or I have to withdraw as your lawyer."

That seemed to get his attention.

"I have a conflict now. I think someone else could be responsible, but that someone is related to me. So the only way I can be your lawyer is if you say it's okay. You have to let me tell you everything I think, and then we have to talk about it. So just shut up, okay?"

Alex folded his arms, fuming.

"I think Ronnie was there. I think after the shooting, you ran to his car, and after you drove away, you switched clothes. You switched clothes so the incriminating evidence wouldn't be on you. The blood. The gunpowder. Ronnie took your clothes, and the gun, and he drove somewhere and dumped them. That's why the cops never found the murder weapon. Or your hat or coat, for that matter. You were wearing Ronnie's leather jacket when you were caught."

She could see, from the sheepish look on his face, that she was right.

"He left you behind because you were already made. Sanchez knew you. So this was the best he could do."

"That's crazy," Alex said halfheartedly.

"You hurt your knee that night," she said. "You fell and hurt your knee. You could hardly move right after. That's how Miroballi was able to catch you. And there's no way you could have gotten half a mile away with the city police descending on the scene. Unless Ronnie had driven you."

She could see Alex's mind race. He seemed unable to concede. "Well, if we were switching clothes and all that to hide the stuff on me, that means I shot him."

"Yes, it does. Or I'm missing something. But remember what I said, Alex. I don't have to prove anything. If I can put Ronnie at the scene, it might be enough for reasonable doubt." She ticked off the points. "Two boys in the alley. No murder weapon to be found anywhere. You were tested for the presence of gunpowder residue and it was inconclusive. So why is it any more likely that it was you than Ronnie? That might be reasonable doubt right there. Especially if I can add more to the story, which I can." She dropped her hands on the table. "We've seen Ronnie on the west side, Alex. We've seen him with Eddie Todavia. I don't think they were getting together to play bingo."

"Bullshit."

"Which means, at a minimum, that he was selling drugs. It might also mean that he's working with the Cannibals. Let me finish," she said as he began to protest. "So take that, and take Officer Sanchez's belief that you were a snitch for Miroballi who had tipped off the Cannibals and, to me, that just means that you confided in Ronnie what you were doing. And he told the Cannibals." She held up her hands. "Or something like that. I don't know and I don't have to connect every dot. I just have to come close and it's over, I think."

Alex had been shaking his head. "You're wrong and I won't agree to that. I'll say it differently at trial. I'll contradict that. How many times do I have to tell you that I shot the guy? I did it. If you put Ronnie there, you just take him down with me. They'll say he was an accessory, right?"

She tapped the table. "Alex, you have to agree that you want me as your lawyer, even though I suspect another boy who happens to be my son."

"I want you to be my lawyer if you don't say he did it."

"That's a different subject. Are you willing to waive the conflict?"

"Whatever. Yeah. I don't care about that. Because he had nothing to do with this, Shelly."

She sat back in her chair.

"Someone's gotta take care of Angela," he said.

Oh. That hadn't occurred to her. Alex might have figured that his goose was cooked—they'd nail him for something; he'd have to do at least some time in jail—and he could trust Ronnie to watch out for little Angela. But if Ronnie went down, too, there'd be no one to help Mary Ellen raise the child.

So *that* was it. Sure.

"You gotta agree that you won't say anything like that at trial, Shelly. That you won't make Ronnie out to be the bad guy."

She thought it through as objectively as she could—making

the case in her mind that self-defense was preferable to pointing the finger at Ronnie. Alex would sabotage any attempt by her to implicate Ronnie. She could make all the suggestions she wanted at trial, but Alex would insist, as he had just said, on testifying, and he would take the fall. In the end, Shelly would have hurt her credibility with a confused jury.

It wouldn't work. That door was closed to her.

And self-defense appeared to be wide open. Talk about a ripe moment to be accusing a cop of narcotics trafficking and fear of the F.B.I. catching him! She thought of yesterday's media coverage of the drug sting. Today's follow-up. It was all over the news. She couldn't have scripted it better. In truth, she *had* scripted it somewhat; she always had planned on this, but she hadn't expected the magnitude of the news coverage.

Dan Morphew would do his best to exclude jurors who had read about the F.B.I. sting. But good luck finding twelve people who hadn't heard. He would be stuck with their lame promises of keeping an open mind and not being influenced. That was fine. The point was, when she came at them talking about dirty cops selling drugs, they'd be nodding their heads. She would put the indicted cops on the witness stand, the F.B.I. agent, the federal prosecutor, and Alex would ride a wave of anti-police sentiment to an acquittal.

Yes. She could feel it now. It made sense. She felt a flood of relief. There would be nothing to gain by putting Ronnie at the scene, so she wouldn't. He would be irrelevant to this case. This would be the same thing it always was. A case of self-defense.

"Alex, I do need something from you," she said. "All of this that we've discussed about Ronnie. You can't talk to him about it." She pointed upward. "They can listen in. You'll be tipping them off."

He looked up, then around the room. "Right."

"The part about Ronnie being my son—I'd appreciate it if you didn't mention that, either. For the same reason. But it's more selfish on my part. I'd rather do that on my own terms."

"He doesn't know you know."

"Not at this point. I'd like to handle that in the—"

He waved her off. "Do whatever. I won't say anything. I

won't embarrass you like that, Shelly. I never would. I'm—I'm really sorry I lied about that. I was scared, you know?"

She put a hand on his. "I know. Forget about it." She removed some files from her bag. "Now we have a lot to go over. So let's get started."

56

Suspect

SHELLY USED ONE of the law firm's conference rooms so she could spread out. She had a master checklist on the windowsill that listed every single item she had to accomplish before trial began. She had checked off many, but by no means all, of the tasks. Serving trial subpoenas on all the witnesses, including all of the newly indicted members of the criminal drug conspiracy courtesy of the F.B.I. That was one of the few tasks she could delegate; Joel Lightner had a guy who did process serving. She had legal research to perform, and pretrial motions to draft that were due three days from now. She had already prepared most of her trial examinations—directs of her witnesses and crosses of the prosecution's people. She had a stipulation from Dan Morphew's office on cause of death, manner of death, and distance between the victim and the assailant, which the county coroner estimated to be about five feet.

She had considered the notion of a plea bargain. She knew the prosecutor was willing to talk, that much was obvious, but Dan Morphew had been right—they couldn't lie down. The best she could hope for, she assumed, was something in the range of twenty to twenty-five years. That had been Paul Riley's assessment as well. Twenty years would be a gift. She knew that. For killing a police officer? And with good time, that number was really ten years. But that assumed two things. First, that the prosecution would come that far down. Second, that Alex could last even ten years in hard time. She had serious doubts about that.

She had worked through it in her mind. He would be twenty-seven when he was released. He would still have a life, and she would see to it that he had opportunities. He would change, irrevocably. But he would still have a chance to go on. He was a smart, resourceful kid. He would probably find some way to survive inside. He was white, and he was close enough to handsome, so it wouldn't be easy. But he would also be a cop-killer. That would buy him something, she assumed.

She shook her head free of these thoughts. She looked at the spreadsheet she had made of all the police officers and others arrested in the undercover sting. Her first task, with Joel and Paul's assistance, had been to group the officers by geography. The police department divided the city into "areas," which were then divided into "precincts." The relevant portion for the purposes of the F.B.I. sting was Area Four. Four of the six indicted city cops, including the sergeant, were assigned to the first precinct of Area Four. The other two officers were assigned to the second, which included the Eduardo Andujar projects and extended to the city's downtown. These officers were named Leonard McArdle and Peter Otis.

Officers Raymond Miroballi and Julio Sanchez were also in the second precinct, along with McArdle and Otis. That explained why the F.B.I. and federal prosecutors had been looking at Miroballi (and presumably Sanchez). They worked in one of the tainted precincts.

She needed to put Miroballi next to the indicted cops, McArdle and Otis. That was one of the many responsibilities she had placed on Joel Lightner, who had been required to go outside his small agency of investigators to hire other private eyes he knew. Shelly didn't want to guess how much all of this would cost Paul Riley's firm, who was footing the bill. Probably a six-figure number, she estimated, when all was said and done. It was against everything she knew to accept such charity, but in the end, it wasn't for her, it was for Alex, and she had no other options. Lucky for her the senior partner was sweet on her.

She got up from her seat and grabbed the file on Eddie Todavia. Morphew had informed her the other day that he was adding Todavia to his witness list. She even remembered his smart-ass follow-up—"Ring a bell?"—which told her that Morphew knew that Shelly had paid Todavia a visit as well. Two days ago, Morphew sent over, by messenger, a copy of a plea agreement between Eddie Todavia and the county attorney. Once they learned about Todavia, the police had sat on him until they could catch him doing something illegal, which must not have been very long. The caught him selling ten grams of crack cocaine on the street and moved in on him.

Then they had him. He wasn't a first offender. This could mean real time for him. So he did what anyone would do in his position—he got creative. In exchange for his testimony in the case of *People v. Baniewicz,* Edward Todavia would receive a get-out-of-jail-free card. Shelly held the plea agreement in her hand. Todavia was being held, pending the trial, in protective custody, and the county attorney would agree to time served when the trial was over.

```
Mr. Todavia will testify that he sold crack co-
caine to the defendant on several occasions
over the last two years in amounts far beyond
personal consumption. He will testify that the
defendant spoke with him about his relationship
as a confidential informant with Officer Raymond
Miroballi. He will testify that he is affiliated
with a street gang known as the Columbus Street
Cannibals.
```

Shelly had already dispatched Joel Lightner to speak with Todavia again. This second conversation, as Joel had put it, was "decidedly less friendly." Todavia, emboldened by his agreement with the police, had refused to speak with Joel at all. His only communicative gesture, Joel had reported, was a middle finger extended upward.

Shelly didn't know how the cops found out about Todavia. Probably it was just good police work. She conceded the possibility that they had found Todavia because Shelly had. The people following Shelly and Joel that day, in other words, were county attorney investigators or cops, not feds. It was not technically illegal for law enforcement to follow around defense attorneys.

Had Shelly led them right to Todavia's door? It was too painful to consider. And unhelpful, at this point, anyway. There was another question burning her mind at that moment.

If they were watching Todavia, did they see Ronnie with him?

She looked up when she heard a knock on the door. Speak of the devil. Ronnie Masters looked like he had just come from school, wearing a buttoned-down shirt and jeans, a navy backpack slung over his right shoulder. The weather had finally broken as June arrived, not the typical seventies but warm enough that Ronnie didn't need the ratty hooded sweatshirt he'd been wearing. That thought brought her back to his presence in the alley that night, the switch of the clothes.

"Hey there," he said.

"Hi." She had forgotten that Ronnie was scheduled to stop by today. He dropped his schoolbag and looked over what she was doing.

She looked him over as well. This was her son. Now there was none of the uncertainty. Had that been it with Alex? Had there been some lingering, unconscious doubt in her mind? Was that why she had been unable to deal with it? She didn't know the answer. She probably never would. But as she looked at this boy—a sizeable kid, the same blue eyes as her father, now that she thought about it, the high hairline from Abigail Trotter's side of the family—she had no doubt. It *felt* right, too. He *seemed* like her son. Could a mother really have such a sensation? Her mind, trained for logical discipline, told her no. Everything else said yes.

This boy was a drug dealer? A gangbanger? It didn't wash. She just couldn't imagine it.

Ronnie helped himself to a seat at the opposite end of the conference room. "So how's it going? Haven't talked to you lately."

"Sorry," she said. "Closer it gets, the busier it gets."

"You heard about the cops being arrested?"

She couldn't suppress a smile. That piece of news had more or less consumed her for the past forty-eight hours.

He opened his hands. "So do I get to hear what's going on? It's hard not knowing."

"Things are going fine," she said. "This thing with the cops being arrested has diverted me somewhat. But we're getting there."

He looked around the room, at the banker's boxes, the accordion files, the piles of paper. "Looks like you need my help again."

"Yeah, I might. We'll see."

"Are you gonna call me as a witness?" he asked.

"Don't know." She busied herself with the papers in front of her.

"Well, you know." He gestured with his hands. "You always said we were gonna prepare or whatever."

"We will, if I need you. I'm not sure I will." She stacked some files together and placed them to the side. She sneaked a peek at Ronnie. He was clearly dissatisfied. He was being kept at bay and he didn't like it. He had always volunteered to help, from day one, and no one had taken him up on it. Shelly looked on these offers now with a newfound skepticism. Ronnie certainly had wanted to keep a watch on things, and now she wanted to keep a watch on him.

He was handsome in the same way that her father was. It wasn't that either of them had magazine-cover features. It was the way they all came together. He would be tall and wide, with a strong face. What else he would be—or was—she did not know. She couldn't even begin to imagine all of the things that she would never know about him.

She knew it now. They had rules for lawyers for a reason. She could never accuse this boy of murder, or even hint at it. Thank God that self-defense was the way that made sense.

Her cell phone rang.

"Shelly, it's Joel. Does the name Robert Eldridge mean anything to you?"

"No."

"He lives in Julian Park."

"No, Joel. Why?"

"Ronnie went to see him last night."

She looked at Ronnie. He had opened up his backpack and removed his cell phone, punched some buttons. He probably had a nicer model than she did, not because he had more money, but because he had probably hunted down a deal on the Internet.

Shelly had just walked into a store and picked up the first one she saw.

"This guy Eldridge works at a consulting firm," Joel continued on the phone. "He's divorced. That's all I know at this point. We just saw him last night. Ronnie went into this guy's house for about fifteen minutes and then left."

Ronnie turned away from Shelly as he listened to his messages.

"Find out whatever you can," she told Joel.

"We will. We'll figure out this guy's story."

Ronnie put down his phone and looked at Shelly.

"That kid is acting weird, Shelly," said Joel. "He's up to something."

"Good, that sounds great, Joel," she said, watching Ronnie. "Keep up the good work. And, Joel? You're just talking to me about this, right?"

"Yeah, of course."

"Good. Keep it that way."

She heard Joel Lightner laugh on the other end of the phone. "That prosecutor's gonna have indigestion when he sees those photos of Ronnie hanging out with Eddie Todavia. Have you sent them to him yet?"

"Not yet," she answered.

Not ever, she now knew.

She clicked off her phone and looked at Ronnie. He was looking at the list of police officers that Shelly had made, with their divisions into precincts, as well as the list of the others arrested in the sting.

"We have to talk," she said to him.

PART THREE

Guilt

57

Subtraction

"THIS IS SHELLY," she said into the phone.

"Shelly. Jerod Romero."

"Hello, Jerod. Did you get the trial subpoena?"

"Sure did, Counselor."

Shelly was in the conference room where she had spread out. She welcomed the chance to stand and stretch her legs. Her back and neck ached. She felt out of sorts physically and mentally. She had gone weeks without physical exercise, where normally she rarely went a day without breaking a sweat.

"Do you really plan on calling me?" Romero asked. "You're calling Peters, too?"

She closed her eyes. Surely, this couldn't be a surprise to the federal prosecutor. Which meant he had a different reason for calling. "You were the ones who grabbed Alex," she said.

"I'm sure this guy Morphew will stipulate that we picked up Alex and flipped him," he said.

Morphew. So Dan Morphew had contacted Romero. She would have loved to have been a fly on the wall for that conversation.

"I guess I was hoping for a little more detail than that," she tried.

"Alex and Miroballi met a couple of times," Romero said. "That's about all I can tell you. That's all we ever knew, besides what your client told us. I told you before—we hadn't built a case against Miroballi."

This wasn't going well. Romero could add a little to that story if he were feeling generous. She thought she had left things with him on a positive note.

"Only, Ms. Trotter"—the tone in Romero's voice, along with the formality, signaled a bit of tension in his attitude—"it seems that the county attorney has a different take on those meetings."

"They're going to say what they have to say."

"Well, I was certainly interested," said Romero. "Alex was an unregistered confidential informant working for Miroballi?"

"That's not true."

"No?" Romero cleared his throat.

"Surely," Shelly said, "you don't know that to be true."

"I don't know it to be untrue, either. And now I'm beginning to see why you wanted to get him immunity from us."

"Jerod—"

"Your client lied to federal agents, Counselor. He made up a song-and-dance when we caught him with drugs. We spent time and resources on that kid. We redirected manpower on that kid. Your boy had us chasing our tails."

"No," she insisted. "That's a load of crap. You don't know that to be true."

"I told you then, I'll tell you now," said Romero. "I knew that kid wasn't being straight with us. The moment we grabbed him, suddenly there's no more conversations with Miroballi. The pipeline goes dry, the moment we catch him."

"That's because Miroballi found out." Now she was giving her closing argument.

"Well—that's fine, Shelly. That's your argument. Go with it and good luck. You ask me, was this kid being strong-armed to sell drugs for Miroballi, or was he Miroballi's informant? I tell you, could be either one. You put me on the stand, I'll say that. Peters will, too. These F.B.I. agents, Shelly, they don't like being lied to."

"Nobody was being lied to," she responded, realizing as she did that Jerod Romero had hung up the phone.

"Well, great," she said, holding the phone at her side. She would cross those witnesses off her list. It wasn't a major loss. And thank God that she had gotten that immunity for Alex—his silence prior to the F.B.I. bust in exchange for a walk. That had been Ronnie's idea, actually, she recalled, one of the few contributions the kid had actually made. Shelly was confident that the immunity agreement would hold, despite Jerod Romero's bluster. He was free of the federal government's reach. But if Romero's reaction to Morphew's argument were any indication, Alex Baniewicz might have a shade more trouble with the state's case.

58
Peers

SHELLY SAT AT the defense table and maintained a pleasant expression as her stomach screamed out at her. Alex Baniewicz was seated next to her, in a blue suit, shirt, and tie. She'd given him more than one pep talk over the last week about his behavior in front of the jury. The majority of the conversation had come from Alex, questions about this or that. Should he smile? Should he look bored?

The most important thing, she had told him, was to maintain a firm belief at all times in his innocence.

She was absolutely exhausted, like she typically was as a trial began. She was not one of those who slept well before trial. It was not a lack of confidence in her abilities but the ever-present uncertainty that a trial brought. Especially a criminal case. She had spoken with every witness and tried to map out every contingency, but without the ability to question the witnesses under oath before trial, it was impossible to be fully prepared. Even when you *could* do that, as in civil cases, there was no getting around the fact that something would happen at trial that you didn't expect.

She had tried in vain to interview each of the individuals arrested by the federal government in the drug sting. Each of them had retained counsel and there was no way they were talking. It was hardly surprising, but she had given it the old college try, nonetheless.

She also had named them all to her trial list and served subpoenas on them. Dan Morphew had objected to the late witness disclosures. Shelly had argued that she couldn't identify any of these people until the arrests were made, so how *could* she have disclosed them? She also argued that Morphew's inclusion of Eddie Todavia was just as tardy. At least be consistent, then, she urged. Morphew had argued that his people had just discovered Todavia and added that Shelly already knew about him, because she had interviewed him before they even knew who he was.

Judge Dominici had allowed Todavia to be called by the state but decided to reserve ruling on Shelly's witnesses until the defense case, a common practice among judges. Leave some uncertainty out there, give the lawyers incentive to settle the case.

Judge Dominici did not allow counsel to question prospective jurors; he took that task upon himself. So Shelly had to sit and take notes. Her job would be to watch the potential jurors, whether they were being questioned at the time or not. She would keep an open mind, and look for facial expressions, body language, choice of words, to suggest any inclination toward or against her client. She had made columns on her pad of paper, one for jurors that she wanted, another for those she didn't want, and a third for those where she wasn't sure. She would write a few notes next to each juror number for a quick reminder. She had given Alex a similarly organized notepad so he would have something to occupy his hands. Plus, he seemed like he had pretty good instincts. A savvy client could be a useful asset.

They sat alone, the two of them. No team of lawyers here. The one person who had lent a hand administratively—Ronnie Masters—was a potential witness, so he could not be at the trial until he was called, if he was called. Technically, he could attend jury selection, but he hadn't been invited at any rate.

Nor would he ever be invited to the courtroom, at least not by Shelly. She put her certainty in that fact at about ninety-nine percent—allowing for the possibility that something could happen that she hadn't predicted. Possibly Ronnie might corroborate Alex's testimony that he was being squeezed by Ray Miroballi, but that was almost certainly inadmissible hearsay.

Each juror was provided a questionnaire seeking basic information—race, age, family, prior service as a juror, criminal record. Shelly and Dan Morphew had supplemented the questionnaire with certain other questions, mostly related to drug use and associations or encounters with the city police force.

First and foremost, however, Judge Dominici addressed the entire bunch on the question of the death penalty. This was a capital case, and people who were opposed to capital punishment on principle—who would never, under any circumstances, vote for death—could not serve on the jury because they were incapable of following the law, the weighing of aggravating and mitigating factors. That, to Shelly, was a considerable loss, not so much because of how these people would vote on the sentence but because of how they would vote on the verdict. People who opposed the death penalty typically carried with them a healthy suspicion of the criminal justice system overall. These were the people who would look for shades of gray in a black-and-white system. These were the ones who would prevent there ever *being* a sentencing phase.

She wished like hell she could do the questioning herself. She had trouble sitting still in the face of action, longed for the adrenaline of the fight. Instead, she sat with a nervous stomach, reassuring her client and making notes as to each juror.

Lawyers were given unlimited challenges to jurors "for cause"—reasons that justified their exclusion from the jury. Each lawyer was allowed five "peremptory" challenges as well, which were essentially freebies. A lawyer could kick out a juror for any reason at all, except for race or gender—the Supreme Court had ruled those two traits to be unconstitutional bases for excluding jurors. Race and gender were the obvious ones, but Shelly assumed that it wouldn't be long before other characteristics—national origin, religion, sexual orientation—would join them. Ten years from now, she figured, there would be no such thing as a peremptory challenge.

None of those characteristics were particularly relevant in this case. White cop, white defendant. Most criminal defense lawyers never met a minority juror they didn't like. The thought was, minorities suffer more abuse from law enforcement than whites and are therefore more skeptical of any prosecution. That was probably true, but Shelly had had enough experience with families in the minority community to pull back the reins on that notion. Some of the most conservative people she had ever met were African American or Latino. Yes, all things being equal, she'd rather have a minority than a white on the jury, but things were not equal. Especially here, where her client was Caucasian; a minority who felt that cops discriminated against them would tend to think that if they were prosecuting a white kid, there must be a good reason.

The jurors seemed like a mixed lot in every respect. Some seemed annoyed to be in the courtroom, others curious, if not impressed, by the spectacle. Some of them might even know that this was that cop-killer case they'd read about some time back. Shelly was undecided, as a generalization, whether she wanted city folk or suburbanites. City dwellers who had experienced unpleasant run-ins with the city police, of course, were more than welcome, but a lot of city residents got along just fine with police. Some suburbanites looked down on the city and would find it perfectly plausible that city cops were dirty. Others, especially those who considered the city as remote to them as Australia despite the fact it was only an hour away, probably hadn't given the subject much thought. Again, there was no set rule, and the lawyers who relied on them were just being lazy. Go with your gut, was Shelly's rule.

Still, she found herself recording the race of each of the first thirty jurors escorted into the courtroom: fourteen were white, seven black, five Latino, three Asian, and one Native American. That seemed to be an unusually high representation of minorities for a county that was still predominantly white. She assumed that this made Dan Morphew and his bunch—there were two other lawyers and what appeared to be a paralegal helping him—unhappy.

The publicity of the federal government's arrest of the six city officers would help Shelly immensely. No doubt, the vast majority of the jury pool had read the accounts. Stories had been splashed on the front page of the *Watch* for a good three or four days, and follow-ups were still present now and then. The city's police superintendent had been pressured to resign but resisted. He had appointed a task force to investigate corruption in the police department which, as far as Shelly could tell, had not yet done anything. Below the superintendent, some heads had fallen. None of these developments over the last week were directly relevant to her case, but they had served to keep the issue front and center in the media.

Jury selection began. Potential jurors always seemed to enjoy the questioning. Having people ask you about your life, your interests, and having the attention of a room was flattering to almost anyone. Shelly saw this in juries and she saw this in witnesses, whether at trial or in civil depositions. People liked being the center of attention.

That was not to say that a number of the potential jurors didn't want out. A week out of one's life, if not two weeks, could be taxing on anyone. One woman was over eight months pregnant and feared an early delivery. An attorney claimed he had a week's worth of depositions next week. A woman who owned a small printing company, a man who managed a catering company, complained that their companies would suffer in their extended absence. Shelly put these jurors in her "Yes" column because anyone antsy to leave would resent the prosecution more than the defense. In a self-defense case, the prosecution would likely have a lengthy rebuttal to disprove the defense's case, which would mean that they, not Shelly, would be blamed for dragging this out.

Judge Dominici paid considerable attention to the F.B.I. sting in his questions. Shelly intently followed how he handled this issue, because it gave insight to his opinion on the impact of that case. The judge noted that all of those people arrested by the feds were presumed innocent, and did they understand that the mere fact that they were arrested did not mean that they were guilty? What conclusions had they drawn from the media coverage? Did they understand that their judgment of Alex Baniewicz had to be based only on evidence that they heard in this courtroom? Were they capable of keeping an open mind?

The good news for Shelly, and the problem for Morphew, was that most people, if asked, would answer that they could keep an open mind. How many people would admit that they were so inflexible that they would take accusations of the U.S. Attorney as true without carefully considering the evidence in this case? Nobody would admit that, to a judge or to themselves. What was undeniable, however, was that this information influenced them. Shelly had instant credibility now accusing a cop of selling drugs and intimidating someone like Alex. Dan Morphew couldn't just roll his eyes at the jury and say that's-what-they-all-say. Not after a federal sting that netted six dirty cops.

Judge Dominici finished questioning the first panel of thirty citizens by three o'clock. Shelly had been putting the panel members into her three categories, and she had found thirteen of them acceptable and three others neutral. Sixteen were okay with her. Four jurors had been excused by the judge on the spot. That left ten she did not want. Those ten she would challenge for cause, which meant she would have to make an argument to the judge for why they were unacceptable. If the judge disagreed, she had the option of exercising one of her peremptory challenges. You had to use those sparingly, because they were not unlimited.

She exchanged her list with Dan Morphew during a ten-minute recess. Morphew found eleven citizens to be acceptable, and Shelly quickly looked for overlap with her list. Eight, by her count. Yes. Eight of them had been found acceptable by both sides. That number was high, in her experience, and she was sure that this overlap hit Dan Morphew the same way it landed in the pit of her stomach—what were they missing, if the other side liked the person, too?

After all of their arguments to the judge for dismissal for cause, nearly all of which were rejected by the judge, the parties exercised their peremptory challenges. Morphew used them on four candidates, all of whom were minorities. Shelly objected and requested a *Batson* hearing, which meant that Morphew had to articulate a nondiscriminatory reason for rejecting these people. It was a game that had become standard since the Supreme Court outlawed race-based exclusions. If nothing else, Shelly was preserving her record here. If she lost this case, she wanted to have this issue for appeal.

The judge found Morphew's reasons acceptable. By the time it was all said and done, the entire jury was chosen from the first set of thirty people. Morphew raised his eyebrows at Shelly. They both knew that this was unusual, but they each had to trust their instincts.

In the end, the jury consisted of seven whites—four women,

three men—and five African Americans—four men and one woman. The two alternates were Asian and Native American men.

"Opening statements tomorrow," said the judge. "Mr. Morphew, you expect to take about three days?"

"That's correct, Judge."

"Your Honor," said Shelly, "the defense would like to defer its opening."

Morphew looked at her. He had been curious, no doubt, about recent developments. She had pleaded self-defense from day one. Seasoned prosecutor that he was, that didn't stop him from preparing to prove his case. Regardless of any affirmative defense the defendant pleaded, the prosecution still had to prove guilt beyond a reasonable doubt, and *then* disprove any affirmative defense beyond a reasonable doubt as well. So he might have expected this move by Shelly: stay quiet and make sure the prosecution could prove its case before arguing self-defense to the jury.

Shelly had been disappointed that Dan Morphew had not tried to re-engage her in plea discussions after she had dropped the bombshell about Alex's involvement with the F.B.I. in its undercover sting. In her estimate, Morphew's case had been substantially weakened with this disclosure—why hadn't *he* thought so? Maybe he was worried. Maybe he was following the lawyer's creed of not bidding against oneself—it was truly Shelly's turn to come forward with a counteroffer. She wouldn't do that, because she didn't want to settle this case. She just wanted to hear Morphew ask again.

"The defense will defer its opening, okay," said Judge Dominici. He wrote something down. "Ms. Trotter? What is the longest your defense case might take?" The question was asked with the understanding that there might be no defense, and that the defense could stop at any time. Or, she thought fleetingly, the judge could throw out the charges after the prosecution's case.

"The longest is seven days," she said. This was a high estimate. Shelly planned on calling every one of the sixteen people implicated in the drug sting. She would ask them several suggestive questions each. They would refuse to answer, invoking the Fifth Amendment. It would be like sixteen mini-closing arguments, because these witnesses wouldn't fight her. She could ask the most self-serving question imaginable and they wouldn't answer at all. *Did you work with Raymond Miroballi to protect drug dealers on the street? I decline to answer. Did Ray Miroballi tell you that he had discovered that Alex Baniewicz was working for the feds and needed to be eliminated? I decline to answer.*

Her job was to find some questions they *could* answer, something relevant that would give her an excuse to haul them into court. The jury would hear sixteen different witnesses taking five; they would have trouble *not* lumping Ray Miroballi in with them.

The twelve jurors and two alternates walked back in the room, one by one, and took seats in the jury box.

"Now for the bad news," the judge told them. Some of them laughed. Some of them groaned. They had already figured, when they were singled out to return to the courtroom, that they had been selected. They would go home tonight and tell their families that they were jurors on the cop-killing case that made the headlines a few months back. Their family members would make comments about the case, offer their opinions. Each of the jurors would make arrangements at work to let people know they were out of service for a week or two. Some would be in a hurry for the proceedings to end. Some would embrace their civic duty and take their roles seriously. They would bring a lifetime of world experiences into their job. They would try to be impartial, try to remember and weigh all of the evidence.

Tomorrow, they would begin to sit in judgment of Alex Baniewicz.

59

Snitch

SHELLY TAPPED HER feet nervously before the jury entered. She had worked over the prosecution's witnesses last night, with Paul Riley playing the witnesses and being an incredible pain in the ass about it. Which was exactly what she had needed.

Alex had been escorted into the courtroom at eight-thirty. He was in a gray suit—the one he already owned—and a white shirt and yellow tie. He looked right. Nothing flashy, and not the prison garb that implies guilt in the minds of the jurors. Subdued attire, highlighting Alex's good looks. He looked like a nice young man, which he was.

Dan Morphew didn't enter the courtroom until ten minutes to nine. His eyes were puffy and red but intense. He was in trial mode, like Shelly. Shelly hadn't slept particularly well either, and hadn't expected to, but she tried to lie still and close her eyes to at least get some rest. She was wearing a blue suit and cotton blouse, her hair pulled back into a clip.

The courtroom was full. There was only one color that filled the first three rows of the gallery. There were about forty uniformed police officers in their dress blue for the first day of trial. Reporters were present and camera crews awaited the proceedings outside the courtroom and in the lobby of the courthouse. The first day was always the biggest for the spectators and the media. Opening arguments were often the most dramatic moments of a trial, before settling into the tedium of witness questioning and admission of evidence, to say nothing of recesses and out-of-court arguments to the judge.

Shelly found herself searching through the rows, looking for someone. She made eye contact with a woman. She was somewhere in her late thirties. She was next to an older woman—her mother, it looked like. Their arms seemed interconnected such that, though it was out of her line of vision, she assumed they were holding hands. The woman was not classically pretty but there was a certain dignity about her, an inner peace that made her flat dark eyes come to life. Her brothers-in-law had been named as potential witnesses, so they would not be here. She had not brought her three children either, for obvious reasons. Sophia Miroballi did not direct hatred toward Shelly. It was more like resolve. She was here to see that justice was done for her husband.

And Shelly, with any luck, was going to rip her departed husband to shreds in front of her.

The Honorable Pietro Dominici entered the courtroom and called for the jury. They entered from an anteroom and took their seats. They seemed impressed with the full house, the rows of police officers showing their loyalty. Shelly smiled at the jurors, a subdued smile, nothing bright or whimsical. She would be pleasant but serious. Story of her life.

The judge instructed the jury that the opening statements were not evidence themselves but only predictions of what the lawyers expected to show. That was true, technically, but many lawyers believed that you won or lost a case in your opening statement. It was the jury's first impression of your arguments. If you didn't believe what you were saying with all your heart, then neither would the jury. If it didn't make sense, even when presented in its best light by the advocate, then it wasn't going to wash.

Shelly braced herself for the opening. She was accustomed to civil practice, where depositions and interviews were more plentiful, where a trial lawyer could predict virtually everything that would happen at trial. In the criminal setting, Shelly was divining the prosecution's theory from its responses to written questions, from the brief conversations she had with witnesses, and from the evidence that the prosecution intended to submit.

A more blunt way to say it was, Shelly was guessing. An educated guess, yes, but still nothing but an estimate. She had to expect that Dan Morphew would say things in the opening that would surprise her. This was why they called it "courtroom theater."

"Mr. Morphew," said the judge.

"Thank you, your Honor. May it please the Court? Ms. Trotter." Dan Morphew was on his feet, nodding in Shelly's direction. He carried a notepad with him, though he seemed to have notes written only on the first page. He did not use a podium as he stood before the jury, holding the pad of paper at his side. He might not score huge points for presentation, but he apparently didn't care. Most prosecutors didn't. They had the facts, truth, and justice on their side, and no one mistook them for the high-priced, expensively dressed trial lawyers that occasionally made their way into the courts for a client who could pay. No flash, all substance, would work just fine for a guy like Morphew.

He placed an enlarged photograph of Raymond Miroballi in full police dress on a tripod. The photo was from several years earlier, showing Miroballi with a proud expression, his thinning dark hair neatly combed, his mouth settled in contentment.

Morphew walked over to a large tape recorder and hit a button. A voice boomed out, the distressed voice of Officer Julio Sanchez filling the suddenly quieted room.

"Dispatch, we have an officer down. Officer down. Officer— we have an—oh, God, Ray."

The jurors recoiled, some closing their eyes, others looking away, wincing as they listened to a police officer calling for assistance for his slain partner. It was the tape from Sanchez to dispatch, which had been premarked and approved as evidence in this case. Shelly couldn't prevent Morphew from using it, even in his opening statement.

Morphew killed the recorder and stood before the jurors. He opened his hand to the photograph. "'Officer down,'" he said. "Words that bring a chill to every police officer. Words that bring a chill to every member of every police officer's *family*." He opened a hand to the enlarged photo. "You're looking at Officer Raymond Miroballi, a husband, a father of three, who lost his life on the evening of February eleventh of this year. What you just heard was his partner, running to him in a vain attempt to save him. He had no chance of saving him, ladies and gentlemen. Because Officer Miroballi, an officer who was trying to keep the streets safe from drugs and gangs, had been shot in the face by this defendant."

Morphew opened up toward Alex with these last words. There was another adverse reaction from the jury, pained expressions, looks of disgust. Most people didn't see violence like this up close. It was hard to imagine anyone being immune to the image of a bullet in the nose.

"Police Officer Raymond Miroballi grew up on the south side and lived there his whole life. He married his high school sweetheart when he graduated, and a few years later, he became a cop. He worked on the street. He worked in neighborhoods where cops aren't so popular. On February eleventh of this year, he was killed in the line of duty. He was shot in the face by a drug dealer. That drug dealer is sitting right there." He pointed at Alex. "We are bringing charges of first-degree and felony murder against that man, Alex Baniewicz."

The defense table was on the left side of the courtroom, and Shelly had positioned herself to Alex's left so that she could look at him as well as the jury. She looked at the jury but kept her eye on her client as well. Alex watched the prosecutor, then the jurors as if he had nothing to hide, and shook his head mildly.

She hadn't told him to shake his head, only to look the jurors in the eye without being threatening or defiant. He had to show them that he was without guilt, not without sympathy.

"At close to eight o'clock on the evening of February eleventh, Officers Raymond Miroballi and his partner, Julio Sanchez, were patrolling the city. The west side of the commercial district, near the train station. Specifically, Bonnard Street. They spotted the defendant, holding a gym bag and stuffing drugs into his pocket. So they stopped. Officer Miroballi got out to approach the defendant. And when Officer Miroballi left his vehicle, the defendant ran. He ran on foot, heading south, and turned down an alley."

The jury was taking notes. Morphew paused a moment.

"Officer Miroballi gave chase and found the defendant in the alley. Officer Miroballi told him to submit to arrest. He told the defendant to show his hands and submit. He didn't draw his weapon, ladies and gentlemen. Didn't pull out his gun. He wasn't looking for a shoot-out. He told the defendant to submit."

Morphew flapped his arms. "So what did the defendant do? He tricked Officer Miroballi. He pretended to submit. He dropped his gym bag, as the officer had instructed. He dropped the gun he had. Which meant that he had complied, right? Wrong. At that moment, the defendant pulled *another* gun from his jacket pocket and he shot Officer Raymond Miroballi in the face."

That was far more detail than she'd heard before. This had to have come from the homeless guy, Slattery, because he was the only one who said that he saw the shooting. But he hadn't said anything close to that to Shelly and Joel Lightner. Morphew had just explained the second gun. She had never played out this scenario in the way Morphew described it. And if it was true, it *was* smart. Alex had dropped his gun and made it look like he complied? Then he pulled out a second gun and shot him? If the person you want to kill is a cop, that's not a bad idea at all. And at this point, as trial had begun, it didn't matter if it was true. It mattered that it was believable.

Morphew turned to Alex again, wagging his finger with disdain. "Make no mistake. It was the defendant. You'll hear from Officer Julio Sanchez, who will tell you that it was the defendant who ran from Officer Miroballi. You will hear evidence that traces of Officer Miroballi's blood were found in the defendant's hair and on his shirt. It was him."

He strolled a step, not even peeking at the notepad he carried. "Now comes the why. Why did this happen? How did this happen?" He walked over to the blowup of Raymond Miroballi. "This was an officer who wanted to wipe out drugs on the street. He wanted to wipe out the people who made that happen. You want to catch drug dealers, you have to work with drug dealers. Sometimes they demand that you work with them confidentially. Confidential informants, you will hear, are an important part of the business of keeping the streets clean. The defendant was one of those confidential informants. The defendant sold cocaine."

Morphew had made sure to allow the jury access to Alex at this point. Most of them looked in his direction with less than pleasant looks on their faces. Shelly had the instant feeling that maybe she should not have held back her opening statement. It had the effect of giving her the element of surprise, but maybe she had overestimated that advantage. Morphew got to make the first impression here and she had no response.

"So Officer Miroballi used the defendant. You will hear testimony that the two of them met on a few occasions. Officer Miroballi was getting information from the defendant. Information about a particular street gang. A gang called the Columbus Street Cannibals."

Shelly had tried to exclude any mention of this gang prior to trial. Their horrific reputation would unfairly taint her client, she had argued. All Morphew had to do, however, was point to Eddie Todavia, who had admitted his affiliation and admitted that he supplied Alex with drugs. That was more than enough, even she had to privately concede.

Morphew shrugged. "Scary stuff. Officer Miroballi patrolled the neighborhoods where the Columbus Street Cannibals worked. Venice Avenue. The Andujar housing projects. The near west side. Part of his turf. He didn't like having gangs selling drugs on his street. He wanted to stop it. So he used someone who worked with the Cannibals." He pointed at Alex. "He used the defendant. He was going to use the defendant to infiltrate this gang. Maybe not take down the entire operation but put a dent in it. Do *something*."

He looked over the jurors. Morphew had an effective delivery, a flair for drama that complemented his unaffected presentation. "What's a cop's worst fear in this situation, folks? You're going after a major street gang and you're using a confidential informant. What's the worst thing that can happen?" He wagged a finger. "The worst thing that can happen is that your confidential informant turns on you. Tells the street gang about you."

That comment seemed to buy something with the jurors. A couple of them gave slow, knowing nods of their head. Morphew let that simmer a moment as he slowly moved to the witness stand. He dropped a hand on the wooden railing. "I wish to God we could put Officer Miroballi in this witness stand and ask him what he was thinking. I really do. All we can know is what he told his partner. He told his partner that the defendant was being dishonest with him."

"Judge, I have to object to the hearsay." Shelly barely got out of her seat and kept her volume low. She didn't want to seem discourteous and, more important, she didn't want to lend added weight to the comment by appearing to be concerned. But she *was* concerned, and she had to make her record.

The judge looked over his glasses down at Morphew. "I suppose, when the time comes, you'll have an argument on this point."

"It's offered only for state of mind, Judge."

"Well—" The judge adjusted his glasses. "Ladies and gentlemen of the jury, I have already told you that what you are hearing in opening statements is not evidence. It is not. We are talking here about a point of evidence, and I have not ruled on that yet. Whether these things Mr. Morphew speaks of will ever come in as evidence remains to be seen."

"Thank you, your Honor." The prosecutor returned to the jury. "That's what the night of February eleventh was all about. Officer Miroballi was concerned that his confidential informant was not telling him accurate information. That he was playing games with him. He wanted to talk to him. He wanted straight answers from this defendant."

Morphew nodded to his assistant, who hit the tape recorder again. Shelly recognized the words from the transcript. She had heard the tape, too, of Officer Raymond Miroballi calling to dispatch, out of breath:

"Dispatch, advise all units that suspect is armed. I repeat, suspect is armed."

Morphew pointed at the tape recorder. "Officer Miroballi knew that the defendant was armed. He knew it, and yet he *still* didn't draw his own weapon. That was probably not smart, in hindsight. But the evidence will show that he didn't draw his weapon on this armed boy because he wanted to reason with this boy. He didn't want to lose his informant. He needed him."

Morphew held out five fingers. "Five feet, ladies and gentlemen. Officer Miroballi was five feet from the defendant when he was shot. You will hear expert testimony on that point. Standing as close"—Morphew paced off the steps walking backward and stopped—"as close as I am right now to you in the front row. This close, and not holding his weapon. That, folks, is a man who wanted to talk to the defendant and only talk."

Shelly wanted to object to the argumentative nature of his comments but held back. Morphew certainly was arguing, and effectively so. He was arguing against self-defense without ever mentioning the words. That was smart. He could not be absolutely sure Shelly was ever going to argue the defense, and he didn't want to make a mark against his own case unnecessarily. So he couldn't come out and say the words, but he had to cover that base.

"We have people who will come into this courtroom and sit on this witness stand"—he moved to the witness railing again—"who will tell you that the defendant ran from Officer Miroballi. Who will tell you that he ran into an alley. That Officer Miroballi chased him in there but only wanted to talk. Never drew his weapon. That the defendant pretended to comply with the officer's wishes by dropping the gym bag he was holding and by dropping the gun he was holding. That the officer then approached him, and as he did so, the defendant removed a second firearm from his jacket pocket and fired on the officer. Shot him in cold blood. And then fled the scene." He walked over to the center of the jury panel. "We will ask you to return a verdict of guilty of murder in the first-degree. We will ask you to return a verdict of guilty for the offense of felony murder. We will ask you to deliver justice for Raymond Miroballi and his family."

Shelly pretended to write a note on her pad. She knew a lot of this beforehand. Some of the details of the shooting were new. But that didn't stop her from making a fresh assessment of the case, now that the words had been spoken, the reactions on the jurors' faces seen. Morphew had done well here. He was off to a strong start.

"Is the state prepared to call its first witness?" the judge asked.

She looked at Alex. He was following her instructions as best he could, which was to say that he remained quiet and rather void of emotion. But his face was ashen. Hearing someone say such things about you could be devastating. If they weren't true—and he had steadfastly denied that he was Miroballi's informant—then it would be utterly terrifying. But what bothered him the most, she assumed, was what bothered her the most. Everything Morphew had said had the ring of truth. Now that it had begun, Alex Baniewicz was feeling the weight of the world in a way previously unknown to him. It was worse than the arrest. Worse than the months of confinement. Now it was happening, the legal mechanism that would determine the rest of his life. She had tried to prepare him for it. She had told him that Morphew would state matters in the most damaging way possible. It won't get any worse than the opening statement, she had told him.

"The People call Edward Todavia," said Morphew.

She sensed that she was about to be proven wrong.

60

Sing

THE WITNESS WAS escorted into the courtroom by armed sheriff's deputies. That was interesting. Shelly had thought that Morphew might ask for a recess and have the witness brought in outside the presence of the jury. Dress him up, remove the shackles and armed escorts, then bring in the jury. But Morphew didn't ask for the jury to be excused. He let them see the deputies haul in this criminal.

Yeah, she probably would have done the same thing, now that she thought about it. What better way to taint a defendant than to show, in very real terms, that his associates are criminals?

Eddie Todavia was wearing a blue jumpsuit. She didn't know the different colors the Department of Corrections used for inmates, but she knew that he was not placed in general population. He still had the shaved head but it looked like he'd had a few days' growth, which made his head look dirty. Still the goatee. He wasn't a big guy but he had a menacing stare, a flat inflection to his voice that amplified the effect. A kid like that knew how to look tough. It was part of his job description.

He said his name for the record. Morphew fronted the arrest and plea agreement, the reason Todavia was here. The questions and answers provided ample detail. He was caught selling ten grams of crack cocaine to a sixteen-year-old boy on Green Street, south of Venice Avenue. City police officers and sheriff's deputies had converged on him. Todavia showed no hint of remorse or hesitation in describing these things. It wasn't pride in his actions but he probably saw something heroic in his arrest. She had seen that before in the kids she helped. There was a drama to the whole thing that captivated them. A badge of pride, to some of them.

He turned a little more reticent when he testified about the plea agreement. That, most definitely, was *not* a source of pride. Cut to the bone, this kid had gotten scared and narced.

"You're not happy to be here, are you, sir?" Morphew asked. He was at the podium placed between the defense and prosecution tables, back just enough so that Shelly's view of the jury was not blocked.

"Nope."

"You understand that if you don't tell the truth here, your plea agreement will be ripped up."

"Yeah, I got that."

"If you don't tell the truth, you could go away for ten years." He nodded.

"You have to give an audible answer, sir. You have to answer out loud."

He cocked his head. "Yeah, I got that."

Morphew pointed at Alex. "Do you know the defendant, Alex Baniewicz?"

"Yeah, I know him."

"Stipulate to identification," Shelly called out in a bored tone. She didn't need Alex to stand up and be singled out.

"Thank you, Counsel." The judge wrote something down.

"How is it that you know the defendant?"

"He's a customer of mine." They looked at each other. "I sold him coke."

"Cocaine."

"Right."

"When?"

"When," Todavia said, as if the question annoyed him. He opened a hand. "Like, 'bout January, maybe, last year."

"January of this year? Or of 2003?"

"2003."

That was about right. It was just after Alex's daughter had

been born, in late 2002, that Alex had decided to supplement his income through illicit means.

"How did this come about? How was it he came to you?"

"We go back. We went to high school together for a while."

"What school?"

"Southside. I's livin' with my mom then. Now I'm on my own." He shifted in his seat. He was slouching, going out of his way to seem unaffected, but it was hard to do so in the unforgiving wooden chair. "Alex comes to me, see. He says he needs some blow. He says he wants a hundo."

This was not hearsay, technically, because hearsay wasn't hearsay when it came from the mouth of the accused. State law exempted the admissions of a defendant from the hearsay rule, and that rule had been extended by the courts to apply to basically any word uttered by the defendant. In any event, she was likely to admit all of this anyway, when Alex took the stand.

"A hundred grams," the witness elaborated at the prosecutor's prompting.

"Did you give him a hundred?"

"No, man. Didn't have no credit with me, know what I'm sayin'? I gave him fifty. He gave me enough for about half that and he owed me." He nodded. "Boy paid me, though. Few months later. We started an arrangement."

"Tell us about the arrangement?"

He threw up a hand. "Boy wanted it all at once. I told him, keep it slow. But he wanted it all at once. I don't think"—he laughed—"don't think he liked comin' out to my 'hood."

She thought of moving to strike the testimony but kept quiet.

"So he would purchase one hundred grams of cocaine at a time from you?"

"Right. 'Bout every six months, he pays me for what he couldn't at first."

"So how often did he purchase this amount from you?"

"Twice, man, is all. First time, like I say, it was fifty then another fifty. Second time, I give him all hundred at once."

And he was caught with 74 grams of it. The cops had never found it, in their searches of his house and automobile, because it was sitting in a federal warehouse.

"When was that?"

"September or October, seems like. Last year."

That was also accurate. It was in November of last year that the feds caught Alex.

"Did you and the defendant ever talk about cops? Law enforcement?"

"Once."

"Where was this? When?"

Todavia rolled his neck. He was doing his best to look bored. He pursed his lips and looked up at the ceiling. "January," he said. "Six months ago."

Shelly froze. This was new, too. She looked at the state's disclosure of Todavia as a witness. It said that the witness would testify about Alex's relationship as a confidential informant with Miroballi. She had no basis for objecting to this, other than her general objection that the witness was disclosed too late, which she had made again before the witness even entered the room.

"January of this year?"

"Yeah. He comes to my house. Says he's got a problem."

"Judge." Shelly got to her feet, which she normally preferred not to do unless she wanted to be noticed, but she had an extended objection. "I don't want to keep interrupting. I want to make a running objection to the hearsay."

"Fine, Counsel. That will be overruled. Mr. Morphew?"

"What was the problem, Mr. Todavia?" Morphew asked.

"He says he's got a cop on his tail," said the witness. "Says this cop is tryin' to put a hole in the Cans."

"The Cans. The Columbus Street Cannibals?"

"Right."

"That's a street gang."

"Right."

"Are you a member?"

"Yeah, I'm C-Street."

"So go on, Mr. Todavia."

"Man, he says he's got this cop lookin' to be a hero, y'know? Says this cop is puttin' a pinch on him."

"Explain that to the jury, Mr. Todavia. A 'pinch,' if you would."

Shelly looked at the jury. She hadn't been watching them, entranced as she was by the witness's testimony. That had been a mistake. Always watch the jury with one eye. Theirs was the only opinion that counted.

Hard to read them, as always. Other than the high points, it was hard to know what was going through someone's head. She could say this much—they did not appear to be on the verge of inviting this kid over for tea. They saw him for what he was. Part of the problem. But that didn't mean he wasn't believable.

"He says to me, this cop has busted him. I say, okay, then take the hit and keep your mouth shut. But Alex, he says no, no. 'This guy wants me to help him,' he says."

"He's lying," Alex said to her, his volume somewhat above a whisper. She saw two of the jurors turn toward him.

"He says this cop is looking to take down the Cannibals. Y'know, make a name for hisself. He says this cop wants him to be, like, an informant or some such."

Morphew put out his hands as if framing the perfect summation. In doing so, he was highlighting the importance of the question. "The defendant told you that a certain police officer was trying to get his help to make a drug bust against the Cannibals?"

"That's what I'm sayin'. He was all upset and shit. He kept sayin', 'What am I gonna do? The guy's got me pinched.'"

"What did you say to him?"

"Told him to keep his mouth shut. Don't do it. Take the hit."

"And can you tell the jury what the defendant said to that, Mr. Todavia?"

Shelly steeled herself. Morphew had told Todavia to "tell the jury" for a reason. It was a device to get the jury's attention; this was something he wanted to be sure they heard. She could guess what was coming at this point, more or less.

Todavia wet his lips and looked at the jury. "This boy Alex, he says to me, 'I gotta get rid of this cop.'"

The gallery reacted to that. The jury did, too, scribbling in their notebooks.

"'I gotta get rid of this cop.' That's what the defendant said?" Morphew asked.

Shelly didn't write the words down, because she didn't want

the jury to see her giving them any credence whatsoever. She rolled her eyes, in fact, but she knew the jury wasn't watching her. She noticed Alex was sweating.

"It's okay," she whispered to him, and nodded for emphasis. She was hoping to convince herself as much as him.

61

Diversion

"OBJECTION, YOUR HONOR," Shelly managed, but there was enough noise in the courtroom that the judge didn't even hear her. So she stood. This was the last thing she wanted to do. Eddie Todavia had dropped a bombshell, and now she was highlighting that fact. The judge finally brought the courtroom back to order and nodded at Shelly.

"Unfair surprise," she said. "We were never given any notice of anything remotely like this—this so-called *statement*. The fact that we were never told about this statement is a disgrace. We have been ambushed."

"It's all there, your Honor." Morphew was referring to the witness disclosure. He was probably right. There was nothing specifically listed about this particular comment, but he was on good paper. There had been much talk around the state of changing the law and requiring every alleged admission by a defendant to be specifically listed before trial by the prosecution, but the legislation had stalled in the state's House of Representatives. So Morphew was under no requirement to list the words, "I gotta get rid of this cop" to Shelly.

They went back and forth with the judge. Shelly hoped, somehow, that she could distract the jury, but they weren't really listening. After a few exchanges, the judge called for a sidebar—a conversation outside the jury's presence but on the record. The court reporter picked up her transcription machine and met the judge and lawyers in the far corner of the courtroom behind the judge's bench, the corner opposite the jury. In hushed tones, the lawyers barked back and forth about the adequacy of the disclosure. The judge was not unsympathetic to Shelly. The disclosure had not been particularly forthcoming. But she had had the opportunity to talk to Todavia, even if he had refused to talk. She had talked to him prior to that, in fact.

"I'll be willing to give you a short recess before you cross, Counsel," the judge said. "Which is more than fair. But I'm not striking the testimony. Let's go back on."

All things considered, it had been about ten minutes since Todavia had testified to Alex's statement. She hoped in vain that the jury had focused their attention elsewhere during that time. She would have done a circus trick right there in the courtroom, if she could, to distract them. Juggling. Cartwheels. But the fact was, the jury had probably taken those ten minutes to let that testimony sink in nice and good.

I gotta get rid of this cop. If those words were spoken, they were not spoken by the boy that Shelly had come to know. Maybe he'd lied to her a time or two, but she couldn't fathom that Alex could speak so casually about committing homicide.

"All right, Mr. Todavia." Morphew resumed his position at the podium. He seemed energized now, and small wonder. "Before this break, you said that the defendant told you he needed to get rid of this cop."

"Yeah."

"Did he elaborate on that? Explain that at all?"

"Naw, man. I knew what he meant."

"Move to strike," Shelly said from her chair.

"That comment will be stricken," the judge said. He then asked the jury to disregard the statement, which was like telling someone to disregard that they had just been punched in the stomach.

Morphew walked over to a tripod and placed the photograph of Officer Raymond Miroballi on it. "Do you know this person?"

"Nope."

"Ever seen him?"

"Nope."

"Did the defendant mention the name Raymond Miroballi?"

"Nope."

"Have you ever heard that name?"

"Just when that chick axed me," he said, motioning toward Shelly. Actually, it had been Joel Lightner who had "axed" the question.

"Right before she kicked me in the stomach," he added.

The judge looked at Shelly. So did the jury. She felt all of the eyes in the courtroom on her, the lawyer who apparently had physically battered a witness.

She got to her feet. "Your Honor, to be fair," she said, "I was aiming for his crotch."

Two of the jurors snickered, then some people behind her, and in that small space of time within which such things happen, the courtroom had erupted in laughter. Even the judge smiled. Courtrooms were often the place for some of the greatest releases of tension, because they were also the sources of the greatest tension. Jurors loved to laugh during a trial. It was such an odd scene, an utterly incriminating bit of testimony placed next to a moment of high comedy. It was a dumb thing to say, her comment, but it was better than cartwheels or juggling and it might buy her something with the jury.

The judge finally settled his look on Shelly, telling her that he had enjoyed the moment but that she had behaved improperly.

"I'll be here all week, your Honor," she said, which sparked some more laughter, but then she held up her hand. "I apologize for the interruption."

The judge settled things down, admonishing Shelly and striking the statements made by both Shelly and the witness. But the smile remained on his face. What was more important to Shelly was that the smiles remained on the *jurors'* faces.

Morphew had regarded her during the spectacle with some admiration, demonstrated by the soft upturn of one side of his mouth. He had bowed his head to her at one point.

"Well, it sounds like you got lucky," he said to Todavia.

So score one for him. He got his share of laughter as well. The judge probably felt like Morphew was owed one, but this was a trial that was heavily covered by the press, and he did not want to be a judge who lost control of his courtroom.

"Let's move on, Counsel."

"Mr. Todavia, after the defendant told you that he had to get rid of this cop, did you ever hear from him again?"

"Nope."

"And Mr. Todavia, do you have any personal animosity toward the defendant? Any grudge or anything against him?"

The witness looked at Alex. "Nope. Me and Alex is all good. We all good." He nodded at him.

Alex nodded, as well, without looking at the witness.

"Thank you. Judge, that's all I have."

Shelly hoped that the comedy stood out more than the drama. But she knew better. Todavia had damaged her self-defense case. He had damaged every part of her case, regardless of which theory she had pursued. Alex was a drug dealer, pinched by a cop, who decided to resolve the problem by killing the cop. All of this, if you believed Eddie Todavia. She had to see what she could do about that.

"Ms. Trotter," said the judge. "Do you want that recess?"

"Why don't we get started and see how it goes," she suggested.

She got to her feet and looked at the jury. Several of them smiled at her. She was their buddy now. The comedienne. She'd been called worse. And you had to work with what you had. She wanted to keep a favorable impression with this jury if she could. That, of course, was where the double standard came in. A man could be nice and charming but still rip a witness's throat out. A woman could only be sweet or tough, not both.

"Hello, Mr. Todavia."

He was openly hostile toward her, especially after he'd been the butt of some courtroom humor.

"You sell drugs, don't you?" She gestured around the room. "I mean, that's why you're here. You sell drugs."

"Yeah."

She wanted to pore over his brushes with the law over the last few years, but he had been a juvenile at the time, and the law did not allow her to impeach Todavia with his juvenile convictions. The judge had ruled, prior to trial, that this area of inquiry was closed. She only had one incident to which she could refer.

"Powder cocaine?"

"Yeah."

"Crack?"

His head inclined. "Yeah."

"Heroin?"

"Time to time. Not much." He scratched his cheek.

"Same was true eighteen months ago. When you claim you sold cocaine to Alex for the first time. January 2003. You were a drug dealer."

"I s'pose so."

"You suppose so, or yes?" She reached for a file and looked back at him.

"Yesss," he hissed with cold eyes.

"You turned seventeen on September sixteenth, 2001, right?"

"Right."

"And on February fourteenth, 2002, you were arrested for selling crack cocaine."

"Yeah."

Seventeen was the age of majority in this state for most drug-related crimes. Which meant Todavia had been tried as an adult. This was when Todavia left high school.

"You served ten months in prison and got paroled at the end of 2002."

"Yeah."

The irony here was that Todavia's incarceration ended just before Alex's first visit to him. She believed in her heart that if Todavia hadn't been around, Alex would not have entered into this trade. It was one thing to go to someone he'd known in high school. She couldn't imagine him hitting up a stranger on the street. Not a kid like this.

"You've been on parole since then, right, Eddie?"

"Right. Well—parole ended—I got twenty months."

"Your parole ended some time this year. January of this year."

"Right."

"So this first time, when you tell us you sold Alex drugs, you were on parole at that time."

"Yeah."

"In fact, both times, you were still on parole."

"Right."

"Part of the condition of your parole, obviously, is that you do *not* sell drugs."

"Yeah, lady."

"And you have to meet with a parole officer."

"Saw my P.O. every month, at least."

"And he asked you, every month, if you were selling drugs." Todavia smiled a worldly smile. "Right."

"And you lied to him."

"Guess I did."

"You lied to him in January 2003."

He waved at her. "Yeah."

"You lied to him in February 2003."

"Okay, lady."

"Every month, you lied to your parole officer about your involvement in narcotics trafficking."

"I'm saying yeah, lady. Yeah."

"Ten straight times, once a month, you lied."

Morphew objected; the question had already been answered. The judge sustained. Through the exchange, Todavia held his stare on her, then slowly smiled. If he was trying to creep her out, he had succeeded. If he thought that this would stop her from questioning his credibility, he had failed.

"You lied because you didn't want to go to prison. Right, Eddie?"

"Yeah."

"And when you got busted for selling cocaine just recently, you knew that it would mean more prison time for you, didn't you?"

"Yeah, I figured."

"And you didn't want to go back to prison, did you?"

"Nope. I sure didn't."

"And for testifying in this case, you get to walk out of jail a free man, don't you?"

"Yes, ma'am." The prosecution had obviously instructed Todavia to be forthcoming on this issue.

"And you also have immunity for any drug dealing that you've done in the past. Right?"

"Correcto."

She crossed her arms and looked over his head. "What about immunity for *this* thing here, Eddie? For the shooting of Officer Miroballi? Did you get immunity for that?"

"Objection, Judge," Morphew said.

"I want his understanding, your Honor. For bias."

The judge took a moment with that. He didn't seem to get her point, but probing a witness's bias was a sacrosanct arena in cross-examination. "Proceed, Counsel."

She looked at the witness. He held up a hand like a waiter holding a tray. "This here crime, I don't know."

"So as you understand it, it's possible that you *could* be prosecuted—you *don't* have immunity—if you had something to do with this officer being shot."

The witness studied Shelly. His eyes moved beyond her. Maybe he was looking at his lawyer, but she doubted it. He'd had a public defender who probably wasn't here. For the first time, he sat up in his chair.

"I didn't have nothin' to do with this here cop gettin' shot."

"Well, that's not what I asked you. What I asked you is, if you *did* have something to do with it, do you think you're covered here?"

"Man, I don't know. You telling me I can be in trouble for *this*?"

It was notable that Morphew wasn't objecting. As Shelly understood the plea agreement, Eddie Todavia was *not* immune from prosecution for this shooting. That was probably because he had nothing to do with it, and it hadn't occurred to Todavia's lawyer to cover him for something that was only tangentially related to the drug bust. Really, all that he was testifying to, in the end, was that Alex had made an obscure reference to killing Miroballi. That didn't put him in the soup in any way, shape, or form. His immunity deal didn't cover him for the Miroballi shooting any more than it covered him for the Kennedy assassination.

But that didn't mean that a kid couldn't get caught up for something, even if he didn't have anything to do with it. And if Shelly believed that, then a kid who grew up and lived like Todavia believed that even more. She had already seen, firsthand, that Todavia had a general fear of law enforcement; she saw him defer to a *former* cop, Joel Lightner.

She read the uncertainty in his eyes. He hadn't expected this. He hadn't expected to be accused of playing a role in the shooting, and he was beginning to think that Shelly was pointing a finger at him.

"Man, no one said nothin' 'bout me bein' up for *this*," he said.

"Well, let me ask you this." She had to play this right. She didn't want to get his lawyer involved, because in the end, Todavia's lawyer would assure him that he had nothing to worry about. She didn't want that. She wanted the witness thinking he was on the hook. She wanted to scare him enough, but not so much that he started shouting out words like *Fifth Amendment* and *lawyer.*

"Didn't you tell us, Mr. Todavia—your words, certainly not mine—but didn't you tell us that Alex all but told you he was going to kill a police officer? And you never *reported* that information?"

"Judge." Morphew stood. "I think the witness—"

"Sidebar, your Honor?" Shelly quickly interrupted. She absolutely did not want the witness to hear this conversation. The judge waved them forward. They all met in the corner, far from the jury and witness.

"Judge, he should be allowed to confer with his P.D.," said Morphew.

"He doesn't need his lawyer," Shelly answered. "I'm just asking him if it's true that he never reported what my client supposedly said to him. That's no crime."

"But she's giving the appearance that it *is* a crime, Judge. He should be allowed to confer with counsel."

"To tell him what?" Shelly asked the judge. Always direct your comments to the judge or risk his ire. "That he has nothing to worry about? He isn't going to incriminate himself, your Honor. He hasn't done anything wrong."

"I'm not going to tell a witness he can't confer with counsel," said the judge.

"I haven't heard him ask, Judge."

"Thank you, Ms. Trotter. If you had let me finish, I would have said that very thing."

"Sorry, your Honor." She raised her hands.

"Do you mind if I continue?"

"Of course not, your Honor. I apologize."

His Honor adjusted his glasses and spoke to the court reporter. "The witness is not in jeopardy with regard to the question of whether he failed to report a vague reference to a future crime. If he wants to speak with his lawyer, I'm going to allow that. But I'm not going to stop these proceedings for a needless exercise until that time." He looked at the prosecutor, almost as an aside. "She can play this game, Mr. Morphew."

They all returned to their places. Todavia was in distress. He seemed to be hoping that, following this sidebar, someone would tell him he didn't have to answer the question. He could lawyer up at any time, so she had to move fast.

"I'll ask you again, Mr. Todavia. If I heard you right before, I thought you said that my client told you of a plan to kill a cop. You said you 'knew what he meant.' And yet you never reported that to the authorities, did you?"

"Man, what am I gonna report?"

"Well, did you really, truly believe that Alex was going to kill a cop?"

He studied her a moment, or he was studying the entire situation. He was doing what they all do, trying to find a middle ground. Shelly was serving it on a silver platter. "No, couldn't a said that for sure," he said.

"Oh." She tried to seem relieved for him. "Okay. So that's why you didn't report it. Because you *didn't* think he meant that he was going to kill a cop."

"No, ma'am." He was gaining momentum now, buying into this position.

"It was possible, for example, that he was kidding."

"Could be."

"Alex, you've known him for a few years, right?"

"Yeah."

"He's been known to joke around, yes?"

"Yeah. Funny guy."

"Funny guy," she repeated. "Alex, you mean."

"Yeah, kid makes lots of jokes. Always joking around, that guy."

Always joking around. Maybe he and Shelly could tour together. A laugh a minute.

"You didn't really take him seriously, did you? Whatever it was he said to you?"

"Nope." Todavia shrugged. "What do I know? Guy says something. Never know."

"In fact, since we're talking here"—she gestured between the two of them—"it was about six months ago now, and you said you didn't take it seriously. Could be, maybe you don't remember word for word exactly what Alex said. Right?"

Todavia squinted at her. She saw immediately that she had overplayed her hand. One question too many, the failure of a lawyer falling too much in love with her own performance. Of course. Todavia could dance around the edges here, but if he came off that statement, he ran the risk that Morphew would pull his plea agreement. She wanted to reach out and grab the words out of the air.

"Well—"

"Tell you what, Mr. Todavia. I'll withdraw that question. Let me—"

"Judge, can the witness finish his answer?" Morphew requested.

Damn. Shelly wanted to kick herself, but she could show no hesitation whatsoever. "Of course." She extended her arm to the witness.

"Man said what he said, is all."

"Okay." She exhaled. That could have been worse. She had been lucky there. Now was the time to scare him. "Mr. Todavia, in this time that you say you and Alex had an 'arrangement,' did you ever introduce Alex to any members of the street gang? The Columbus Street Cannibals?"

"Lady, I told you before. I didn't introduce nobody to Alex."

He told her before at his house, he meant. "As far as you knew, did Alex know any of the other members of your gang?"

He laughed. "Alex? No, lady. Alex didn't know none of my friends. Look at that boy."

She couldn't have scripted a better answer. It was more or less the same thing he'd said at his house. "Okay, Eddie. You told us that Alex said he had a cop on his tail who wanted to take down the Cannibals. Remember you told us that?"

"Yeah."

"According to your testimony, this cop wanted to use Alex to help take down the Cannibals."

"Right."

Shelly had slowly moved toward Todavia. "If Alex is going to help take down the Cannibals, and you're the only Cannibal he knows, that meant he was going to have to take *you* down. Isn't that right, Eddie?"

Morphew rose to object. "Assumes facts not in evidence. Speculative."

"I just want his state of mind," Shelly said calmly, as if it were a no-brainer.

The judge slowly nodded. "I'll hear the answer."

Having turned to the judge, she saw in her peripheral vision that Alex was squirming. She looked at him and he summoned her with his eyes. "A moment, Judge?" she asked. When she reached Alex, he stood and leaned over the defense table.

"Shelly, what are you doing?" he whispered urgently. "You can't accuse this guy of murder."

"I'm not. Relax." She motioned him down and turned back to the witness. "You know what? I'll rephrase." It gave her a chance to say the whole thing again for the jury's benefit. She moved a step closer to the witness, whose demeanor had turned decidedly sour again. This was about as unexpected to Todavia as the kick to the abdomen. She ticked off points on her hand. "You said you believed Alex when he said that this cop wanted to take down the Cannibals, and that he was going to use Alex to do it. You said that as far as you knew, Alex didn't know any other Cannibals besides you. So from your standpoint, Eddie, didn't that mean that this cop had become a threat to *you*?"

Todavia sat back in the seat and folded his arms. "Now you sayin' *I* had somethin' to do with this here beef. I ain't talkin'." He directed an emphatic finger downward. "I got my rights."

Perfect.

The judge turned to the witness. "Sir, you do, in fact, have a Fifth Amendment right to refuse to answer this question. Is that your intention?"

"Nobody said nothin' 'bout this thing here." He continued to point downward. He could have punched holes in a can with that finger.

"Sir. Are you choosing to remain silent?"

"That's right. I'm remainin' silent."

"Okay," Shelly said. This was a freebie for her, if she handled it right. That was a big *if.* She hadn't really expected to be here. She hadn't known precisely what Todavia was going to say, and she had done her best to twist his words. Now she had him in a vulnerable spot. She could run off a series of incriminating questions that he would refuse to answer—and look bad for doing so. *Didn't you plan the murder of Raymond Miroballi? Isn't that gun sitting there on the table yours?* He would probably refuse to answer, which would be the next best thing to admitting them. But this kid was unpredictable. He might shout out a denial, too.

She liked her odds on that score, but there was a very real danger of being too cute here. She was planning a self-defense argument. If she proceeded down the present course—suggesting that Todavia had something to do with this murder—she would be telling the jury the defense was pleading a straight not-guilty, that Alex didn't do it. And then later, she would tell them that Alex *did* do it but had legal justification. The jury would lose their trust in Shelly. They would think the defense was saying anything and everything. Morphew would crucify her in closing arguments. No. She had to make the call right now, go forward here and abandon self-defense, or shut the hell up. She would have loved a continuance, but Morphew would grab Todavia and talk some sense into him. She had to make this decision now.

Oh, she had his jugular exposed and she was going to let him go. But it made sense. Sure. Morphew was going to have the chance to clean this up, anyway. No matter what kind of misdirection she tried here, Morphew would set the record straight with a more confident Eddie Todavia this afternoon.

So if she wasn't going to make the jury think Eddie Todavia was a killer, she could at least make them think he was a liar.

"Mr. Todavia, tell me if you agree with this statement. *If* my client said that he was being forced by a cop to help him go after the Cannibals, and *if* you were the only Cannibal he knew, wouldn't that give you a motive to want to eliminate that cop? Or Alex?"

"Object to the form."

"Sustained."

She didn't agree with that ruling but she didn't really care. She just wanted Todavia and the jury to hear the question. She was approaching the witness again. "And Alex, quite obviously, is still with us, isn't he? Whereas a certain police officer is dead."

The witness had curled into a ball. "Man, I ain't sayin' nothin'."

"If Alex really said all those things to you about a cop being on his tail and wanting to take down drug-dealing Cannibals like you, then I don't blame you for taking the Fifth."

"Objection."

"Sustained. That question is stricken. The question is improper."

She nodded her head, acknowledging the court's admonition, but she wasn't looking at the judge. She had reached the witness stand. She placed a hand on the railing. "Is it worth it, Eddie? Get out of a drug-dealing beef and fall into a murder beef?"

"Man, I want my lawyer."

"The truth is, Eddie, that Alex never said any of those things to you. Right? You lied to stay out of jail, isn't that the truth?"

"I want my lawyer."

That was fine. That was better than a denial.

"He never said any of those things to you, because if he had, you wouldn't have stood for it. You would have killed either Alex or the cop."

"Object to the form."

"Sustained."

She gave a long look at the witness, then at the jury, who seemed quite attentive.

"That's all I have," she said.

62

Trust

MORPHEW DID WHAT she expected. He asked for a lunch recess as the hour drew near twelve. With that time, he was going to explain to Todavia, or have his lawyer do so, that there was nothing illegal about a failure to report a crime. He might even give him immunity for the Miroballi shooting, but that would be a bad move for him; immunity acknowledged guilt, some participation. In any event, he would clean this up. He would get Todavia on the straight path on redirect and have him clearly state that Alex alluded to killing a police officer.

"You're a good lawyer," Alex said to her as he took a bite of a peanut butter and jelly sandwich Shelly had made this morning. They were in a holding cell below the courthouse. It was dark and depressing and had the faint smell of urine.

She had done all she could with Todavia. Her tricks would not work the second time around, after he was redirected by Morphew.

"You tied him up real good," he added. "Made him look bad. For a minute there, I thought you were gonna get us all killed. That guy's C-Street, Shelly. You don't mess with a guy like that."

She shrugged. "He said you two were 'all good,' Alex."

"That was before you made him look ridiculous."

"I hope so. I think the jury believes he's capable of lying. The question is whether he *was* lying."

"He was."

"Well, I'm saying—it's all what the jury thinks." She put

down her sandwich. "That was a very damaging piece of evidence, Alex. Not just the part about getting rid of the cop, but the whole conversation."

It was damaging to *her,* at least. If this story were made up, that meant that the prosecution had a hand in it. Dan Morphew had fed lines to a witness in a pinch. She was not ready to make that assumption about Morphew. She'd seen that kind of prosecutor, but she didn't think Morphew was capable. Add to that the fact that Shelly's father was the county attorney's political ally, and it didn't wash. The jury knew none of this, of course. They had to be viewing Todavia's testimony with some skepticism. But Shelly had to concede that, in the end, she thought Todavia was telling the truth.

"You talk to Ronnie lately?" he asked.

She shook her head no. "Not for a few days. You?"

"No." He wiped his mouth. "I think he's trying to be careful about not talking to me, since he's a witness and all. But you're not gonna call him, right?"

"Doubt it. Don't see why I would."

Ronnie had offered his testimony, in whatever form she wanted, on so many occasions she had lost count. He would willingly lie for Alex. Whatever corroboration Shelly needed, he would provide.

"You told him, didn't you?" he asked.

She had told him. She had confronted Ronnie in that conference room right after her conversation on the cell phone with Joel Lightner, who had reported a strange visit by Ronnie to a man named Robert Eldridge. *That kid is acting weird,* Joel had said to her. *He's up to something.*

Why, she wondered, had she chosen that moment to confront him with the fact that she knew he was her son? She wanted to tell herself that the timing was right, or she had an irresistible urge. A mother's urge.

Nonsense. The evidence had been building up against the boy. He was seen consorting with Todavia. He was at the scene of the murder. Alex's defensive overreaction every time she broached the subject of Ronnie only confirmed her suspicions. She knew why she had chosen that moment for the heart-to-heart.

She was going to warn him.

I know you were involved. I won't say anything but don't do anything stupid. Stay away from Todavia. Keep your mouth shut. Stay as far away from that courtroom as possible.

Something had made her stop. Ethics? Rules? Something like that. Something about right and wrong, she assumed in hindsight. Regardless, she hadn't warned Ronnie. She hadn't said anything about his involvement in the shooting of Officer Miroballi.

Instead, in that moment when her heart had raced and she felt the building perspiration, she had simply said, *I know I'm your mother.*

She had put forth all of the information to him—her personal check of the birth records, Alex's admission, her father's knowledge—to spare both of them the embarrassment of his possible denial. That, unfortunately, did not do the trick. He still denied it, first with a laugh, then more adamantly, until finally he was throwing things. Out-of-control angry.

So what the hell are you gonna do now? he had asked. *You're not gonna help Alex now?*

I'm still going to help him, she had said.

How are you gonna help? You gonna say self-defense? Or someone else did it? Which one?

She had refused to answer. She couldn't. Not anymore. If Alex chose to do so, against her wishes, that was his prerogative. But she could no longer assume that Ronnie and Alex were on the same side.

That, of course, had sent Ronnie into even more of a rage. He had finally stormed out without another word. It was the last she had spoken to him.

It was obviously not the reaction she had hoped to elicit. The anger and frustration, she could understand. He was entitled to a number of adversarial feelings toward the mother who gave him up years ago. That wasn't it. It was the other part of his reaction. He had seemed worried. Fearful. It had gone a long way toward confirming her suspicions about Ronnie. He had been keeping close tabs on this case—one would presume out of brotherly love and concern—and he seemed quite concerned that he no longer knew where the fingers were pointing. He was being shut out, and that scared him.

Was she doing her job here? Yes, she had proceeded to have yet another conversation with Alex on the subject, and he had responded in exactly the same way the second time: *Forget Ronnie. He wasn't there. I won't say he was. Stick with self-defense.*

Yes, she could say that she was following her client's wishes and putting forth what, under the circumstances, was the best case. A case of self-defense. Sure. A panel of lawyers investigating her ethical performance would probably say she did everything she could do and then took her best shot for her client.

"Todavia's testimony," she said to Alex now. "About your conversation. Getting rid of Miroballi."

"It didn't happen, I'm telling you."

"The jury could believe it, Alex."

He nodded gravely. "But I thought you turned it around on him okay."

"Well, it opened a door. It gave me a reason to point the finger at him. A reason that I didn't have before now, because I didn't know about this conversation."

Alex raised his hands in defense. "There was nothing to tell. It didn't happen."

She shook her head. "The point is, Alex, that I had his head on a guillotine in there. It's still there, I think. We could make a case against Todavia."

"No," he answered, before she had even elaborated.

"Alex." She opened her hands. "The jury would happily buy that. I was playing some lawyer games in there with him, but I think it worked, and it worked because it made sense. If Todavia thought Miroballi was going after the Cannibals, that *did* mean him. He was in danger. He would have a good reason to eliminate Miroballi. And the jury is ready to believe that."

Alex did not seem ready to accept that. "If you're saying I didn't do it, that means you'll point at anyone."

"I won't point at Ronnie." She was surprised at the speed of her response. "I'm talking about Todavia."

Alex ran his fingers through his hair and stood up, paced the small cell. After a long moment, he shook his head. "No. We stick with our story."

She lacked the energy to fight. Now was not the time to decide this, anyway. Shelly hadn't even made an opening statement yet.

She could walk this tightrope, she felt. In her cross-examinations during Morphew's case-in-chief, she could dance along the line between self-defense and implicating Eddie Todavia.

"God, Alex," she said, more to herself. "If I had known this about Todavia, I could have spent the last three months building something against him. I thought this was a kid you saw once a year. Now I hear you're having conversations about Miro—"

"We didn't *have* that conversation," he said, snapping around from the bars of the cell door. "Just"—he waved his arms—"you did good today. You made him look like a liar. Don't make him out to be a killer. Just let it go, all right?"

Alex nodded at the guard, who appeared at the cell door.

"Time to head up," he said.

"Right." Alex seemed eager to end the conversation.

Shelly walked over to him as the guard fumbled with the lock on the door. She whispered in his ear. "You don't want me going after Todavia because he's connected to Ronnie. Is that it?"

He broke free of her as the guard opened the door and put him in handcuffs. Alex would be taking the back elevator up to the courtroom, like all prisoners, while Shelly took the elevator on the other side of the hallway.

"Stick to the story," Alex said as he walked away with his armed escort.

63

Identities

THE AFTERNOON MOVED quickly. Morphew put Eddie Todavia back on the stand for redirect and basically asked him the same questions. He made sure that the jury understood that Alex really, really said that he "had to get rid of that cop." He emphasized that, while Todavia had allowed for the possibility that Alex was joking, Alex did not smile, smirk, or laugh when he made that comment, nor any of the other comments.

Shelly saw no utility in an extended recross. She asked Todavia if he had ever heard of the word *sarcasm*. She asked him if he had ever made a joke without smiling. "You heard the one about the rabbi, the priest, and the elephant with three legs?" she asked with the most serious expression she could muster. The witness stared at her, and she back at him. One of the jurors picked up on it, and pretty soon several of them were smiling.

She didn't know what it was with her and comedy all of a sudden. She was usually accused of lacking an appropriate sense of humor. She had stumbled upon it, though, and it seemed to be working to her favor with the jury. She considered working on a monologue for tomorrow.

A forensic specialist with the County Attorney Technical Unit next testified that the bullet that penetrated Ray Miroballi's brain had traveled approximately five to six feet. Shelly did not quibble with the estimate. There was nothing of a technical nature with which Shelly could quibble, so she did the next best thing with an expert of this kind—asked the witness questions she could not answer that helped Shelly's case:

"This forensic analysis you performed doesn't tell you whether the slain officer had his gun drawn, does it?"

"It doesn't tell you whether the slain officer had intended to shoot the person who shot him?"

"You were not able to look at the weapon used to shoot the officer, were you?"

Of course, the witness could not speak to any of those issues, which allowed Shelly to make a closing argument in her questions.

The judge recessed the proceedings at four o'clock. Shelly sat in her office after five o'clock and reviewed her notes. A Monday evening, the place was buzzing. She much preferred this place on Thursday through Sunday evenings, when even a high-powered firm's lawyers tended to be around less.

It was possible that there could be as many as four witnesses tomorrow—Officer Sanchez, the other two eyewitnesses, and the county medical examiner. That was probably optimistic, but she had to be ready. She had been over the reports and the evidence a number of times, but she had made a point of not reviewing them over the weekend. She wanted a fresh look at the stuff the night before. She had prepared her cross-examinations of these witnesses weeks ago but was prepared to make adjustments. Then, of course, she would have to make more adjustments on the spot, after the witnesses actually testified. Things always changed once the trial got going; strategies were modified and, of course, witnesses' testimony could never be predicted with complete accuracy. It was clear from Morphew's opening statement, for example, that the homeless man was going to say that Alex had two guns and had tricked Officer Miroballi into believing he was unarmed when he threw down the first gun.

She became vaguely aware of someone in her peripheral vision. Paul Riley was wearing a white dress shirt and beautifully patterned tie of powder blue. Matched his eyes. He looked tired. He had been on trial himself until a week ago. But he loved it here, she could see, lived off the energy of the toiling attorneys around him. That could owe to the fact that part of every hour that these attorneys worked went into his pocket. But that wasn't it with this guy. This wasn't just a job to him, like with many lawyers. He loved the law. He cherished the competition and high stakes and his rather coveted place in the legal community.

There had been a subtle change in their relationship since their "attorney-client" conversation a few weeks back. Was it because she had confided in him that she had a son? No. Paul had a daughter. He wasn't a twenty-year-old afraid of commitment. It was the other topic of conversation that day. She had told him that she had some reason to suspect Ronnie. He had strongly urged her to come clean with Alex, of course, and she had done so. But she sensed that he had the same feeling she did—not simply that pointing the finger at Ronnie was a better course of action, but that Shelly had not necessarily done the best job of trying to convince Alex of this. Maybe, she conceded, Paul disapproved of her conduct here, and he was trying to put some distance between himself and Shelly, at least on an intimacy level.

He hadn't said any of this, which seemed to be his trademark. He spent many an hour with people accused of wrongdoing, often justifiably so, and he had grown comfortable with keeping his judgments to himself. He had spent much of the weekend helping Shelly prepare for the cross-examination of many of the witnesses without offering a word of advice on the best theory of defense. He had never even mentioned Ronnie.

They talked about the day's events. Morphew's description of how the shooting transpired. Eddie Todavia's testimony. Most of Paul's questions were about the jury. How did they like Morphew? How did they like Shelly? Did they believe Todavia?

They discussed a couple of evidentiary issues. This, more than anything, was where Paul had been most valuable. Shelly had been on trial dozens of times, but the vast majority were in juvenile court, where they never heard of the hearsay rule and most rules of evidence were relaxed; or in civil court, where witnesses rarely took the Fifth and there was scant talk of things like coconspirators.

She slid her chair back from her desk. Her stomach ached badly. She never ate well during a trial but she was usually spared indigestion. She had never felt such stress, and it was only during down moments like this that she noticed its effect on her. She had seen it in her father, as well, the last four years as the state's chief executive. Each of them had probably aged prematurely from stress, and yet each seemed to want, more than anything else, to remain in these positions that placed such burdens on them.

"And how are *you,* Ms. Trotter?" Paul asked. "Other than stressed and sleep-deprived."

"Shows that much, huh?"

He smiled. "You're the type, if you aren't working past midnight and skipping meals, you think you're not working hard enough."

She allowed for that. That was a major difference between Paul and her.

"You feeling okay about things?" he asked.

A vague question. "The trial? I think so."

He cocked his head. "Not really what I meant."

"Ah. Our privileged conversation."

"Those rules are more important than the case," he said. "I know that must seem hard to swallow. But it's true. And when a case becomes more important than those rules—well, that's when you know that maybe you shouldn't be working the case."

"I'm being lectured now."

He wagged a finger and gave a soft smile. "Reminded. It gives me comfort, Shelly, to think about that. I get invested in my clients' welfare just like anybody else. But then I think of the rules that govern my role, and it reminds me that I just have a role. I don't have this person's life. I do everything within my power to play my role as best I can, but that's all I do."

Her head rocked back. She stared at the ceiling.

"I realize your circumstances aren't quite the same," he acknowledged. "But the principle is. Do the best you can, and realize that's all you can do."

"Okay." Easier said than done.

"And get some food tonight," he said as he left the office.

Her smile widened as he walked out. She realized that he really hadn't been lecturing. He was trying to put her at ease, in his way.

She picked up the folders and began reading over reports and notes. She couldn't help but think of the mystery that was Ronnie. So many questions about this boy. Could he really be working with a street gang? A kid with a scholarship, a hardworking, ambitious boy? A caring young man who showed such a willingness to take care of a baby that wasn't his? And why exactly was it that he had sent Alex to see her that first time at the legal clinic? Why send Alex to do his dirty work—

Her heart skipped a beat. Something within her stirred. She was missing something. Better put, she was looking for something and couldn't find it. She closed her eyes and tried to relax. When you're searching for something, it's easier to look at everything than to look for that one particular thing. So she let the images come to her and absorbed them as best she could, using all of her senses. Alex in the park with Ray Miroballi on two separate occasions. A boy leaving the City Athletic Club in a long coat and cap. Ronnie and Alex in the photos with Angela. The view from the south of the crime scene, the nineteenth floor looking down on bodies and tops of heads. The surveillance photos of Ronnie with Eddie Todavia. The basketball in Ronnie's room, that she had tripped over. Alex's words to Shelly about Ronnie, a year ago. *He saved my life once.* Ronnie had come to Alex's rescue after Alex and his drunken freshmen buddies had hot-wired the wrong guy's car. What had Ronnie done to help Alex? Taken a beating for him? *Killed* the bad guy? It didn't matter. The point was, Alex felt he owed Ronnie his life.

She opened the folders. She read over the police report and Joel's notes of their conversations with the eyewitnesses, Monica Stoddard and Joseph Slattery. She tapped her own memory about her conversations with Sanchez and the others.

She leapt to her feet. She closed her eyes and worked it through. Yes.

Yes?

They hadn't switched jackets that night, after all.

She dialed Joel's cell phone before she could stop herself.

They had switched identities.

"Joel, it's Shelly. Remember when you went to the City Athletic Club on open gym night? You showed Alex's photo around?"

"Yeah. What's today—Tuesday? You want me to go back tomorrow night?"

"Yes," she said. "But show them Ronnie's photo."

64

Messenger

"RONNIE WAS THE drug dealer," Shelly said into the Dictaphone. She had never used the transcription device before, felt odd holding a small tape recorder to her mouth. It came with her office supplies, and she felt the need to speak out loud and bounce her thoughts off someone. She couldn't go to Paul. She couldn't go to anyone. So she would go to herself. She would play the tape back later and see how it sounded.

"We know Ronnie has been seen with Eddie Todavia," she continued, pacing around her office. She had closed the door for privacy. "We know that there were drugs in the car behind their house. We have assumed they belonged to Alex. Maybe—maybe Alex and Ronnie both were dealers."

She touched the wall, a piece of peeling paint that was giving way to gravity. Truth was like gravity, a law professor had once said. In the end, both prevail. Shelly had always found that professor annoying.

"Ronnie was the confidential informant," she said. "He must have been busted by Miroballi and flipped." She held her breath. "But he worked with the Cannibals, so he didn't want to be seen with a cop. So he sent Alex. Alex *was* feeding information to Miroballi. Sanchez was right about that. But the information was coming from *Ronnie.*"

She clicked off the recorder and said a silent prayer. She stared at the tiny device a moment. She considered throwing it out the window, if she could even get the window open. Then she set it on "Record" again.

"When the feds saw Alex with Miroballi, they busted him. Alex couldn't give up Ronnie. No way he'd do that. But then the feds start talking about Miroballi and selling drugs, and using Alex to catch Miroballi. So what can Alex do? He can't give up Ronnie. So he takes their bait. He says, yeah, Miroballi was making me sell drugs for him."

Yes. The F.B.I. had never really trusted Alex, and now she knew why. Their instincts had been accurate. He *had* been screwing with them.

"So somehow, Miroballi starts suspecting that Ronnie hasn't been straight with him. Or that Ronnie is telling the Cannibals about him. Something. So he goes to find the person who has been playing around with him. He goes to find the snitch who, he thinks, has turned on him."

She looked at the door. How much she wished she could walk out that door and leave this case behind her.

"He went to find Ronnie," she said. "Ronnie, who was returning from a game of basketball at the open gym. Wearing a cap and a long black coat. He had his back to Sanchez the whole time. Sanchez probably never saw him. The other witnesses sure didn't. Why the black coat, which Alex normally wore? We don't know. Probably, because he was the only one going out that night, and the long coat was warmer than that leather jacket. These two shared everything else. They probably shared coats, too."

She moved back to her chair and collapsed in it. "Ronnie shot Miroballi. And Alex got there, too late, and helped Ronnie escape. Alex figured that he wouldn't look too bad as a suspect because he hadn't fired the weapon. So Ronnie left with the gun and his bloody clothes. Alex stayed behind, because he hadn't fired the gun and didn't have blood on his clothes. He took the hit for his brother, for the boy to whom he owes his life."

She sighed. "But if Alex thinks he won't be implicated, he's wrong. Turns out, Alex *did* get a little bit of blood on himself, probably from contact with Ronnie. And it turned out that Miroballi's partner, Sanchez, didn't know about Ronnie. The only person he knew about was the guy Ronnie was sending to give information to Miroballi—Alex. Alex was the person who had met with Miroballi in the park—meetings that Sanchez watched from his car. Sanchez has probably never heard the name Ronnie Masters. So now Alex goes from not looking guilty to having Miroballi's blood on himself *and* being identified as Miroballi's snitch."

She clicked off the recorder. She felt uncomfortably warm. Her heart was drumming. Her stomach was a barren wasteland of acid. She desperately needed something in her system but couldn't even consider the thought. She lifted the Dictaphone back to her mouth. "We don't know the details. Did Ronnie shoot in self-defense? *Was* Miroballi going to kill him? Or did Ronnie commit this murder on behalf of the Cannibals? It doesn't matter. It doesn't matter because Ronnie's not my client and I don't have to prove any—"

Her throat closed on her. Yes, it was all finally coming together. It all made sense, and suddenly nothing made sense. She couldn't implicate her own flesh and blood in a cop's murder, but she couldn't imagine how she could let this pass, either. Not now. She had solved the puzzle, she was sure of it, and it exonerated her client. And she couldn't use it because her client wouldn't let her, would contradict her, in fact, by taking the witness stand and denying Ronnie's participation.

And she didn't *want* to use the information.

She felt a draft and drew her arms around herself. She desperately wanted to go for a run but she was in courtroom attire and low heels, and she probably couldn't have made it far anyway, from lack of sleep and poor nutrition. She tried to map out the turns this case had taken and how it had all come to this. This, she decided, was her punishment. She needed a priest, like Paul Riley had said. Or a philosopher. A theologian. She considered flipping a coin. *Heads, my client goes down. Tails, my son does.* All of these momentary diversions as the mind worked at warp speed were preferable to a reality that she wanted so desperately to avoid.

She removed the tape from the Dictaphone, dropped it to the floor, and smashed it to pieces with her heel.

65

Angles

SHELLY REMOVED THE *Daily Watch* from the newspaper stand at the bus stop. She skipped the front page and went straight to Metro, where she would expect to see coverage of the trial yesterday. She reacted audibly to the headline.

DEFENSE BLAMES DRUG DEALER
IN MIROBALLI TRIAL

She laughed, because she didn't know how else to respond, and touched her eyes. The reporter, not surprisingly, had missed the subtlety and just taken out portions of quotes from the cross-examination. Yes, she had alluded to Todavia's guilt, but that was hardly the highlight.

Still, this was interesting. If this was how a reporter viewed the evidence presented yesterday, is that how the jurors saw it, too? For all of her posturing on Todavia's reliability, did they walk away thinking she was accusing him of murder? She wondered if any of the jurors would violate their oath, intentionally or otherwise, and catch that headline. Would they have the same reaction Shelly did?

For someone whose ultimate goal here was to argue self-defense, this was not the impression she was trying to give. *Was* she still pleading self-defense?

God, what a case. She longed for the easy stuff again, the

school disciplinary cases, the civil lawsuits, even the juvenile stuff, where one's assignment was largely straightforward.

She forced some breakfast down her throat in the court cafeteria below the courthouse. She drained two cartons of orange juice but barely touched the grapefruit or toast. She read the entire article only because it was possible that some of the jurors had done the same, and she wanted to know what might taint their opinions.

The reporter expressed surprise at the turning of the tables on Todavia, after the defense had notified the prosecution of a self-defense theory. The first day of trial was entertaining theater, said the writer, ranging from a damning opening statement to one particularly humorous episode to a tough cross-examination of the admitted drug dealer.

Little of substance, other than the reporter's complete misreading of her strategy. She tapped the table and headed up to the lobby of the courthouse. She saw a camera crew and a news reporter pacing in circles. She had almost slipped past when the man called to her. She refused comment but she couldn't exactly run; she was in a line for the metal detectors. Used to be, lawyers could flash their credentials and get past all that, but security-conscious officials would have none of that now. Everyone got checked.

So she was a captive audience. The reporter threw several questions at her as she looked into the lights and saw the red button light up on the camera. She muttered a couple of professional pleasantries, but he wouldn't leave.

"Are you giving up on self-defense?" No comment. "Do you think someone else killed Officer Miroballi?" No comment.

"Are you supporting your father's re-election campaign?"

She looked at the reporter and smiled. "That's my business."

Finally, it was her turn through the metal detector, and she was on her way to the courtroom at eight-thirty. Alex was seated in his chair. He looked positively dreadful. Cleaned-up and appropriate, sure, but up close, the purple circles beneath his bloodshot eyes had darkened.

She patted him on the shoulder. "You clean up nice," she told him.

He looked at her and flashed a glimpse of his old self. "Death row chic," he said, tugging his suit collar.

"Hey, come on now."

Shelly looked over her notes one last time. Alex had his pad of paper out as well. He had taken notes and slipped the occasional comment or question to Shelly. She invited his participation. If he was anything like her, he had to feel like he was doing something.

The courtroom was just as blue as the day before, possibly more so. She sensed that some of the police officers in the front rows were different from yesterday. She imagined that it was considered an off-duty obligation to attend the slain officer's trial.

Sophia Miroballi walked in with her mother, presumably, just before nine, but a space had been kept open for her. Notably absent was any familial representation from the defendant's family. Elaine Masters—Laney—worked the day shift and probably had difficulty moving it around. That assumed she had *tried* to make such arrangements. Shelly couldn't be sure of that. She had adopted Ronnie late in life—typical for attorney adoptions— and her husband had died, leaving her and Ronnie with little in terms of financial support. Laney, in rather dire straits herself, had taken on another boy, Alex, which said something about the kindness in her heart. But somewhere along the way, she had lost control. Laney had turned to booze. Shelly was not unsympathetic but, for Christ's sake, the woman could offer a modicum of support for Alex right now.

Dan Morphew rushed in just under the bell. He seemed harried, and he was taking it out on his two assistants. Why the long face? She felt a bit of relief, regardless. Always nice to see your adversary sweating. She tried to watch him without watching. He was whispering something quite serious to a young assistant, and then he pointed at Shelly.

The jury entered the room and took their seats. Shelly wore her pleasant face. Morphew hardly even looked up when he spoke to the judge. "Call Monica Stoddard," he said.

The witness walked into the room and caught some attention from the audience. She was tall and athletic and not unattractive.

She was dressed her best in a blue suit and heels, simple jewelry. She seemed nervous as she was administered her oath. Many people were when they got in that box.

"Good morning, ma'am," said Morphew, making it to the podium with a notepad. "Please state your name and spell your last name for the record."

He took her through her job description and background. He seemed to spend a little too much time on her education and positions as an architect over the years. He was building her up so she could buttress the testimony of a homeless person, the only other eyewitness to the shooting. Finally, Morphew made it to the building where she worked, the Forrester Insurance Building, which was across the street and to the south of the alley where the shooting occurred. She was working late in her office on the nineteenth floor. He took her to the relevant date and time.

"I saw a boy running from a police officer. He was wearing a coat and a cap." She was using her finger to point at her imaginary view. "He ran into the alley and the officer was behind. The officer was not as fast."

"Go on," Morphew urged.

"Well, the boy disappeared out of my view. The officer made it to the alley and stopped somewhere in there, but still in my view."

"You couldn't see the entire alley from your window?"

"No. The officer ran for just a couple of seconds. Well, here." She adjusted in her seat. "He stopped first at the very front of the alley. Like, still on the sidewalk. He had a radio in his hand and I think he said something into it. Then he walked a few steps. He didn't go that far."

It didn't seem that Morphew had prepared this testimony very well. That seemed odd. She was not a critical witness, but still. What had been occupying Morphew's time since yesterday at trial?

"Then tell us what you saw."

"I saw the officer talking. I mean, I couldn't hear anything. But he seemed like he was talking to someone. Then he seemed to jerk, kind of, and then I saw him fly backward and fall on the ground. He'd been"—she ran a hand across her face.

"He'd been shot in the face?"

She closed her eyes. "Yes."

"Ma'am, you mentioned that the officer had a handheld radio in his hand."

"Yes."

"What about his other hand?"

"I think it was free. He wasn't holding anything."

No. Shelly checked her notes on that. No.

"What about when he was talking to whoever it was—did he do anything different with that hand then?"

"Not as far as I could see, no."

"And you could—well, that's fine. That's fine. Now, did this officer do anything, at any time here, that you would perceive as threatening or aggressive?"

Shelly thought to object but she would lose, and that would highlight the testimony.

"I didn't see him do anything like that, no."

"Did you ever see this officer, at any time, draw his weapon?"

"No, I didn't."

"And did these events take place in the city, county, and state in which this courthouse is located?"

"Yes, they did."

Morphew nodded. "That's all I have, your Honor."

Shelly had little for this witness. She stood at her chair. "Good morning, Ms. Stoddard. I'm Shelly Trotter. We've met before."

"Yes. Good morning."

"Just a few questions. You couldn't see this other person, whom the officer was chasing?"

"No, not once he went far enough in the alley."

She put her hand on Alex's shoulder. "You can't identify this young man as the person who was running, can you?"

"No, I can't."

"Your view wasn't sufficient to see his face."

"My angle wasn't, no."

"Sure." She moved away from Alex now, toward the podium. She didn't want to discuss this other person while standing next to Alex. "This boy, once he left your line of sight, he never came back into your sight."

"That's right."

"So you couldn't tell us whether, for example, he had his hands up?"

"No, I couldn't."

"You don't know what kind of a conversation they had."

"No."

"Or even *if* they had a conversation."

"That's right."

"The part of the alley you couldn't see—you can't tell us how many people were in that alley, can you?"

Alex's head whipped around at her. She avoided his stare.

"How many people?" The witness grimaced. "Other than that one boy I saw, no."

"There could have been more than one person out of your sight line and you wouldn't know."

"That's right. I would have no idea."

Alex cleared his throat, still directing arrows at her with his eyes.

"Your Honor," Shelly said, "one quick moment with my client?"

The judge nodded.

Shelly walked over. Alex got out of his chair and put his mouth to her ear. "What are you doing?"

"I'm trying to show that she doesn't know anything."

"No, you're not. You're saying it wasn't me."

She looked at him for a moment. She moved to his ear. "Alex, you sit down and shut your mouth. Do not ever glare at me like that again with the jury present. Or I swear to God, I'll go to the prosecutor right now and tell them all about Ronnie."

She smiled at him, for the jury's benefit, and tapped him playfully on the shoulder. "Okay?" she said sweetly. "Sorry about that, Ms. Stoddard." She moved away from the defense table and the podium, into the well of the courtroom. She was trying to stand directly between the jury and Alex. She heard him take his seat behind her.

"Ms. Stoddard, you said that the officer had a radio in one hand, and as for the other hand, I believe you said, you *thought* he wasn't holding anything. Isn't it more accurate to say that you aren't sure about that?"

"Umm." The witness looked up at the ceiling, squinted. "I don't remember seeing a gun in his hand."

"Let me put it this way, Ms. Stoddard. Can you rule out the possibility that he didn't have a gun in his hand? You can't, can you?"

"Rule out the possibility." She played with that. "I guess it was my understanding that he didn't have a gun in his hand."

"Your understanding." Shelly looked over at the prosecutor. "Do you mean someone *told* you that?"

"Oh, jeez." She sighed loudly. "Well—"

"Ms. Stoddard, do you remember when I paid you a visit?"

"Yes."

"And I brought a gentleman with me."

"Yes."

"And didn't you tell us"—Shelly made a point of retrieving her notes and reading from them verbatim—"didn't you tell us that 'he had a walkie-talkie in his hand, but I don't know about the other hand.' Isn't that what you told us?"

She seemed embarrassed by the question. Shelly smiled at her with sympathy. She wasn't trying to berate the witness.

"I said that?"

"I'm asking you, ma'am. Didn't you tell us that you didn't know about that other hand?"

"Well. It was dark." She threw up her hands. "I don't really remember that he had a gun, but I don't have a real specific image in my head of that hand. It was more like—a big picture sort of thing? I saw a police officer chasing a guy. I guess on the specifics of whether that officer had a gun in his hand—I guess I'm not positive one way or the other."

"You don't know about that other hand," Shelly summarized, tying the witness to precisely what she had told Shelly and Joel in her office.

"I guess I don't, no."

"Okay. Let's move on then. You said that the officer 'jerked' before the shooting."

"Yeah."

"Would you mind, Ms. Stoddard, standing up and showing us exactly what you mean by that?"

The witness shrugged and got up. "Well, I guess it's hard to replicate."

"Sure."

The witness feigned a quick spasm of her upper body. Her body seemed to rotate to the right. "It was like something surprised him or something."

Ouch. *Surprise* was not the word she wanted to hear. "Looks like"—Shelly tried to replicate the witness's movement—"looks like he was pivoting a little."

"Maybe. It was really quick. I didn't really analyze it."

"Of course. You can take your seat, by the way, thank you. So, his upper body sort of twisted or moved or something."

"Something like that, yes."

"His feet were planted."

The witness recoiled, as if she were being asked too much. She thought about it a good long while, moving her body slightly as she tried to reenact the image.

"I mean," Shelly tried, "he didn't jump backward or forward, did he?"

"No. He didn't do that." The witness sighed, and slowly nodded. "I guess you're right. His feet didn't move."

"Okay, great." Shelly squinted over the jurors' heads as if she were trying to get to the bottom of this. "Seems like—you tell me—seems like when you just did that, it was sort of like a shiver that started from the left side of his body and moved to the right."

"Oh"—she dropped her head back—"that sounds right." She looked at Shelly. "I mean, 'shiver'—it would be an awfully bad shiver."

"Okay, we'll use your word. 'Jerk.' The officer jerked in a way such that he turned slightly to the right. Isn't that what you showed us?"

"Yeah, that makes sense."

"You said, Ms. Stoddard, that the witness had a radio in his hand."

"Yes."

"I didn't hear Mr. Morphew ask you *which* hand was holding the radio. It makes me curious."

Morphew, at the sound of his name, looked up from his notes at Shelly with an expression that said, *I'd object to the cheap shot but it's not worth it.*

"Left hand," said Ms. Stoddard.

"Left hand. Radio in his left, right hand you're not sure." She did the twist again, though slower than the quick jerking motion the witness had described. "He jerked to the right, and his right hand maybe had a gun in it, maybe was free."

"Correct."

"You didn't happen to see what his right hand did, when he jerked to the right?"

Stoddard was following Shelly's right hand, which moved toward her right hip. She seemed to get the point, too. "No, actually, I didn't specifically notice that." She heaved a sigh. "I guess I wish I had taken notes or something."

Some of the jurors smiled, so Shelly did as well. Shelly patted her right hip with her free right hand. "His holster was on his right side, wasn't it?"

"Oh, wow. I have no idea about that."

That was fine. That much could be easily established.

"And one more topic, Ms. Stoddard. The other officer? Do you recall that he was back at the car when the shot was fired? Back at his patrol car?"

"Yes."

"Now, I assume you weren't paying much attention to him while these events were taking place."

"No."

"When did you next become aware of him?"

"Oh, at some point after that, I saw him jogging down to the alley and he went in. Then he ran to the other officer and he held him."

"Did you see him do anything else?"

"I think—I was going to the phone to call 911. But then I heard a siren, so I figured they already knew."

"There was a gap of time there, when you weren't watching."

"That's—that's right, yes."

"Thank you very much, Ms. Stoddard."

Shelly took her seat. Alex leaned into her and said, "That last part was better."

"Thanks."

"You never at any time saw the officer brandish his firearm, did you?" Dan Morphew had barely waited for Shelly to make it to her seat to begin his redirect examination.

"No, I can't say that I specifically recall that."

"And you can't sit here and tell us, with any certainty whatsoever, that the officer was even *reaching* for his weapon when the shot was fired."

"No, I can't."

"Nor can you tell us what the officer was seeing if, in fact, he did reach for his weapon."

"I couldn't see what he was seeing, no."

"You can't tell us, for example, whether the officer—if in fact he did reach for his weapon—whether the officer did that because the young man in the alley had pulled a gun on *him.*"

"Objection." For this one, Shelly stood. "That question assumes facts not in evidence, your Honor." She pointed at Monica Stoddard. "This witness never said that a 'young man' pulled a gun or shot anyone. There has been no testimony about *who* did that shooting. This witness specifically said that this 'young man,' whoever it was, left her line of vision and did not return."

"Oh, for God's sake," said Morphew, as if the point were elementary. "It's an inference clearly drawn from the evidence."

The judge stared at Morphew a moment. "The objection is sustained. Rephrase it, Counsel."

Morphew adjusted his stance a bit to show displeasure, then framed his hands. "Ms. Stoddard, if we were to assume—*assume*—that Officer Miroballi was reaching for his weapon just before he was shot—you couldn't tell us if he did that in response to *someone* pulling a gun on *him.*"

"No, I have no idea."

"And we know that someone *did* shoot the officer, right?"

"Yes."

"Thank you, ma'am. That's all."

"No recross," Shelly said.

"Let's take five minutes," the judge said. "Mr. Morphew, do you have your next witness ready?"

"Judge, we do—could I beg for ten minutes?"

"Okay. Ten minutes."

"Julio Sanchez," Morphew said to the bailiff. Then he hustled out of the courtroom.

66

Price

SHELLY CLOSED THE door behind her. She and Alex were in the evidence room on the side of the courtroom. The prosecution was in charge of custody of the evidence and brought it into the courtroom every day. It served as a confidential meeting place for an attorney and client with a short break.

"Sit there." She pointed to a chair. She positioned herself on the table, which was holding various exhibits. "I am going to handle this in the way that I think is best. You can give me your opinion and I'll take it under advisement. But I make the trial strategy." She patted her chest. "If you don't like it, you can fire me. Try. Tell the judge you want to fire me. See if he lets you, at this late date."

"I told you," he answered. "I won't let you say that Ronnie or Todavia did this."

"I haven't. I'm laying the groundwork. We can decide later."

Alex brought his hands to his face.

"These people want to execute you, Alex."

He opened his hands, silently pleading. They stared at each other a moment before he finally spoke.

"I did it, Shelly. I'm the one who shot him." He held up his right hand. "God as my witness. I shot him."

His voice had a different quality to it. Deeper yet quieter, as if he were confiding in her. At that moment, she believed him. She had ample reason not to, but she did.

She moved to him, knelt down so she was face-to-face with Alex in his chair.

"I don't care," she told him. "Let's put Todavia next to you in that alley. The jury will be happy to go that way." She took his hands in hers. "Don't you see this, Alex? At most, the only person who puts that gun in your hand is a homeless man with mental and social problems. I'll do what I need to do to him. All you have to say is Eddie Todavia did it and"—she took a breath—"you could walk out of that courtroom."

He pulled his hands away and got out of the chair, moving around her. He moved to the door and put his hand on it. "And then what?" he asked.

"Then what?" She got to her feet.

"I have more than myself to think about." He turned around to her. "I accuse Todo of killing this cop and what happens to Angela? What happens to Ronnie?"

She nodded. "He's a Cannibal, you mean."

"Shit." Alex shook his head. His face was crimson. A sheen cast over his eyes. "I just"—his voice cracked; he swallowed hard—"I just got away from this guy." He began to pace the small room. "I can't go back to that. You get me out of one death sentence and into another one."

"I would take care of Angela." The words startled her, both because she was acknowledging the possible outcome of this case and because—well, she meant it. Angela was not technically her flesh and blood but Ronnie hadn't made that distinction, and so neither would she.

Alex, whether from relief or fear, broke down. He collapsed in the chair, head in his hands, and wept like she had never seen a boy cry. The tremble of his body, the sounds of anguish emanating from this boy, had the opposite effect on Shelly, emboldened her to action. She gave him his space, taking note of the time—they only had another minute or two, at most. Then she moved to him, knelt beside him again.

"I'm going to help you with Angela either way, Alex. Either way. I'll do whatever I have to do to make sure that Eddie Todavia never lays a glove on your family."

"One stupid mistake," he said. She didn't know what he meant. It was as if he hadn't heard what she had said.

She wasn't following. What mistake did he mean?

"What did you mean before?" she asked him. "You just got away from Todavia. What does that mean?"

It took Alex a moment to calm. He looked up at her, his face washed out, streaked with tears. "The car I hot-wired," he said. "When I was a freshman?"

Right. Okay. Ronnie had helped Alex out of that. Saved his life, Alex had said. He had hot-wired the wrong guy's car—

"It was Todavia's car you took," she said.

Alex nodded his head. "I didn't know it was his. But I was the driver. I was the one everyone knew about. Man, of all people, I hot-wired the car of a C-Street Cannibal."

"He was going to kill you," she said. "Ronnie talked him out of it."

"But nothing's for free."

"He put you to work for him. He made you sell drugs for him. Oh, Alex."

Me and Alex is all good. Eddie Todavia had nodded at Alex when he said that yesterday. Alex had nodded back. Now she got it.

Alex opened his hands. "He beat the piss out of Ronnie and then he told me that if I would work for him, he'd let me skate."

"But that was freshman year. You didn't start selling until 2003, right? Sophomore year."

"Todo got busted, like, a month after this happened. It bought me a year. Ten months. Whatever. But he had a good memory. He had moved out to the west side after he served his time. He said he could use a white kid to sell to the professionals that don't want to come out to his 'hood to score. He also said he'd heard I had a daughter now." He deflated. "I got the point."

Shelly stood again, reached for the wall to steady herself. "So you started selling drugs to settle a debt to Todavia."

He nodded. "I liked the money, too. I admit it. But yeah, that's how it started."

"And what Todavia said in court yesterday—you were 'all good'—he was saying the debt was paid now. He screwed you in court so he felt he owed you one."

Alex took a deep breath, settled now. "Yeah. I'm free of him now. You go after him, he'll come back harder."

"Was it Todavia in the alley with you, Alex?"

He looked at her with a look that told her she knew better. "C'mon, Shelly. You know it wasn't."

She did know. She had never truly thought so. She just liked the idea because it worked. It was convincing. But there was more here. *You know it wasn't,* Alex had just said. Alex was admitting, without saying so, that *someone* was there. He was telling her they both knew who that someone was.

And truly, Shelly had known that, too. She had lived with the small residual doubt that Alex's denials had given her. She had taken every morsel of rationalization she could to avoid what she knew to be true. Ronnie was the one in the alley.

A knock on the door. One of Morphew's assistants poked her head in.

"One minute and we'll be there," Shelly said.

The door closed again.

"You were a confidential informant for Miroballi, weren't you, Alex? The reason you met with him was you were trying to get him to bust Eddie Todavia. Right? Because if Todavia were arrested, you'd be free of your debt. *That's* why you were meeting with Miroballi."

Alex smiled. She couldn't read the expression.

"Everything I say, you have a new story," he said. "I guess that's why you're a good lawyer."

Another knock on the door, and this time the assistant said, "We really need you out here, Counsel."

"One second." Shelly turned back to Alex as the door closed. "Listen to me, Alex Baniewicz. We are going to put Eddie Todavia in that alley with you. I *will* do that. I'll make sure that kid never gets near you. You have my word on that. No one with any credibility is going to say that it *wasn't* Todavia. I'll make the jury believe that. And you don't get an opinion on this."

She opened the door and went into the courtroom, where all eyes at the prosecution table were fixed on her. Dan Morphew walked over to her and handed her a videotape and a file.

"We have a new witness," he said.

67

Flipper

SHELLY LOOKED AT the videotape. It had a sticker on it that said DEPARTMENT OF CORRECTIONS. She looked back up at Morphew.

"We took it last night," he said. "They're not family, Shelly, in case you were going to argue confidentiality. We checked the D.O.C. regs last night. Before we even looked at it. Ronnie Masters isn't related to your client any more than the prime minister of Japan is."

She opened the file folder. It was a plea agreement between Ronnie Masters and the county attorney.

"I told the judge about this," he said. "I told him you'd want to see the tape right away. There's a VCR back there."

They went through the same door the judge used, passed his chambers, and went to another room where a television and VCR were assembled. While Morphew worked the machine, Shelly looked through the file. She saw the form signed last night by Ronnie Masters—signed by every visitor to a corrections facility, in fact—acknowledging awareness that the government could record conversations unless the visitor was either the detainee's counsel or blood relation.

"Nobody really reads these things before they sign them," she said, hardly even pretending to accept her own argument.

"That dog won't hunt," he said. "Here we go."

He stepped back and the screen came alive. The hidden camera in the detention center was angled so that the person in clearest focus was the detainee, who sat in the same spot every time—the end of the table where the chain from the prisoner's handcuffs was locked down. Smart. Guaranteed that you'd get the prisoner on tape clearly.

She held her breath as she watched the tape.

Ronnie Masters walked over to Alex with a piece of paper rolled up in his hand. "What the fuck is this?" he asked, slapping the paper down on the table.

"I don't know," Alex answered, seated in the chair with his hands in manacles. "What is it?"

Ronnie kept a distance but pointed at it. He couldn't stand still. "That's the paper tonight. The Watch, *on-line. Look at the fucking headline."*

Alex read it aloud. "'Defense blames drug dealer in Miroballi trial.'"

Ronnie paced a small area and pointed at it again. "It says Shelly's not going with self-defense anymore. When the fuck did that happen?"

Alex looked at Ronnie. "Take it easy—"

"I'm not gonna 'take it easy,' okay? I'm not gonna be the scapegoat here, got me? I'm not going to jail for you. I'll tell them. I'll tell them everything."

"Ronnie"—Alex came out of his chair, as best he could with his hands shackled. "What the hell are you doing? They can—"

"I don't care what you or your lawyer says. I'm not—"

"Ronnie, shut up! What the hell are you doing?" He nodded his head upward.

Ronnie looked around the room. He seemed to understand the reminder. He moved closer to Alex and pointed a finger at him. "Do not mess with me," he warned in a softer, but no less firm voice that came through perfectly clear on the tape.

"What the hell are you—"

"Alex." He moved away but kept his finger directed at Alex. "Don't forget what I said. Don't make me do anything here."

He left the room. Alex called after him but to no avail.

Shelly fell back in her chair. "That tape isn't coming in," she said.

Morphew sat next to her in a chair. He was a gentleman, more or less, and he seemed above outright gloating. But he was awfully pleased. "Who needs the tape?" He pointed at her file. "The tape just explains how we first came upon him. It shows we're not springing this on you."

Morphew motioned to the plea agreement he'd given Shelly. "We got him last night and finalized the deal this morning," he told her.

The plea agreement was signed, only an hour ago, by a public defender representing Ronnie. That answered the question of why Morphew had seemed preoccupied. In exchange for receiving immunity for obstruction of justice charges, Ronnie Masters agreed that he would truthfully testify to the following:

(1) That he was present at the place and time of the shooting of Officer Ray Miroballi, to wit, February 11, 2004, at approximately 8:00 p.m., in an alley intersecting the avenues of Gentry (200 south block) and Donnelly (200 south block);

(2) That the reason for his presence at that place and time was that he was driving to the City Athletic Club, at 155 South Gentry, to pick up the defendant, Alex Gerhard Baniewicz, from a basketball game;

(3) That at the aforesaid place and time, he witnessed the defendant, Alexander Gerhard Baniewicz, discharge a firearm that resulted in the death of Officer Raymond Miroballi;

(4) That at the aforesaid time and place, after witnessing said shooting, he drove his car back to his residence;

(5) That he was aware, after the fact, that the defendant, Alexander Gerhard Baniewicz, had met with Officer Raymond Miroballi but that he was unaware of the reason for these meetings;

(6) That on February 25, 2004, between the hours of 8:00 and 9:00 P.M. at the location of the defendant's detention, the defendant, Alexander

Gerhard Baniewicz, admitted to meeting with Officer Raymond Miroballi on more than one occasion in the past and stated that he had "been
playing   a   dangerous   game"   with   Officer
Miroballi;

(7) That he knowingly and deliberately failed
to disclose the aforementioned facts to law enforcement despite being asked for any information relating to this matter; and

(8) That he knowingly and deliberately lied to
law enforcement about his whereabouts on the
night of the shooting.

"Oh, Ronnie," she mumbled. He had kept himself entirely
out of the fray. He didn't know why Alex was talking to
Miroballi, he was going to say. He didn't participate in a cover-
up of the crime. Sure.

She looked up at Morphew.

"Sorry, Counselor," he said, and she sensed that, on some
level, he meant it.

"You've been recording everything all along?"

"Actually, no. We really don't do that as much as we should."
He shrugged. "I got to thinking that somebody must have helped
your guy. I mean, we never found the gun. Where could he have
put it that we didn't look? That meant Ronnie. So a few weeks
ago, I got the bright idea. Only Ronnie hadn't been coming
around. He stormed in last night and we were ready for him."

"But he didn't admit to disposing of the weapon."

"No, he didn't."

She waved the paper in her hand. "Have you given me everything on this kid, Dan? You're expecting me to believe that this
all came about as a hunch?"

"I am. Because it's true." He leaned into her. "You think I'm
going to withhold evidence from *you*? That's not a smart career
move." He straightened again. "We've been by the book all
along, Shelly, and you know it. C'mon, let's go talk to Petey."

They went to the judge. Shelly objected to the "ambush" but
she had no chance. The prosecution was entitled to continue
their investigation. They had just come upon this tape, and it

spawned an interrogation of Ronnie Masters. He waived the right to counsel—Shelly had been provided the waiver as well—and ultimately had secured the services of the public defender to work out a deal.

"I'll allow a brief continuance, Ms. Trotter," the judge offered. "After we finish our witnesses today."

Only twenty minutes ago, she had said the words to Alex—that she would put Todavia in that alley, the gun in his hand. Nobody, besides a homeless man, would say otherwise. It was a good case. And now this.

She got up from the chair in a daze. She felt like she'd been hit over the head with a brick. She had only one thing going for her.

Ronnie had made the decision easier for her.

She was allowed all of five minutes to show this to Alex. "Thank God," he said, when he learned that Ronnie was off scot-free. "There's no way Ronnie gets in trouble now?"

"That's right. Tell me what's true and what's not," she said, referring to the numbered paragraphs that would constitute Ronnie's principal testimony.

He reread the allegations and looked at Shelly. "Every word of this is true."

She felt like the floor had collapsed beneath her. She was back at the bottom of the mountain again.

"We still can say self-defense," Alex offered. "This doesn't say it wasn't self-defense."

"Let's proceed," said the judge as the jurors took their seats. "See what we can get in before lunch."

"The People call Julio Sanchez," said Morphew.

68

Partners

"My name is Julio Edgar Sanchez." Ray Miroballi's partner was in uniform, his hat in his lap. The sizeable witness stand, the high railing, dwarfed him. His hair was neatly combed; his skin was smooth and almost glossy, possibly the result of perspiration. This would be a tough memory for the officer, and his encounter with Shelly when she accosted him had not been the most pleasant, either. All in all, there were probably many places Sanchez would rather be.

Dan Morphew was comfortable directing police officers, something that came with every case. He moved with efficiency through the essentials—shield number, years on the force, assignment to the second precinct of Area Four.

"Ray was my partner for three years," said Sanchez.

Shelly had to continually work her way out of the avalanche that had just fallen on her. Ronnie Masters would put the gun in Alex's hand, when no other credible evidence could have. Ronnie had turned on Alex out of fear. And Alex was letting him.

"Take you to February eleventh of this year, Officer." Morphew now used the lectern centered between the prosecution and defense table, but moved behind it so the defense could look at the jury, and vice versa. Shelly had continually reminded Alex that the jurors would sneak glances at him throughout the trial, not seeking confrontation but wanting to look at the person they were judging.

"We got started that day at one o'clock. We worked the precinct."

"You were patrolmen."

He nodded.

"Officer, an audible answer, please."

"Yes, we were patrolmen. We drove a patrol car. Squad Thirteen."

"What was your shift?"

"One to nine."

"And describe the day for us, Officer. February eleventh."

"Well, I can't remember every detail, y'know. But it was a normal day. We drove around the second."

"The second precinct?"

"Right, the second precinct." Sanchez described the boundaries of the second precinct in Area Four. The precinct included such neighborhoods as the Andujar projects on the west side and the city's downtown.

"We made a couple arrests that day, I'm pretty sure. Like every day. Nothing big happened, though. Not until later."

"And what happened around seven-thirty that evening, Officer?"

"We were by the train station. Ray said he wanted to head over to the City Athletic Club. We were going to pay a visit to his confidential informant."

"Now, when you—"

"Objection." Shelly got to her feet. "Move to strike based on lack of foundation, your Honor. This witness has no idea about any confidential informant."

The judge nodded. "Lay the foundation, Counsel," he said to Morphew.

"Yes, Judge." Morphew pointed at Alex. "Officer, before the night of the shooting, had you ever seen the defendant before?"

She could object to that, too, but she didn't want to show her hand.

"Yeah, I saw him a couple of times before."

"Describe these times."

"Ray met with the kid a couple of times."

"Where? When?"

"They met at Abbott Park. It's down south of the commercial district. I think the first time was right around Thanksgiving—"

Right. The first time Alex had met with Miroballi was November 24 of last year.

"—and the second was, I think, beginning of December."

Also correct. December 1, 2003, was the second time they had met.

"I went with him. Ray said you never knew with a confidential informant. He said he wanted some backup just in case."

"Object to the hearsay," said Shelly.

Morphew was prepared on this point, naturally. These were critical facts for him. "These statements go to state of mind. They aren't offered for the truth of the statements. They're offered for the fact that they were made."

"I'll allow them," said the judge.

"Judge." Shelly was on her feet. "State of mind, at this point, has no relevance. This is a thinly veiled attempt to establish—"

"I said that I will allow it, Counsel. Your objection is overruled."

The word on Judge Dominici was that he was a prosecutor's judge. Most, but not all, former prosecutors who assumed the bench were. This didn't mean that they jumped up and down and applauded the prosecutor and booed and hissed at the defense attorney. It was always more subtle. Subtle, as in, at a critical evidentiary juncture of the case, you go the prosecutor's way.

The judge was wrong on this, and she had to make her case for the court of appeals. She argued, despite the judge's attempt to close debate, for the better part of a minute.

"You are overruled," the judge repeated.

"So I watched from my car," Sanchez continued at Morphew's prompting. "Both times. Alex over there and Ray talked for a while. Then Ray would go back to his car and I'd go home, too."

"On each of those days, Officer, did you ask Ray afterward what had happened?"

"Yeah."

"And what—what information did he give you?"

"Information about the Columbus Street Cannibals."

They had rehearsed this well. They were dancing around the hearsay rule.

"What kind of information did Officer Miroballi say to you, after he had talked with the defendant each of those times? Can you be more specific?"

"Information on the Cannibals' drug dealing. Places. Amounts. Future plans for drug purchases."

"Did Officer Miroballi tell you the defendant's name?"

"No."

"Did Officer Miroballi, to your knowledge, register this confidential informant?"

"Objection."

"Overruled."

"Judge," Shelly said, "now it's Mr. Morphew making the assumption that my client was somehow a confidential informant."

"Counsel." The judge removed his glasses. "There has been more than enough foundation to demonstrate that the defendant had been supplying information about drug deals to Officer Miroballi."

"There hasn't been any," she said quickly. The judge's words had hurt badly, said as they were in the jury's presence. She felt the heat come to her face. Her objection had gone south on her. Now the judge was placing his official stamp on the prosecution's theory. "This is assumption stacked upon assumption."

"You are overruled, Ms. Trotter. You've made your record and now we're going to continue, if that's all right with you."

"We move for a mistrial, your Honor. This is unbelievably prejudicial and unfair."

"That motion is denied. Mr. Morphew, proceed."

Shelly took her seat. She didn't know if she was angrier at the judge or herself.

"No," Sanchez answered. "Ray didn't register the defendant. Something like this—drugs and especially the Cannibals— people want to be sure of privacy. Ray, he didn't even tell *me* his name. It's, like, a trust thing."

Morphew paused a moment. "All right, sir. Now let's go back to what we were originally talking about. Seven-thirty, the night of February eleventh, 2004."

"Okay. Ray said he wanted to go see his informant."

"Did he say why?"

"He—y'know, like I said, he didn't want to tell me too much. I think he was worried for me, too."

"Objection."

"Overruled."

"Go on, Officer Sanchez."

"Ray, he didn't say much detail or anything. He said to me, 'I think this kid's playing with me.' He said—"

"Objection."

"—'I gotta get some answers from this kid.'"

"Goes to state of mind, Judge," said Morphew. "Based on what the defense has pleaded pretrial, the state of mind of the officer is very much at issue."

"No." Shelly got to her feet. "No, it is not. His *actions* are relevant. *My client's* state of mind is relevant. What was going through the officer's head is absolutely not."

"I don't agree with that," said the judge. "I'm going to allow it."

"This is"—Shelly opened her arms—"this is simply wrong, Judge. This is entirely unfair. All of this so-called 'state of mind' evidence is entirely unreliable and inadmissible."

The judge leaned forward on his elbows, staring at Shelly. "Counsel, the officer's state of mind informs his actions. This is relevant testimony."

"We are talking about an objective standard," she said, referring, without using the words, to self-defense. "A reasonable-person standard from the standpoint of my client. Unless the officer was transferring his thoughts by telepathy to my client, his state of mind is of no relevance whatsoever."

The judge didn't seem to appreciate the sarcasm. "Over," he said, "ruled."

"Tell us again, Officer, since there was an interruption—"

"Ray said, 'This kid is playing games with me. I gotta get some answers from this kid.'"

"He didn't say anything about hurting that kid, did he?"

"No. Just talking. Getting some answers."

"Okay." Morphew looked at the jury. "Now, did you see the defendant when you got to the City Athletic Club?"

"Not at first. Then he came out. So we drove over to him."

"Did your partner say anything else about the defendant?"

Sanchez nodded. "Ray told me he saw the defendant holding drugs."

"Objection," Shelly said. "Total and complete hearsay."

"Goes to state of mind," said the judge. "Overruled."

"What happened next?"

"Ray radioed it in."

"To whom?"

"Dispatch. Police dispatch."

"Did you turn on your overhead lights?"

"Yeah, we did."

"Go on, Officer."

"Ray got out of the car. He started walking toward the defendant."

"What did you do?"

"I got out, too. Walked over, too, but not as far as Ray. Not over to the defendant. Kept a distance. That's what we do. So I can see the bigger picture."

"What did Officer Miroballi do?"

"He walked over to the defendant."

"And?"

"The defendant ran."

"How did the two of you respond?"

"Ray ran after him. Told me to get back to the car."

"Was that unusual, in your experience?"

"No, it was normal. Standard. One chases by foot, the other by car."

"What happened next?"

"Ray, he"—the officer caught himself, paused, cleared his throat—"well, the defendant over there ran into an alley about ten, fifteen yards away. Turned and went down the alley."

"And Officer Miroballi?"

Sanchez gestured, swatted the air. His eyes had filled.

"You need a moment, Officer?"

Sanchez took a deep breath, then finished the story with his exhale. "Ray chased him into the alley. Few seconds later, I heard a single gunshot. I'd barely had the chance to get the car going. I—I got there too late." He licked his lips nervously, as a single tear streamed down his cheek.

Morphew waited a moment out of respect, and to allow the jury to absorb the sorrow. He was starting with the emotional aspect of the testimony, trying to win the jury early and then pile on corroboration.

"You drove to the alley?"

He shook his head. "I got out and went over there on foot. I— I found Ray."

"He was dead."

"That's right."

"Your Honor." Morphew had moved to the defense table. "I'd rather not have to show the officer these exhibits. But if I could publish." They were the death photos. They had already been ruled admissible, so Morphew didn't need anyone to authenticate them.

"Certainly," said the judge.

Morphew passed them around, one by one, and the jurors passed them, wincing and holding their breath. Using them now had a good effect, probably a better impact than with the medical examiner who would testify later. The prosecutor gave the jurors all the time, and more, that they needed to go through the grisly pictures. Then he collected them and entered them into evidence, without objection from Shelly.

"What did you do next, Officer? Can you describe the scene?"

Sanchez was looking over everyone's heads, into his memory. "I held him. I just held him and prayed for him. I don't remember the scene."

"Of course. Did you see the defendant?"

He shook his head. "No. He had left by then."

"That alley. It ran all the way through from Gentry Street to the next street to the east?"

"Yeah. You can run all the way through to the next street."

"Other than your partner, of course, did you see anything else in that alley? Can you remember anything at all?"

"Yes." Sanchez cleared his throat. "Yes. I saw some drugs— what looked like a couple of packets of drugs, and a gun, a ways down. To the east. In the direction he had run away."

That was objectionable, but there was little denying that Alex—or Ronnie—had run through the alley.

"And what about Officer Miroballi's gun?" Morphew asked.

"Holstered."

"His weapon was in his holster when you found him dead?"

"Yes."

Morphew flipped through his notes to make sure he had covered everything. Shelly had forced him to go out of order by her objections. Morphew had covered the confidential informant testimony before he had planned. Finally, after flipping pages back and forth, he looked up at the witness.

"And, Officer, these events took place in the city, county, and state in which we are sitting today?" A basic jurisdictional question, to establish that this court had the right to be hearing this case. Morphew probably asked now before he forgot.

"Yes."

"Okay, Officer. I'd like to move to another topic." He waved a hand. "Was Officer Raymond Miroballi, to your knowledge, involved in illicit drug dealing in any way at all?"

Sanchez straightened his posture. "Absolutely not. No way." His voice was suddenly stronger, his tone indignant.

"To your knowledge—"

"Ray hated drugs. Never took them, never put up with them. He used to talk about the damage they did to kids. We saw them, you know." He was talking to the jury. "We saw strung-out kids every day. It made Ray sick. He always talked about wiping out the drug trade completely. He hated drugs, he hated gangs. He hated everything they represented. He used to, he used to point at kids running around in the projects, and he'd say, 'That could be my kid.'" He shook his head. "Ray wanted to take down the street gangs. Not work with them."

Shelly wanted to cut him off but opted not to. She was playing a popularity contest, in part, with the jury. Besides, with follow-up questions, Morphew could elicit this information, anyway.

Morphew approached the witness and extended his hand. "Officer Sanchez, thank you very much for doing your duty here."

Many questions here. Some issues to explore. Shelly wasn't sure where to start first. She calculated the damage, prioritized it, as she rose for cross-examination.

69

Dance

SANCHEZ REGARDED SHELLY with wariness, watching her out of the corner of his eye. That told her something. The last time they spoke, it was out of compulsion, due to the blackmail photos Shelly had. She still had them, of course. And Sanchez obviously hadn't told anyone about it, at least not Morphew. So he still had something to lose. Then again, he wasn't going to go overboard and sell out the case. He had probably figured, correctly so, that Shelly wouldn't use the photos, unless perhaps he completely betrayed her. She could expect him, at a minimum, to stick to what he told her before. It would be a delicate dance.

"Good morning, Officer." Shelly stood at the podium. She had a single page before her with bullet points. She wanted to go after him, but the emotional tone had to subside somewhat first. She would start easy. "Over the months that preceded this shooting, Officer Miroballi seemed troubled, didn't he?"

"Maybe so."

"He was upset about something. Something he wouldn't share with you."

"It seemed like that. I'm not a mind reader but it seemed like that."

"He seemed stressed out."

"Yeah, I'd agree with that."

"He wouldn't tell you why."

"No."

"He told you he was a good cop, right?"

"Uh-huh."

"Yes?"

"Yes."

"He made a point of telling you he'd never taken a payoff."

"He said that."

"You wondered why he was telling you that stuff."

"Ray, he didn't always open up. I figured he'd tell me if he wanted to."

He hadn't exactly answered the question, but he was doing fine. "You suspected that your partner was doing something illegal."

"Objection," Morphew said from his seat. "There's no foundation for that."

"Sustained."

Shelly expected the objection and didn't really mind. She had planted the seed with her question, and she wasn't sure Sanchez would go along with it anyway.

"He started acting like this in November or December of last year," she said.

"Yeah, that's about right."

"Ordinarily, your partner really enjoyed Christmas," she said. "Last year, he didn't."

"Right."

"And the day of February eleventh of this year. You partner was not in a good mood that day."

He looked away from her. "I suppose not," he conceded.

"He seemed nervous."

"Maybe."

"It was your partner's idea to go to the City Athletic Club."

"It was, yeah."

"And as you approached the City Athletic Club, Officer Miroballi became more nervous, didn't he? As far as you perceived it?"

Sanchez blinked, wet his lips. He was thinking. Shelly felt a surge. One of those things that defy description; something in the direction of his eyes, the twitch of his mouth. There was something there. She'd always suspected. But the officer's decision to speak up would not come from her threats or compulsion. Shelly always had thought the guy was okay. A religious man. He was pitting department loyalty and friendship against the truth.

She didn't know the answer to this question—she was violating a cardinal rule of cross-examination—but with each passing moment, she felt more confident of her guess.

"A boy's on trial here, Officer." She motioned toward Alex.

Sanchez looked at Alex, then back at Shelly. The jury was picking up on his hesitation.

"He asked you to back him up out there, didn't he? Officer? He told you—"

"No." Sanchez swallowed hard. "I don't recall anything specific. Just same old stuff. Just talking about how the day went, that sort of thing."

Shelly fixed her stare on him. "You sure about that, Officer?"

"Objection."

"Sustained."

She shook her head with disappointment, for the jury's benefit.

"Let's go the scene, Officer, on February eleventh." She moved to the podium and placed on it a diagram of the crime scene, showing South Gentry Street, the alley running horizontally across the page, Donnelly Street to the east. A key in the corner showed the top of the page pointing north and showing a bracketed distance to represent one yard. It was drawn to scale by a trial graphics company—something else Paul had popped for—and Morphew had stipulated to its accuracy.

"This boy on the street," she said, "he ran, after you and your partner got out of the car."

"Yes."

"Then you went back to the car."

"Yes."

The measurements couldn't be exact. Nobody could precisely place Alex at a particular spot on the sidewalk when the car approached them, and nobody could precisely pinpoint the car, either.

"Your car was about, say, about twenty yards north of the alley."

Sanchez looked into the air. "Something like that, yeah."

"And you had walked about how many steps from the car when the boy started running?"

"Just a few, I guess. I stayed back. Maybe five or ten steps."

"And it is stipulated that Officer Miroballi was nineteen feet into the alley, from the sidewalk on Gentry, at the time he died. You have no reason to disagree with that, do you?"

"No."

"Okay. And—I'm sorry—when the boy started running, how far away from the vehicle was your partner?"

"He was, maybe—if I had taken five steps, he had taken more like ten."

"So he was still a good, oh, ten yards from the alley."

"Sounds about right."

"Okay. And—the car was still running, right? You didn't turn it off."

"Yeah, of course it was still running."

"So to get to the car, you just had to move a few steps."

"Yeah."

"And Officer Miroballi ran ten yards to the alley, plus another nineteen feet or so into the alley."

The witness watched Shelly. "That's right."

"So you were in the car before your partner had even reached the alley."

"Okay."

She nodded and moved from the lectern, behind the prosecutors and toward the jury. "If I told you, Officer, that there has been testimony that your partner had some kind of a conversation in that alley with that boy—based on your memory of the timing of things, sir, would that surprise you? Would it surprise you that Officer Miroballi would have had time to have a conversation with that person before you arrived? In fact, before you even put the car into drive?"

Morphew objected, but the judge allowed it.

Sanchez had figured out where she was headed. Maybe everyone had. Officer Sanchez had ample time to get to his car and drive to the alley, or wherever, if he was helping in the chase. By the time his overweight partner made it to the alley, then traveled nineteen feet and had a conversation with Alex, Sanchez easily could have moved the car forward at least an inch.

"I gave them some privacy," he conceded. "Ray said he wanted to talk to the boy. So I let him."

"Okay. So you weren't part of any 'chase,' were you, Officer?"

"No. You don't come between a cop and his snitch."

"So it was your intention to let your partner do whatever it was he was going to do. You were going to stay back."

"He was going to talk to the boy."

"That's what he told *you*."

"That's—yes."

"Sure. I mean"—Shelly placed a hand on the jury railing—"if you knew that Officer Miroballi's real plan was to kill this boy, then you'd be in quite a lot of trouble for sitting back and letting that happen, wouldn't you?"

"Objection."

The judge had the court reporter read back the question, which was fine with Shelly. "Goes to bias," she said, as if the point were elementary.

"The witness will answer."

"That wasn't what Ray was going to do."

"And that's what you *have* to say, isn't it, Officer? Or you lose your badge."

"It's the truth, is why I'm saying it."

"You said Ray kept to himself."

The witness gathered himself. "Yes, I said that."

"You couldn't read his mind, could you?"

"I couldn't. No."

Shelly wasn't done. This line of questioning had been scheduled for the finale of this cross-examination, the way she had planned to end things. That was the problem with her methods. She went with her gut, and sometimes a grander plan got lost in the process.

She took a deep breath as a segue. She was now standing next to the jurors. Generally speaking, on direct examination, you want the jury to watch the witness, so you stay out of the jury's view. For cross-examination, the lawyer wants to be the center of attention, because it is her words, more than anything, that she wants the jury to hear. In a perfect world, the witness would simply answer "yes" or "no" to every question, such that the jury was really hearing a mini-closing argument from the lawyer.

She strolled away from the jury into the center of the courtroom so that the jury could look at both her and Sanchez. "You don't know for a fact that my client was a confidential informant, do you?"

Sanchez played with the characterization. "Ray said he was."

"Sure, *Ray* said he was. But you don't know that, do you?"

He shrugged. "I saw them meet. He was giving Ray information."

"You don't know what was said when those two met, do you, Officer?"

"Well, not firsthand—"

"*Ray* told you what was said."

He sighed. "That's true."

"So all of your reasons for thinking that my client was a confidential informant come down to what your partner told you."

"I suppose so. But I saw them together. I don't know why else they would be meeting."

"Exactly," she said. "You don't know."

"No, I don't."

"So you have to concede the possibility that Alex may *not* have been your partner's confidential informant."

"I—I suppose that's possible."

"And if that possibility were true—if Alex was not an informant for Officer Miroballi—that would make you reconsider the events that led to his death, wouldn't it?"

"Objection, Judge," said Morphew. "Argumentative and speculative."

"I will—I'm going to allow that."

Sanchez opened his hands. "I don't know what you mean."

She nodded. "Your partner reported that the boy he saw walking down the street had drugs in his possession, right?"

"Right."

"You didn't see those drugs, did you?"

"No. Doesn't mean he didn't have them."

"Well, wasn't your view of the boy as good as your partner's?"

"Not really. I was looking around some. Checking out the street."

"Oh. You didn't get such a good look at the boy."

"Not really."

"I guess that makes sense," Shelly said, as if to herself. "He had his back to you, right? Because he was walking south-bound, away from you."

"That's right."

"He had on a long coat."

"Yes."

"A cap on his head."

"Yeah."

"It was probably hard for you to see anything about this boy at all."

"That's right."

She imagined that Sanchez was eager to say such things. He wanted to put some distance between himself and the events, for the sake of the Internal Affairs Division's review of this case. The less he saw, the better.

"You didn't see his pockets."

"No."

"Didn't see his face."

"No."

"Didn't really see—he had a cap on. You probably couldn't see his hair, either."

"No."

"This thing was all your partner's, wasn't it? He wanted to see the boy. He's the one who said he saw him with drugs. He's the one who wanted some 'privacy' with the boy."

"That's right."

"You didn't see the drugs. You didn't give chase. You didn't even see his face."

"That's right." Again, Sanchez was more than eager to comply. Shelly was surprised, frankly, that Morphew hadn't worked with Sanchez more on this.

"And since you never saw his face, or his hair, or any part of him from the front, Officer," she said, her heart drumming—because this could fall under the heading of one-question-too-many—"you can't even sit here and say that it was *this* boy that you saw, can you?"

"I—" Sanchez cleared his throat. "Ray said it was his snitch."

"*Ray* said." Shelly knew now that she had the answer she wanted. "*Ray* said. You can't say for sure that it was my client who you saw walking down that street, can you?"

"Ray saw his face. When he first came out on the sidewalk. We were about a block away to the north. I wasn't looking. But Ray saw his face. He said, 'There he is.'"

"*Ray* said," Shelly repeated. "Please answer my question, Officer. You didn't actually see my client, did you? You cannot sit here, under oath, and identify Alex Baniewicz as the person you saw, can you?"

Sanchez answered in a quieter voice. "It was my understanding that both Ray and another man on the street identified your client—"

"Move to strike—"

"—as the one who shot my—"

"Your Honor—"

"Stop." The judge leaned forward with his hand out. "Everyone stop. The answer is stricken as unresponsive. The jury will disregard that testimony. Officer, answer the question, please."

Sanchez looked at the judge. "I didn't see him with my own eyes, no."

Now she was finished. There was an audible reaction from the jury. Based on his earlier equivocation, they had to have known his answer, but actually hearing it made an impact. Shelly felt a rush. The homeless man was the only person left who could identify Alex as the shooter.

Well, no. There was the small matter of Ronnie Masters.

70

Silence

THE REDIRECT OF Officer Sanchez went well into the afternoon. Morphew did well with the cop, but it was nothing new. It was just nice to restate the favorable points. Morphew made the point that "the boy" was wearing a coat he had seen on Alex Baniewicz at the park, and that the height and build of "the boy" matched that of Alex.

Ronnie could have worn the coat, obviously. Yes, Ronnie was about two inches taller and thicker in the chest and shoulders than Alex, but how well would any of that come out when he was wearing winter clothing, a long wool coat and cap?

In her lengthy preparation of the cross of Officer Sanchez, Shelly had obviously considered the idea that she could get Sanchez to admit that he didn't see Alex. She knew he wanted to distance himself from what happened—put it all on his partner—and she thought, in his effort to do so, she could trap him.

Now, she wasn't sure that she could chalk up his admission to her courtroom skills. She believed that Sanchez was telling the truth. There were a million reasons for him to believe it was Alex without seeing him. Sanchez thought "the snitch" referred to Alex. Alex was arrested that night with Miroballi's blood on his clothes. And Shelly, almost right out of the gate, had pleaded self-defense, which meant that Alex was the shooter. Maybe he had unconsciously revised his memory and assumed that he saw Alex, until pressed on the point.

The judge adjourned the proceedings at three-thirty. He told

Shelly, out of the presence of the jury—and for the sake of a higher court that might review this case—that he wanted to give her some extra time to prepare for the testimony of Ronnie Masters tomorrow. If she did not feel prepared to go tomorrow, he advised her, he would grant her additional time.

"Very good," she told him. She was not going to thank him. He had screwed her today. He was wrong in allowing all that testimony about what Miroballi said to Sanchez about Alex. She felt sure of it. But she realized that a higher court would need more than that to overturn a conviction. Appellate courts in this state liberally applied the "harmless error" rule, under which a court found that the trial judge made an error but that the error was not enough to warrant a new trial. A fair trial did not mean a perfect trial.

She spoke with Alex at length after the adjournment. He was pleased that Ronnie now had immunity. It meant that his daughter, Angela, would have someone to take care of her. Technically, Ronnie had only been given immunity for obstruction of justice, because that was the only crime to which he had admitted—withholding information from the cops and lying to them. But short of a confession by Ronnie, he would never be prosecuted for anything related to the Miroballi shooting.

After speaking with Alex, she went immediately to Ronnie. Ronnie was being held, pending his testimony, at county lockup, in segregation, but when she arrived there, she was told that the detainee did not wish to speak with her. She demanded to hear this from Ronnie's mouth. Eventually, the deputy warden was called down. Detainees had the right to refuse a visitor, he told her, but she jumped up and down and threatened enough that he finally agreed to a face-to-face. Shelly wondered if the fact that her father could have this guy fired had anything to do with the change of heart.

She was shown to a small room not unlike the one Alex had been in. Ronnie stood at the doorway of the detainee's entrance and shook his head. "I don't want to talk to her," he told the deputy warden. "I don't have to talk to her."

She stared into his eyes, but he looked away. "You sure about that, Ronnie?" she called out.

"I'm sure," he said to the deputy warden.

Shelly watched him walk out. The door closed. She was out of luck. She looked at her watch as she left the building. It was six-thirty. She had a long night ahead of her. On her way to her office, her cell phone rang. It was, as always, Joel Lightner.

"I'm over at the City Athletic Club," he said. "I got three guys who said they've played hoops with Ronnie Masters at this open gym."

"Okay." She was not the least bit surprised. "You have your trial subpoenas?"

"Yeah."

"Serve them," she said. "We'll need those guys in a few days."

71

Bait

SHELLY SAT AT the defense table next to Alex. She had had the benefit of exactly three hours of sleep from the prior evening. There was a point in time at which it did no good to go to bed, because the small amount of sleep one received was woefully insufficient and the brief interlude of sleep left one fuzzy-headed. For Shelly, three hours was the minimum amount necessary, else she would forgo sleep altogether.

She had gone back over everything in preparing for Ronnie's cross-examination. In truth, she had known, before she started, the questions she would ask. She had made the case against Ronnie in her head for weeks now, gathering information along the way to buttress her position.

She looked at the headline from today's edition of the *Watch*.

SECOND COP CAN'T IDENTIFY DEFENDANT

The story borrowed liberally from the prior day's edition, again noting the turn in developments as defense attorney Shelly Trotter—yes, *that* Trotter, the governor's daughter—now appeared to be heading full force down the path that the prosecution got the wrong guy. There was news, according to the article, of a new witness being disclosed by the prosecution for today's proceedings, but the prosecution had refused to disclose the identity to the media because the witness was a juvenile.

On the front page of the *Daily Watch,* below the fold, was a story about Governor Trotter's opponent, Anne Claire Drummond. Her support, in little over a month, had dipped considerably. The story attributed the drop to a combination of two things: first, her initial surge was due to her status as the "new kid," the fresh-faced challenger (ironic, though, since she had served six terms in Congress), and second, it was still rather early in the race and the voters weren't hearing much from Drummond. In mid-June, most candidates were spending their time raising money and seeking the support of the critical interest groups—in Drummond's case, the unions and teachers and seniors. Ideas were being formed, strategies plotted, but the initial glow of her candidacy was temporarily dimmed.

A political columnist for the *Watch* wrote that the race was "clearly Trotter's to lose." The economy was rebounding, security-conscious citizens liked Republicans (even though state government had little to do with antiterrorism), and people just generally liked incumbents, especially G.O.P. governors. Nothing short of the revelation that the governor's daughter had given up a boy for adoption, who in turn had murdered a cop—and did we mention that the governor had tried to persuade his daughter to have an abortion?—nothing short of that could lose the race for him.

The judge entered the courtroom and asked Shelly if she was ready.

She told him she was. She didn't tell him that she had been ready for a while now.

Alex fidgeted. He had been put at ease when Ronnie got his deal, but he still was not looking forward to this day. "Don't push him," he whispered to her.

"People call Ronnie Masters," said Daniel Morphew.

"What does *that* mean?" she asked Alex.

"Just—don't hurt him too bad."

She looked at Ronnie as he entered the courtroom. He did not stop as he passed the defense table. He was wearing a button-down blue shirt and khaki trousers. His hair was combed and parted. She thought that a couple of the female jurors, and one of the male ones, found Ronnie attractive. She could see that.

Ronnie spoke with a strong voice as he gave his full name and spelled his last name. He explained that he lived with his mother, Elaine, and Alex in a small home in Mapletown, a neighborhood to the south of the commercial district. Ronnie testified for a long while about his life with Alex.

"I'd do anything for him," he said. "He'd do anything for me."

"Would you lie to protect him?" Morphew asked.

"Well, I guess I did do that," he conceded. "I would always try to help him."

"Are you here today of your own free will?"

"No, I'm not. I'm here because you made me come. And you're making me testify under oath. So I have to tell the truth."

They talked about the plea agreement for several minutes. Ronnie had been approached by police and investigators from the county attorney two nights ago, after his visit to Alex Baniewicz at the detention center. They had told him they suspected his involvement in the Miroballi shooting. He had requested a public defender and entered into a plea agreement.

"You understand, Mr. Masters, that if you tell a single lie in this courtroom today, we will rip up this plea agreement?"

"Yes."

"And you can be fully prosecuted for the crime for which you currently have immunity? If you lie."

"I understand that."

"All right. Let's talk about the eleventh of February, this year. Take you to seven o'clock that evening. Do you remember that?"

"Yes. I was getting ready to pick up Alex from the club where he plays basketball."

"Alex Baniewicz, the defendant?"

"Yeah."

"What club was that?"

"City Athletic. They have an open gym every Wednesday night. Alex plays until eight. Sometimes it goes on a little. So I left around, maybe seven-twenty. It takes me about twenty-five minutes or so but you never know."

"You drove to the City Athletic Club to pick up the defendant?"

"Yeah."

"And tell us what happened next?"

"Well, I was driving down Bonnard—that's the street just to the south of the club."

"The club is on Bonnard and Gentry?"

"Right. Bonnard's the east-west street. So I was driving east on Bonnard, after getting off the highway. Anyway, I get to the intersection and I see a police car with its lights flashing. And I saw someone that looked a lot like Alex running from a cop."

"What did you do?"

"Well, these guys were to my south. I saw Alex run into an alley. So I went east past Gentry to the next street, Donnelly. I went south down Donnelly to the alley. Like, the alley from the other side that Alex went in."

"Donnelly is a one-way street going north, is it not?"

"Yeah, it is. I went the wrong way down a one-way street."

"Why the urgency?"

He shrugged, offered a plaintive smile. "You see your brother running from the cops?"

Morphew nodded. "What were your intentions in going there?"

"I don't know. I just, sort of did it."

"Did you, in fact, reach the alley by car?"

"Yes. Well, pretty much. I pulled my car up just a little past the alley and walked over to it. Ran, is more like it."

"What did you see or hear when you made it to the alley?"

"I saw Alex and a cop."

"Did you know who the cop was?"

"I had never met that person before in my life. I knew Alex, of course."

Never met that person. That didn't mean he didn't know who he was. Ronnie was being cute here, she sensed.

"It was the two of them," Ronnie continued. "Alex and this cop. I saw the cop and Alex going for guns. Alex pulled out his gun and shot the cop."

Morphew paused a good long moment, then pointed at Alex. "You're sure it was Alex—the defendant—who shot Officer Raymond Miroballi?"

"Yes."

The jurors seemed impressed with this. Shelly realized how

much Dan Morphew must have worried about proving that Alex, in fact, was the shooter. He had probably taken for granted that Shelly would concede that fact, given her plea of self-defense; his heart had probably done a few leaps when she cross-examined Eddie Todavia, and then more so when Sanchez said he couldn't identify Alex.

He was putting Ronnie Masters on the stand, even though Ronnie was testifying that both Miroballi and Alex went for their guns. That was consistent with self-defense. Morphew must have felt desperate to put the gun in Alex's hand if he was willing to live with this testimony from Ronnie.

Shelly's stomach was cramping up. She felt the perspiration in her hairline, her underarms.

"Now, Mr. Masters," Morphew continued, "you say that when you first came into the alley, the defendant was removing his gun from his pocket, and Officer Miroballi was reaching for his?"

"Yes."

"And whose gun got out first?"

"I saw Alex's first."

"And you said that you saw nothing before this moment?"

"I did not."

"You heard nothing?"

"I did not."

That was the best Morphew could do. His point being, Miroballi was probably just trying to react to Alex. The fact that Alex got out his gun first meant that Alex was the aggressor. That was the one dent that Morphew could put in the self-defense case, making Alex the initiator of the events because he pulled the gun first. Although Ronnie had simply said he *saw* Alex's gun first.

Being cute again?

"What happened next, Mr. Masters? After the shooting?"

Ronnie adjusted in his chair. "Alex turned around and ran."

"Did he see you?"

"Yeah. I ran to my car and left. I didn't look back. I was scared."

"And do you know what Alex did?"

"No, I don't."

"Where did you go?"

"I went home."

"Later that night, did you receive a visit from police officers?"

"Yeah."

"Did they ask you questions about Alex and the shooting?"

"Yeah."

"And you lied to them, didn't you?"

"Yes, I did."

"You lied to help Alex."

"Yes. I didn't—I didn't want to hurt him."

"Are you telling the truth now?"

"Yes."

"Were you aware that the defendant had met with Officer Miroballi?"

"Before the shooting? No, I didn't know."

"Did you talk to the defendant about Officer Mirohalli?"

"Well, only after the shooting. I didn't know he'd been talking to the guy before that."

"When did you talk to the defendant about that?"

"One time when I visited him. It was a couple weeks after he was arrested."

"Was the date February twenty-fifth, 2004?"

"Yeah. I went to see him at the detention center. I asked him what the deal was with him and Miroballi."

"And what did he say to you?"

"He said he'd been playing a dangerous game with Miroballi."

"A 'dangerous game,' he said?"

"Yes."

"Did he elaborate on that?"

"No."

Morphew leafed through his notes. "Thank you. I have nothing further."

Shelly felt her stomach flip.

"Are you ready for cross-examination, Ms. Trotter?" the judge asked.

She pushed herself slowly to her feet. She was ready.

72

Foundation

THEY LOOKED AT each other for a long while. She didn't know what to make of his expression. Challenging, to put a word on it. He seemed anxious, but who wouldn't in this situation? He did not take his eyes off her. So much passed between them at this moment.

She had tried, she told herself. She had tried to give this boy a good life. The circumstances—most notably the fact that her father was an elected official averse to embarrassment—had led her away from a conventional adoption, to a private attorney adoption procedure that often connected older people, too old for the state agencies, with the not atypical result that his father died when Ronnie was young. His mother, Elaine Masters, was a good woman but not strong enough to persevere. She was an alcoholic who provided some, but not enough, for this boy.

A mother is responsible for how her child turns out. Not completely, no, but to a large extent. Was all of this her fault on some level? She didn't know the answer. It was pointless. Objection, irrelevant. Her job was at hand. She had avoided it with all her might but now it was time.

If you had told me, she did not say to him, *we could have figured something out.*

Shelly decided to forgo the lectern and stood before Ronnie, her arms together behind her back.

"Mr. Masters." Her voice was flat, hoarse. "We know each other, don't we?"

"Yes, we do."

"You and I have talked about this case, haven't we?"

"Yes, we have."

"You never told me that you were there in the alley that night of the shooting."

"I never told you a lot of things."

"You—" Her throat caught. She ignored his comment and kept going. Her legs were trembling. She considered, for a moment, returning to the defense table and questioning him while seated. "You never told me that you saw Alex shoot the officer, did you?"

"No, I didn't."

So he was cooperating so far. Surely, he did not have an agenda here. He obviously had wanted to keep himself out of the soup. He had accomplished that with his plea deal. But surely he wasn't looking to bury Alex. Surely he would work with her as much as he could.

Right?

"You said that you saw Alex's gun first."

"Yes."

"You can't tell us, can you, which person reached for a weapon first."

"No. I can't. For all I know, it was the cop that went first."

Good. Good.

"You didn't see a second gun on the floor of the alley, did you?"

"No. There wasn't a second gun that I could see."

"So if someone were to say that Alex had dropped a first gun—in an attempt to 'trick' Officer Miroballi, let's say"— because this was exactly what Morphew *had* said in his opening statement—"you would say that this wasn't true."

"It wasn't true," said Ronnie. "There was no second gun. Not then."

She watched him. Obviously, his testimony was excellent so far. He returned the stare with a life to his face that hadn't existed on direct examination. Was he trying to tell her something?

No, she could not trust this boy. This child of hers.

"You never saw drugs in Alex's possession during the time you were in the alley, did you?"

"No. Alex? No, he ran right past me and I didn't see anything fall out."

"Did you see the drugs at all?"

"No. I told you what I saw. I saw the cop and Alex with their guns. Alex shot him in self-defense."

Dan Morphew leapt to his feet. "Objection, your Honor. There is no basis for that testimony. It is a legal conclusion and it—there are no facts to support it. No foundation. This witness"—Morphew wagged a finger at him—"this witness said he saw nothing until the moment the defendant went for his gun. He said he knew nothing of a relationship between Officer Miroballi and the defendant until later."

"That's true," said Ronnie.

The judge held out a hand toward Ronnie. "Son, there is no question before you. The objection is sustained. The testimony relating to 'self-defense' is stricken."

The blood had rushed to Dan Morphew's face. It was not simply a reaction to an adverse piece of testimony, Shelly assumed. It was the fact that Morphew himself had sponsored this witness, and now he might be heading south on the prosecutor.

She was more interested in Ronnie. He had readily agreed with Morphew's objection. And now he was looking to the side of Shelly. She turned, followed Ronnie's line of vision to Alex, who was shaking his head slowly with a cold stare. He was saying *no* without words.

Alex caught Shelly's eyes on him and sighed. He dropped his head and continued to shake it, now more furiously.

What was going on here? Was she being baited by Ronnie?

Shelly took a step toward Alex and then stopped. She had conferred enough with Alex, who had stymied her every move. She was going with her gut. She was betting that Ronnie Masters would help Alex.

"Mr. Masters," she said, "you said before that you had never met Officer Miroballi. But did you know *of* him?"

Ronnie's chest heaved. "I knew he was a cop. I knew he had cops for older brothers, too."

Shelly's eyes narrowed. She looked again at Alex, who stared at the table. Then back at Ronnie. Her mind raced as if her life flashed before her eyes. Ronnie had been the one who advised her to get rid of the federal case against Alex—because, she realized, he knew that the truth of what happened, when borne out at trial, would not be what Alex had told the F.B.I., would expose Alex as a liar to the F.B.I. She pictured Ronnie going to Alex last night, full of bluster, against her repeated warnings not to talk in that interview room because the government could listen—

Her mouth opened, ever so slightly. A soft moan of recognition escaped from her throat.

Okay. Ronnie had known exactly what he was doing last night when he marched in there. He wanted to be recorded. He wanted to get the county attorney's attention.

Why?

She looked at Alex. It was like a tennis match for her now.

Alex hadn't let Ronnie say something that Ronnie had wanted very much, apparently, to say. Ronnie had a story to tell, and he didn't want anyone stopping him. Not Alex, not Shelly, not anyone. So he got the prosecution to put him on the stand and give him this opportunity, in open court, where nothing could be reversed.

"I'm sorry," Ronnie whispered to Shelly, under his breath.

The judge leaned forward. "The witness will only answer questions put to him."

Shelly nodded. "What did you know about Officer Ray Miroballi and his brothers, Ronnie?"

"His brothers covered for him, Shelly. His older brothers were cops."

"Objection!" Morphew was on his feet again. "There is no evidence that the deceased officer has done anything wrong in this case, your Honor. In fact, the only testimony has been that Officer Miroballi was not involved"—Morphew stopped himself. "Judge, we object to the lack of foundation."

"I will sustain that objection. Ms. Trotter, I realize that you are entitled to some leeway here, but I want foundation laid before there are any more outbursts like this. Lay the foundation. And Mr. Masters"—he looked down at Ronnie—"you will only answer questions put to you."

Shelly held her breath. "Ronnie, do you have evidence that

Officer Raymond Miroballi committed a crime that is related to this case?"

"I do," he said carefully.

"Related to this case?"

"Very much so. And I have more than evidence. I have proof. I have absolute, total proof."

"With your own eyes?" she asked, following the judge's admonition.

A sound came from his throat. Not quite a laugh. "With my own eyes," he said. "My own nose. My face. My hair. My arms and legs."

She kept her eyes on him. His eyes. His nose. His mouth. His—

"No," she heard herself say.

She took a step back. She brought a hand to her mouth. Of all things, she thought of Governor Langdon Trotter in the midst of a re-election campaign that was his to lose.

"Ray Miroballi is my father," Ronnie said.

Shelly made an effort to turn away, toward the defense table, to look for her chair as if it were a life-preserver.

"He raped you, Shelly, and they covered the whole thing up for him."

She became vaguely aware of Alex rushing from the table toward her, then everything turning upside-down.

And then everything turning black.

73

Refuge

DAN MORPHEW WALKED into the office within the judge's chambers, a room typically reserved for the clerks and interns who worked in the state courts. Shelly was seated on a couch, her elbows on her knees.

He handed her a glass of water. "Drink," he said.

She accepted it from him and he was right, it did help somewhat, the cool water in her mouth.

It was early in the afternoon. Several hours had passed since Ronnie had testified in open court. Shelly had been taken into the judge's chambers after fainting, where she rested for over an hour. Finally, when she had regained some measure of strength, the judge had summoned Ronnie Masters and his lawyer into his chambers, along with Morphew and Shelly.

Ronnie's public defender had freely offered a blood test for his client to confirm that he was linked by DNA to Ray Miroballi. Nobody in the room seemed to doubt this fact, but Ronnie submitted to a blood test nonetheless. Shelly also agreed to do so tomorrow. And the state had plenty of Ray Miroballi's blood for a comparison.

Dan Morphew looked like he had gone fifteen rounds with a heavyweight. Shelly probably looked like a zombie. And the judge, who on some level probably appreciated the courtroom theater, nonetheless did not enjoy spectacles during the most prestigious case he had handled in his short tenure as a judge. He told the lawyers that they had tomorrow off. The obvious explanation for this would be concern for Shelly's health. A lawyer who passed out during trial was probably dehydrated, malnourished, and sleep-deprived to the point of exhaustion. But Shelly figured the judge wanted the parties to have the chance to talk, to perhaps make this case go away.

Morphew took a seat at a desk near the couch where Shelly was sitting. It was just the two of them now. The judge was in his chambers. He had dismissed the jury for today and tomorrow.

"You feeling better?" he asked.

She took another sip of the water, made an equivocal noise as she drank.

"You didn't know any of that, did you, Shelly?"

She set the cold glass against her forehead briefly, then down on the floor.

"I found out about two weeks ago that Ronnie was my son," she said. "And I talked to Alex about it. But that is the only piece of information that I knew."

"I need a beer." Morphew had his tie yanked down, his sleeves rolled. He was enjoying the refuge of the judge's chambers as much as Shelly. A carnivorous media awaited the lawyers just outside the courtroom doors, and neither of them was anxious to venture through the crowd. Morphew looked at her out of the corner of his eye. "Well, Counselor, whatever happens here, I can say this much. I'm sorry that happened to you when you were a kid, and I'm even sorrier that you had to have this on public display."

"Thanks." She looked at her watch. "Where's Ronnie?"

"Back in lockup," he said, which made sense. Ronnie's testimony was not completed, so he was still being held as a material witness.

"Your client is downstairs in holding," he added.

She got up tentatively and stretched her arms. "What are we going to do here, Dan?"

Morphew chewed on his lip a moment, shaking his head slowly. "Miroballi was trying to cover up a dirty secret? Christ, I don't know. Sounds like neither one of us got it right."

"Let's end this now, Dan. This isn't a drug case. This isn't about a cop. This is about a man trying to bury his past."

"Aren't we all." Morphew lifted himself from the chair,

wincing with the bad back. "Listen, Shelly, I'm sympathetic. But you can't expect me to drop this."

"I can. I do."

"Then you're not thinking this through."

Morphew's estimate was probably right. If Elliot Raycroft simply dropped the charges at this point, the media would assume that Governor Trotter had intervened. That would be no help to Lang Trotter in his race for reelection, nor would it be something that Raycroft would want the voters remembering two years from now when he re-upped. Under these circumstances, the county attorney actually would have to take a tougher stand than he otherwise might. That was the irony of having a powerful father. Special treatment, perhaps, but not always more favorable.

"A cop still died," he added.

"A cop who committed rape. You get those blood tests back, it's absolute proof. You have indisputable evidence of statutory rape. And Miroballi knew that, Dan. That's why this happened. You can sell this."

Morphew stared off in the distance as she spoke. "Your client was carrying a weapon. And he was probably extorting Miroballi."

"And he's a juvenile. Those things won't transfer."

"I know, Shelly. I know. Let me see what can be done. I'll be in touch tomorrow." He reached the door and turned back to her. "You really kicked Todavia in the gut?"

"I sure did."

Morphew thought about that for a moment, chuckled to himself, and left the room.

74

Why

THE JUDGE ALLOWED Shelly to take the back elevator down to the holding cells, so she was able to avoid the feasting reporters outside the courtroom. Alex Baniewicz was lying on the thin cushion in the holding cell. He bounced up when he saw her.

"How are you?" He reached her and embraced her.

"I've got my sea legs back," she said, patting his back. She pushed him back so she was holding his shoulders at arm's length.

"Why you?" she asked. "Why you and not Ronnie? Coming to see me at the law school? Confronting Miroballi? Why did Ronnie send you?"

His expression softened, as if in embarrassment. She held firm on his shoulders.

"Give me one straight answer this entire case, Alex. You owe me that."

"Ronnie didn't send me." Alex nodded off in the distance. "He had no idea."

"Why you, then?"

He focused on her, gave her a look as if the answer were obvious. "Money, Shelly. I wanted money."

She dropped her hands from his shoulder.

"Think about it," he said. "Ronnie and I look up your birth records. We find out that his real mother is the daughter of the governor. I figured you would probably do a lot to keep Ronnie a secret."

She put her hands on her hips. "You were going to—blackmail me?"

"Yeah." He shrugged. "Ronnie would've killed me if he knew. But, yeah."

"So why didn't you?"

He smiled. "Because I liked you. I went in there with a plan, I admit it, but then I got to know you. You were an okay chick."

"I was an okay chick."

"And then you told me about—that incident. It was about a year ago."

"Mother's Day, last year, to be exact," she said.

"Oh, yeah, right." He pointed at her. "Right. So anyway. After that, I don't know—"

"After that, you found an even better blackmail target," she finished.

He shrugged. "Yeah. That was part of it. Yeah. I admit it. But also—y'know, I felt like this guy should probably answer for what he did."

"So you used that same investigator who found me to find Miroballi."

"Yeah. This guy goes through the police records, whatever. He comes up with the name of a witness. Dina. Dina Patriannis."

A shiver ran through her. *Dina.* Yes. Shelly remembered how she envied that young woman, her glamour and grace, the way a young girl romanticizes someone older.

"She knew about the whole thing, Shelly. She knew Ray Miroballi. She knew he had gone into that bedroom. When the cops came to her, she gave them his name. That's how the cops knew about Miroballi."

"I can imagine how the police reacted to that," Shelly mumbled.

"Right," Alex said. "Sure. He had two brothers on the force. They covered the whole thing up. They got you to drop it. They told Dina that you had dropped the charges."

"God." Shelly closed her eyes. That all made sense now. And Shelly had complicated things back then by giving Dina and her friends a fake name and age. She had given the police plenty of fodder to force her into dropping the case.

"So I went to Miroballi, after I knew all of this," Alex continued. "I showed him what I had. The report you had filed with the cops. I even gave him some of Ronnie's blood. I told him it was mine. I told him I was his son. I told him, test it if you want."

And he had, Shelly now realized. That was the reason Miroballi had gone to a medical center, not the one covered by his health care. He had told his partner, Sanchez, that it was a urinalysis. But it was a blood test. He was checking his blood against the blood given to him by Alex. It was a paternity test, not a urine drop.

"What you didn't know," said Shelly, "was that the feds were searching around for dirty cops. So when they found you in these clandestine meetings with Miroballi, they followed you and nabbed you. They got in your face about Miroballi and drugs, and you gave them what they wanted."

He nodded along with her narrative. "I was feeling pretty tough, y'know? I've got this cop who seems pretty worried about me. I thought I was the big man. Then, the next thing you know, I got federal agents breathing down my neck, and I'm shaking in my boots. What was I supposed to do? They caught me with drugs. And they were so damn sure that I was selling for Miroballi. So I let 'em believe it. Hell, if they were so sure about him, I figured maybe he *was* selling drugs. I was hoping maybe they'd come up with something against him without using me. I was just buying time."

"A dangerous game," she said.

"Dangerous, yeah. But what am I supposed to do? And I couldn't exactly go back to Miroballi at that point and demand cash from him. They were watching. And I had told them that he was the one who contacted me."

"They thought you were working for Miroballi," Shelly summarized. "Turns out, you were blackmailing him."

"Yeah."

"And Miroballi didn't know about Ronnie?"

Alex shook his head no. "He didn't know there *was* a Ronnie. He thought I was his son."

She accepted that. It made sense. Alex had done the same

thing with Shelly, assuming Ronnie's identity. "Ronnie knew nothing about this?"

He blew out a sigh. "Ronnie knew I had met you that first time. He thought that was the only time. He thought I just went because I was curious. And he had no idea I was talking to Miroballi. He had no idea I found out who his father was. You know him, Shelly—he would've kicked my ass. But after I was caught by the feds, I told Ronnie. My back was against the wall. So I told him everything. After that, he followed me around like a puppy. He was worried that Miroballi might come after me. Which is exactly what he did." Alex pointed to his head. "That boy, he's got a good brain on him. He was exactly right about that."

She tried to digest all of this. She walked along the cell. "Let me ask you the sixty-four thousand dollar question."

He raised his eyebrows. A kid his age probably didn't even understand the reference.

"Why, Alex—why in God's name didn't you *tell* me all of this?" She waved her arm. "All of this misdirection and deception? I'm looking at Ronnie. I'm looking at Todavia. I'm thinking about Miroballi and drugs. I understand why you bluffed the F.B.I. But why *me*?"

"Because you would have used it," he said easily.

"Because—" She stared at him. "What?"

"You would have had to tell everyone you were raped."

She drew back. "You were trying to protect *me*?"

He raised his shoulders. His eyes suddenly filled. "All the time I've known you, Shelly, you only asked me for one thing. You asked me to keep one secret. After everything else I had done, I thought it was one thing I could do right."

She put a hand on her forehead. "Alex, I think I would have made an exception where you were looking at a *death sentence*."

"Yeah, yeah. I know. It sounds ridiculous." He looked out through the bars. "This whole thing was my fault, Shelly. I was the one who did all of this. I got caught up in drugs because of that stupid thing with Todavia's car. I got greedy looking to blackmail you, and then Miroballi. I got caught by the F.B.I. I just kept screwing things up because I was doing the wrong thing. I

thought I could get this one thing right. I felt like I owed you."
He looked at her.

"I guess." She drew a circle on the floor with her shoe.

"Besides," he added, "we had a pretty good defense, right?
The F.B.I. thought Miroballi was making me sell drugs. You did,
too. Why couldn't we convince a jury of that? I thought we
could."

"Okay."

"Any other questions, Ms. Trotter?"

She scratched her head. "I can barely process what you've already told me."

"Then I have a question for you," he said.

"Shoot." She winced at the pun.

"You asked me the other day about me hurting my knee that
night. How'd you know about that? I never told you."

She looked at him.

"Ronnie told you, didn't he? Must have been him."

"It was."

"All casual-like, I bet." He laughed. "You see what he was
doing."

"Actually, no," she conceded.

"He was trying to draw you to him. He wanted you to wonder how I had gotten so far away from the alley in such a short
time, on a bad knee."

"You're saying he wanted me to think that he had helped
you," she said. "He wanted me to suspect him."

Alex nodded. "He really wanted you to put him on the stand,
so he could do exactly what he did—tell the whole world the
truth. He wanted *someone* to put him on the stand, whatever it
took. And you weren't going to call him as a witness. He was doing whatever he could to get your attention."

"He could have told me the truth."

"I wouldn't let him. He probably figured I'd sabotage it if he
tried. He wanted to give you no choice but to call him."

"I'm not sure I would have." She sat down on the bed. "I
struggled with it more than you could know."

"Because he was your son. That's why he didn't want you to
know that. He didn't want you to feel loyal to him. He wanted
you to *accuse* him."

She recalled Ronnie's reaction when she confronted him on that point, told him that she knew he was her son. His anger, his frustration.

"He finally figured out a way to get the prosecutor to call him," Alex continued. "He came to visit me in that interview room and shouted all kinds of bad stuff to me. He was hoping that the government was watching."

And they were. Dan Morphew had eaten it up. In one fell swoop, Ronnie Masters had gotten himself immunity for any role he played and, more important, had been given the forum he had badly craved to announce the secret to the entire world.

"He's a smart one," said Alex. "It must be the good genes."

"No doubt."

"That boy would do anything to protect me."

Shelly thought through the last couple of weeks. "Ronnie went to see Eddie Todavia a few times," she said. "Why?"

"Same reason." Alex shook his head, smiling. "Trying to draw someone's suspicion. Hoping someone, anyone, was watching. I'll bet he was obvious about it. He was in broad daylight with Eddie, right?"

She recalled the photos Joel Lightner had taken. It was true. Ronnie was walking down the middle of the street with Todavia. She laughed. "He couldn't have been *more* obvious."

Alex tapped his temple. "Smart, I'm telling you."

"What about this other guy he went to see, Alex? Robert El-something. What was—"

"Robert Eldridge. He went to see him?"

She looked at Alex.

"Robert Eldridge," Alex explained, "is Dina's ex-husband. That witness from way back? He was trying to find Dina to help tell the story all over again."

"Or hoping that we'd follow him and make the connection ourselves."

"You or anyone else," Alex said. "If it had come down to it, I'm sure Ronnie would have just marched into the judge's chambers and spilled the whole thing. But I don't think he trusted the legal system. He always complained about the rules. If he just went to you, or to the prosecutor, he was afraid that he wouldn't be allowed to testify. That someone would say that the rules of evidence prevented it or something. Better to make one of you call him, put him on the stand, and then tell a room full of reporters and the jury the truth. Then, nobody could stop him. Any excuse he could come up with, just to get into that courtroom."

"Right."

"I pulled all this shit, Shelly, and Ronnie saved me. You got a good kid there."

She *did* have a kid. She had always known it, and was even able to put a face and name to the concept over the last few months. Now, for some reason, as things were coming to a close, the notion seemed to have more meaning. Something she couldn't put her finger on, that stirred her emotions in a way that she had never felt.

The tears surprised her, how quickly they came. She was in a fragile state in every way, but still. She wasn't a crier. She wiped at her face.

"So—what's gonna happen now, do you think?" he asked.

She composed herself after a moment. She walked over to him, placed a hand on his shoulder. "We're not on tomorrow. The prosecutor and I are going to see what can be done."

"You think they'll drop the case?"

She sighed. "Honestly?"

"No, lie to me."

"I don't think they'll drop this case, Alex. And I don't think the judge will throw it out, either. The heat is too great. There's politics. There's a dead cop."

Alex seemed to deflate. He apparently thought that things would change with this revelation.

"Get some sleep," she told him. "Let me be the lawyer. I'm going to talk to Ronnie, and I'll come back tomorrow and we'll get prepared for the rest of this."

"Okay," he agreed. "But you're the one who needs sleep."

She kissed him on the cheek and left him in the cell. She reached into her bag for her cell phone, which had been turned off. When the screen lit up, it told her she had four messages. She listened to her voice mail as she waited for the elevator to the courthouse lobby. The reception was less than perfect, but she had no trouble making out the callers, because all four messages, spread out over the last hour and a half, were from the same person.

Maribelle Rodriguez, the chief of staff to Governor Langdon Trotter.

She could imagine the chaos in the state capital, or wherever he was. It would have taken the press all of two minutes, after the revelations in court hours ago, to hunt down the governor and ambush him with questions. And she hadn't called to warn him. Never mind that she had been lying unconscious on a courtroom floor. That was a distinction that would be lost on an elected official, in the heat of a re-election campaign, who suddenly had a great deal of explaining to do. He would want to co-ordinate his comments with Shelly, and perhaps add a few private comments of his own.

Well, he'll have to wait, she said to herself.

75

Beginning

SHELLY WALKED INTO the interview room at the county lockup. Ronnie Masters still wore a blue button-down shirt and khaki pants, looked like he was readying himself for church.

He looked different to her, though, more at ease than ever before. All of the calculating was over. He had had a mission all along, and that mission was apparently accomplished.

"How are you doing?" he asked her.

"The bump on my head is fine," she said. "I'm not sure about the rest of me."

"What are they gonna do about Alex?"

She sighed. "I don't know. Probably keep going."

"But you'll win now."

"Probably. You and I need to talk about your testimony. That's one of the reasons I'm here."

"What's the other?"

"The other—" She looked up at the ceiling. She thought of all the times she had spoken with Ronnie about Alex, back when she thought Alex was her son. All of the questions Ronnie had asked. Was she ashamed of her son? Was she mad that her son had come to find her?

She opened her hands. "I'm sorry, Ronnie."

"Why are you sorry?"

"I'm sorry because—because—"

"Because you gave me up for adoption?" he asked. "That wasn't such a bad move."

"Because I didn't come to find you. Because I didn't try."

She felt another shiver run through her. She could never pin-point exactly why she had never looked up her son. There were plenty of rationalizations. She didn't want to burst into a happy child's life and cause chaos. She feared her child's rejection. She would never know the reasons. Maybe that was no longer the point.

"The whole thing was probably tough on you," Ronnie said.

"Tough on *me*." She grimaced. "Ronnie, I—" She felt her throat close, the emotion rise. She thought of her own parents, the years lost after Ronnie was conceived.

She walked over and sat next to him. "Listen. I don't really know what I'm doing. It's not like there's a manual or anything." Her hand lingered in the air.

"A manual for what?"

"I—" She framed her hands in the air. "I—we need to—I want to be a part of things. I don't know how this is going to work. I just—"

"Just be my friend, Shelly. I already have a mom." He said it with such simplicity. Shelly was impressed by his strength, grate-ful for his generosity.

She touched his hand. "I can do that. I want to do that."

Her cell phone rang. She held her breath. This was the fifth phone call.

"You should answer that," Ronnie said.

"It can wait. We have to talk about your testimony."

"Maybe it's important."

"It can *wait*." She went to her bag and removed a notepad. Then she put it down. She thought of her father. She thought of family. She looked back at Ronnie.

"I have always loved my child," she said, surprised at the strength of her voice. "I didn't know if it was a boy or a girl or anything else. But I have always carried around so much love for that child. I know it's hard to understand, because I didn't do anything about—"

"You think it's hard for *me* to understand?" Ronnie stood up. "You loved someone you had never met. So did I. I understand. Is that what you need to hear? I forgive you. Okay? It was tough, and you have all kinds of thoughts swirling around your head.

It's a lot different when it moves from the abstract to real. Believe me, I get it. Just—don't get so worked up about labels. Let's just—y'know—hang together. Watch each other's backs. Have some fun once in a while. Stay a—a part of each other."

She walked over and extended a hand. He took it and pulled her into a hug. "There," he said. "Not so bad, was it? Friends hug."

"Okay." Her throat choked, but she felt unimaginable relief. He was making this so easy for her. "Now, as inappropriate as it may seem, we really do need to talk about your testimony." She grabbed his shoulder, then moved to the other side of the table and picked up her notepad.

"Can I have ten bucks for the movies tonight?" he asked.

She laughed.

"Can I stay out past my curfew?"

"Cease and desist." She raised a hand.

"Can I sleep over at Billy's?"

"Only if you clean your room. Now, can we talk about your testimony?"

"Hey—" He shrugged. "You're the one who wants to make up for lost time."

Lost time. Time lost. She had spent so long pining over it, she had forgotten to turn her head forward. Her cell phone rang again. She reached for it and turned it off.

76
Messy

SHELLY FOUGHT THROUGH reporters that had gathered around the county jail, and jumped into a cab. A taxi to her house from downtown could set her back as much as twenty dollars and was typically unheard of for her, but she couldn't fathom the thought of dozens of reporters following her to the bus stop. Safely in the taxi, she dialed the number Mari Rodriguez had left her.

"Mari, it's Shelly."

"Shelly—God, I've been calling you all day."

"I take it the news has reached you."

"You could say that. He wants to see you, Shelly. He's been in a budget meeting all day but he told me to pull him out when I got hold of you."

"I'm heading home."

"I'll tell him."

"This news isn't—" She wasn't going to apologize. No. There was nothing for which she needed to say she was sorry.

"Mari," she said, "I didn't want this. I had no idea who this cop was."

"I understand."

"This is going to hurt, isn't it?"

A pause. Mari was a good sort.

"You could say that," she said.

Shelly clicked off the phone and dropped her head back on the carseat. She thought of the headlines for her father. She tried to rationalize each piece of information. A private adoption was not a crime. His grandson's involvement, in some way, in a cop shooting. His loose-cannon daughter. It was the collective whole. Messy, is what it was.

Her phone rang again.

"Shelly, it's Joel. Jesus Christ!"

"Hi, Joel."

"I'm reading this on-line. The *Watch*. Ronnie's your *son*? Miroballi—"

"All true," she said.

" 'A grandson who's never been acknowledged by the Trotter family.' 'A daughter, outcast from the family—' "

"It says that?" She came forward in the seat, felt a wave of nausea.

" 'Did the governor involve himself in the prosecution?' 'Did his daughter know this all along?' "

"Oh, Jesus."

"It's not pretty, Shel. Did you really faint?"

She moaned.

"And I got some news for you, Counselor."

"Tell me it's good, Joel. I can't take anything else right now."

"Depends on your perspective. Guess which west-side drug dealer woke up this morning without any arms?"

"No."

"Mr. Edward Todavia, one and the same."

She did a quick calculation. Ronnie Masters was in the county lockup last night. She immediately scolded herself for even considering it.

"That's the Cans for you. He got notorious. They don't like publicity."

"I think I'm gonna be sick," she said.

"Not in my cab, lady," the driver called back.

"That's one less scumbag on the street," Joel said. "Don't lose sleep over that guy."

"It's up here on the left," she told the cab driver.

"You got plenty else to lose sleep over, I'm afraid," Joel added.

77

Regrets

SHELLY WALKED DOWN the hallway upon hearing the whine of the intercom buzzer. She hit the button for entry into her building and walked over by the door. She unlocked it and found herself taking steps backward, away from the door.

The state plane from the capital would have landed, by her estimation, about twenty-five minutes ago.

He came in by himself, without any security detail. He seemed startled, for some reason, to see her. Perhaps he'd been lost in thought. Perhaps he'd been busy calculating the damage to his political campaign. There had been some talk of a vice presidential bid down the road, perhaps even the top spot. Why not? He was a tall, handsome, personable conservative from a large Midwestern state.

That was over now. No question. Stuff like this? Just too messy. He'd be lucky to hold on to his current job now.

"I'm sorry, Dad," she said, standing firm. She immediately regretted the capitulation.

He looked at her with a quizzical expression, cocked his head. And then she saw something she had not ever seen before. She saw tears in the eyes of her father.

"You're sor—" His throat closed. Something else she had never seen.

It was a moment she couldn't describe, one that she never would be able to explain. A breakthrough. A spark, maybe, that each of them had been awaiting. She didn't know who moved to whom. Later, she would remember that they met in the middle. They held each other tightly, desperately, their bodies trembling. No words were spoken for what seemed like forever, as if they were trying to recover so much with this embrace. Just like that, and she felt it sweep over her, felt time melt away.

His head turned, his mouth moved to her ear. "What kind of a father am I?" he whispered, his voice trembling. "What kind of a father am I, when my beautiful little girl can't tell me that she was—that somebody had—had hurt my little—"

"I should have told you, Daddy. I'm so—"

"No," he whispered gently. "It wasn't your job to tell me. It was *my* job to *ask*. I prosecuted so many of those cases, and when it came to my own daughter—" He stroked her hair. "I thought you were being stubborn. I swear that's what I thought. I swear."

She didn't have a reply to that. She just held on to him as tightly as she could.

"You had to go through all of that alone. And I made you feel *worse*. Oh, God, Shelly, can you ever forgive me?"

"I already have." She pulled back from him. She tried to smile, but her lips were still trembling.

He cupped his hand around her chin, and this seemed to calm him. "I am so proud of you and so ashamed of myself."

She shook her head but couldn't speak.

"I want my daughter back," he said.

"She's back," she managed. And she meant it. Could that really be all it took to erase years of barriers and resentment? Was that, in the end, all she ever really wanted, to hear these words?

He smiled at her. His steel-blue eyes were entirely bloodshot now. The strong, stoic mask was washed away. It seemed appropriate, somehow, that she was seeing something new in him at this moment.

He touched the back of her neck tenderly. "You hurt yourself today. You fainted."

"I'm fine," she answered, and then chuckled. "Do you think I could have possibly found a more public way for this to come out?"

He smiled. They both did. "It doesn't matter," he said.

"This is going to hurt you—"

"It doesn't matter." He slowly shook his head.

Their breathing evened out. They looked at each other, their smiles slowly growing. He petted her hair, wiped the tears from her cheeks.

"I'm going to do something I've never done before," she told him.

He looked into her eyes, noted the expression on her face. He tilted his head so their foreheads touched. In some ways, nothing had changed. He could still keep a step ahead of her.

"You're going to vote for me," he said.

78

Rewind

FEBRUARY 11, 2004. A feeling he cannot escape: Someone is watching. He has no visual confirmation but it's a sense, his gut telling him that he's not alone as he stands on the street outside the athletic club on the commercial district's west side. The bitter evening air stings his sweaty body, the light wind shooting over the top of his long black coat and filling the space within his sweatshirt. His fellow players have left in their various directions, to high-priced condos along the city's lakefront or, in some cases, to student housing at whatever school they are attending. Not so for this young man. He will walk four blocks to the Austin bus that will transport him to the city's south side, to his middle-class home.

Alex Baniewicz looks at his watch. It's early. Seven-forty. Open gym at the City Athletic Club usually goes until eight, maybe eight-thirty. Ronnie Masters, who was going to pick him up—who has been so protective of Alex since he learned about Alex's meetings with Ray Miroballi—wouldn't be here yet. Kicked out of the gym as he is, Alex decides to head to the bus. He certainly doesn't want to linger out here.

The streets on the southwest side of the commercial district are empty. It has been dark since five, and most of the professional buildings in the district are to the east and north, so it is quiet as he walks toward the bus stop. Quiet is not good, not anymore. These days, he prefers noise and company to drown out the howling in his head.

He hears it before he turns his head and sees it behind him, to the north. Squad cars are unmistakable, even from a distance. This particular police vehicle is headed south on Gentry, toward him. The car has just crossed Bonnard Street, which puts it less than a block away from him. The boy finds it difficult to walk with his head craned back, but he will do what he can to be non-chalant. There is no reason to panic. He doesn't know the offi-cers' intentions. More than likely, it's a routine cruising. He's a white kid in a long coat and sweats, obviously leaving the City Athletic Club after a game of hoops. They might not think any-thing of him. Or they might stop him. They might even ask him what's in the gym bag he's carrying. But he doesn't know this, and he can't react preemptively because that would draw suspi-cion, could turn a nonevent into something.

He hears the squad car stop, short of him. That seems odd, because there is nothing behind him that would draw their inter-est, no reason to stop. He doesn't know how to respond. He lis-tens a moment, slowing his pace. He hears another car drive by, on Bonnard Street north of the officers. That car, headed east, sounds like it's moving quickly, which might normally catch the attention of police officers on a sleepy night. But he hears no re-sponse from the cops, which means something else—some*one* else—has their attention just now.

They are looking at him.

He tries to be casual as he turns and looks back at the squad car. He tries to catch a glimpse of the car he heard speeding by. He hopes it was Ronnie, just arriving and seeing a scene that would make his blood boil. The illumination of the street is de-cent, with the towering lights, and he sees two of them inside the car. The driver—it's Miroballi. Miroballi and that partner of his. Miroballi is speaking into a radio.

Alex turns and continues walking, stifling the instinct to run. His heart is drumming now. Perspiration on his forehead, when it's only ten degrees or so outside.

He hears car doors open, then close, one after the other.

He will not run, not yet. If nothing else, he will let them walk a sufficient distance from the vehicle, so that if Alex does run, it will take some time before they can return to the vehicle, if that is their choice. He assumes that only one of them will give chase—Miroballi—but he can't know this.

He looks ahead of himself now. He is walking among high-rises, so there are few options. Buildings will be closed, or open only to the extent that he could approach a security guard. Wait—an alley, before the end of the block. His mind races as he taps his recall. The alley goes through to the next street. Yes. He can cross through the alley to the next street. Yes.

"Hey," Miroballi calls out.

It has happened in a finger-snap. He has been identified and called out. Until now, it has been something of a game, Alex pretending not to notice Miroballi. Now a line has been drawn.

Alex tries to calculate the amount of time that has passed since he heard the car pass by to the north. He prays that it was Ronnie, that somehow Ronnie will come driving up the street now.

But he's been called out, so Alex runs. He's in the perfect outfit, sweats and court shoes, though a sixteen-year-old probably doesn't need such advantages against a large man pushing forty. It takes him under thirty seconds to reach the alley. He hears the officer calling to his partner, something about the car, which means that the vehicle will be giving chase soon as well.

He looks down the alley. Bags of garbage next to full dumpsters, an old fire escape running up one wall. A parked car on the next street over. Something in the shadows, maybe his eyes playing tricks.

No. It's Ronnie, lurking in the shadows, waving to him. An escape route. Ronnie has the car waiting on the next street over, he assumes. Alex turns and runs down the alley, his heart lifted now.

He hears Miroballi again, talking into the police radio as he gives chase.

"—in pursuit—"

He looks back for signs of the officer as he's running. A mistake. He knows it before it happens. His foot catches something, a pipe, probably, and he falls. His gloves rip against the uneven pavement. Worse, his knee. His kneecap, even with the protection of the wool coat, has landed awkwardly onto the tattered concrete. He can't diagnose the damage. It just hurts like hell.

"Shit," he hears Ronnie say in a violent whisper.

Alex gathers his gym bag and manages to get to his feet. He is shrouded in the darkness of the alley, only indirect lighting from the street allowing him to see at all. He can't run anymore, will probably need a moment before he can even put weight on his leg. He is not even midway between the two streets now. He couldn't possibly escape.

"I just want to talk to you, kid. Relax." Miroballi is standing at the threshold, casting an ominous figure with the light behind him. One hand on his police radio, the other extending forward. But not holding a gun. The officer shakes his head, even shows the palm of his open hand, as if to decelerate the threat. He is moving cautiously toward Alex, shuffling his feet as each one eyes the other.

"See those hands," he calls out. "Lose the bag."

Miroballi moves slowly, his gaze alternating between Alex and the gym bag. Alex shows the palm of his free hand as he moves backward. It actually hurts less to backpedal, but he still moves with a limp. His heartbeat drums, not from the physical exertion. He swallows hard and feels a hot, sickening taste in his mouth. He asks himself, in a flash of a moment, how it could have come to this.

Miroballi pulls his radio close to his mouth, speaks urgently but quietly. Then he moves closer to the boy, his index finger still extended. Do-not-move.

That's smart, Alex thinks to himself. Miroballi has come forward without his weapon drawn, in peace, because he didn't want Alex to run. He thinks he has fooled Alex, when the only reason Alex isn't running is because he cannot.

"I said drop the bag," he says to Alex. "Let's just talk a minute."

Alex drops the bag. Raises his hands to waist level. His fingers are spread out, his palm showing, but his hands remain there, at his waist. He continues to move backward, away from the streetlight's faint illumination.

Miroballi's right hand falls to his side, sweeping gently at his leather jacket, exposing for the first time the holster, his weapon. The boy waits another beat, looks into the eyes of the police officer.

"I haven't said anything," Alex says. "I won't. I swear."

The officer looks at him, seems to note for the first time Alex's limp. Then he brings his radio close to his mouth. He mumbles something into the radio that Alex can't make out.

But Alex hears him the second time.

"I repeat," Miroballi says in a louder voice. "Suspect is armed."

Then he clicks off the radio, moves toward Alex. Alex keeps his eyes on Miroballi's right hand. He does it quickly, gracefully. Slides the gun out of his holster and holds it at his side.

"No, I know you won't say anything, kid." He closes the distance on Alex, again watching the gimp in his movements. He knows it now. Alex won't run, can't run. He slowly raises the gun so it is pointed at Alex. "I just wanted to tell you one thing, and that's all. I wanted to tell you that your mother was one hell of a good fuck—"

A noise, a bottle smashing, to Miroballi's right and slightly behind him, shattering into pieces on the pavement. Miroballi jerks to the right and behind him, points his gun in that direction as well.

It has happened just like that. That moment in which the officer turns, shifts his weight, to look. The moment he takes to redirect his weapon in that direction. The moment spent measuring the situation, realizing it was glass, then realizing that someone from behind Alex must have tossed it. Or—was it someone behind Miroballi? That momentary limbo, unsure of the who or how of that shattering glass. That moment spent readjusting, bringing the weapon back to the forward position and refocusing on a boy who has had time now to remove a weapon of his own from his coat pocket.

Miroballi's face explodes, a shower of blood. Alex stands in disbelief, holding the gun in his hand but not sure of how long he can keep holding it. Not sure of anything, really. Time passes, but he could not possibly estimate seconds. It feels like a lifetime.

A hand on his back. A hand removing the gun. A force, pulling him back. And he is running, with some help from Ronnie. An alternating limp and run.

Out of the alley now, onto the next street over. Ronnie's car is running. He moves to the passenger door but Ronnie is behind him, stripping him forcefully of his gloves, then his coat, then his sweatshirt. Then the car door opens and Ronnie shoves him in.

Ronnie squeals the tires forward, moving three, four blocks away in what seems like an instant. He pulls around a corner and quickly sheds his own leather jacket. As he pulls off his sweatshirt, Alex is suddenly aware of Ronnie.

Ronnie.

Alex opens the car door.

"What the hell are you doing?" Ronnie asks as Alex fumbles out of the car.

Alex leans in and takes the sweatshirt and the jacket from Ronnie. "They know me," he says. "If I run, they'll come to the house. They already got me."

"Get the fuck back in the car, Alex."

"*You* get out of here," Alex answers, turning his back on his brother. He walks a few steps, onto the curb, staggering forward. It seems like an eternity before he hears the squeal of tires behind him. Alex collapses to the pavement as the sirens grow louder.

SHELLY TOOK a step closer to the jury box, looked at each juror individually before continuing. "This is the truth, ladies and gentlemen. It is the truth as told to you by Ronnie Masters and by my client, Alex Baniewicz. And it is not only the truth, because let's remember who has the burden of proof here." She pointed at Dan Morphew. "The state has the burden of proving that this shooting was *not* committed in self-defense. Who has refuted this testimony? Who? Certainly not Monica Stoddard, the woman who came in here and testified that, from her office on the nineteenth floor, she saw only Ray Miroballi, that the rest of her view of the alley was obscured, that she saw Miroballi make movements that were consistent with him turning to his right, then coming back forward. That is perfectly consistent with Ronnie's and Alex's testimony."

Ray Miroballi, not Officer. He was no longer a cop, at least not for the purposes of her closing argument. He was acting outside his role as a peace officer, and she would cut him no slack.

"And all this stuff Mr. Morphew told you in the opening statement? About Alex dropping one gun, duping Miroballi into believing he had surrendered, and then pulling out another one? Remember how bad all of that sounded? I sure do. But guess what, folks? This case is over now, and we never heard a *lick* about that. That is a promise to you that was broken. There is no evidence about those kinds of games or tricks whatsoever. Nothing."

Shelly felt a bit bad laying it on Morphew like that. The truth was, as he had told her, he was not unsympathetic to her position. Shake him awake in the middle of the night, and Morphew would probably say that Alex didn't deserve to go to prison. And in that spirit, Dan Morphew had reinterviewed the homeless man, Joseph Slattery, who had been the one who gave that version of events to the state. Morphew had conducted the interview himself this time—as opposed to the police officers who originally took his statement—and he had come away not believing in his witness. So he had done the right thing. He had refused to call him. Shelly firmly believed that Morphew was inclined to drop the charges altogether, but the politics of the situation would not permit it, and maybe this was the best Morphew could do. Surely, he had to know that she would crucify him for this in closing argument. One of the cardinal rules of opening statements was, don't make a promise to the jury you can't keep. And by not calling Slattery, Morphew was breaking a promise. He knew she would do this.

"The version of events as told to you by Ronnie and by Alex stands uncontroverted. There is absolutely no evidence whatsoever to disprove the notion that Alex acted in self-defense."

Shelly paused. She was running on empty, and she had been arguing for over an hour, nearing the end of her argument with her second recount of Alex's and Ronnie's testimony. She had covered almost everything she could think of. She was just about done but wanted to discuss Ray Miroballi's partner in more detail.

"This isn't about a cop," she said. "This is about a man who happened to be wearing that uniform. He directed the events that night. He went to find Alex for no legitimate reason. No reason pertaining to law enforcement. Alex wasn't Miroballi's snitch. We all know why Alex had met with Miroballi in the park on those occasions—it was a question of paternity. It was a question of criminal sexual assault years ago. It was a man being confronted with his past."

She took a step to the side. "This whole 'snitch' thing was made up by Miroballi, and willingly accepted by his partner, who frankly didn't want to know *what* was going on. I can't sit here and tell you that Julio Sanchez is a bad man. I honestly don't know. But I do know this, and so do you. He was being a cop's cop that night. He was letting his partner do his thing and not asking questions. He may not have known precisely who Alex was, and he may not have known why, but as sure as we're all sitting here, he absolutely knew that Ray Miroballi was going to eliminate Alex that night. How do we know that?"

Shelly went to the defense table and handed out copies of the police dispatch, which had been entered into evidence. Then she walked over to the tape recorder, which had been queued up.

"This was the call from Miroballi's radio at 7:47 P.M.," she said. She hit the "Play" button and the voice echoed throughout the room:

RADIO 27: Dispatch, advise all units that suspect is armed. I repeat, suspect is armed.
DISPATCH: Copy that, Twenty-seven. Vehicles are responding. Where is he running? Twenty-seven? Twenty-seven, do you copy?

"The next transcript, from Sanchez in the patrol car—Squad 13—came at 7:48 P.M."

SQUAD 13: Dispatch, this is Radio Twenty-six. I'm in the squad car.
DISPATCH: Give us your location, Thirteen. Thirteen, advise of your location. Two hundred block of South Gentry? Thirteen?

"This final transcript, from 'Radio 26,' was Officer Sanchez's handheld. This call came two minutes later—7:50 P.M."

RADIO 26: Dispatch, we have an officer down. Officer
    down. Officer—we have an—oh, God, Ray.
DISPATCH: Twenty-six, paramedics and ambulance are
    responding. Keep your man alive, Twenty-six.

Shelly pointed at the recorder. "According to my client and
Ronnie, the shooting happened just after Miroballi called in that
the suspect was armed. Not two minutes later. But even if you
don't believe Alex—let's think about this. Sanchez must have
heard the gunshot when he was in the car, right? But he didn't
report shots being fired. He didn't say a word to dispatch. He
didn't say a thing until he saw *who* had been shot. That's not
only contrary to department policy, but it tells us that Sanchez
was leaving the show to his partner. He assumed that *Miroballi*
had fired the shot, so he wasn't going to call in 'shots fired.' He
was going to let his partner do it."

She looked at the jury. "When he heard the shot, he assumed
it was his partner who had done the shooting. He sat there and
did nothing. Then, as even Monica Stoddard told you, Sanchez
'jogged' down to the scene. He wasn't in a hurry. Why not? Your
partner is involved in a shoot-out, and you don't call it in? You
don't sprint to the scene? Not if you know that your partner is
planning to rub someone out. No, in that case, you hang back,
like Sanchez did. You wait for your *partner* to call in that he shot
a suspect. You let your partner take care of everything. He
doesn't want your help, and you don't want to know. You just
stay out of his way."

Shelly shrugged. "Maybe we should give Sanchez the benefit of the doubt. He didn't know Alex. He admitted that. He
didn't know Alex. Maybe he assumed Alex was a bad guy.
Maybe he thought this was some kind of rough street justice.
I'm not a cop and I don't live in their world. What matters,
though, is that Sanchez's deliberate unwillingness to involve
himself in this confrontation proves my point even more. This
whole thing was a setup. Miroballi finds the guy he wants to
eliminate, and just before he does so—just when he has his target pinned down, helpless and injured in a dark alley—he calls
in, 'Suspect is armed.'"

She flapped her arms. "Sure. Of course. Suspect is armed, so when I shoot him, I can claim self-defense. But what does Miroballi need to make this happen? He needs a second, unregistered firearm. He needs a couple of packets of cocaine. Nothing that would be hard for a cop to get hold of." She wagged a finger. "That gun that we have seen in this case wasn't fired, but it was going to be fired. It was going to be fired right after Ray Miroballi killed Alex. He was going to kill Alex, then put a gun in his dead hand and fire it into the wall. Then Miroballi has an airtight justification for killing Alex. He was chasing a perp who was carrying drugs. The perp fired at him. He fired back and killed him. All of this happening in a deserted downtown on a very cold and dark February evening. And if it hadn't been for Ronnie Masters tossing a bottle to distract him, his plan probably would have worked."

She flipped her hand. "Let's go back to Sanchez now. We know he heard a gunshot and did nothing. We know he eventually 'jogged down' to the alley. Then, of course, he saw something he never expected to see. He saw his partner lying dead. So then he calls it in. But what about this unregistered firearm sticking out of Ray Miroballi's belt, or tucked in his jacket, or wherever it was? And what about these packets of cocaine Miroballi brought along to plant?"

She shook her head. "No. No good. Those can't be found on Miroballi. That wouldn't just make Miroballi look bad. It would make *Sanchez* look bad. So he tosses them in the general direction of where Alex ran. He tosses the gun. He tosses the cocaine. That story, at least, could sell. Then he waits for the cavalry to arrive."

She looked at the prosecution. "Mr. Morphew has a rebuttal. He gets the last chance to talk to you. Let's hear what evidence he has to prove I'm wrong. Because he has no evidence that puts that second gun in Alex's hand, or Ronnie's hand. He has absolutely, positively no explanation for that second gun—or for that matter, for the cocaine. What—we're supposed to believe what Ray Miroballi said? Sanchez didn't see any cocaine. He knew what his partner was doing. This whole thing was a setup, I'll say it again, and we know why. Ray Miroballi was undeniably guilty of sex with a minor—a simple DNA test of Ronnie,

Miroballi, and—well, me, would prove that. And he knew that. This is a man who would lose his job, and maybe his wife, and be on the hook for child support. He couldn't have any of that. Easier just to kill the boy who you think is your son. Kill the boy and get on with your life. And since you're a cop, it's easy enough to set the whole thing up."

She looked down and lowered her volume. "The reason we're still here—the reason this case is still going on—is that the person who died was a police officer."

She was referring to the prosecution as well as the judge, who in Shelly's estimation should have directed a verdict of not guilty after the state closed its case. Judge Dominici lacked the fortitude to make the tough call, and so did Elliot Raycroft.

"But this case has nothing to do with cops. This isn't about sending a message to police, one way or the other. This is about a man looking to commit a cold-blooded, premeditated execution who happened to wear a blue uniform. And since no one else has the courage to do the right thing, I'm asking you to do it." She looked at the jurors' faces. "All of you know that Alex acted in self-defense. But you don't even have to go that far. All you have to find is that the prosecution has not proven, beyond a reasonable doubt, that Alex *didn't* act in self-defense. And that, ladies and gentlemen, is an easy call."

She walked over to Alex and put her hands on his shoulders. "One man already tried to take away Alex's life. I'm asking you to give him his life back."

79

Slow

PAUL RILEY PUSHED the remaining half of his dinner away. "Well, Shelly Trotter, I have to tell you that I've seen quite a few cases in my time, and heard lots of interesting stories about people's lives, but—"

"I'm topping the charts."

"Hey." He shrugged. "All's well that ends well."

It had ended rather well, she would have to say. The jury had returned a verdict of not guilty by reason of self-defense after four hours of deliberations. Alex had slept in his own home for the last two nights. His legal problems were over. He had already pleaded out his drug case with the U.S. Attorney, and now his murder charge was beaten. There was always the possibility that the county attorney would charge him for extorting Ray Miroballi, but there would be no way to make that case. Alex hadn't admitted to that on the stand. He had testified, when pressed by Dan Morphew, that he had never asked Ray Miroballi for money, and there was no one alive to refute it. And she was relatively sure that the county attorney would never have the appetite to prosecute Alex for that, anyway.

Ronnie Masters had not been entirely forthright in his plea agreement with the county attorney. It was debatable whether he had lied about a material fact, which is what would be required to tear up the plea agreement, but at a minimum he had omitted some important facts, which would be grounds itself. In the end, however, all legal technicalities aside, Ronnie had simply helped Alex after the fact in a crime for which Alex had been acquitted. And the county attorney had suffered some embarrassment. Elliot Raycroft had informed Shelly yesterday that he considered the matter closed with regard to Ronnie.

Did her father have a hand in that? She had to concede the probability. This was different from dropping the charges in the middle of a cop-killing trial. This was a fairly technical application of the law concerning a broken plea agreement, which was not particularly interesting fodder for the press. The media had been far more fascinated with the facts that Ronnie disclosed on the stand than in whether he had technically played loose with the county attorney. This gave plenty of leeway for Raycroft's office, and for whatever reason—a political favor, the desire to put the entire affair behind them, or the feeling that the interests of justice did not require charging Ronnie—Raycroft was taking a pass.

"I can't thank you enough for everything you did, Paul. Your advice. Your firm's financial support. You have been wonderful."

He responded in typical fashion, deferring the praise. She saw something more, too. Paul was trying to read between the lines. This, she knew he was thinking, sounded an awful lot like goodbye.

He clapped his hands together. "So what are your plans now?"

She hadn't thought that far ahead. "I was thinking about going back to the law school."

"Mm-hmm. That's where your heart is, I suppose. You could stay with us. Run our pro bono program full-time. Christ knows, we need someone to do it."

She smiled at him. "That's very kind of you—"

"Make three times the money and do a lot of the same stuff."

She looked down. "I think you hit on it. The school is where my heart is."

That, she was sure, was something Paul Riley could understand. The law was his passion, too, even if it took a different form. She missed that place dearly, she now realized. She missed Rena, the students, their fresh idealism and commitment.

Paul was watching her. There was a sense of loss about him. She imagined that Paul Riley rarely felt vulnerable.

Oh, he really was such a wonderful guy. Beneath that polished exterior were a compassion and tenderness that he had willingly allowed her to see. She had kept him at arm's length and he had accepted it; he had been patient with her. It was just—just—

Not now.

She had so much time to make up with so many members of her family. She would be thrown into the fire when she returned to the law school. "Paul," she began, keeping her eyes down, "I want you to know—"

She felt his hand on her wrist. He looked at her with an intensity she had never seen from him.

"Let me in," he said. "For Christ's sake, *let me in.*"

She looked up at him sheepishly.

He shook her wrist. "Or tell me you have no feelings for me. That—that I could accept. But this. *This* I can't accept."

"What is the 'this' you're referring to?"

"This whole act of yours. This whole thing about keeping everyone at bay. Would you just take your goddamn foot off the brake?"

She put a hand on her chest in defense. "My foot's on the brake?"

"Hey." He softened his grip on her wrist. "Look. I see things about you that I didn't before. You went through some terrible stuff. You experienced some real trauma. You separated from your family. But look at you. Look at what you've accomplished, in spite of all that. You're a talented, beautiful, compassionate, courageous person. You can have so much if you would just come out of that damn shell—"

"I get it, Paul." She withdrew her wrist from his grasp. "Fear of commitment, I get it."

"I'm in love with you, Shelly. Don't ask me why or how, the way you've been stiff-arming me. But I am." He drew his hands back and forth between them. "See what I'm doing here, Counselor? I'm putting myself out there. I'm opening up. I'm taking a chance." He looked up, held open his palms. "And I don't see the sky crashing down."

She realized that her mouth had fallen open. "Well."

Paul trained a hand in the air. "I—look. I certainly don't expect you to return the compliment, Shelly. I'm just saying, Think about it. Just think about what I said and maybe—get back to me. Okay?" He signaled for the check.

The waiter arrived shortly. They knew each other and chatted briefly. The waiter made a joke about his wife and walked away. Paul smiled and watched the waiter leave, probably because he didn't want to return his focus to the table. "Anyway," he said. "Enough of the serious talk. I'm sorry, it just sort of came out. This was supposed to be a celebr—"

"I'm a vegetarian," she said to him.

He didn't catch her point. "I know that."

"Yeah, but I don't even really like seeing other people eat meat."

He watched her a moment, then chuckled. "I can't swim."

"I have a scar like you wouldn't believe from the Caesarian."

He pursed his lips. "I don't like olives on pizza or anything else, but I love them in martinis."

"I think I snore."

"How would you know?"

She smiled. "I woke *myself* up once."

He raised his eyebrows. "I don't like being judged for liking meat."

"I have a teenaged son whom I plan to spend a lot of time with."

"I have a legal practice that is rather demanding as well."

The waiter arrived, cracked another joke with Paul. He signed the receipt and handed it back with a remark of his own. Somehow, Paul seemed to know that this young man was putting himself through college. He looked back at Shelly with a measure of expectation.

"You really can't swim?" she asked.

"Just flop around in the water like a drowned kitten."

She released a laugh. She didn't know what the term *ready* meant. Paul was right; she had spent so many years with the brakes on, she couldn't even find the accelerator. But it felt—what was it with him?

Possible. Yes. Possible.

"Slow," she said to him.

"Hey, slow is good," he answered. "I like slow."

80

Forward

A RECENT POLL in the *Watch* found that Governor Langdon Trotter had suffered a drop in popularity in recent weeks. The article attributed it less to the revelations in the Miroballi trial than to his reaction to it. The governor had issued a single statement on the entire subject, which Shelly could recite by heart: *My personal life will remain personal and not public. I hope the voters will have the wisdom to judge me on my four years as governor. I will gladly stand on that record. I expect my opponent to direct her attacks at me and not my family.*

The media, in typical fashion, had chased the various tentacles of the story, from the Miroballi shooting to Shelly's sexual assault complaint years ago. A story last week, from an anonymous source in the police department, indicated that the Internal Affairs division was focusing closely on whether Officer Julio Sanchez had tampered with the crime scene after the shooting. That same source indicated that Internal Affairs had opened a review of the circumstances surrounding Shelly Trotter's report of her sexual assault years ago, and whether illegal means were used to conceal facts and pressure Shelly into dropping the charges.

Shelly didn't know how they obtained half the stuff they did, but the reporters had dug up some good information. They learned that the detective who had initially fielded the case was a woman named Jill Doocy, now living out east and raising her children. The case had then been transferred to another junior detective named Howard Stockard—the man who had convinced Shelly to drop the charges. It was unclear why the case had been transferred, but it was known that Howard Stockard had worked in the same station for a time with then-Officer Anthony Miroballi, who was now a lieutenant.

Stockard was deceased, and Jill Doocy said that she did not recall the specifics, which might or might not have been true. What was true, however, but unknown to Shelly as a teen, was that the crime Shelly had reported was statutory criminal sexual assault—it was rape regardless of whether Shelly consented, because she was a minor at the time and Ray Miroballi was not. The fact that she gave birth to his son was indisputable proof that Ray Miroballi had committed a felony. Thus, Detective Stockard's questions back then—his suggestion that she had consented to the sex but was having remorse after the fact— were entirely improper if he knew that the person who had raped Shelly was Ray Miroballi.

And he did know. Because the media had found Dina Patriannis, just as Alex's investigator had, and she confirmed that she had identified Ray Miroballi to Detective Stockard.

Shelly sat on the park bench and enjoyed the sun on her face. Soon, the police would be contacting her about that long-ago incident, she imagined, and she would tell them what she knew.

She knew now, for certain, what she had suspected all along—Ray Miroballi's brothers had been the ones who had broken into her apartment and threatened her. She had thought at the time that they had acted out of familial loyalty, or because they were involved in drugs along with their deceased brother. She knew differently now. They knew who Shelly was, obviously, from way back when. They must have hit the ceiling when they learned that Shelly Trotter, of all people, was defending the person who killed their brother. What the hell was *she* doing on this case? They were afraid. They were afraid that Shelly knew that Ray Miroballi had raped her, and if she knew that much, it wasn't much of a leap to implicate Tony and Reggie Miroballi in the cover-up of that rape.

It would never be proven. She couldn't possibly make a case against them. And in the end, it probably could never be conclusively proven that the Miroballi brothers pulled strings for their little brother back then. With Detective Stockard dead, there would be ample reason to think that Tony Miroballi used a chit with Stockard, but no proof. There almost certainly would not be criminal charges against the Miroballis, if for no other reason than the statute of limitations probably had expired. And in all likelihood, there would be no departmental disciplinary action against them, either. Shelly would have to rest with the comfort that anchors would be attached to their legs in the department; they might keep their jobs but would not move up.

And she wasn't sure how much she cared about that. She had made a commitment to remove the "Rewind" button from her brain. She preferred to look at what was in front of her.

Alex sat in a sandbox in the park with his daughter, Angela, who wore a set of pink overalls, preferring to scoop the sand with her hands instead of the tiny shovel provided to her. From her spot on the bench, Shelly saw the look of relief on Alex's face. Things were not perfect for him. He had lost half of his junior year of high school while incarcerated; with that setback and tough financial times for him and his daughter, he was inclined to drop out and get a full-time job. Shelly had used all of her powers of persuasion, including the offer of financial assistance, to convince him to stay with it and graduate. That, after all, was what she was best at—keeping kids in school.

Elaine Masters—Laney—finally had been informed of the relationship between Shelly and Ronnie, though Shelly had not been present. According to Ronnie and Alex, she had not appeared to have particularly strong feelings one way or the other about Shelly. That was because Laney was an addict, and alcohol had become the consuming focus of her life. Shelly wanted to help, but it was not as if she could pounce into their lives and start making changes. She could only hope that, someday, Laney would find the strength to want to help herself. And if she did, Shelly, Ronnie, and Alex would be there to help.

Ronnie Masters, standing only a few feet away, was filming Alex and Angela with a camcorder (courtesy of Paul Riley), providing running commentary and trying to coax Angela to speak for the camera. Ronnie would definitely graduate, and he had that legislative scholarship to Mansbury College after his senior year of high school. Mansbury was just a car-ride away, so Ronnie could commute, stay close to Alex and little Angela. And Shelly.

His grades were excellent, and all things considered, he had done well with very little to start with. Still. She had seen State Representative Sandoval on occasion, on a school issue, and she would love to ask him how it was that he had decided to direct one of his coveted scholarships to a boy who had not even applied for it, whether the idea might have come from a certain governor looking for a favor.

She smiled at that thought. The scholarship had been awarded months before Alex shot Officer Miroballi, before Langdon Trotter had any idea that Shelly would discover anything she ultimately learned. She had underestimated her father. Then, and all along. It was amazing to her, having been a lawyer herself for almost ten years, having seen so many stories between the lines, so many shades of gray in a black-and-white system—that she had painted her father with such a broad brush.

It was with a twinge to her heart that she noticed Ronnie's thick dark hair, the face that before her eyes was starting to square at the jaw—the tough Italian features he had inherited from his father. It was true. He looked like Ray Miroballi, at least the photos Shelly had seen of him. But there was also the light blue of his eyes, the fullness of his mouth, that made Shelly think of her own father.

Ronnie turned the camcorder suddenly and approached Shelly.

"We're talking with Shelly Trotter," he said in an official voice. "Vigilant defender of troubled youth by day, beautiful karate black-belt by night. Shelly, what's your secret?"

She blushed. "I don't have any secrets. Not anymore."

"Is it true that you're my mother?"

"That is true," she answered. "And I'm proud of it."

"Then don't just sit there," he said. "Go get me some lunch."

She winked at him and waved him away. Maybe she saw some of herself in him, too.

ACKNOWLEDGMENTS

I have relied on the efforts of so many people in completing this novel. For explaining some of the technical aspects of adoption, I would like to thank Illinois State Representative Sara Feigenholtz, who has been a wonderful friend as well as a source of information. On details concerning law enforcement, especially on the federal level, thank you to John Lausch, a federal prosecutor in Chicago, for his comments and insight.

A special thanks to Vince Connolly, a former top federal prosecutor in Chicago and now one of the most successful white-collar criminal defense attorneys in Chicago. Vince provided technical assistance as well as a read of an early version of the novel. His help and friendship have been greatly appreciated.

Any mistakes or inaccuracies on these technical issues are not to be attributed to these very generous people, but to me.

Thank you to those who read over earlier drafts of this novel and offered their valuable input: Missy Thompson, Adam Tullier, Dan and Kristin Collins, my mother, Judy Ellis, and my father-in-law, Ed Nystrom.

Thank you to all of my family for their love and support: July Ellis; Jennifer, Jim, and Jenna Taylor; Ed and Sally Nystrom; and Angela, Mike, Elizabeth, Matthew, Thomas, and Nicholas Riley.

A special thanks to Jim Jann, who once again has volunteered a great deal of his time and energy to offer his input on this novel. Jim has one of the best literary minds in the business, and he isn't even in the business. I hope to be editing one of his novels soon.

Thanks to everyone at my law firm for their support and enthusiasm over the years: David Williams, Doug Bax, Dan Collins, Kerry Saltzman, Lisa Starcevich, Chris Covatta, Michelle Powers, Adam and Grant Tullier, Rebecca Johnson, and Debbie Philips.

Thanks to David Highfill, my editor, who worked with me on the rather arduous journey that was the writing of this novel. Thank you to everyone else at Putnam for their faith in me. Thanks to Jeff Gerecke, my agent, for once again helping me to keep a steady hand.

Thank you, finally, to Susan Nystrom Ellis, my wife, editor, consultant, lawyer, psychiatrist, and best friend. You are everything to me.

Penguin Group (USA)
is proud to present
GREAT READS—GUARANTEED!

**We are so confident that you will love
this book that we are offering a
100% money-back guarantee!**

If you are not 100% satisfied with
this publication, Penguin Group (USA)
will refund your money!
Simply return the book before
May 1, 2005 for a full refund.

**With a guarantee like this one,
you have nothing to lose!**